PROAGNON'S REVENGE!

BY

RONAN STROBING

08/05/1976 – 20/10/18

Books by the same author

To Avenge the Father
Terror Reigns Again
Revenge of the Scimitar

Books in the same series
Terror Reigns Again
Proagnon's Revenge

To Andrew
A good friend as well as a cousin

Proagnon's Revenge is the follow up novel to Terror Reigns Again and covers events from the end of Terror Reigns Again to a similar point a year later; the year in question being 2013 – 2014 and is an adventure story that charts and follows events of many terrorist attacks, however there is an underlying factor that runs throughout the book.

Both organisations (HART and *Proagnon*) have new leaders following the end events of Terror Reigns Again and their style of leadership is a little different from that of their predecessors.

From the cold climate of Scotlands to the hot and sultry climate of Saudi Arabia nothing and nobody is safe. Proagnon's Revengeis a fast paced, high action, book

Acknowledgements

I should like to thank everyone who has helped me shape this book in the form it has taken, and who has assisted me in contributing ideas. I should also like to thank my friends, and members of my family, for being supportive of my writing of this book.

All the characters featured are fictional as well, and any resemblance to people (both living and dead) is purely coincidental and not intentional.

Foreword

The events contained within the pages of Proagnon's Revenge are total fiction, and do not reflect events that might occur in the future.

PROLOGUE

NEW BEGINNINGS!

The assassin stared down at the two, now seemingly lifeless, HART operatives, and then casually walked away back into the underground bunker from which they'd emerged. The assassin knew that they could reach the bunker; where the surviving members of *Proagnon* had gathered. Once the person had gathered everyone together they would, all return, along with the surviving vehicles, to the adjoining bunker in Iran.

The assassin would then emerge, make their way to Tehran and the *Imam Khomeini* Airport, and then board a plane for one of London's airports. Finally, from the airport she would take a taxi and go and see the man Dr Q once reported to.

*****

One of the two HART figures slowly stirred; he got, unsteadily, to his feet and surveyed the scene, of carnage, around him. He looked down, at his companion, evidently a woman, judging by the size of the body, but which one? Was it Celia Most or Lucy Lang? As the face of the figure was turned away from him, he couldn't tell which of the, two, female commanders the body belonged to. Plus he wasn't sure if whoever it was dead or was just unconscious, as he had been.

Next the man turned and surveyed the wreckage of the palace, and the HART convoy. How many had been killed? If his memory served him correctly there had been two Jeeps, both had contained two soldiers; the cattle truck, which had contained driver, soldier, and the 30 soldiers who had helped to storm the palace; finally, there was the HMMWV cargo/troop carrier, this had contained a driver, soldier, and each of the 5 HART Commanders. Therefore a total of 41 out of the 43 HART personnel, along with Dr Q/Adam Barker of *Proagnon* were now dead.

Realising all this he sat on a rock and broke down in tears. *Was she still alive?* He wondered, and climbed off the rock he was sat on, "Lucy," he shouted at the female form, "Commander Lang." There was no response, so he tried again, "Lucy." Knowing it was futile to keep trying he seated himself on the ground, his back against the rock and broke down, in tears, again.

*****

Back at HART's temporary headquarters, at the Diyarbakit air force base in Turkey, the radio operator, Faruk Dissar, had been ordered by the base's commander, John Craig, to try and contact the HART convoy as nothing had been heard from them for several hours.

Everybody, at the base, had heard the explosion that had destroyed the palace, and the following explosion which had destroyed the convoy; however, nobody had connected the second explosion to the destruction of the HART convoy, they'd all assumed that the two explosions were linked and, therefore, just part of the same one.

Faruk tried the radio but all that came back was static, radio operator Dissar reported this fact to his superior, his superior ordered Dissar to keep on trying, on the hour every hour, until midnight. If nothing was heard by then John Craig would then explore other options that were open to him. So, having received his orders, Faruk Dissar kept trying.

*****

The person who'd shot at the HART operatives, in the desert, had communicated, via hand held radio, and requested transport to take them back to Iran. A BTR-60 was deployed and picked them up and had them taken back to the *Proagnon* bunker under the desert of Iran. Most of the remaining, *Proagnon*, soldiers were already assembled there. Mitchell Walker, somehow he'd survived, asked, "What happened?"

"Well," their new leader began smoothly, "as you all know the Iraqi palace was totally reduced to rubble. However, the five HART commanders, together with their prisoner, Dr Q, escaped the explosion, and boarded a convoy of, waiting, vehicles. These were then destroyed by an apparent suicide bomber, the resulting explosion carried throughout the four vehicles killing everybody, including Dr Q. Two HART operatives were thrown clear of the burning vehicles, one male and one female; I emerged from where I'd hidden myself, shot and, presumably, killed them both; once I'd performed that task I made my way back here. At least I assume that's what happened"

"Very commendable I'm sure," replied Mitchell, his tone of voice tinged with sarcasm. "What makes you so sure these two people are dead?"

"I shot them, didn't I?" retorted the other member of *Proagnon*. "Okay I didn't wait around to see the end results, but I'm pretty sure they're both dead, and so will you be," they raised the Makarov semi-automatic pistol, "if you try to usurp my command."

"Fine!" answered Walker and left the room in a huff. *Proagnon's* new leader smiled to themselves, and was left to contemplate their next move.

*****

Back in the Iraqi desert the man from HART, Commander Ronan Strobing, suddenly felt a, light, touch on his shoulder; he spun round, almost falling off the rock he was leaning against in the process, to see who had touched him, standing behind him was the figure of Commander Celia Most. "So you survived as well," he began, "it looks like we're the only two. " There was suddenly a look of immense relief on his face.

"So it would appear," replied Celia calmly, "now we have to get back to base. Any ideas?" Sadly Ronan shook his head

"There must be something we can do, c'mon Ronan think!" She was almost having to shout at him now, as he just appeared to be lost, and had no sense of the urgency required for the current situation they found themselves in. "I suppose we could check each vehicle's radio, you never know one might have survived intact." Reluctantly, or so it seemed, Commander Strobing climbed off the rock he was seated upon and wandered over to join his fellow Commander.

Carefully, avoiding any flames that were still lingering and avoiding touching any of the vehicles exterior surfaces, they checked the radio equipment in each of the four vehicles. All that came from each was static, the situation appeared absolutely hopeless. "Just a minute," announced Ronan Strobing, suddenly, startling Commander Most, "wasn't the HMMWV (High Mobility Multipurpose Wheeled Vehicle) fitted with an external satellite dish?"

"I don't remember, let's take a look." So both of them walked around the side of the HMMWV and looked above the door, trying to ignore the dead soldier who was staring out the vehicle at them.

"There we are," announced Commander Strobing triumphantly, pointing upwards. "Now Celia, have you still got your hand held radio?"

"Yes, what's your idea?" She handed her radio over.

"If I can patch the radio through the satellite and get a good enough signal perhaps we can contact headquarters, in Turkey, inform them of our situation and, maybe, they'll mount a rescue operation, otherwise we'll freeze to death." With that Ronan got to work; firstly he slid the back from the radio exposing the circuitry inside, next he checked that the satellite dish hadn't been burnt too badly and could, therefore, be suitable for their purpose.

He then selected two wires from inside the handset and lifted them out, Celia watching all this activity with renewed interest – it was as if her fellow Commander had, suddenly, come back to life. It was then that Ronan disconnected two of the leads from the back of the dish, and tried to connect these to the wires from the radio; suddenly, there was a flash and then a shout of, "Oh damn!" As she watched her companion dropped the wires, and then turned to her; sheepishly Ronan said to her, "Whoops, wrong wire to the wrong connection. Oh well, back to work."

He turned back to the task in hand and tried another set of two wires, there was no dramatic flash this time; motioning Celia over and crossing his fingers Ronan activated the communications equipment, "HART assault squad calling headquarters in Turkey. Come in please," static was all that was heard. "Oh well," muttered Commander Strobing, dropping the radio handset, "it was worth a try;" just as he spoke a faint voice was heard coming from the handset. "This is HART headquarters in Turkey, please identify yourself and state your position."

Ronan picked up the handset and spoke loudly into it, "This is Commander Ronan Strobing, along with Commander Celia Most. The rest of the Commanders who came here, and the HART soldiers, are dead, all of them wiped out in an explosion that has completely destroyed the HART convoy."

"Understood. Shall mount rescue operation within the hour, base out." Ronan, joyfully, hugged Celia to him and held her tight, briefly he looked down at her, and her eyes seemed to have some hesitation in them, as if she were going through some mixed emotions. Once he'd let go of her Commander Strobing disconnected the radio handset from the satellite dish, on the HMMWV, replaced the wires and back cover, and then handed it back to Commander Most.

"Thank you," he said to her, and then said, "let's find somewhere to shelter and wait, we're in for a bit of a wait yet."

*****

At HART headquarters, at the Diyarbakit air force base in Turkey, the radio operator, Faruk Dissar, had reported the brief transmission, from Commander Strobing, to the base commander. "Do we have the convoy's last known position?" asked John Craig.

"Not exactly," replied operator Dissar, somewhat hesitantly, "however, the lead Jeep was fitted with a tracking device."

"Good idea of Peter's that," he moved over to another operator, who was seated at another computer terminal. "Operate the GPS tracking system." The computer operator saluted and activated the system that would link up with the orbiting satellite overhead; the satellite, once it was fed with the right information would, hopefully, be able to pinpoint the convoy of HART vehicles. As the computer whirred and hummed with power Craig was joined by the four HART Lieutenants: Ben Smith, Lloyd Samuels, Mike Hunter and Dennis Cutler.

"What's the latest sir?" asked Ben Smith, who was Commander Strobing's lieutenant.

John turned and looked at them all, "We are attempting to pinpoint the convoy's position. According to Commander Strobing the convoy has been completely destroyed along with all personnel, apparently only Celia Most survived, along with him; therefore, we will be mounting a rescue operation, which I would like you four to take part in, once we have received their current whereabouts."

"Right you are sir," Ben replied on behalf of each of them, and all four of the lieutenants saluted their commander. Just then the tracking computer sprang to life, and hummed with power, as the coordinates of the convoy's position were received. John Craig peered at the screen, as did the other four men, and noted the coordinates that were currently displayed on the screen.

"Can you bring up a reference map?" John asked the man at the computer.

"Certainly sir," was the reply; the operator pressed a few switches, entered some instructions and pressed a further button, on the keyboard, and a map of Iraq appeared on screen, with a flashing *red* light marking the convoy's position. "There you are sir."

"Transfer that computerized reference map to the HART SUV vehicles designated one, two, three, and four. Lieutenants, as you are to assist you will each board one of these vehicles, Ben – HART 1, Lloyd – 2, Mike – 3, and Dennis…"

"Don't tell me," began Lieutenant Cutler, "4."

"Correct," responded John, "now, everyone, to your vehicles." The four men rushed out of the computer room, and journeyed down the corridors of the base to rendezvous with their designated SUV. HART 1 was a Toyota Mega Cruiser – this had been used in Geneva the previous year, HART SUVs 2 and 3 were both Toyota Land Cruisers, whilst HART 4 was a Range Rover.

*****

The Toyota Mega Cruiser was a large, heavy-duty sport utility vehicle introduced by Toyota in 1995. The largest SUV ever built by Toyota, it resembled the military's Hummer H1, and like the Hummer, was designed primarily for military use with the Mega Cruiser often seeing duty as infantry transports equipped with mounted howitzers and mobile Surface-to-air missiles in the Japan Self Defence Forces.

Exclusively sold in Japan, the Mega Cruiser had also been used by the prefect police and fire/rescue departments, although a limited number were sold to civilians. This vehicle was intended to test designs that would eventually make their way into mass produced Toyota SUVs (like the Land Cruiser), but the Mega Cruiser was financially unsuccessful for Toyota.

The Mega Cruiser featured a 4.1 L turbo diesel I4 engine capable of producing 155 horsepower. The engine focused on producing high amounts of torque at low revolutions. The SUV featured front, centre, and rear differentials, as well as four wheel steering. The vehicle also had a 4-speed automatic transmission, and it was capable of carrying up to six people.

*****

The Toyota Land Cruiser is another of the series of four-wheel drive vehicles produced by the Japanese car maker Toyota Motor Corporation. Design of the Land Cruiser initially began in 1951 as Toyota's version of a Jeep-like vehicle and full production began in 1954. The Land Cruiser had been produced in convertible, hardtop, station wagon, and utility truck versions. It had once been Toyota's flagship 4WD.

The Toyota Land Cruiser, that HART were using, was the redesigned version that had been introduced in 2008. Known as the 200 Series, it shared the 2008 Lexus LX's platform and its overall design. Though many time-honoured Land Cruiser supporters had welcomed this re-invigoration of the mechanical aspects of the vehicle, the 200 Series had also encountered much criticism due to its controversial body restyling, with some claiming that Toyota had *overdeveloped* the classic trademarked Land Cruiser identity in its efforts to fit the Land Cruiser in to modern 21st century motoring. Toyota presented the completely redesigned Land Cruiser at the 2007 Australian International Motor Show held in Sydney. The vehicle entered production in the September and started to become available for sale in November 2007. Although the new Land Cruiser was presented at its first motor show in Sydney, it was already on sale in Japan, as it was launched there in September 2007. It also became available in Venezuela for sale early in November under the local nickname of *Roraima* (Taken from Mount Roraima in Venezuela). The 200 Series was offered in three different levels of trim in Australia and Oceania: There was the GXL, VX, and Sahara versions.

The 200 Series, offered numerous features and upgrades over its predecessor not limited to the cosmetic changes made to the body and interior, including: Smart Entry - A sensor was triggered when the remote was brought near the vehicle, allowing the user to simply touch the door handle to open it. Smart Start - Start/Stop push button for ignition; a key was not required for this. 4-zone climate control on the Sahara models, with the outlet vents increased in number from 18 to 28 10 airbags (VX & Sahara), plus a stronger and lighter frame

Various driver assist technologies not offered on previous models included: CRAWL; a four-wheel drive control system that operated like an off-road cruise control, automatically maintaining a low uniform vehicle speed using the brakes and throttle. A Downhill Assist Control A newly developed ABS system, the multi-terrain anti-lock braking system (ABS). Kinetic Dynamic Suspension System (KDSS), allowed for greater wheel articulation

Engine and transmission improvements had included: An all new optional V8 Diesel engine, the 1VD-FTV (also used in the earlier 70 Series). An Automatic transmission standard across all levels of trim of the 200 Series, 5-speed manual transmission was offered only with the 4.0L GX models (in selected regions). A five-speed automatic gearbox was assigned to the 4.7L petrol models, while the 4.5L diesel models received a six-speed automatic.

*****

The Range Rover was a four-wheel drive luxury sport utility vehicle (SUV) produced by Land Rover in the United Kingdom, which was owned by the Indian-based Tata Motors. It was initially introduced in 1970 and was still in production; there have so far been three major generations. The original model was known simply as the Range Rover until almost the end of its life, when Land Rover introduced the name Range Rover Classic to distinguish it from its successors. The second generation had the internal Land Rover code name *P38A*, and the latest generation is internally designated *L322*.

The model which was the basis for HART 4 was the armoured Range Rover; this was first introduced in 2007. This was a version of Range Rover Vogue developed by Land Rover Special Vehicles as an integral part of the new Range Rover Vogue programme. Development work had been carried out by Land Rover Special Vehicles and working closely with one of the world's leading armouring specialist companies, Armour Holdings Group, which included O'Gara Hess and Labbe. Testing of the vehicle's armouring was done by QinetiQ.

The vehicle was then certified for European B6 ballistic protection standard. Other changes included Side blast and under floor grenade protection, independent ballistic and blast certification, updated suspension, handling and braking system, wheels fitted with run-flat tyre system, fuel cut off over-ride. Optional security features included Tinted windows, Anti-tamper exhaust and Intercom. All of which were standard on HART 4.

Engine choices for this vehicle included the 4.4L V8. In 2010, a 5.0L V8 engine was introduced, and fitted.

*****

Once each of the HART lieutenants had boarded their designated vehicle, along with the driver for each, they radioed the communications room to let base commander John Craig they were aboard and ready to depart on their mission. The voice of John Craig came back to them all, "Once you're fully ready, and you've got your map coordinates locked into your vehicle's SAT NAV equipment, you may depart and I wish you every success." The men aboard the SUVs acknowledged this message, about a minute later all four vehicles left the base grounds, the Mega Cruiser leading the way, the two Land Cruisers following, whilst the Range Rover brought up the rear; all the SUVs were painted *black*.

*****

Over in the United States of America, as in Russia, a new president had been elected and sworn in. In America Arnold Smee, who after all had only been the caretaker president, had run for election but, after his confession about his past, hadn't been re-elected; a relatively unknown senator from the state of Michigan, Roger Theobald, had run against Arnold Smee, and been elected as the 46th President of America. Meanwhile President Vladimir Krushkev had been succeeded by President Sergey Kasporov, again another relative unknown.

Both new presidents were known to be HART haters and refused to do business with them. So now the only people HART could rely on were the Europeans, and some of them disliked the counter terrorist organisation, because of the previous year's happenings.

*****

In London, England, the Queen's consort, Gareth Andrews, had informed Queen Charlotte Pendragon that he had received some news from his brother, and needed to stay with him at his London residence. He then promised Miss Pendragon he would return to her side as soon as he was able to. Charlotte told him she understood, yet at the same time she was rather frustrated that he had chosen this time to go away, plus the commander of HART, Peter Roberts, had not yet brought the head of *Proagnon* to face her. She didn't know of the tragedy that had occurred in the Iraqi desert

*****

The head of *Proagnon* boarded a taxi that would take them to the Tehran's *Imam Khomeini* International airport which had now replaced *Mehrabad* as Iran's main international airport. This airport was located 30 kilometres (19 miles) south of the country's capital.

*****

The construction of the airport began before the Islamic Revolution of 1979. The original design was based on Dallas Love Field. The original designers for the project were TAMS, a consortium of US designers. A local joint venture was formed and this was called TAMS-AFA to carry out the full design and supervision of construction.

After the Islamic Revolution, the project was abandoned until the government of Iran decided to design and build the airport using local know-how. The French firm ADP was selected to head the local designers and the engineering firms. A turnkey design and build contract was awarded to a local general contractor company, Kayson, to carry out and manage the construction process. After two years this contract was abandoned and was awarded to a Bonyad, the Mostazafan & Janbazan (M&J Foundation), which was a public cartel.

After construction of the main terminal was finished by M&J Foundation, the Iranian Civil Aviation Organisation decided to turn the management of operations along with the construction of the second terminal to the TAV (Tepe-Akfen-Vie) consortium of two Turkish (Tepe and Akfen) and an Austrian (Vie) companies.

The original opening was scheduled for 11 February 2004, the onset of the auspicious *Ten-Day Dawn* (1-11 February) celebrations, marking the anniversary of the 1979 Islamic Revolution.

There were numerous issues surrounding the construction of the airport including the supply of fuel to the new airport, and a delay in signing a deal with the Iranian oil ministry forced a delay in the opening of the airport until 8 May 2004.

Just prior to the opening on 8 May, two local airlines refused to switch to the new airport. *Economic Hayat-e No* daily quoted Ali Abedzadeh, director of semi-privately-owned Iran Aseman Airlines, as saying *We are not flying from an airport run by foreigners.* TAV officials were ordered to withdraw their personnel and equipment from the airport on 7 May 2004, and operations were handed over to Iran Air. *I think they (the armed forces) were given false reports that the Turks were still on the site, while they had all evacuated the airport by Friday*, airport manager Hossein Pirouzi said.

However, on 8 May, a few hours after the opening of airport, the Revolutionary Guards of the Iranian Armed Forces closed it, citing security fears over the use of foreigners in the running of the airport. Only one Emirates flight from Dubai was allowed to land. The second flight from Dubai, which was an Iran Air flight, was forced to land in Isfahan International Airport, because the *Mehrabad* Airport did not allow it to land there after the *Imam Khomeini* airport was closed by the armed forces. The rest of the flights were diverted to *Mehrabad.*

On 11 May, in a meeting of the Turkish Foreign Ministry Undersecretary Ugur Ziyal and Iranian Foreign Minister Kamal Kharrazi, the Turkish expressed uneasiness about the actions of the Iranian armed forces. The airport then reopened on 13 May, as deputy head of Iran's Joint Chiefs of Staff Brigadier-General Alireza Afshar stated *because foreign companies will no longer be in charge of the airport's operation, security obstacles are removed.*

TAV officials, who had agreed to clear out for two weeks for the dispute to be settled, also stated that they believed the memorandum of understanding they signed with the Iranian government the previous year to operate the airport's Terminal 1 was still in effect.

In April 2005 the $350 million *Imam Khomeini* International Airport was reopened under the management of a consortium of four local airlines—Mahan Air, Aseman, Caspian Airlines and Kish Air—although no formal contract appeared to have been awarded. Further complicating matters, on 29 April 2005, the United Kingdom and Canada warned its citizens against using the airport due to alleged safety concerns concerning the runway, which had been claimed to have been built over ancient *qanats* (subterranean waterways). Iranian officials countered these claims by stating that there were no safety issues and that the International Civil Aviation Organization had inspected and approved the airport.

The Sepah Pasdaran were announced as temporary operators after Iran Air resigned its post in January 2008. However, the Iranian Government sent a request to IETA for an extension on the Sepah's operation of the airport until August 2009.

*****

The *Proagnon* leader boarded the 15:30 (local time) *Iran Air* flight 862 to London's *Heathrow* airport; the only luggage this person took on board with them was a rather official looking briefcase. Settling themselves down in seat 3G aboard the Boeing 767 they brought down the table from the back of the seat in front of them, set the case on the table and waited.

Once all the 258 passengers had boarded the aircraft and had fastened their safety belts, plus the stewardesses had gone through the, usual, safety talk, the *Proagnon* agent smiled to themselves. Flight 862 then began to taxi to the top of runway 11 L /29R, which was 13,772 feet (4,198 metres) long and prepared for, take off. Slowly the twin engines built up thrust and, suddenly, the aircraft gave a lurch and started to power down the runway it was on, building up speed as it went. Finally once it had reached its take off speed the Boeing 767 lifted off the runway and ascended towards the sky, to reach its cruising altitude of 36,000 feet (10,972 metres).

Once the plane had levelled off at its cruising altitude the captain's voice informed the passengers that the aircraft would be landing at *Heathrow* airport, in England, at 20:30 (local time) as the aircraft was travelling at 500 mph (804 kph). This suited the agent's purposes well, hopefully, if all went to plan many of the 258 people on board would arrive at their destination complaining of severe stomach infections.

The agent pressed together the catches on the briefcase; with a hiss of escaping air via two nozzles within the cases exterior lining the briefcase opened revealing a laptop computer, a pair of black, leather, gloves, a parachute (if needed), and an oxygen mask. The nozzles hadn't just released air into the cabin; they had also released a mild virus. Donning the gloves and mask the agent opened the laptop, which would be running on battery power, and powered it up; in just a few minutes the agent had broken into the flight's main computer, having bypassed several firewalls and inputted several varying security clearance codes, the agent then watched as the flight went on its way, and knowing that they could doom flight 862 and all of its 258 civilian passengers.

However, could they do it, or just sit back and let the journey continue, thus letting the virus infect as many passengers, and cabin crew, as possible. Realising that the best option, at this current moment, was to let the aircraft continue on its journey to *Heathrow* the *Proagnon* leader exited the plane's main computer, shut down the laptop and replaced it in the briefcase, and then placed the briefcase under the seat.

Already a few people were starting to get up and rush to the toilets aboard the aircraft pushing past anyone who got in their way. The agent watched all this commotion with something close to amusement; this sure would be a long, and possibly messy, flight.

*****

In the Iraqi desert the convoy of four HART SUVs were travelling eastwards towards the location that was shown on their SAT NAVs. HART had sent all four SUVs in case there happened to be any equipment that could be salvaged, plus the extra 3 vehicles were to bring back the bodies of the other three commanders; a *Hercules* transport plane would be deployed to collect the two M151 Jeeps, HMMWV, cattle truck, together with all the remaining bodies of the HART soldiers. *Proagnon* had struck a blow at HART but, luckily, it hadn't been a decisive blow.

The convoy arrived, in a little over an hour, and while the two surviving members of HART climbed aboard the leading SUV the four lieutenants walked around the military convoy and inspected the damage to the military vehicles; as they moved onto the HMMWV cargo/troop carrier they peered inside at the four, dead, bodies. Not knowing whose body was whose the lieutenants removed all four bodies and loaded them aboard the two Land Cruiser SUV vehicles.

Once everything had been done, and whatever equipment and weapons (mainly M16 rifles) had been salvaged Lieutenant Ben Smith climbed back aboard the Mega Cruiser and contacted the base, at Turkey, that all survivors had been picked up, and all equipment that could be salvaged had been; he then requested tat a C-130J *Hercules* be deployed – with winching capabilities – to collect the four vehicles, complete with the bodies of the fallen soldiers, and return them all to the HART compound outside Geneva. A message was relayed back informing Lieutenant Smith his request would be granted. When the radio transmission had finished Ben turned the communications equipment off, and turned to face his two, rather bedraggled looking, passengers, "Sir, Ma'am, it's good to have you back. We didn't know what to think when we hadn't heard from you for several hours. If I may say so sir I know we've had our differences, in the past, but I'm glad you survived; I admit it would have been better if this tragedy had never taken place and everyone had survived."

"Your sentiments are duly noted Ben," said Ronan, looking Lieutenant Smith straight in the face.

"And ma'am," continued Ben respectfully, addressing Celia, "I shall freely admit that even though I have never really known you, or rated you as a commander, I understand better now why Commander Roberts promoted you to commander. I mean you survived a car accident, last year, and then earlier this year you were almost gassed but thankfully you survived. Most people I know would've given up by now and left HART, but you didn't and I fully admire you for sticking at it."

"Thank you Lieutenant Smith," Commander Most answered. Just then they all heard the roar of the *Hercules'* 4× Rolls-Royce AE 2100D3 turboprop engines overhead. It landed just south, on the road, of the burnt out convoy; the roadway had been closed because of the burnt out vehicles therefore the C-130J could land safely.

Once the transport aircraft had landed the ramp at the back of the plane was lowered and the winch was activated, the loadmaster emerged from the interior of the transport aircraft pulling the winch rope behind him. Reaching the first of the two M151 Jeeps he attached the winch hook onto the front bumper. Reaching inside his uniform tunic he produced a hand held radio and spoke into it; the winch mechanism inside the aircraft was activated and, slowly, the Jeep was dragged inside the interior of the aircraft, the loadmaster followed the vehicle inside, and unhooked the Jeep. The winch was deployed again and, carefully, leading the rope round the vehicle he emerged back out into the sunlight. Next was the turn of the HMMWV, afterwards the cattle truck, and then finally, the second M151 Jeep. Once the whole operation was completed the rear exit ramp was raised, the convoy of SUVs started to drive away from the area, and then the *Hercules* manoeuvred to face the opposite direction. When the SUV convoy was clear the pilot of the C-130J started the four turboprop engines enabling the Dowty R391 six bladed composite propellers to start their clockwise revolutions. Slowly the aircraft built up enough thrust to enable it to take off; it lurched, and then hurtled forward the distance of 3,127 feet (953 metres) that was needed for full take off; climbing to a height of 28,000 feet (8,615 metres) which was its maximum altitude the *Hercules* then levelled off and began, at its cruising speed of 400mph (643 km/h), the 2500 mile (4023 kilometre) journey to the compound outside Geneva, in Switzerland. At their current speed the journey would take approximately eight and a quarter hours, still the passengers wouldn't mind

*****

Iran Air flight 862 landed at *Heathrow* airport at about 20.48 (local time) and the new *Proagnon* leader, dressed like any other returning tourist in jeans and a yellow blouse, exited the civilian airliner, carrying the briefcase, and walked inside the terminal building. Making their way through the exit doors and from the building they hailed one of the numerous black cabs that were found in London, they climbed inside and instructed the driver to drive to a particular residence in southern London.

As they drove along the streets the agent looked out the window, much had changed since the previous year; many structures (especially houses) had been rebuilt, while some had had to be pulled down. The taxi crossed the newly rebuilt Tower Bridge into southern London, finally the cab parked up outside a large house, the driver turned to his passenger, "There you are. That'll be ten pound and fifteen pence."

The agent put their hand in their jeans pocket as if trying to find the correct money. "Come on, I haven't got all night," the driver said, somewhat annoyed. *Taxi drivers are all the same*, thought the passenger, *so impatient.* It was then they produced their *Corvo* knife, and stabbed the driver of the vehicle, and then slit his throat. The agent then replaced the *Corvo* long bladed knife (it was similar to a bread knife).

Exiting the vehicle, briefcase in hand, the agent bounded up the set of seven stone steps and knocked, loudly, on the wooden door. The door was answered a few moments later by a young looking man with only a towel wrapped round him, it was obvious he'd just come from the bath or shower, "Ah there you are," he said as he saw who was standing on the doorstep, "do come in my dear." The person stepped inside, he glanced outside to check nobody had seen her enter this particular residence – it was then that he noticed the taxi and its, now, dead driver – satisfied there was nobody about who may have seen his contact enter his residence and, therefore, nobody that could connect the two of them he closed the door. Turning back around he found his companion admiring him from behind. He, hurriedly, said to them, "You go and make yourself more comfortable whilst I go upstairs and finish off dressing. Then when I come down we'll discuss where we go from here" Reluctantly his guest agreed and went off to the sitting room while he carried on upstairs and dressed himself in jeans and T-shirt.

He ventured back downstairs after about ten minutes to find his guest sitting on his dark red, leather, settee with a glass of wine in their hand, the briefcase on the seat next to them. He went and seated himself on the other end of the settee and looked over at his guest, "You told me Dr Q was dead." This was more a statement than a question.

"I did indeed. It was me who helped bring about his downfall," his guest answered, totally aware of the consequences this action may bring upon them, but they wanted to be truthful with this man.

"Why did you resort to taking this action, knowing the repercussions you may bring upon yourself?" he then asked.

"Simple," his guest started, "I felt he had outlived his usefulness to me, sorry us, I didn't want power. Don't get me wrong but I felt *Proagnon* could do with a new leader, one who could see the bigger picture; all Dr Q or, to give him his real name, Adam Barker seemed focused on was getting revenge on Peter Roberts, by whatever means necessary. So I felt that the time was right to end it all, put him out his misery, and, therefore, lead *Proagnon* to greater glories."

"What you said about Adam Barker simply wanting revenge on Peter Roberts is very true, but he was, ultimately, my puppet; if he had managed to dispose of Roberts and bring down HART as well I would've found other uses for him." Next he asked the question that really surprised his guest, "Now how can I make use of you?"

"We'll discuss that while we're in bed."

"You're remarkably single minded, I like your spirit, let's go then." The two of them then got up and left the room. "Before you make your final decision about whether you want to be my puppet there is someone I think you ought to meet," he told his guest as they were climbing the stairs.

"When do I get to meet this person?" his companion asked the man, as they reached his bedroom.

"In a few days, in the meantime let's just enjoy being together again," and with that they threw caution to the wind

*****

The convoy of four HART SUVs had reached headquarters in Turkey, and currently the Commanders were meeting with base commander John Craig. Craig was saying, "I've been in contact with HART headquarters in Geneva and informed them of everything that has happened; apparently now, with the death of Commander Roberts HART are leaderless and, therefore, in turmoil. Dr Schaiffer is holding things together as best he can, along with Gwyneth Jones, but he is no natural leader and is more suited to dealing with injured patients. So the job as overall HART commander should fall to the next in seniority."

"And that person would be me!" announced Commander Strobing, suddenly realizing that he was next in seniority.

"That is correct," reiterated John Craig, "unfortunately this cannot be conferred on you here. You will have to wait until you both return to HARTs main headquarters, but as far as I can see there will be no opposition to you assuming overall command."

"Right," announced Commander Strobing suddenly, "let's get the four lieutenants in here, and see what sort of losses HART has incurred since coming to Iran."

Craig called up the computer file while the lieutenants were found; once all six men and one woman were seated in the base commander's office he produced a print out of the file, and then turned round to face them across the desk. "Now, according to this we have lost, since HART came to Iran, 16 men and 3 vehicles in Iran, and we've lost 135 soldiers and 14 vehicles in the desert battle, that includes the vehicles we have just deployed back, aboard the *Hercules*, to Geneva; so, unfortunately, that means that the rest of the base staff, plus you six, are the only HART personnel left on this site. On the plus side it means there are fewer vehicles to transport back, and you will be taking 20 fit men back with you. "

"20 soldiers!" announced Celia, surprised. "How many did we bring with us?"

"Counting you six, 177," responded John evenly. "I know it doesn't seem many, but you must remember war claims many casualties."

John then contacted main headquarters, in Geneva, and requested that the C-17 Globmaster III, C141B Starlifter, and the C-5 Galaxy be sent over to collect the remaining, undamaged, vehicles and men. Next John contacted, via the outside phone line, *Esenboga* International Airport, in Ankara, and requested that a *Learjet 55* be readied for take off in the next couple of hours.

Once this had all been done he replaced the STU-8 handset and looked across at the senior officers again, and said, "I think that's everything. The SUVs will take you to the airport at Ankara. Safe journey home." Then the two Commanders, along with the four lieutenants left the base commander's office, and made their way back to where the SUVs were stored.

They boarded the Toyota Mega Cruiser and the Range Rover, and then, once the vehicles engines were started, the two vehicles left the base grounds and began their journey towards Ankara, the capital of Turkey, and *Esenboga* International Airport.

*****

Ankara was the country's second largest city after Istanbul. The city had a mean elevation of 850 metres (2,800 ft), and was of 2007 the city had a population of 4,751,360, which included the eight districts under the city's administration; probably the population was nearer to 8,000,000 by now – if not more. Ankara also served as the capital of the Ankara Province.

As with many ancient cities, Ankara had gone by several names over the ages: The Hittites gave it the name *Ankuwash* before 1200 BC. The Galatians and Romans called it *Ancyra*. In the classical, Hellenistic, and Byzantine periods it was known as □γκυρα (*Ánkyra*, meaning *Anchor*) in Greek. The local Armenians called it *Enkare*. The city was also known in the European languages as *Angora* after its conquest by the Seljuk Turks in 1073, and continued to be internationally called with this name until it was officially renamed *Ankara* with the Turkish Postal Service Law of 1930.

Centrally located in Anatolia, Ankara was an important commercial and industrial city. It was the centre of the Turkish Government, and houses all foreign embassies. It was also an important crossroads of trade, strategically located at the centre of Turkey's highway and railway networks, and served as the marketing centre for the surrounding agricultural area. The city was famous for its long-haired Angora goat and its prized wool (mohair), a unique breed of cat (Angora cat), white rabbits and their prized wool (Angora wool), pears, honey, and the region's muscat grapes.

The historical centre of Ankara was situated upon a steep and rocky hill, which rises 150 m (492 ft) above the plain on the left bank of the *Ankara Çayı*, a tributary of the *Sakarya* (Sangarius) river. The city was located at 39°52'30" North, 32°52' East and about 351 km (218 mi) to the southeast of Istanbul, the country's largest city. Although it was situated in one of the driest places of Turkey and surrounded mostly by steppe vegetation except for the forested areas on the southern periphery, Ankara could be considered a green city in terms of green areas per inhabitant, which was 72 m^2 per head.

Ankara was a very old city with various Hittite, Phrygian, Hellenistic, Roman, Byzantine, and Ottoman archaeological sites. The hill which overlooked the city was crowned by the ruins of the old castle, which added to the picturesqueness of the view, but only a few historic structures surrounding the old citadel have survived to date. There are, however, many finely preserved remains of Hellenistic, Roman and Byzantine architecture, the most remarkable of these being the Temple of Augustus and Rome.

*****

The airport was located in the north-east region of Ankara. They arrived at the airport and were left to book in. Luckily each of them was carrying his/her HART passport which, usually, fast tracked any HART personnel; sure enough the six people were shown straight through to the airside lounge for the *Learjet 55* which would take them home to Geneva's *Cointrin* International Airport.

*****

Esenboga International Airport was an airport located 28 km (17 mi) east of Ankara. It had been operating since 1955. The name of the airport came from the village of Esenboğa (the g is silent), which literally meant *healthy bull*.

In 2008, ESB served 5,692,133 passengers, 4,444,311 of which were domestic passengers. It ranked 3rd in terms of total passenger traffic, 2nd in terms of domestic traffic and 7th in terms of international traffic among airports in Turkey.

Esenboga International Airport was awarded as the best airport in Europe by ACI Europe (Airport Council International) and the award presented to airport officials on 17 June 2009 in Manchester. The award was given in 4 categories every year and *Esenboga* was in the 5-10 million per annum category. It was the first time an ACI award was granted to a Turkish Airport. According to ACI-Europe, *As with number of the top candidates in this category, the airport excels in all the keys areas of operations, however the judges singled it out for its work in the area of environmental innovation, securing an incredible 25% energy savings stemming from its recycling of exhaust gases to power its air conditioning plants*.

*****

The jet that was to take the six people to Geneva was finally rolled out the hangar at about 15.02 (local time) and taxied to the edge of the terminal building to receive its six passengers.

*****

The Learjet 55 *Longhorn* was a business jet that had been manufactured by Gates Learjet. The introduction of the Learjet 50 series occurred at the 1977 Paris air show. The winglets on the Learjet 55 were developed by NASA, thus the winglets gave the 55 the nickname *longhorn*. Construction of the Learjet 55 began in April 1978 after extensive testing and much work on the wing design which came, initially, from the Learjet 25. The Learjet 55 first flew on 19 April 1979, while the first production aircraft were produced starting on 18 March 1981. 147 Learjet 55 aircraft were delivered.

Since 2008 any redundant Learjet aircraft had been bought up by HART, to be used, along with any redundant aircraft from the Gulfstream series, to transport any HART agent to, or from, a foreign country where they were needed. The agents boarded the Learjet *55*; actually it was a 55C/LR which carried an extra tank of fuel, for long distance flights, in its tail cone. However, as this flight was 1500 miles (2400 kilometres) in distance the extra fuel would probably be needed.

The jet, so they were informed, would be travelling at 462 mph (774 km/h), which was the jet's cruising speed, so the business aircraft would arrive at its destination in approximately four hours, probably a little less. Once everyone was safely aboard, and the safety procedures had been followed the two Honeywell/ Garrett TFE731-3AR engines. The TFE731-3AR engine produced 3,700 lbs of static thrust when operating at sea level with the additional Automatic Power Reserve *APR* capable of producing up to 3,880 lbs of thrust when it was operating. Whilst they were travelling the six passengers aboard chatted, quietly, amongst themselves, exchanging opinions about the previous year's war and contemplating what would happen now that it was all over.

Yet the war was far from over as the next few months, possibly longer, would prove.

*****

The three of them, two men and one woman met in a small, London, café about three days later; they sat at a corner table so, hopefully, nobody would overhear them, they all ordered steak pie and potatoes, together with three mugs of tea – the café that they were in, the *Contigi*, had a very good reputation. As they were waiting for their food the man from London introduced his guest, who was staying with him, to the new arrival, "I would like to introduce you to Dr. Simon Forrestor, I believe he can assist us in our ambition."

"Oh yes," responded the woman, "and how, exactly, does Mr Forrestor intend to assist us?" Her voice was dripping with sarcasm, as if dismissing this man as being of no use.

"My dear," Simon said to her, "my work involves dealing with many unwell people."

"Yes buddy," she replied, more sarcasm, "but we want to kill people not make them better, or hasn't my companion," she looked over at him, "informed you of that?" While her attention was away from him Simon produced a hypodermic from inside his jacket and broke her skin with it. "Ow," she cried, turning quickly back, Simon removed the needle. "What have you injected me with?"

"Absolutely nothing," Dr Forrestor responded with a grin. "Now imagine if I had injected a poison into your bloodstream. You might survive a few minutes, hours or days, or the effect could be instantaneous. I have my own, secret, laboratory at *John Groggins* Hospital, in Norwich, where I study the poison's effect on the human body, and then, if I feel it is needed, I develop it into something more lethal."

"You mean?" asked the woman, now thinking of what could be achieved, and smiling at those thoughts. "Yes I believe you could help us achieve our ultimate ambition," looking over at her partner and smiling mischievously at him.

It was then that the food arrived and having no time for further conversation, at that moment, they all tucked in heartily. The food was hot, as it should have been, and the three mugs of tea were steaming. They each drank the hot liquid, gratefully, and then the man went up and paid for their meal, whilst Simon Forrestor and the woman talked about the development of this poison.

Once the bill had been paid, the two people accompanied Dr Forrestor back to his car: a, lime green, Renault *Megane*. As the three of them were making their way through one of southern London's, numerous, parks the woman turned to Mr Forrestor and asked, "Tell me Mr Forrestor do you have a wife?"

"Why yes Miss erm…"

"Turner," she said quickly. "Carol Turner."

"Yes I do Miss Turner. My wife Rebecca and I have been married for thirty years. May I enquire as to why you're asking?"

"You may. The answer is quite simple, if you wish to prove yourself worthy of *Proagnon* I simply would like you to develop a killer poison that will bring about instant death and use it on her. I also wish you then to develop an airborne version of this poison."

"What?" he asked, suddenly, her words sinking in, and turned to look at her. "You want me to kill my wife of thirty years, that's murder. I won't do it."

"You will," Miss Turner retorted, producing the *Corvo* knife. "You will give her the lethal injection, photograph her dead body – I assume you have a camera on your mobile phone, and then send the picture to my companion's mobile phone. His number is, I believe, 07*********; this photograph will prove that you are serious about helping us."

"And if I refuse?" he enquired, thinking he already knew the answer.

"Simple, I will kill you here and now and we," looking over at her partner who nodded, "shall dispose of both your car and body, and make it look like an accident."

"Now I ask again, Dr Forrestor, are you with us or not?"

"Yes, I'm with you," he responded, somewhat reluctantly. "You shall hear from me in the next few days."

"We'd better," the woman called Carol Turner told him. With that he gave them both a wan smile, and then got in his car and drove off.

*****

The Learjet *55* touched down at *Cointrin* International Airport at 18:50 (local time) and the six HART personnel were met by receptionist's Joshua Smith and Ben Gillespe in two *Apollo II* cars. The two commanders, plus Lieutenant Smith, climbed into the lead automobile, with Joshua Smith, while the other three lieutenants climbed into the following car, "Welcome back, sirs, ma'am," Joshua said to his passengers enthusiastically, as the convoy of vehicles left the airport compound.

The automobiles travelled the, relatively, short distance of fifteen miles to the compound that was the headquarters for the Human Alliance for the Retaliation against Terrorism (HART) counter terrorist organisation. The two commanders left the lead vehicle and went to their separate residences to clean themselves up; likewise the four lieutenants returned to their barracks to make themselves look more presentable. The two receptionists, meanwhile, returned to the main building, their job was done for today.

Once they were ready the commanders, along with all four of the lieutenants, marched over to the main building. Inside they took the elevator to the fourth floor, and found nobody about; there was nobody in reception or in any of the offices. Assuming some emergency had arisen the six personnel made their way to the conference room; reaching the double doors Commander Strobing opened them, behind the doors and seated at the rectangular table were: Hans Schaiffer, Gwyneth Jones, Lisa Bell, Joshua Smith and Ben Gillespe. "Welcome home commanders, lieutenants," Dr Schaiffer said to them. "We all know what fate befell the other HART commanders and a good number of our soldiers. Now we need a new overall commander, and I believe, Ronan, you are, actually, next in the chain of command."

"Who? Me," Ronan said, surprised but he knew this was coming.

"Yes, you," replied Dr Schaiffer. "Either you or Mrs Most, I cannot take command, I am more suited to the medical side of things, while the rest of us," he gestured around the table, "are mere receptionists and not worthy of such a high ranking job. Plus Mr Strobing you are the more senior HART commander here. Therefore, do you accept?"

"Erm," answered Commander Strobing, now a little unsure – the job would probably come with added responsibilities, and then there was his son to consider – sure he was growing up, fast, but would he want his father, his only parent, to put himself in more danger – yet Simon didn't know his father was a HART operative. Yet it was his decision to make, no one would make it for him; after what seemed an eternity, to those waiting, though it was only a few minutes Ronan reached a decision, a decision that could well change his life forever.

He looked at the ten assembled people in that room, and then looked Dr Hans Schaiffer straight in the face and said calmly, "I accept the leadership of this organisation and all the responsibilities the job entails."

Commander Ronan Strobing then made his first speech as overall commander, "There will be one or two minor changes but nothing drastic. I require that Commander Most act as my number two, plus I promote all four of the lieutenants gathered here to the position of commanders, to replace the commanders of their squads, be those commanders alive or dead. You five people, whether doctor or receptionist, shall continue with your, ordinary, everyday duties; that is all, carry on; you five commanders with me." Dr Schaiffer and the receptionists left the room after swearing their allegiance to their new commander.

Next out came Commander Strobing and the other five commanders. He led them all into, what used to be, Peter Roberts' office. "Please be seated," he said to the others while he seated himself behind the desk. Once everyone else was seated he began, "Now we have suffered many casualties over the past few months. Therefore, we are down to the people in this room, the five people that were in the conference room, the twenty soldiers that are returning from Turkey, the four soldiers that were in Germany, and our full compliment of ten medical staff. Therefore, that is just forty five. As for our new squads of soldiers you new commanders will only have six soldiers under your command, for the time being."

"Unfortunately *Proagnon* have dealt us a big blow, but we will recover. Let's just hope they, I assume there's some members left, don't decide to strike again too soon. In fact I hope we aren't called upon for a while"

Little did Commander Strobing know how wrong he could be!

CHAPTER 1

PLANS & A MOVE!

In the house, in southern London Carol Turner informed her partner, who was using the name Floyd Maxwell that she was returning to the underground base in Iran, and would transport part of the *Proagnon* force to a different base; they had located an old, now disused, sea fort off the northern coast of Scotland – this belonged to the Maxwell consortium, of which Floyd Maxwell was head while Carol Turner was his *sleeping* partner.

The sea fort was large and round with a helipad on top, and several moorings for sea vessels; the actual fort was extremely spacious inside, containing crew quarters, radio room, numerous laboratories, canteen along with adjoining dining room, armament stations, etc. The exterior was built out of a concrete type substance with a watch tower situated on top, along with the helipad. Altogether the structure was a magnificent looking sight, and looked impregnable.

The rest of the *Proagnon* force, the soldiers, would stay in the Iranian bunker until such time that they were needed. With that both Floyd and Carol exited the house where Floyd lived, and climbed into his car, a grey Subaru saloon, and he proceeded to drive her to *Heathrow* airport. Carrying her briefcase she walked inside the main building to check in, after kissing him and promising she'd return to his side soon; cheerily he waved her off and then left for the house where he lived, when he got back he noticed the black cab was gone – he'd left instructions for a friend of his to come and tow the cab away, and then destroy it, it looked as though these instructions had been carried out.

*****

At *Heathrow* airport Miss Turner checked in on the 17:10 flight to *Imam Khomeini* airport, in Tehran; as she was only carrying a, relatively, empty briefcase, apart from a pair of leather gloves the decision was made to let her carry it on board, and not to store it in the hold of flight 781. However, she had no, actual, luggage to speak of, no suitcases; she did inform airport security that she was a travelling rep and was now going back to the organisation that employed her. She did begin to wonder firstly about how the 258 people she'd already infected were getting on and secondly if Simon Forrestor had carried out his task yet. Still she would be returning to England in a few days.

*****

At HART headquarters Ronan was seated in his office when there was a knock at the door, "Come in," called Commander Strobing, the door opened and Gwyneth Jones walked in. "Yes Mrs Jones," he said.

"Sir, we've had an urgent communication from John Craig, in Turkey, it seems that one of the four other bodies that was brought in has mysteriously, got up and walked out the base, nobody saw a thing."

"Do they know who it was?" enquired the Commander.

"No," answered Gwyneth honestly. "They are awaiting dental records from England and the United States of America, but they are pretty sure it wasn't Lucy Lang. However, they want to make certain."

"Damn!" Ronan said angrily, smashing his fist down on the desk in front of him. "You say the body just got up and walked out?"

"Yes sir," replied Gwyneth hesitantly.

The commander now looked very angry. "Obviously there is a lapse in security over there. Tell them to step up security." Just then they heard the engines of the last of the transport aircraft overhead.

"That'll be the Galaxy bringing the Abrams tank," Mrs Jones said to the commander – as if he hadn't guessed, "it had to be delayed because of a, temporary, lack of fuel for the plane. I've also brought you the condolence forms to sign." Ronan remembered the last time he'd had to sign these types of forms, it was only last year, plus he'd only had to sign three, this time he had to sign over thirty. Still he had accepted this job with his eyes wide open.

Mrs Jones carried on, "The twenty soldiers, as well as their commanding officers, are being checked over by Dr Schaiffer and the medical staff. Perhaps you should get yourself checked over sir."

"I'll go when I can," he answered her, "now if you'll excuse me I've got forms to sign." The new commander didn't seem his usual self at the moment, so Gwyneth decided to withdraw.

"Yes sir," she remarked, "I'll leave you now, once you've finished signing those if you'll let me have them back."

"I will Gwyneth, sorry if I don't seem myself at the moment but I'm still readjusting"

"Of course sir," and Gwyneth Jones withdrew from the office, leaving Commander Strobing to work in peace. As she was returning to her receptionist duties she noticed a figure watching her from the shadows, "Hello," she called to it. The figure didn't respond, it just retreated further into the shadows, and then disappeared. It was then that Commander Most appeared from round the corridor corner; seeing the puzzled look on the receptionist's face Celia wandered over and said to the woman, "What's the matter?"

"Oh hello Commander Most, nothing's actually wrong with me, it's just I'm sure I saw a person shaped figure standing over in the shadows; I'm sure it was watching me as I left Commander Strobing's office."

"Did you recognise the figure you allege you saw?" enquired Celia, thinking it may just have been an out of place filing cabinet, or cupboard.

"Commander Most," the other woman said, indignantly, "there is absolutely nothing wrong with my eyesight, I know what I saw. The figure in question may have been as tall as a cupboard, maybe marginally shorter, but believe me the figure was there, I assure you." Gwyneth was most insistent that she was telling the truth it was hard not to believe her. "And no I didn't recognise the figure." Finally she asked, "Do you think I should report this?"

"No, I shouldn't report it, after all it may have been nothing," Celia told the other woman calmly.

"You're probably right," Mrs Jones said to her senior, "Commander Strobing's got enough to deal with at the moment." Gwyneth looked down at Celia Most, "Still you know him better than most. Try and persuade him to get himself checked out by Dr Schaiffer."

"I will," Mrs Most promised her junior colleague, Mrs Jones then made her way back to reception.

*****

Miss Turner arrived back in Iran at 01:45 the next morning, she disembarked the *Iran Air* flight designated 781, walked through the airport building, found the vehicle that had been sent to meet her and it took her back to the *Proagnon* bunker. Once the car pulled up to the bunker she climbed out, deposited the briefcase in her, private, quarters, and then called a meeting in the - main - conference room.

All the *Proagnon* soldiers, along with Mitchell Walker – who had been promoted to deputy leader; she seated herself at the head of the table and spoke, "My contact and I have enlisted the assistance of a doctor in our quest for, global, power, plus we have located an old sea fort off the northern coast of Scotland which is owned, presently, by the Maxwell consortium. Therefore I suggest you will all be able to vote in a moment, that we divide our forces; those of you that have scientific knowledge will be transferred, and join up with Dr Simon Forrestor, should he have completed his task successfully."

"And what happens to those of us with no, or very little, scientific knowledge?" one young soldier asked, evidently he was one with very little scientific knowledge.

Miss Sandy Tulliver looked over at him, "All those other soldiers will remain here, under the command of my deputy Mitchell Walker. Now we shall put this to a vote, all those who feel this would be a good plan?" Many hands were raised. "I think that settles it – twenty for – so I assume you five are against." These five soldiers nodded.

Sandy spoke again, "We shall use the couple of remaining HIND D class helicopters to transport the men to the sea fort; this activity will take place at night. Now hands up those with scientific knowledge." Several men raised their hands. "Only ten of you," Sandy asked, totally aghast and shocked.

"So it would seem," announced Mitchell.

"Right, I'd like you ten men to report to the HINDs immediately. I shall be along, in a minute, to issue your pilots with their flight plans." Once everyone had left the room she spoke to Mitchell, "I am leaving you in command of the soldiers, in this bunker. If you need me you can reach me at this number," and she wrote the number down, "use the STU-9." She then looked directly at him, "And Mitchell."

"Yes ma'am?"

"Look after yourself."

"And you," he responded with feeling, but those feelings weren't real. He despised this woman and still had no idea why Dr Q had chosen her as his deputy – when he would have been a much better choice.

*****

Miss Tulliver then left the conference room and made out the flight plans for the HIND pilots; once this was done she went and issued these flight plans to the pilots. After handing over command of the bunker to Mr Walker she left to catch her return flight to *Heathrow*. She had decided to return by aircraft as she wouldn't be needed on the fort.

*****

In his house in southern London Floyd Maxwell received a text message, with a picture attached, from Mr Forrestor, all the message said was 'job done!' The picture showed Forrestor's, now, dead wife, her tongue hanging out her mouth; it wasn't a pretty sight. Admittedly, she'd probably been beautiful once, but not now, she also had several, small, growths on her face, and some, even, on her tongue.

He knew his partner had requested Forrestor kill his wife, but it was a horrible death; and now she wanted the doctor to mass produce this poison as an airborne virus, that would be used to kill off as many of the world's population as possible – starting with Britain. This was a barbaric thought, but it was necessary.

He would show her the picture when she, eventually, returned. In the meantime he had work to do, on the internet. If he was right, the information he turned up would change her life, in more ways than one.

*****

The flight from Iran touched down at *Heathrow* at 11:40 (local time) a couple of days after she'd departed, she'd slept on the flight back but still felt rough. Of course she was carrying her briefcase when Floyd collected her. "You look rough," he said as she climbed into the automobile he was driving.

"Thanks for the vote of confidence," Miss Turner muttered to him. "I'll rest at your place. Incidentally I may need you to make some transport arrangements for Dr Forrestor."

"That's fine by me," he told her. "Actually I've got a surprise for you, back at the house."

"Don't tell me you're out of milk," Carol responded, trying to make it sound like a joke.

"Not at all," Floyd replied, laughing, "it's better than that." He carried on driving back to his house, his companion deep in thought at what this surprise might actually be. They, eventually, pulled up outside his house and went up the steps and inside.

Sunlight streamed through the kitchen window, and, out into the hallway flooding it with light. Carol hadn't noticed before but Floyd had a collection of assorted weapons, from around the world, mounted, in a glass case on the wall. While Mr Maxwell busied himself, making them both a cup of tea, in the kitchen, Carol went through to the sitting room to wait for his return.

When he did return, about five minutes later, he was carrying a tray with the tea things and a plate of biscuits on; he set the tray down on the table in front of her, "Before we have tea and biscuits," he produced his mobile phone, "I have something to show you." Carol, suddenly, sat more upright on the leather sofa she was sitting on; "here we are," and Floyd handed her the mobile phone.

"Well, well, well," she announced, "it looks like Dr Forrestor's prepared to help us after all. We will need to contact him, to congratulate him." She was looking at the picture of Mrs Rebecca Forrestor, now deceased. "Not a pretty sight is she?" she asked, looking up at Floyd, who nodded in confirmation. "Still we had to make sure the substance worked, and she made the perfect guinea pig."

Mr Maxwell turned and said to Miss Turner, "You may use my phone to contact Simon Forrestor, now we know the poison works. If need be we can travel to the hospital where he works and kidnap him, if he isn't willing to leave, along with his notes."

"Good boy," Carol responded with plenty of sarcasm in her voice. "I see my influence is rubbing off on you."

She then looked up and told him, "I'm sorry but I don't think I can face any tea and biscuits. I'm growing tired."

"Okay," he responded, now showing concern for her. "You go and get some rest." She left the room and started up the stairs.

*****

Dr Simon Forrestor had been born in 1961, the only child to his parents Matthew Forrestor – known as Matt – and his German mother Helga Lutendorff[1]. He figured he was their only child until his elder sister, Julia Fuller, appeared on the scene, in 1974, she being the child of his father's sister and his father.

As time went on his sister found herself a boyfriend named Mark Hindle, whilst Simon had found himself a girlfriend named Rebecca Morris; actually, he'd known Rebecca since secondary school and had always liked her. Sadly, when Simon's mother was killed in an automobile accident one winter the whole family had been reunited for one final time, for their

[1] See To Avenge the Father.

father's sake. Now Julia and Mark were married, they had been since 1979, and living in Dawlish, Devon.

When Simon's mother had died he had decided to study medicine, and one day become a doctor, which he'd achieved at the age of twenty five. At that time he'd already been married to Rebecca for five years; he'd sometimes, in the earlier days of their marriage, found it difficult to fit in his time at medical school around the marriage, but with time and the support of his wife, they'd got through that rough patch.

Simon, as well as treating patients, had been studying the effects of certain toxins (poisons) on the human body and therefore working on vaccines – at least that's what his wife had been told by him – however, what she didn't know was her husband had a secret laboratory, on the floor below the basement at *John Groggins* Hospital, where he worked.

He'd always seemed such a happy person until his meeting in London, once he'd returned to Norwich his mood and demeanour had darkened considerably. He'd, suddenly, thrown all his regular work aside, and started to study poisons again with renewed interest and vigour. Rebecca wasn't sure why he'd changed but she'd soon find out.

A few days after he'd returned from London the good doctor had injected his wife with a substance 'a harmless mild sedative' he'd told her. Thinking that he'd been telling her the truth she'd ascended the stairs to go to bed, unaware of the poison coursing through her veins, reaching the top of the flight of steps Rebecca felt slightly dizzy. "Simon," she called weakly, "I don't feel very good."

He appeared at the bottom of the stairs, "I'm sure you'll be okay after a good rest," her husband reassured her. "Don't worry." He'd then returned to the sitting room and tidied up, make the place look neat and tidy – that's how she liked it; pausing in his work, for a second, he checked his watch – five minutes had elapsed since he'd administered the lethal injection; couldn't be long to go now.

Quite suddenly, he heard a crash from upstairs so he rushed to the bottom of the stairs just in time to see his wife's body falling down the stairs. Knowing what had happened he rushed to get his mobile phone, and also put on some surgeon's gloves, sauntering back he, carefully, prised her lips apart and withdrew her tongue; it was then he noticed several, small, growths on her face. Then he took a picture of her dead form, and sent it along with a text message to the number he'd been given.

Once his task was completed, he collected the files and books he'd been working from, along with his computer records, and placed them in a box which he loaded into the boot of his car, climbed in the car and drove away; once he was about ten miles away he phoned the authorities to inform them of what had happened. He knew he was guilty of her murder but, hopefully, *Proagnon* would look after him, after all they needed his skills.

*****

Back at HART HQ Commander Ronan Strobing was looking out his office window; it was a reasonably sunny day, he was looking out over the scenery around; he was still wondering if he'd made the right decision accepting a job with so many responsibilities. He did want this job, yet he also wanted to be a father to his son, Simon. So he was faced with a dilemma.

In fact he was so deep in concentration he failed to notice the office door open and the fact Commander Celia Most had entered the room. She looked at him, a look of concern on her face, "Ronan," she called, no reaction. "Commander Strobing!"

"What?" he turned to face her then, and his face looked, suddenly, so old. "Oh it's you; sorry, I was lost in thought. Please have a seat." Celia sat herself, on a chair, on the other side of the desk.

"You were lost in thought," started the female HART commander, "I could've been an assassin and killed you easily. Now tell me what's wrong?" Celia had known him, for such a long time, she knew when there was something bothering him. *Was he that predictable?* Ronan wondered.

"It's all this, Celia, I didn't ask for all this responsibility, at least not yet. All I wanted was to be a good father to my son, and to do my job, as best I could. Yet, suddenly, my whole world's been turned upside down, my wife and daughter are killed, I'm involved in an automobile accident, the two agents who are with me, in Russia, are killed, I'm nearly killed myself, and to top it all we've lost many friends and colleagues in Iraq including Peter Roberts, Leon Bigship and Lucy Lang."

"You know you can still rely on me," soothed Celia, "and as your deputy I'm willing, in fact more than willing, to take over, temporary, command if you ever feel a week, back in England, with young Simon is what you need. You don't need to shoulder this burden by yourself."

"Thank you Celia, I would like to take you up on your offer." Ronan then handed the *gold* star of leadership over to his deputy, and promptly left the office leaving Celia Most in command. "If anyone wants me I'll be at my residence," he announced. With that he was gone.

Commander Most sat in the chair of command, thinking to herself, *Peter will be worried that I'm here, in charge, while Commander Strobing goes home. Still, as my husband knows, he's always known, duty comes first as does my loyalty to Ronan, plus Mike can look after himself nowadays. Anyway, I'm sure if Ronan remembers he'll go and see my husband – put his mind at rest.* She looked around the desk, Ronan had put up several pictures of his family there was one each of his children – Simon and Zoe, although Zoe was now dead. The third was of his wife Mandy, but she too was dead now, one was of Mandy and himself, on their wedding day, whilst the final photo was a picture of all four of them on a holiday somewhere.

Celia Most knew some people may disapprove of the photos with Mandy and Zoe in but if that was how he wanted to keep their memories alive that was Ronan's business. The only photo that gave her a twinge of regret was the one of the Strobing's wedding; if things had turned out different it would have been her and not Mandy in the photo.

Dragging herself back to the present Celia suddenly thought about the lack of soldiers, around the compound, so called up a file on the computer called *Reserves* and printed a copy of the list out. With the computer printout in her hand she went through to the main reception, Joshua Smith was manning reception today as Gwyneth Jones had the day off. "Josh," she said, thrusting the list under his nose, "please call the people on this list, they're meant to be reservists, and request that they come in as HART needs them."

"Right away ma'am," Joshua said to her. Then he asked, "Where is Commander Strobing?"

Commander Most chose her words carefully, "He's had to take, temporary, leave to go and see his family, in England, so until he returns I'll be in command." Mrs Most then started to wander back to the commander's office.

As she was crossing the corridor, Celia caught sight of a fleeing figure, "Halt," she shouted but the figure didn't stop, it just kept moving; Celia drew her Beretta 92 and started to run after the figure. She thought she recognised the person she was chasing, in fact she was pretty certain, but until she caught the fleeing figure she couldn't be absolutely sure. "Halt, she shouted again. "I am an armed HART operative and will use my weapon if I have to," with that she fired a warning shot at the person's feet. The 9mm cartridge hit the floor just behind the fleeing figure.

They were running down the corridor that led to the main entrance, "Lower the shutter," Commander Most shouted to the guards on duty. "Stop that person." The door shutter started to be lowered, Commander Most thought that they'd trapped the figure but it dived through the open gap between the shutter and the ground and then the shutter clanged shut. Commander Most sighed resignedly, they'd lost their quarry. "Get that shutter raised," she shouted; the guards looked at her quizzically, "you heard me, just do it!" The men shrugged their shoulders and operated the mechanism that would raise the metal shutter.

As soon as the shutter had been raised far enough Celia ducked under the shutter and stepped out into the, relatively, cool air, even though bright sunshine was shining down; of the figure there was absolutely no sign, it was as though they'd never existed. Sighing in frustration Commander Most walked back inside, past the two guards on duty, and returned up to the fourth floor, where the commander's office was located.

Once in the corridor outside she looked towards the office and suddenly stopped dead, in her tracks; the door to the office was open. Drawing her re-holstered firearm Celia, cautiously, made her way over to the doorway, nothing seemed out of place; however, she, carefully, ventured inside – she remembered that her lack of caution many months ago had nearly ended up costing her life – she didn't intend to repeat that mistake or next time the consequences might be of a more fatal nature.

Once she was more or less in the room she kicked the door shut, with a flip from her heel, and whirled around, pointing her Beretta semi-automatic pistol in every direction, finding nobody else, in the office, she relaxed and started to re-holster her firearm.

Suddenly, somebody knocked on the outer door, making her jump – quickly Celia withdrew her weapon again but then realised if this was an assassin, come to kill Commander Strobing or herself, why would they knock on the door; hastily she perched on the edge of the desk and called cheerfully, "Come in."

The door opened and Joshua Smith walked in, "I've contacted the people on the list you gave me, and forty out of the seventy people on the list have confirmed they are able to come in and assist us."

"Okay, what about the other thirty people?"

"Some I can't get through to, either they've changed their phone number and not informed us or there's some other reason; whilst others are away with their loved ones," Joshua informed the base commander.

"Has there been any further word from Commander Craig, in Turkey, regarding their, mysterious, disappearing body?" Celia Most enquired.

"Not as yet, but I intend to chase them up later if you require me to," he replied to her question. The look she gave him confirmed that he should enquire further. "Right you are ma'am, I'll just leave the list of names with you – I've circled the ones that can come in." He laid the sheet of paper on the desk, saluted, and left the office to return to his work in reception.

Just before he left her Commander Most called, "Josh, have the four, new, operational commanders convene here as soon as possible."

"Yes ma'am."

*****

Over in England, Carol Turner was just getting up after her, what she thought was a, short nap; she dressed in a white blouse, this time, as well as her jeans, as she passed a clock on the sideboard she was stunned to see it was already 19:00, she'd come up for a rest at 16:00. Carol left the bedroom and wandered down the stairs.

Floyd Maxwell was waiting in the sitting room for her. When she went in he turned the TV off, he'd been watching some film, got up from his seat and went over and kissed her, tenderly, on the cheek. "Come with me," he said to her and led her from the room, through the kitchen, and out into the conservatory – at the rear of the house; there were two wicker seats and a table situated in this extra room. They seated themselves in the chairs and sat there looking out at the garden, and lawn beyond. As it was June the sun was beginning to reach its full height in the sky, and also it's most powerful; Carol got up from her seat after a few minutes, wandered outside through the open conservatory doors and lay down, on her back, on the lush green lawn.

Eventually, she walked back into the conservatory and sat back in the chair she'd vacated earlier. Looking across at Mr Maxwell she said, "When Mr Forrestor has developed an airborne version of his killer virus I think we should use people to release by means of a deodorant spray – up north, for a start. Speaking of Mr Forrestor I believe we should journey up to the hospital where he works, have the helicopter meet us there."

"Agreed, on both counts," Floyd responded to her, and then he said, "why delay further? Let's go and get him now." The two of them walked back through Mr Maxwell's house, and climbed into his, silver, Vauxhall *Vectra* – he had several different cars - and he started the automobile up; the vehicle pulled away from where it was parked and began the, nearly, 114 mile (183 kilometre) journey to *John Groggins* Hospital, up in Norwich.

*****

The plane carrying Commander Strobing, a Gulfstream *G650*, left *Cointrin* airport at 17:30 and landed at *Robin Hood* airport at 18:45, but due to the time difference it was only 17:45 in England. He disembarked the plane with the luggage he'd brought with him, and presented himself to one of the airport staff, who immediately recognised him as a HART operative and went and fetched the keys to his Hyundai 4 x 4 from the security office.

Ronan then drove the 48 mile (78 kilometres) journey to his in-laws house, in Hull, to see his son. When he reached the house he knocked on the door, politely, which was answered by Elle Stevens. "Hello Ronan," she said when she saw who it was outside, "I guess you've come to see Simon, he has missed you, please come in – he's in the sitting room watching cartoons." She stepped aside as he came in. It was then that Ronan noticed the tray, on the side, with a couple of sandwiches and a glass of, what looked like, milk on it. "I'm sorry; I'll make you a cup of tea when I come down from attending to Arnold."

"What's wrong with him?" the HART commander asked curiously.

"He came down with a stomach bug a couple of weeks back," Elle answered, "he dismissed it as nothing, you know what he's like. I tried to get him to see a doctor, but he refused, anyway last week he took a turn for the worse so he did go to the doctor's; the doctor told him he'd got a type of flu and to get plenty of rest, so I'm having to look after him, as well as Simon. So I'd be grateful if you'd take Simon home, as I feel I may be coming down with something as well."

"Of course I will Elle," Mrs Steven'ss son-in-law told her. "But tell me, if I have to go away again, where do I take him?"

Mrs Stevens thought about this, and then looked back up at Ronan.

"Couldn't your parents look after him?" she asked. Ronan considered this.

"No Mrs Stevens, they're both too old, is there anyone else?"

"There's always Melissa," Elle told him, "although I know you and her don't - exactly - get on."

"No we don't and never have after that incident a couple of months after I'd married Mandy," he told her, his disdain for his sister-in-law apparent. Mrs Stevens found a pen and paper, and wrote down her younger daughter's phone number, anyway. She didn't, Ronan noticed, enquire what the incident was.

"Take it, just in case," she told him firmly, pressing the paper into his hand. "Now take Simon home please." Elle then picked up the tray and proceeded upstairs to attend to her husband. Ronan fetched Simon from in front of the television, and they left, Ronan closing the door to the Stevens house.

They climbed in the 4 x 4 and Simon's father drove, slowly, away, to begin the journey home.

*****

As he was driving Ronan thought about the sort of relationship he had with his younger sister-in-law.

Melissa had been Mandy's younger sister by two years making her five years younger than himself admittedly he'd never known much about her apart from what Mandy had told him.

Apparently, through their more teenage years Mandy Stevens had been shy and studious, while Melissa had been one for the boys, and seen as a bit of a rebel at school. This hadn't changed much after they'd left school, while the elder sister had stopped in most nights to help her parents her sibling had been out partying, and had ended up with a different man each night; but she'd never brought any of them home, in fact at that time her bed was rarely slept in.

This had been due to two things; her behaviour, and the types of clothes she wore, many leaving little to the imagination.

When she was younger than twenty six Melissa had, usually, aimed her charm at men that were older than her, however, now she was older than twenty six she preferred the company of younger men, and black men at that. She'd never brought any of them home to meet her parents because Arnold disapproved of her behaviour. Therefore, she always met them at the flat she rented.

Even though she still lived fairly local she'd never attended Zoe's birth, or Mandy and Zoe's funerals. In fact she hadn't even visited Mandy in hospital. Melissa was the, proverbial, black sheep of the Stevens family. However, she was Simon's aunt and he had a right to see her every once in a while, and Ronan supposed Melissa had a, sort of, right to see Simon; he couldn't help what Simon's aunt got up to.

Actually, Melissa had tried it on with Ronan when he and Mandy had only been married a couple of months. One evening Mandy had gone to a friend's party, while Ronan had decided to stay home; Melissa had just happened to drop by and told him she'd just come to keep him company for an hour or two; they'd got talking and Melissa had tried it on.

Of course, Ronan had refused her telling Melissa that he loved her sister. Luckily her elder sibling had returned then; Melissa had left and gone back to her, little, flat.

*****

Since Mrs Strobing had died there had been nobody else in his life, okay he'd had a brief fling with Commander Lucy Lang, but now she was dead – killed when the HART convoy had been blown up in Iraq. Now he had no female in his life and wasn't that bothered by this fact as he still had Simon, admittedly his son was only eight and would, eventually, one day leave his father, but until then Ronan would enjoy every moment they spent together.

Suddenly his son turned to him and asked, "Why are you so quiet Dad?"

"Just thinking about work," Ronan lied. "And how lucky I am to have you," that bit was the truth. He drove the 4 x 4 down numerous streets until they reached their, modest sized house.

Ronan handed the door key to Simon and told him, "Go let yourself in, I'll just park in the garage, get the luggage, and be in then."

"Okay Dad," was the cheery response from the eight year old, and Ronan stopped on the drive to let his son out. He parked the car in the garage and unloaded it; before he went in he stood looking at the vehicle thinking to himself *as there's only the two of us now perhaps I should get something smaller. I've had my eye on a Ford Mondeo for a bit so maybe I'll get one of those.* With that thought he gathered up the luggage and walked indoors.

He found Simon in the sitting room watching cartoons on TV; he looked up as his father entered. "Simon," Ronan began, "there are a couple of things I need to talk to you about. Please come here." Grudgingly his son switched the television off and went over to sit by his father.

"Yes Dad."

Ronan had decided that now was the right time to tell his son everything. How Simon would take it all was up to him.

*****

The Vauxhall *Vectra* pulled into the at the *John Groggins* Hospital parking lot at 23:00, two and a half hours since they'd set off from his residence, in the south of London, and were surprised to see his Renault Megane still in the parking lot. As Floyd parked the automobile they were in the two of them observed Dr Forrester taking boxes from the boot of his car, and into the hospital. He would carry a box each one looked like it contained files or folders, inside, and would emerge about five minutes later empty handed. After he'd, practically, emptied the boot of boxes Carol emerged from the *Vectra* and leant against the side of the lime green automobile.

The doctor returned to his car after taking the final box inside; he had, then, intended to drive off, find a B+B and stay there until *Proagnon* came for his help, therefore he was most surprised to see Miss Turner leaning against his *Megane*. "What do you want?" he asked suspiciously.

"We got your message," she answered bluntly. "So after much discussion my partner, Floyd, and myself," Simon Forrestor then turned to see Mr Maxwell walking towards them, a Walther PPS semi automatic pistol levelled at the doctor.

*****

The Walther PPS (Police Pistol Slim) was a semi-automatic pistol that had been manufactured in Germany by the Carl Walther GmbH Sportwaffen company. It was first shown in 2007 and was a slim polymer framed weapon of similar size to the Walther PPK. The 9mm version featured magazines of 6, 7, and 8 round lengths so the shooter could customize the grip to his hand size and concealment needs.

It also featured a partially cocked striker system like the Walther P99 Quick Action model. This particular variant was called QuickSafe and the primary change from the Quick Action was that removing the pistol's back strap would disable the gun for safe storage.

The Walther PPS had a weight of 549 grams, an overall length of 6.3 inches (16.002 centimetres), while the barrel length was 3.2 inches (8.128 centimetres). Plus as well as the 9mm version there was a .40 S&W version.

*****

Simon stared at the weapon, "What is the meaning of this?" he demanded to know, turning to the woman called Carol Turner. Floyd Maxwell had now come to stand beside them, the pistol still pointing at the doctor's head.

Dr Forrestor," Floyd started, "we are here to arrange your travel needs."

"My travel needs, I work here."

"Not anymore Mr Forrestor," Carol interjected, she lowered her voice so it was just above a whisper, "since you killed your wife you are a wanted man, all it would take is one phone call." Her voice was filled with hidden menace, as she produced a mobile phone; she dialled 999 and then let her finger hover over the *call* button.

"Okay, okay, there's no need to use those tactics."

"Shame the battery isn't in," Carol told him.

"Bitch!" snarled Forrestor. Then Maxwell pressed the gun against the side of the doctor's temple. "I'll do what you want, no need to shoot me."

"I believe you've made the travel arrangements Floyd," Miss Turner remarked, a cruel smile crossing her face.

Mr Maxwell replied that he had, and the transport would be with them by 23:55. As it was 23:50 they didn't have long to wait. Around two minutes later they all heard it – the unmistakeable sound of a helicopter.

The helicopter's spotlight, situated underneath the aircraft shone down, illuminating the three people by the lime green automobile. Finding a suitable spot the air vehicle landed, its five rotor blades kept turning whilst Miss Turner looked over at Mr Forrestor, she had to shout to make herself heard over the roar of the air vehicle's single Allison 250-C20 turboshaft engine, "Take what you need and climb aboard. The pilot knows where you're going."

Rapidly Simon gathered, from the boot of his car, his laptop computer carrying case, which contained all the information and computer files that he would need for his research, and a box containing laboratory equipment such as test tubes, Petri dishes etc. He climbed aboard the *Hughes* MD helicopter (model 500C) and then looked behind him. The other two were walking back towards the *Vectra*, "Aren't you coming?"

Carol turned and shook her head, "Good luck," she mouthed and then turned away. Dr Forrestor then climbed into the interior of the helicopter and closed the door.

*****

The MD Helicopters MD 500 series was an American family of light utility civilian and military helicopters. The MD 500 was developed from the Hughes 500, a civilian version of the US Army's OH-6A Cayuse/Loach. The series currently includes the MD 500E, MD 520N, and MD 530F.

Prior to the OH-6's first flight, Hughes announced it was developing a civil version, to be marketed as the Hughes 500, available in basic five and seven seat configurations. A utility version with a more powerful engine was offered as the 500U (later called the 500C).

The improved Hughes 500D became the primary model in 1976, with a more powerful engine, a T-tail, and new five-blade main rotor; a four-blade tail rotor was optional. The 500D was replaced by the 500E from 1982 with a pointed nose and various interior improvements such as greater head and leg room. The 530F was a more powerful version of the 500E optimized for hot and high work.

McDonnell Douglas acquired Hughes Helicopters in January 1984, and from August 1985 the 500E and 530F were built as the MD 500E and MD 530F Lifter. Following the 1997 Boeing/McDonnell Douglas merger, Boeing sold the former MD civil helicopter lines to MD Helicopters in early 1999.

*****

The air vehicle then began its vertical ascent, up to 10,000 feet (3048 metres) at a rate of 1,700 feet per minute (8.6 metres a second); once it had obtained this height the helicopter started the 375 mile (605 kilometres) journey northward. Carol and Floyd watched it depart, and then climbed into the silver *Vectra* – Carol driving this time, so Floyd could get some rest, and set off on the 114 mile journey southward.

*****

The *Proagnon* scientists, who'd left the bunker in the HINDs, had already arrived at their destination, and had been busy, over the past day or two, getting things ready and making the base habitable; they'd checked all the communications equipment they'd brought, as Mr Maxwell had arranged for a sea vessel from Fraserburgh to take supplies to the sea fort, plus any other items that needed taking, back to Scotland for special delivery to some of Maxwell's other agents.

Just under three hours later the *Hughes* helicopter carrying Dr Forrester approached the fort and landed on the helipad. Forrester departed the air vehicle taking his equipment with him, and went below to the interior. Fuel lines were attached to the MD 500C and the helicopter was refuelled. Once refuelling was complete the pilot of the *Hughes* started the four bladed top rotor and the twin bladed tail rotor, and the aircraft took off and ascended vertically into the overcast night sky and began the journey home.

Forrestor was shown to one of the crew quarters and went to bed; it had been a long night and the weeks ahead would be even longer.

*****

Simon Strobing listened as his father informed him that he worked for an organisation known as HART (Human Alliance for the Retaliation against Terrorism) and this meant he had to travel all around the world, fighting terrorists. His son listened, in awe, at his father's exploits.

"So you're like James Bond?" Simon asked eventually.

"Sort of," Ronan replied, "but don't be fooled, it isn't all about always saving the world and getting the girl. Admittedly that might happen once in a while, but it is very rarely like the movies make out. Plus people do get killed, lots of people."

Ronan paused and Simon noticed the regret and upset cross his father's face, "We've lost some good friends and colleagues, I've lost good friends, men and women. Okay most of them knew what they were letting themselves in for and that they may be killed in action one day, but when it does happen it still comes as a shock."

"In fact," Mr Strobing continued, "you remember that man who joined us last Christmas, and that woman at work I told you about?"

"I do," his son responded, "don't tell me they're both...," he let his voice trail off. His father, solemnly, nodded. "I am sorry," Simon said, "I know I never met the woman you were interested in, but I liked the man." Ronan smiled weakly, his son really seemed to be maturing maybe it was due to the loss of his mother and sister the year before.

"This has got to remain our secret," the elder Strobing said, "not even Gran or Granpa know. And no telling people at school; never glamorise my job because, as I've told you, it's very different from what you see in films."

Simon, solemnly, promised that he'd not mention it to anyone.

*****

Over the next couple of days Arnold Stevens took a turn for the worse again, leaving Elle more scared than ever; he suddenly, one night, started thrashing about in bed, this carried on the next few days and Elle began to fear for her life as she'd never known him be violent before. Hadn't the doctor said it was just a strain of flu? Maybe he had but all this wild behaviour was most out of character, and she now knew this was much more than flu; so after three further nights of this behaviour she finally plucked up the courage and dialled 999. An ambulance and a doctor were with her within five minutes.

*****

Once the doctor had given him a sedative to make him sleep, Arnold was placed on a trolley in the ambulance and taken to Hull Hospital, Elle then contacted Ronan and informed him of the news.

"Why didn't you ring me sooner," Ronan enquired. "I could've helped."

"The doctor I got Arnold to see, eventually – after much persuasion, told him he'd picked up a flu bug and to get plenty of rest," Elle protested. "So that's what we assumed it was and he'd be better after a day or two. However, now I know it's something far worse"

"Do you know where he may have picked it up?" asked her son-in-law.

"No I have no idea. All I can tell you is we took a trip to Iran a couple of weeks back, and after the flight home Arnold started to feel unwell. That reminds me is Simon okay?"

"Yes, he's fine I'm worried about Arnold though. I know we haven't always seen eye to eye, but I'm generally worried about him. Does Melissa know?"

"Not yet, I decided to call you first as you're like a son to both of us. Okay Arnold may not always show it but, believe me I know how he feels about you really."

"Ronan," she continued, "will you take me to see him?"

"Tell you what," her son-in-law told her, "contact Melissa and ask her, if she can't, or won't, call me back. I've got another call to make, in the meantime, if I don't hear from you within the next ten minutes I'll assume Melissa has taken you."

"Okay Ronan," and Mrs Stevens rang off. Ronan walked through to the sitting room and told Simon about what had happened, as far as Ronan knew, to his grandfather.

He then crossed to the study, dusted off his STU-8 and phoned HART headquarters, Ben Gillespe answered, "HART headquarters."

"Ben, put me through to Commander Most."

"Commander Strobing?"

"Just do it Ben, it's urgent," snapped Ronan. "In fact it's a matter of life and death."

"Putting you through, now, sir." The STU rang three times and then Celia picked up at her end.

"What's up Ronan?" she enquired.

"Celia, I need a favour, do you think Mike'd look after Simon for an hour or two?"

"I'm sure he would," she responded. "But why?"

"My father-in-laws in hospital and I might have to take my mother-in-law to see him."

"I am sorry," she told him, with genuine sympathy in her voice.

"Thanks Celia, I owe you," and he replaced the handset of his STU-8. Suddenly, the main phone began to ring so Ronan dashed back through to answer it. As he'd assumed it was Mrs Stevens, apparently Melissa didn't want to take her mother as her father would only start on at Melissa about the various men in her life.

Ronan knew it was really a case of Melissa just not wanting to see her father. He agreed to take Elle to see Arnold and would be with her as soon as he could. Hurriedly he got Simon ready to go and told him he would be staying with a friend while Ronan took Simon's grandma to see his grandfather.

They climbed in the 4 x 4 and Mr Strobing drove to the Most household, Mike was expecting him as he'd received a phone call from his mother. Simon went inside with Mike and Ronan drove off to pick up Elle and take her to the hospital. She was standing on the path, outside her house, waiting for him.

She climbed in the passenger seat, buckled herself in, and Ronan drove the 4 x 4, on the journey, to Hull Hospital. When they reached their destination they weren't allowed to see Arnold because the doctors were running some, initial, tests on him.

"What sort of tests?" Elle asked, fearing the worst.

"Just routine tests to see what we might be up against, and to check his general health," the doctor told them. "You can observe through the panel in the door."

The two of them thanked the doctor and turned to the observation panel, they saw Arnold being restrained, in the bed, by several doctors and nurses. They were having to strap his hands to the bed sides, to stop him harming himself – so Elle and Ronan had been informed. An IV drip was attached to him, via a needle in the back of his hand, and he was hooked up to several monitors.

One of the doctors then came out the room and said, mysteriously, "Follow me please." The two of them followed the doctor into a nearby office. "Please sit down," so Mr Strobing and Mrs Stevens seated themselves on the seats provided. The doctor then moved to the other side of the desk and seated himself, and then he opened a drawer and withdrew a folder which he placed on the desk between himself and the two others. The doctor's name, according to his name badge, was Charles Lighten.

"Now we have taken a blood sample from Mr Stevens, and have found some strange anomalies in his bloodstream," he then produced a plastic sheet from the folder, there was a black and white diagram printed on it, he held this up to a light projector and the other two in the room looked up at it.

"As you can clearly see," Dr Lighten said to them, "there are several anomalies in his bloodstream; they may just be extra blood cells which need draining off, however, they may be something nastier. That's all I can tell you, at the moment, as these are only preliminary tests. Once we have performed brain and body scans we should be able to tell you more."

"Thank you doctor," Mrs Stevens said to the man seated behind the desk.

"I thought you should know," he responded. "Now can I ask if either of you know any reason for this sudden deterioration in his health?" Mrs Stevens looked at Ronan as if wondering whether she should tell the medical man what she had told him, Ronan simply nodded. "What is it?" asked Dr Lighten curiously.

"Well," began Elle, unsure, "a couple of weeks back my husband, myself, and my grandson took a brief break in Iran. My grandson," looking at Ronan, "is fine, but a couple of days after we returned my husband – Arnold, complained of feeling unwell. Unfortunately, he is a stubborn man and refused to seek a proper diagnosis; however, a couple of days later he took a bit of a turn for the worse, so I, finally, managed to persuade him to see our local doctor."

"He told Arnold that he'd probably picked up a flu like bug and advised him to have plenty of rest and he should be okay. Earlier he took another nasty turn, started thrashing about like he was possessed, that's when I phoned for an ambulance."

The doctor considered this after Mrs Stevens and Mr Strobing had left. Where was the connection, if there was one? Had Mr Stevens been poisoned, somehow? If so where had he contracted the infection? There were too many questions, at the moment; however, the test results might show something.

Ronan drove Elle home and then collected Simon from the Most household, and drove home.

*****

At HART headquarters Celia Most was finishing up after another day in command. She wandered back to her residence with the idea of having a long, hot, soak in the bath and then something to eat and drink, and then she'd watch a bit of television before she finally retired to bed.

With this in mind she crossed from the main building to her residence. As soon as she entered Celia went upstairs and set the bath running. Walking through to the bedroom she threw off her gun belt, and proceeded to undress; once she was undressed she took her Beretta 92 pistol and went through to have her soak. Placing her weapon on the side, after ensuring the safety catch was on, Mrs Most stepped into the bath and started to wash herself, the hot water easing her aching muscles and joints, so much so Celia lay down and closed her eyes.

After about a quarter of an hour Commander Most was awakened by the sound of breaking glass; for a start she didn't know what was happening, but then several loud crashes followed indicating, as they sounded pretty close, that whatever was happening was happening in her residence. Jumping out the bath she grabbed the pistol, wound a towel round her body and, slowly, made her way down the stairs, her footfalls light and wet droplets glistening on her skin.

Reaching the bottom of the stairs Celia padded to the edge of the sitting room and peeped round the frame of the door. There was a figure in the room going through the drawers, with a start she realised it was the same figure she'd chased earlier but they'd disappeared. Swinging into the doorway Celia shouted, "Halt or I fire."

The figure just grunted, turned and ran past her, pushing her sideways and knocking her off her feet. She fell to the floor, letting go of the towel, and landed flat on her back, just for a moment she thought she'd seen the face of the figure, and recognised it as that of her fellow agent, Commander Leon Bigship, but that was ridiculous and absurd. He was dead, wasn't he?

Hang on, Celia suddenly thought; *hadn't there been that incident in Turkey when a body, that had been presumed dead, had just disappeared in mysterious circumstances?* That question still remained unanswered, so Celia got up, grabbed her fallen towel and Beretta, and went back upstairs to bed. She was too exhausted now, to face any food and drink.

*****

The working day had begun, on the sea fort with a light breakfast and then the *Proagnon* scientists, along with Dr Simon Forrestor, got down to work on the virus; Simon consulting the notes he'd made on his computer as he went. He took a blood sample from one of the other scientists and examined it, the blood was clear of any types of impurities, and then he poured the blood he'd taken into one of the test tubes he'd brought with him. He had also taken a quick sample from his wife's, dead, body and had brought this sample with him. Simon placed the two tubes of blood side by side and looked at them in turn, the blood he'd taken from his wife was starting to turn a different colour and becoming thicker, more glutinous and jelly like, and there seemed to be spores developing in it; Simon knew this would ultimately happen, but he had only killed Rebecca the previous evening, so this change was very rapid. Why was that?

Then it suddenly hit him. This had been a, more, concentrated version of the poison, so if he refined it, it would, hopefully, be slower acting but would still have the same ultimate effect. Deciding on this he now went back to the notes he'd made, seeing if they would give him any clues on how to refine it. He knew, from his discussion with Miss Turner that the *Proagnon* scientists had developed a similar virus but it lacked the end result that his did, so that was why they had come to him. If he could get a sample of their virus and add a little of the substance his wife's blood had become it may work, but then he'd need a second human guinea pig to try the resulting substance on.

Simon Forrestor had made many friends in the medical world, primarily when he was at medical school, but others when he'd been on placements at various hospitals. When he had been at medical school he'd struck up an extremely good friendship with another training doctor named Charles Lighten. Lighten, once he'd finished his training, had moved up to Hull and currently worked at Hull Hospital, both men hadn't seen each other for years and Forrestor decided, that once the virus was ready, the two men ought to meet up again. Maybe Charles would have a sick patient he could try the virus type substance on. If the virus did, eventually, cause death then that could simply be attributed to a bad reaction to the virus or the drugs used to fight it.

Simon had, actually, engineered the poison he'd injected into his wife so that when the heart wasn't pumping any further blood around the body the spores within the poison, or in this case the virus, that were created would evaporate and disappear. Afterwards, once examined, the body would show no trace of spores; so this would be the ultimate killer virus.

*****

Dr Lighten telephoned Elle Stevens about a day after her husband had been admitted to Hull Hospital, and had informed her that the further tests had been carried out and the results showed that Arnold had heightened activity in his brain, why he didn't know; he could only guess that this activity was due to him trying to fight the infection. However, his body scan had shown that certain organs were on the verge of shutting down, if that were the case the heightened brain activity told the doctor Arnold was, actually, accelerating the effects of the virus. Therefore Elle needed to prepare herself for the worst case scenario that he may, eventually, die; or at best he may stay alive but become paralysed to the effect he may have to have care.

*****

Commander Ronan Strobing decided, after a week at home he might as well return to work; begrudgingly he found Melissa Stevens's number and phoned her up. After about ten rings a female voice answered, "Hello," she said in her best feminine voice.

"Greetings Melissa, Ronan here."

"Ronan? Ronan? Oh it's you," she said, remembering who he was.

"Melissa," the HART commander replied, trying to keep the contempt he felt for his sister-in-law from his voice. "I need a favour; I'd like you to look after Simon for a few weeks."

"No!" she said firmly, "I'm busy."

"Go on," he responded, I bet you'd love to see him really."

Melissa's voice softened then, "You must be desperate. Go on then, just for a few weeks." She gave him her new address, as she'd moved recently.

"I'll bring him over on the way to the airport. Thank you." He then rang off.

On the Saturday morning, it was a hot day, he took Simon round to Melissa's; he knocked on the front door which was answered about five minutes later by a young woman with long blonde hair, this was Melissa, hastily fastening up her lime green bikini top, "Yes, oh it's you," the contempt for her brother-in-law evident. Then she turned to Simon, "Hello Simon darling, my how you've grown. Come in." Simon rushed past her; Melissa then looked at Ronan, "Would you like to come in for a moment."

Ronan didn't want to but found himself agreeing. Melissa led him to the backyard where two sun beds were set up. "Who's the other one for?" Ronan asked, "Or do you pretend you've got an imaginary friend."

"The other sun beds for me," said a deep voice from behind them; Melissa smiled. Ronan turned to face the newcomer who was a black man, no surprises there, dressed only in dark red trunks, he was also a few inches taller than Ronan, and about ten years younger than Melissa.

"Aren't you going to introduce us Melissa?" enquired her brother-in-law.

"Sorry," she answered, not really sorry, "Ronan this is, my latest man, Isaac. Isaac this is my brother-in-law Ronan." Suddenly Simon burst outside, "And this, little man, is Ronan's son Simon."

"Pleased to meet you," said the HART commander, shaking Isaac's hand. "I must be off now Melissa, but take good care of Simon. Simon, be good for Aunt Melissa and Isaac." He then left the house, instantly regretting the decision to leave Simon with that tart and her new bloke, but he had no other option.

CHAPTER 2

GHOSTS FROM THE PAST!

Ronan Strobing climbed back into his 4 x 4 and pulled away from the kerb outside his sister-in-law's house, he had one further matter to attend to before he made his departure from England to Switzerland, and HART headquarters, via *Robin Hood* Doncaster-Sheffield airport.

He drove through the streets to see his-mother-in-law, once there Ronan informed Elle Stevens that if Dr Lighten called with any further news on Arnold's condition she should contact Mike Most, inform him who she was, give him the message and then ask him to contact Ronan. "Why can't I do it direct, and who is Mike Most?" demanded Mrs Stevens.

Ronan explained, "Firstly you won't be able to contact me as I don't know where I'll be, and Mike Most is the son of my colleague, Celia Most, and he can contact his mother and pass the message on, she in turn will be able to contact me and give me the message."

"I see now, I think I do," Elle told him. "By the way, where's Simon?"

"He's with Melissa and her new friend Isaac."

"I guess you must have had to swallow your pride to leave him there," she remarked.

"Yes I did, and you should see Isaac, he must be about ten years younger than her."

"Will she never learn?" Mrs Stevens added as an afterthought. "Still, I hope you have a good trip wherever you're going."

"Don't worry about me, you look after Arnold. Oh, and if you can keep an eye on Melissa, I only left Simon there as I had no other choice." With that they said their farewells, Ronan climbed into his *Hyundai* and continued with his journey, onwards, to the airport.

He showed his HART pass to one of the airport staff, and then handed over to them the vehicle's keys; the member of staff drove the vehicle round to the airport's garages and parked the *Hyundai* in the garage numbered one. Satisfied the HART commander entered the airport's main building, once he'd shown his pass to a member of staff inside Ronan Strobing, along with his luggage, was fast tracked through to the airside departure lounge where he waited; about five minutes later the Gulfstream *G650* that had brought him over to England rolled up.

Commander Strobing departed the airside departure lounge and boarded the aircraft where he was greeted by the pilot, Alan Lockhart, and the co-pilot, Greg Zuckermann. Once he was seated and strapped in the aircraft taxied to the top of the secondary runway where it waited for a vacant slot. Once one had been found the executive business jet powered up its two Rolls Royce turbofan engines and started to move down the concrete runway, as it went the aircraft speeded up to its maximum speed of 610 miles per hour the plane's undercarriage slowly lifted off the concrete surface and the aircraft slowly rose into the sky, up to, he was reliably informed by the pilot, 40,000 feet. The jet levelled off and began its 658 mile journey to *Cointrin* airport, just outside Geneva.

At the plane's current speed of 582 miles per hour the journey would take one and a quarter hours, then there was the fact that Switzerland was one hour ahead of England, so Ronan had left England at 15:00 and would arrive in Switzerland at 17:15; by the time he'd left the airport building it would probably be something like 17:30. Finally by the time he re-entered the main HART compound it would be close to 18:15.

The *G650* started its descent to the 12,795 feet long runway below the plane seemed to sway to one side. Suddenly the pilot's voice came over the intercom, panic in his tone, "Our *port* (left) engine has developed an electrical fire, we are trying to deal with it but please standby." The jet was approaching the runway when the intercom came into life again, "Major electrical fault has developed, we can't lower the landing gear so are having to divert onto the grass runway which is not as long. Hang on Commander Strobing, this could be a rough landing."

This isn't happening, thought Ronan. *This can't be happening*. All of a sudden the business jet landed on the earth runway, with a thump, and seemed to come to a standstill; all the lights aboard went out and there came the smell of something electrical burning. Ronan had memorised where the exit doors were but then he thought to himself, *Are the crew okay?*

Hesitantly he unbuckled his safety belt and made his way forward, he then, carefully, opened the door between the cabin and the flight deck; both pilots had fallen forward, hitting their heads on the flight controls. Unbuckling the pilots harnesses he eased both men out of the flight deck, opened one of the exit doors manually and breathed in the fresh, evening, air, and then he passed the two crew members into the waiting arms of rescuers, who had - quickly - appeared on the scene. "Now you sir," said one of the rescuers.

"One second," Ronan replied, ducking back inside.

"Now sir!" demanded a fireman; suddenly there was a rumbling sound from the, underneath, workings of the plane, Ronan suddenly appeared in the doorway. "Jump sir." Ronan jumped towards the man, suddenly there was a flash and a loud bang, and the Gulfstream *G650* jet exploded creating a huge fireball. Once the smoke cleared of the plane and the rescuers there was no sign.

*****

The explosion was so great it was seen at HART headquarters, it was then that the phone, in reception, began to ring; Lisa Bell, who was on the night shift snatched the receiver up, "Hello," she said. She listened for many minutes, in silence, "thank you," she said afterward and replaced the receiver.

"What is it?" asked Ben Gillespe, who was just finishing some paperwork, noticing Lisa had suddenly turned deathly white.

"I think we should get the commander here," Lisa told him. "Apparently there's been an accident."

Ben buzzed through to Commander Most, who was just filling in a requisition form for some new weaponry, "Yes," she said.

"Commander," Ben started, "we need you here quickly please."

"On my way." Celia Most left the office, crossed the hallway, and entered the reception area. "Okay, what's happened?"

Lisa looked up, "There's been an accident at *Cointrin* airport involving a Gulfstream *G650* aircraft."

"Can't the authorities handle it? Why should that involve us?"

"Ma'am, Commander Strobing was on board," Lisa said to the commander, simply.

"What?" snapped the woman in charge. "Find me Dr Schaiffer, and have him meet me at the garages. We are organising a rescue mission, and taking the Mega Cruiser. Is that understood?"

"Yes ma'am," both receptionists replied, and set about trying to contact Dr Hans Schaiffer, whilst Commander Celia Most left the reception area and made her way towards the area where HART 1 was stored – the vehicle, as well as HART 2, 3 and 4 (Land Cruisers and Range Rover), had been transported back from Turkey using one of the transport aircraft.

*****

Dr Schaiffer, meanwhile, satisfied his patients were in good hands, left the medical area of the main building, and started to wander down the corridor towards the elevator. Suddenly his page started bleeping; annoyed the German looked at the number of the person who was trying to contact him, it was the number of someone in main reception.

With haste, instead of taking the elevator to the ground floor, as he'd, originally, intended he pressed the button for the fourth floor and hurried into reception. "What's the matter?" he enquired of the two people there.

"Commander Most wants you to join her at the garages. There's been an accident at *Cointrin* involving Commander Strobing," Ben told him rapidly.

"So basically," remarked Hans, "you got me up here for nothing. Now I have to go all the way back downstairs, still it should keep me fit." He turned and ran back the way he'd come, his coat tails flapping behind him; Dr Schaiffer and the four receptionists were the only members of HART that were allowed to wear *civvies*, all combat trained personnel had to wear uniforms consisting of a khaki coloured tunic, or top, beige coloured combat trousers, black calf high boots and black leather gloves (these weren't essential though). Also these personnel had different uniforms for different missions, jungle or desert.

Jungle uniforms consisted of khaki coloured trousers, boots with holes in to let the air in, green floppy hats to avoid getting sunburnt, and face netting to prevent creatures from getting on the skin. In contrast the desert uniforms had beige coloured tunics instead of khaki ones.

*****

Hans Schaiffer arrived at the garages - containing the vehicles - slightly out of breath. "Not as young as I used to be," he wheezed, as he drew up beside Celia. She was standing outside the door to HART 1. "Which one are we taking?"

Celia smiled at him, "The Mega Cruiser of course." With that she entered the storage area, climbed aboard the SUV and powered up its powerful 4.1 litre turbo diesel engine, and selecting *drive* she manoeuvred the 6,395 lb (2,901 kg) vehicle from its garage. Dr Schaiffer got in the, left hand, passenger side and they exited the compound and turned in the direction of *Cointrin*.

As Celia drove the huge SUV onward through the traffic at a steady 55 mph (89 kph) down the main highway she started to come up behind some traffic leaving work. Each time she came up behind a slower moving vehicle she would flash the, large, SUVs lights at the traffic in front, most would then get out her way but any stubborn drivers who held the HART vehicle up she would overtake, once she was sure the other carriageway was clear.

Finally the Mega Cruiser reached its ultimate destination; a security guard, on duty, stopped them, “HART,” Celia said, holding her pass out the window so he could examine it, “here to examine the plane wreckage.”

The guard who, obviously, had just come on shift and not been informed about the significance of the crash to HART told her, “Sorry ma’am, sir,” he threw a glance at the German, “HART has no jurisdiction here. This is an internal matter.”

”Bollocks!” she snapped at the man, even making the man beside her cringe, and she withdrew the pass, revved the engine up and hurtled through the perimeter gate. They spotted the wreckage of the *G650*, it was still smouldering, and Commander Most drove the vehicle over the concrete runway to the jet, but not too close.

“Nein,” remarked Schaiffer, reverting to his native language for a moment. “That is one, seriously, wrecked plane.”

“It is indeed,” agreed his commander as she pulled the Mega Cruiser to a halt. They both climbed out the vehicle and proceeded to begin with their examination of the *G650*. “Ronan,” called Celia; getting no response she shouted, ”Commander Strobing.”

Dr Schaiffer began his examination on the side furthest from the open exit door; looking down, he didn’t know what made him look downwards, he spotted a scrap of burnt trouser, he knelt down to examine it further and spotted a body under the fuselage of the plane, “Commander Most,” he called.

She was at his side in moments, “What is it?” she wanted to know. He pointed at the body, partially hidden in the dirt, by the fuselage. “Commander Strobing, but how did he get there?”

“May I suggest we take him back to headquarters, so I can examine him in the medical unit,” Dr Schaiffer suggested. “While you load his body aboard, for the journey home, I shall go over, to the main building, and see what shape the flight crew are in. Bring the Mega Cruiser over when ready please.”

"Okay," responded Celia, loading Ronan's - apparently lifeless - body aboard the SUV whilst Hans rushed off in the direction of the airport building, his coat tails flapping behind him.

*****

Once the deputy commander had loaded her superior's body on board, she climbed aboard the SUV and drove over to the main building to await Dr Schaiffer's appearance. After a few minutes the German doctor came out of the building shaking his head. He resumed his position, in the passenger seat, and they drove away in silence. Presently Commander Most looked over, at the man, and asked, "The flight crew, are they…?" she didn't finish her question as the doctor's face said it all.

The doctor suddenly aged as he said to his commander, "Unfortunately pilot Lockhart and co-pilot Zuckermann were pronounced dead on arrival. I can only hope I can save Commander Strobing," he glanced back at Ronan's body, "I just hope he hasn't been injured too badly."

*****

Once they reached headquarters, Celia had radioed ahead, the vehicle was met by a medical team, who loaded Commander Strobing's body onto a trolley and wheeled the trolley, followed by a concerned looking Dr Hans Schaiffer, into the building, he would definitely not get much sleep tonight; Celia parked HART 1 back in its garage, and walked back to reception. As she entered the room Lisa Bell, who was now the only receptionist in there looked up, at the commander, from the typing she was doing. "What happened?" she asked.

"Much as what Ben told us, the business jet crash landed, probably a fault of some sort, and exploded a few minutes later," Commander Most responded, "the crew were killed upon impact and Commander Strobing…," her voice faltered.

"Is he…?" Lisa enquired. Tears started to form in her eyes; she had, actually, started to develop feelings for her, ultimate, superior but had never shown them. Now here the young receptionist was – only 25, with Commander Celia Most, showing those feelings.

However, what Miss Bell didn't know was that Mrs Most, even though she was happily married, still harboured certain feelings towards her superior. Probably these feelings weren't strong enough to lead to anything but they were there. "We, Dr Schaiffer and myself," continued Celia, "found his body laid next to the wreckage of the plane. We brought the body, we think he's still alive, back to headquarters and he was rushed to the medical unit."

"May I go and see him ma'am?" Lisa enquired of her commander.

"No you may not," snapped Celia; Lisa visibly jumped, Celia had never used that tone of voice before, had the commander guessed how Lisa felt or did she already know? "You are needed here I shall go and see him. You may visit when he feels up to visitors, if indeed he ever does," Celia continued with a slight air of superiority.

Commander Most then turned and marched out of the reception area and along the corridor to the elevator which she took down to the third floor; from there she marched along the wooden panelled corridor to a set of swing, double, doors that led into the medical unit. She entered the medical reception area, the fluorescent lights shining above, and, ignoring the doctors and nurses, found Dr Hans Schaiffer's office and knocked on the door.

"Enter," called a voice from inside and Celia went inside. "Commander Most," said the doctor, "a pleasant surprise, please sit down." Celia plonked herself down on the other, plastic, chair in the room and looked across at Schaiffer.

"How is he Hans?" she asked the German, concern was evident in her voice; the doctor consulted some notes he'd made before replying.

"He is a very lucky man, he has suffered, superficial burns to some areas of his skin – only mild – but these wounds will clear up in time, in the meantime he will have to wear a dressing, on his back, under his uniform. However, at the moment he is in acute shock; once he has come to terms with what has happened he will be allowed to leave – say a week, two at the most."

"When can he have visitors?" she then enquired.

"In a day or two," the German responded, "once he's adjusted."

"Thank you Dr Schaiffer," Celia said to the medical man, "and I mean that." With that she got up, left the office and wandered back the way she'd come, deep in thought. In fact she was so deep in thought she didn't notice the figure of a man coming towards her.

*****

On the sea fort Simon Forrestor had received a small amount of the virus *Proagnon* had used and was now mixing different chemicals with it, relatively harmless chemicals but, if mixed together right, the chemical produced could prove very potent, and lethal. Once this was achieved he added a small amount, only a few drops, of his wife's, mutated, blood; and then added a drop of the mixture, that had been produced, to the healthy blood he'd taken the other day.

Nothing happened at first; then Simon realised as it was a slow infecting virus he'd need to keep checking on it, and if it worked as planned the other scientists, as well as himself, would need to produce the virus in large quantities, and transport it aboard the supply ships from Fraserburgh, to the mainland for mass distribution by Mr Maxwell's agents – these weren't *Proagnon* agents, just regular civilians with loyalty to Maxwell.

*****

Forrestor took a microscope from the medical equipment he'd brought along with its slides (there were only five). He then added a drop of blood to each slide, added a tiny amount of virus and then placed the slides, at various points in the workroom. Once this was done he exited the room, and went about making checks on how the other scientists were getting on.

After a day he checked the five slides through the microscope, the blood had turned a lighter shade of red but that was all. He continued checking them over the next couple of days; there was no, dramatic, change until the fourth day when tiny spores started to appear; over the next week these spores seemed to enlarge and multiply, plus they appeared to develop small spikes around their edges. After a further week the spores seemed to release a substance into the bloodstream which started to make the blood seem to thicken, more than normal, and start to mutate.

Finally, after the fourth week he checked and the blood he'd placed on the slides was now all gone. The virus had done its job; it could also – probably - with a tiny bit of alteration be turned into an airborne virus. He still had the original, more concentrated, substance in his secret laboratory under *John Groggins* Hospital.

He disliked having to be made to wait but he knew it was necessary. The latest supply ship docked alongside the fort and Simon decided he needed a few days on land instead of being cooped up on the structure in the Moray Firth; he had contacted the mainland about a week beforehand and made his request. Surprisingly he had been granted a few days shore leave.

*****

At Hull Hospital Arnold's condition hadn't got any better, yet it hadn't become any worse; Dr Lighten plus the many colleagues/experts he'd called in were all at a loss to explain this; however, he'd received a call from his long time friend Simon Forrestor, who had been working in Scotland, saying that he was coming to see Charles in a day or two. So it was with some resignation he'd phoned Elle Stevens and informed her that her husband's condition was seemingly stable, but he was receiving a visit from a friend in a couple of days and that he may be able to give her more information then.

As good as his word Dr Forrestor arrived at Hull Hospital two days later. He was shown to Dr Lighten's office where Charles greeted him. As they sat at Lighten's desk Charles happened to say to his friend, "I see you've brought a box with you. What's in it?"

"This," answered Simon producing the hypodermic, "is a new vaccine I've been working on. According to my initial tests it has proved highly effective against many types of virus related diseases."

"Is it safe?" Charles enquired.

"Perfectly," Simon assured him with a smile on his face.

"I have a patient, brought in a week or two back, who I'd like you to look at, give me your diagnosis of his condition." Lighten then produced, from his desk drawer, a folder that contained Arnold Stevens notes and the results of the scans that had been performed on Arnold. "Please look at these first," he held the transparent sheet of plastic with Arnold's blood results on it. Dr Forrestor saw the spores in the bloodstream and, immediately knew the man had the *Proagnon* virus. "Odd isn't it?" said Lighten.

"What? Oh yes very odd," responded Simon quickly.

"I wonder if your new vaccine, which you've been working on, might be effective in his treatment."

"We can but try and hope," said Forrestor lightly. Charles, who was two years older than his counterpart, then led Simon from his office, Simon bringing his new wonderdrug with him, and down the hospital corridor to room 3A, a private room, in which was the sleeping form of Arnold Stevens, a young woman and a small child were at his bedside. As the two doctors entered the room Forrestor heard the boy say, "Please don't die Granddad."

It wasn't what the boy said, but the way he said it and the look on his face, that seemed to move Simon Forrestor inside. Could he really murder this boy's grandfather? He would have done it without a moments thought if only the woman had been there. Then there was Dr Lighten, would he insist that his friend use the vaccine? Then Simon had a sudden thought, could he add the vaccine subtly maybe making it less effective? Making his mind up he said to Lighten, "Charles, I feel instead of injecting the vaccine it should be added to the saline solution."

"But that would mean halting the intravenous drip, for a moment or two, and I'd prefer not to do that. I think an injection into the back of the patient's hand will suffice."

"Okay Charles," Simon reluctantly agreed, "you are the more senior of us." The doctor then looked down at the boy who smiled at him.

"Are you going to make my grandfather better?"

"We're certainly going to try," he ruffled the boy's hair. "Is this your mummy?" he indicated Melissa.

"No," she said firmly, "I'm his aunt, Simon's mother, my sister, died last year along with my niece."

"I am sorry," he said, looking up at Melissa.

"Come on Simon, Isaac'll be wondering where we've got to."

"Okay," the boy responded, not wanting to leave his grandfather but Melissa assured him the doctors would take very good care of him. The two of them left the hospital room and the hospital.

Once they'd gone Dr Lighten said to his colleague, "You can inject the vaccine now; Simon selected a vein in the man's arm and broke the skin, and then pressed the plunger on the syringe; the new, deadlier strain of the virus was injected into Arnold's bloodstream. Possibly as Arnold had been infected before the older virus may try to fight the newer virus off, only time would tell.

The two doctors then left the room, as Dr Forrestor passed to leave behind his colleague he paused and whispered to the sleeping form, "I'm sorry."

"What was that?" called Lighten, having just heard his colleague whisper something.

"Oh nothing, just whispering to myself," Simon assured the older doctor. "Let's go." Dr Lighten walked back down the corridor to his office, Dr Forrestor following. Charles then invited Simon home with him so they could talk about old times, Simon readily agreed; Lighten placed the container with the replaced vaccine in, in his safe, "Don't worry," he said, seeing his friend's reaction, "it'll be quite safe until we return in the morning. Now come on." The two of them then left the office, and made their way out the hospital; they climbed into Lighten's red Honda *Civic*, a bit ancient nowadays as it was 2013, and journeyed to Lighten's house which was a, renovated, country cottage; it was only a small dwelling but it suited Charles and his wife Mary. They pulled up in front of the cottage – located just outside Wawne – and exited the vehicle, the front door of the cottage flew open and Mary rushed out; when Dr Forrestor saw her, she was about ten years younger than her husband, he was taken aback by how much she looked like his own wife, Rebecca, had when she was alive

He now felt regret about having to kill her like he had, if he'd had his way she'd still be alive now, he was guilty of her murder; had he now condemned another man to death at Hull Hospital, yes he might have succumbed to his original infection – he was over sixty – or even if he survived would he remember anything about what had happened?

Seeing Simon Mary said to him, "Go on in Mr Forrestor, make yourself at home." Simon went inside the cottage and seated himself in the main room, Charles and Mary following him; Mary made them a meal of steak pie, potatoes, vegetables and gravy. As they ate Mary casually asked their guest, "How's your wife nowadays Mr Forrestor? Rebecca isn't it?"

Simon stopped eating and replied, "Sadly Rebecca passed away a few months back, it was all very sudden."

"Sorry bout that," Charles said.

"Yes we are truly sorry for your loss," followed up Mary. "I'm sorry if the memory's still painful for you."

"It's okay," Simon said, "I admit it was painful talking about it at first, but as they say time's a great healer." He carried on eating, "We only had family attend the funeral that's what Rebecca wanted. I admit I should have told you before but I forgot as I've been very busy."

"Understandable old chap," remarked Mr Lighten, "you had a lot on."

"That's why I've been in Scotland; I'm still working at *John Groggins*, but was doing research in Scotland."

"Researching what?" enquired Mrs Lighten, more out of curiosity than anything else.

"Simon's discovered a new wonderdrug, my dear, a vaccine which is effective in combating many types of virus," replied her husband. Simon smiled at them both.

Later on Simon Forrestor informed his hosts that he was going to go to bed, as it had been a long day for him. Mary led him through to the rear of the cottage where the bathroom and bedrooms were situated, Simon thanked her and went into the bathroom and closed the door; unfortunately the door didn't quite shut so Mrs Lighten had a good view of him as he undressed – not that it wasn't anything she hadn't seen before – however, when he turned and she saw the scar across his leg, it seemed healed but was still noticeable, she let out a small gasp.

It was then Simon realised that the bathroom door wasn't quite closed, so he turned and shut it fully, blocking the view from the outside corridor. He then showered himself down, dried off, gathered up his clothes and peeked out the door to check there was nobody outside. Finding nobody about he quietly and quickly, crossed to the room he'd been allocated, and settled himself in the bed, in the room.

About half an hour, maybe an hour, later, Simon heard Charles and Mary Lighten retire to bed. Mary popped her head round the door, while Mr Lighten preceded her into their bedroom; Simon was most surprised to see her, "I'm sorry I peeked at you earlier," she told him.

"Please think nothing of it," with that they said their good-nights and Mrs Lighten left him, and closed the room door behind her.

*****

In the HART medical unit Commander Most was visiting Commander Strobing who had been allowed visitors. "Can you remember what happened?" Celia asked him.

Ronan looked into her youthful looking face and said, "Everything's a bit vague but I'll try. The plane was coming into land when it gave, what you might call, a sway. Suddenly, I was informed, via the intercom, that the jet had developed an electrical fault; a few moments later I was informed, again via the intercom, that the landing gear had developed a fault and couldn't be lowered, I was told to prepare for a crash landing. Subsequently a few minutes later the plane landed on its fuselage."

He paused, "Once the plane had stopped I made my way to the flight deck to find both pilot and co-pilot had fallen forward, they were both unconscious. I managed to drag them both from their seats and pulled them to the cabin door, which I managed to open, to find a rescue truck waiting outside. I passed the bodies over to the man on the rescue truck and was told to jump. I jumped and then everything went black. Tell me what I missed."

"Okay," replied Celia, "we, at HART, got a call about the accident, so Dr Schaiffer, along with myself, attended in, the SUV designated, HART 1 and found the plane had exploded. We found your seemingly lifeless body and, whilst I loaded you into the Mega Cruiser, Dr Schaiffer went to check on the other two people."

"How are they?" asked Commander Strobing suddenly and quickly.

"Regrettably I have to inform you that they're both dead." A look of shock crossed Ronan's face, "there was nothing you could've done." Celia then went on to tell him about the reaction she'd gotten from Lisa Bell, upon their return.

"What are you trying to tell me?" the male HART commander enquired of his female counterpart.

Commander Most simply smiled at him, and then said to him, "I think our Miss Bell is either developing, or has developed, certain feelings for you. Call it women's intuition but I wouldn't be, at all, surprised if she doesn't visit you soon."

It was hard to read his expression, or gauge his reaction as he just said, "Hmm." Commander Most was unsure whether to tell her superior about the break in at her residence while he'd been away, and that she was pretty certain, now, that Leon Bigship was still alive; maybe it would be best to wait until he was back in the chair of command, after all she hadn't told anybody else about it.

She told Ronan she'd be back later and kissed him, lightly, on the forehead, and then left the side of his bed. Ronan watched her go and lay back down to rest; his back was still pretty sore, probably when the plane had exploded the heat given out had, mildly, scorched him, still his back would heal given time.

*****

As predicted, a couple of hours later, though to Ronan it felt like days, Lisa Bell appeared to see him. Commander Strobing sat himself up in bed as Miss Bell came into the room; she seated herself, on the bed, leaned over and kissed him; he was a bit taken aback by her sudden show of passion towards him, but hadn't Commander Most told him that she thought Lisa felt this way? He, himself, couldn't understand why she was interested in him, he was twelve years older than her, Ben Gillespe was more her age.

They talked about what had happened to him, his life, her life, and then Lisa opened up and said, in a low voice to him, "I don't like Commander Most, get rid of her." Ronan then opened up to her and told her the history that had occurred between the two of them, and why he felt he couldn't get rid of her, just on Lisa's say so.

It was, at that moment, Celia entered the medical unit and saw, through the room window, Lisa Bell kiss Ronan Strobing. Commander Most felt something inside of her, something she hadn't felt since looking at that photo of Ronan and Mandy Strobing, on their wedding day – jealousy! Why should she feel jealous now though, it was her who'd ended their relationship all those years ago. Yet here she was – feeling jealous of this younger woman, she knew she shouldn't, but she did.

In the room Ronan was saying to Lisa, neither of them knew Celia was watching, "I'm sorry Lisa, but I just can't involve myself with anyone yet. I may feel different in a few months, therefore I'm not saying never; just not yet. You do understand don't you?"

Miss Bell sighed, "Of course Ronan, sorry Commander Strobing, I understand. I forgot your wife's only been dead a year, so I'll bide my time and wait for you to come to me." With that she kissed him again, much to the annoyance of Celia Most, and left his side. Just before departing she looked back and told the man in the bed, "When you're ready," and then made her way towards the door. Ronan watched her go, part of him knew he wasn't ready for a new relationship yet – he'd had that brief fling with Miss Lang but now she, too, was dead, while there was part of him that could see the two of them together. Plus he guessed he didn't want to hurt Celia, okay they'd been over for a long time but, oh he couldn't work it out.

He spirits had, actually, been lifted by seeing the young receptionist, again he didn't know why, maybe he did care for her, more than he was letting on.

As Miss Bell exited the room she bumped into Mrs Most. "Oh hello," Lisa said and snapped a quick salute, "I've just been in to see Commander Strobing, he's looking much better," what she didn't know was that Celia had been watching through the room window. "I'm just going back to reception now."

With that Lisa Bell left the medical unit, Commander Most watching her go, as she watched she noticed Lisa had a *spring* in her step which hadn't been there before. *How would you know he's looking better*, Celia thought, *you never saw him when he came in*.

Commander Most walked into the room and greeted Commander Strobing. "Two visits in one day, aren't I the lucky one?" Ronan said to his female counterpart.

"I suppose you are," Celia answered her commander, and sat in the chair beside his bed, she didn't tell Ronan that she'd seen Lisa and him through the room window, but what she did say next both surprised and shocked him, "Get rid of Lisa Bell and replace her, she's no good as a receptionist."

"You've never complained about her before," said the man she was speaking to, knowing deep inside there was more too it than that, so he decided to tackle Celia head on. "What's the matter? Just because she's younger than you, and some may consider her prettier."

"It's not that, it's just I feel she's too young for her job," was the dismissive answer he got.

"Don't tell me you still have feelings for me," Ronan asked her outright. The look on his fellow commander's face told him everything he needed to know. She did.

"Okay Ronan, I admit I do. I know I shouldn't now, I didn't think I did but after seeing you two together these feelings of jealousy just built up inside me."

"When did you see us together?" Ronan demanded to know.

"When I arrived, a few minutes before Lisa left, I looked in through the window," she admitted to him honestly.

"How could you?" he enquired. "I feel betrayed now, but I know that by admitting your feelings for me I know you're only looking out for me, so I guess I forgive you."

"Anyway," demanded Celia angrily, "you're a good one to lecture me after you crawled into my bed, while we were in Iran."

Ronan was taken aback by his deputy's tone of voice and decided to try and smooth things over, "'I'm sorry about that, that was a terrible mistake."

Celia and Ronan chatted a little more, before she rose from her seat and told him she was leaving to resume command.

Once she'd left Commander Strobing lay there thinking about the past; first he'd loved and lost Celia Sancton, next he'd loved, married and eventually lost Mandy Stevens, finally he'd loved and lost Lucy Lang. Now there was Lisa Bell, could he risk her safety? Then there was Celia Most, she'd admitted she still had feelings for him, but she was married so she was off limits. With these thoughts and others running through his head he closed his eyes and was soon fast asleep.

*****

Over in England Simon Forrestor's shore leave was now over. He said his farewells to Charles and Mary Lighten, he told Charles he hoped Mr Stevens would be better soon, gathered the container he'd brought with him – that contained the vaccine he'd created and made his way to Fraserburgh, in Scotland. Once there he boarded one of the supply ships and finished the journey to the sea fort.

*****

Over the next few weeks Arnold Stevens condition deteriorated. He started to develop ulcers and abscesses in and around his mouth. These were horrible to look at as some of them, on his skin, started to leak a decidedly evil looking yellow substance; the sores in his mouth looked even worse. All nurses and doctors who entered room 3A, including Lighten himself, were advised to wear contamination suits, just in case.

Mr Stevens was given another brain and body scan which now showed a much larger number of the spore like things inhabiting his body; plus there was a large build up of spores in his bloodstream close to his brain. Dr Lighten didn't know what any of this meant, but he knew one man who may be able to help, Dr Forrestor had disappeared again, except this man was in Geneva, he dialled the main hospital switchboard and asked them to ring a certain number.

The phone rung several times and then a young female voice answered, "HART headquarters."

"Ah hello," said Dr Lighten, into the handset. "My name is Dr Charles Lighten and I work at Hull Hospital. Is Dr Hans Schaiffer around?"

"I'll just check for you Mr Lighten, please hold," there followed about two minutes of some music, and then the female voice came back on the line, "just putting you through to the medical unit now."

"Thank you," Charles said politely, another few rings later and the phone was answered, "Dr Schaiffer here Charles, what can I do for you?"

"Dr Schaiffer," Lighten said, "we have a patient at Hull Hospital with some, very, mysterious symptoms."

"Can you describe them?" asked the German. Dr Lighten described the symptoms and the abnormalities in the body. When he was done he waited for Dr Schaiffer's response, he didn't have to wait long. "Nein! I shall be with you as soon as I can; in the meantime keep Mr Stevens warm." With that he replaced the receiver.

Dr Schaiffer then picked up the receiver handset again and dialled the main reception again, “Yes,” said Lisa Bell.

“Miss Bell, Dr Schaiffer here, I’d like you to arrange a *Learjet* business jet to take me to *Robin Hood* Doncaster-Sheffield airport, in England, please; preferably within the next hour or two.”

“Of course, Dr Schaiffer, is there anything else?”

“Not at the present time, but will you inform Commander Most I am going to England for a few days.”

“Of course.” Lisa heard the *click* as Dr Schaiffer replaced his handset. She then dialled the commander’s office number and informed Commander Most where the German would be for the next few days.

*****

Mr Stevens was starting to thrash about more now, sometimes trying to rip the needle that was attached to the saline drip solution from the back of his hand.

Dr Lighten gave him a powerful sedative and then instructed two orderlies to tie his arms and hands to the metal sides of the bed, which they did. This helped for a while but then Arnold started to thrash wildly again. Dr Lighten wondered whether to call Arnold’s family in; no, he would wait until Dr Hans Schaiffer arrived.

*****

Dr Schaiffer left the HART compound at about 18:10 in his *Apollo II* car and drove to *Cointrin* airport. There he boarded a Learjet *55* and it made the 515 mile journey to the airport in England, landing at around 18:30 (due to the time difference); he exited the airport and took a taxi for the seven mile journey to Doncaster railway station. The train he boarded at the railway station (19:00) took him the 49 miles to Hull railway station, he arrived there at 19:45, and then walked from the railway station southwards down Ferensway, avoiding any oncoming traffic, he then turned right and walked along Anlaby Road; finally about a third of the way down he turned right, again, into Lansdowne Street where the hospital was located.

He entered the hospital's main entrance at 20:18, informed the receptionist who he was and why he was there; the woman on reception gave him directions on how to reach Dr Lighten's office.

He thanked her and walked off in the direction of the lifts, upon reaching these he took one up to the third floor; exiting the lift the HART medical man proceeded to enquire at the reception, on this floor, where Dr Lighten's office was to be found. Again following the directions he was given he found his English colleague's office and knocked.

"Come in," called a voice from inside, Dr Schaiffer entered and found Charles Lighten, seated at his desk, studying medical records; he noticed the name on the folder was Arnold Stevens. At last he looked up, "Ah Dr Schaiffer, these are Mr Stevens medical notes, he is the patient who I called you about, the one with the mysterious symptoms."

"Can I have a look at the notes?" enquired Hans politely, seating himself on one of the other chairs in the office. "Make my own decision?"

"Oh yes sure," answered Charles handing the notes, including the plastic, see through, sheets across the desk. Dr Hans Schaiffer studied the sheets thoughtfully.

Finally he said, "When did this all start to happen?"

"He was brought in last month, June, and we performed a quick blood test on him, and performed a couple of scans – you have the results there. Anyway we hooked him up to a saline solution, via an intravenous drip connected to his lower arm, and he seemed to be showing signs of recovery; however, a couple of weeks back a colleague of mine – Simon Forrestor - from medical school, came to see me with a new type of vaccine." He paused to allow his German friend to digest what he'd just said.

"Anyway," Lighten continued, "I allowed him to inject this new vaccine, he assured me it was quite safe and could treat most diseases related to virus's, into the patient, it was then Mr Stevens condition deteriorated so we conducted more tests and scans, where we found - as you can plainly see - that these spore like things had multiplied, rapidly, and seemed to be mostly collected around the brain."

Dr Schaiffer listened to all this while he studied the results. Eventually he asked, "You say this build up started after Dr Forrestor injected him with this new vaccine?"

"What? Oh yes I believe so," answered Charles, wondering what Dr Schaiffer was getting at – he thought he knew but didn't want to accept what might have happened. Hans now looked straight, across the desk, at him.

"Isn't it at all possible that this Dr Simon Forrestor may have injected Mr Stevens with this new vaccine, knowing that it would do more harm than good? Might I suggest a new blood sample be taken for study I shall require one sample that I can study in the hospital laboratory, whilst the other sample will return with me to HART headquarters for further study and analysis, should I come up with no result here."

"I shall see to it at once," Charles assured him.

"By the way," Hans said to Lighten, "this Dr Simon Forrestor, where does he work and live?"

"As far as I can recall he works at *John Groggins* Hospital, in Norwich, near where he lives. Although he did tell me he's been doing some research in Scotland."

"Do you know where in Scotland?"

"I don't think he said. Is it important?"

"It may be," responded his German counterpart, "anyway, look its 21:05. Shall we call it a day and resume tomorrow."

"We can do," said Charles. "Tell me Dr Schaiffer, have you got anywhere to stay tonight?"

"No I haven't," he answered truthfully.

"That settles it you're coming home with me tonight." The two, old, friends left the hospital together, climbed into Dr Lighten's Honda *Civic*, and they made the journey to Charles Lighten's cottage dwelling just outside of Wawne.

*****

At HART headquarters, in Switzerland, Commander Strobing had sufficiently recovered to leave the medical unit, he still needed his bandages changing but not so regularly now, plus the bandage on his back was much smaller now. He looked much better, and also felt better in fact he was back in the seat of command, which had been temporarily held by Commander Most – who was, even now, seated across the wooden desk from her superior. "Commander Most, you wished to see me."

"Ah yes sir, its just I've been having a bit of trouble."

"Trouble!" exclaimed Ronan, "What sort of trouble?"

"I suppose it is wrong to class it as trouble," she told him.

He peered intensely at her, "Please explain what you mean, and leave nothing out," her superior ordered.

"It started when you went back to England sir, there was this figure hanging about and I found the office had been ransacked. I think that the figure, it looked like a person, did it – they were looking for something – anyway, I chased this person from the building but then lost them." She looked at Ronan to see what his reaction would be. The look that crossed his face told her he didn't disbelieve her, and he was interested to hear anything else she could tell him.

"Anyway," continued Celia, "I was in my residence a few nights later, having a bath, when somebody broke in; I grabbed a towel, and my Beretta 92 pistol, and rushed downstairs to challenge the intruder. I caught them in the sitting room, overturning drawers; again they seemed to be looking for something. I burst in the room and challenged them, but they just pushed past me, knocking me to the floor, and exited my residence," she paused, unsure whether to go on. However, the look on her superior's face told her he wanted to know everything, "When the person pushed past me I thought I recognised them. The person was a man."

"Who do you think it was?" enquired Ronan Strobing. Just then the phone rang, Commander Strobing answered it and listened quietly, after the other person had finished speaking the commander simply said, "You are fully authorised to take whatever action you see fit." He then replaced the handset and turned his attention back to Celia, "Well, who do you think this person was?"

"Leon Bigship," she responded simply. Ronan's face was a picture; he looked really shocked at this piece of news. "You remember we received reports that one of the bodies, in Turkey, had mysteriously vanished. Well I, now, believe it was that of Commander Bigship."

"But how?" he asked quietly, "how did he survive?"

"We'll find out when we catch up with him," Commander Most told him. Suddenly there came a knock on the office door.

*****

Dr Lighten and Dr Schaiffer were, both, similarly dressed in contamination suits in room 3A, the room that contained Arnold Stevens, Dr Schaiffer looked at the man aghast; he'd never known a virus, if that's what it was, that had produced such horrific effects so rapidly. "Horrible isn't it?" Dr Lighten said, seeing the look on his German counterpart's face.

The German simply nodded, as Charles prepared to take the two blood samples; he took from a side trolley the equipment he'd need – this equipment consisted of a plastic hub, a hypodermic needle, and a vacuum tube for collection of the blood. Charles selected the median cubital vein, on the anterior forearm (the side within the fold of the elbow) of the right arm - this was where blood was most commonly obtained from – plus this vein lay close to the surface of the skin, and there was not a large nerve supply.

He then made the vein more pronounced, swabbed the area, he was going to use, with antiseptec and, carefully, pierced the vein with the hypodermic needle; and then, once he'd got a good flow of blood attached a vacuum tube. The needle, of the hypodermic was double ended; the second shorter needle was being shrouded for safety by the holder. When the Vacutainer test tube was pushed down into the holder, its rubber cap was pierced by the second needle and the pressure difference between the blood volume and the vacuum in the tube forced the blood through the needle and on into the tube. Once the tube was full it was removed and the other was inserted and then filled in the same way. It was important to remove the second, full, tube before withdrawing the hypodermic needle, as there may have still been some suction left, causing mild pain upon withdrawal, but this patient knew nothing of what was happening to him.

Charles finished with the procedure and handed both tubes to Schaiffer. "The laboratory is located on the basement floor, you go and examine the blood whilst I go and call the family."

"Okay," announced Hans Schaiffer, took the tubes, which were sealed in a clear, plastic, bag, and hurried from the room. The German, once out of his containment suit, located a lift that would take him down to level minus one. The lift stopped with a slight *bump* and once the doors were fully open the HART medical man walked down the corridor and finally found the laboratory for the analysis of the blood sample.

Even though the laboratory was located in the basement the room was light and airy; technicians in the room looked up as Dr Schaiffer entered. "As you were people, I'm just here to analyse a blood sample." The technicians resumed the tasks they were doing.

Dr Schaiffer took one of the blood samples from the plastic bag and began to analyse it. He examined the structure and make up of the blood, there was definitely something nasty happening here but what, he couldn't tell yet. It was as if something had been injected by this Dr Forrestor into Mr Stevens bloodstream, if the effects hadn't been accelerated by the second injection, was there even a first, Mr Stevens might have recovered by now. Knowing, ultimately, he would probably have to do further tests once he returned to Geneva, he, resignedly, left the lab and made his way back to Lighten's office.

When he reached the office he was most surprised to find Charles talking to two women. The older one was probably Mrs Stevens, while the younger of the two ladies was probably the daughter. As if to make his presence known Dr Schaiffer cleared his throat, loudly, and both ladies turned to look at him. "Mrs Stevens, Miss Stevens, may I present my esteemed colleague, from Switzerland, Dr Hans Schaiffer. Dr Schaiffer, Mr Stevens's wife and daughter."

"Pleased to meet you," the HART medical man told them. Hadn't Commander Strobing married a Miss Stevens? Surely this wasn't the same family; however, when he looked into the face of the Miss Stevens he was being introduced to he knew, at once, that this young woman was Ronan Strobing's sister-in-law. Even though the German'd never met Ronan's wife, he'd seen a picture of her once, and this young woman – he could tell – was her sister.

"Dr Schaiffer," said Lighten, "I have explained to these two ladies about Mr Stevens, present condition, and why I have called you in. Now tell us what did you ascertain from your study of the blood sample?"

"Much the same as we already knew, Charles, there's definitely something nasty going on, and, as I explained to you earlier, the effects seem to have been accelerated by the injection this Dr Forrestor gave him – whether this is a mild side effect or he did it on purpose we will never know. In my opinion if Mr Stevens hadn't been injected he would be better now."

Melissa Stevens suddenly piped up, "I never liked the look of that Dr Forrestor. He just seemed too shifty."

Both Elle Stevens and Hans Schaiffer stared at her. Finally Dr Schaiffer broke the silence, in the room, and asked, "You've met him, when?"

"A couple of weeks back, I brought my brother-in-laws son, Simon, to see his grandfather, Dr Forrestor was here then," she told them. Now Hans Schaiffer knew, for certain, that this family was indeed related to Commander Strobing. Had he not been certain before he was now.

The German turned back to his English counterpart, "Dr Lighten, as I suspected this is a type of viral infection and will need further study. I will study, in more depth, the other blood sample we took, upon my return to Switzerland. Once I have gathered as much from it, as I can, I will be in touch."

"Right you are," Dr Lighten said, "when will you know?"

"A few days, as I have a few other things in England to do before I, ultimately leave for Switzerland." The doctor then excused himself and left, he exited the hospital, walked back to the railway station and booked himself on the next available train(s) to Norwich. The full journey time would be approximately four hours and five minutes.

As the train pulled into the station Dr Schaiffer got up from where he was sitting and stepped forward, once the train had come to a complete halt the carriage doors were opened – there were ten carriages in all – and the carriages disgorged their passengers; when everyone had got off the passengers who were waiting, including Hans Schaiffer, climbed aboard. Once everyone was aboard the doors were closed, the guard, on the platform, blew his whistle, and the engine pulling the carriages moved off.

The train travelled on, through the countryside, and stopped at many small stations along the way for passengers to disembark or come aboard, towards its destination of Doncaster. Here the German, along with some of his fellow passengers who were also travelling to Norwich, had to change trains; their next destination was the station at Peterborough where they again changed trains and travelled to the station at Ely.

Here more passengers got off and some climbed aboard. Again when they were all ready the train moved off to its final destination, Norwich Upon reaching the station at Norwich the German exited the train station, hailed a taxi and went to *John Groggins* Hospital where he asked for Dr Simon Forrestor.

"I'm sorry sir," the receptionist, at the hospital, told him, "but he hasn't been in for a couple of months. His office is all locked up as well."

"Do you know where he could be?" enquired Schaiffer.

"No, sorry, but his car's still outside, that green *Megane*."

Hans thanked the receptionist for her help, he now knew that this Simon Forrestor was either very elusive, or he had disappeared on purpose possibly because he had something to hide. He walked outside, it was a reasonably warm day, and taking pen and paper from his jacket pocket he wrote down the registration of the Renault *Megane*.

He then produced a cell phone, from another pocket and rang the DVLA; although the operator that answered gave him the address the vehicle was registered to, Hans thanked her and then ended the call by thumbing the *kill* switch.

Schaiffer nipped back inside the hospital and asked the receptionist for directions to Just Avenue; she gave him directions and he set off walking, when he reached the Forrestor's dwelling there was absolutely no sign of life. He knocked on the front and rear doors, and peered in all the windows, the house seemed totally empty. Hans was just making his way back down the front path when the door to the house next door opened and a woman, in about her sixties Dr Schaiffer assumed, said, "Are you a friend of Simon Forrestor?"

"A work colleague," responded the German. The woman looked unsure as to whether she believed him or not, nevertheless he ploughed on. "What's happened to his wife?" He knew from what Forrestor had told Dr Lighten what had happened but he just wanted to be sure.

"Rebecca died just before he disappeared," she responded with certainty. Yet hadn't Forrestor told Lighten she'd died many months ago; more mystery. Dr Forrestor seemed to be the key to this particular mystery, but where was he. With a heavy heart he set off back to the hospital.

*****

At HART headquarters the door to the commander's office opened and a figure stood framed in the doorway, the figure of a man. The man stepped inside and reached inside his pocket; it was then Ronan and Celia recognised the figure, "Leon!" they both shouted joyfully. "What happened?"

"You left me to die," Leon replied angrily, and then produced his Beretta 9000 and pointed it at them. "Now you must die!"

CHAPTER 3

THE FIRST WAVE OF CASUALTIES!

Commander's Strobing and Most looked at the semiautomatic pistol that was pointed directly at them, and then peered upwards into the face of their colleague. There was, now, a huge amount of tension, and silence, in the commander's office.

Commander Strobing's own Beretta 9000S 9mm lay on the desk in front of him, it's shape not dissimilar to Leon's, the only difference was Leon's semi automatic pistol - most Beretta pistols were semiautomatic - had wooden hand grips whereas Ronan's hand grips were plastic ones – which were black. As Commander Ronan Strobing, slowly, reached for the weapon Leon fired his own.

The 9mm cartridge skimmed the desk top making Ronan flinch and hastily withdraw his hand, it harmlessly struck the wall behind Ronan; even Commander Most was shocked, and surprised, at her colleague's sudden change in behaviour. "Leon, why are you doing this to us?" enquired the superior HART commander.

"You left me for dead, you could've rescued me but you didn't." Celia had now drawn her, own, Beretta 92 pistol and was pointing it, straight, at Leon.

"Don't make me use this," she told him. The look on her face told him she would if she was provoked.

"We're all friends here," Commander Strobing said in a gentle tone, and then in a more authoritative tone, "Celia, lower your weapon, Commander Bigship isn't going to shoot either of us."

"But sir."

"Just do it!" Celia Most lowered her pistol, still a little unsure, "I know what I'm doing." Next he turned his attention back to the man who was holding the pistol on them. "Sit down Leon," Ronan said calmly but authoritatively.

Leon reluctantly sat across the desk from the other two, in the chair recently vacated by Commander Most, but kept hold of his weapon. "Now," said Ronan gently, "I know you think we deserted you, but please tell us what happened, in your own time."

Seemingly more reassured now Commander Bigship said to them, he noticed Commander Most had pulled up a chair next to her superior; Leon's voice was slightly shaky, "As you may recall I was in a seat at the very back of the HMMWV cargo/troop carrier, near the tail flap. When the vehicle started to explode I saw that you two were thrown from the vehicle, I wasn't sure where you ended up, but, evidently, you both survived."

"Anyway, I was thrown to the floor and ended up face down, totally unconscious I think. After a while somebody picked me up; when I did finally awake I was laid on a bed in a medical unit, I knew it was a medical unit as there were numerous medical instruments scattered about. Plus there were numerous beds with several bodies on them. I looked at the bodies, the ones next to me were unrecognisable; so I climbed off the bed I was on, there was nobody about, and I, calmly, walked out the back entrance. There were no security personnel about so I found an unlocked shed and hid inside it."

"Eventually, I heard a vehicle drive past, I risked a peek out and saw it was a HMMWV that we'd brought with us – it stopped briefly outside, the soldier driving it climbed out and went inside one of the other buildings, so I stole out and climbed in the back, covered myself with a tarpaulin, and waited; presently the driver came back and drove the vehicle I had hidden myself in - I assumed - aboard a transport aircraft; this was confirmed when I heard, though the sound was muffled, the engines firing up."

"When the aircraft eventually landed the HMMWV was driven from the plane, a while after the vehicle had come to a full halt I risked a peek from under the tarpaulin; there was nobody about so I exited the vehicle, it was then I knew the vehicle had been parked in a garage. I found the door, it was locked, as I'd suspected it would be, however, I managed to force the lock and escaped. It was then I noticed I was back at the main HART headquarters; it was then I came to the main building – always keeping to the shadows – and ventured inside."

"What about security?" asked Commander Most suddenly. "Surely someone saw you."

"As I say Mrs Most I was careful," Leon answered her calmly.

"Anyway, I made my way to this office and set about looking for the star of command."

"You mean this," Ronan said, producing the *gold* star from his uniform pocket.

"Yes."

"So it was you I chased from the building," Celia said, realisation finally dawning on her.

"Yes it was, and it was me who broke into your residence, I apologise for that. You caught me again, I thought you were out, by the way you've got a magnificent body." Celia suddenly went bright red with embarrassment as she remembered the evening in question. "I knew you were both here today, so I decided to make my move."

Celia and Ronan looked at each other, as if contemplating on how next to proceed. "A remarkable story," Ronan eventually told the other man. "Now where do we go from here."

Leon, now aware of the overall situation, suddenly, announced, "I shall understand, completely, if you wish me to turn in my firearm and badge, and resign completely from HART."

"Nonsense Commander Bigship, I won't hear of it, you're too valuable. I have promoted your deputy, Lieutenant Samuels, to the position you held, only because we assumed you were dead; however, like Mrs Most here, you will become my second deputy – therefore in both our absences you will become overall commander of HART."

"Thank you sir," he responded, it was only similar to the job he'd done before, but he'd, sort of, stepped up a place. Just then there came a knock on the office door.

"Come in," called Ronan, it was good to have the three of them there; he was still saddened at the deaths of Commander's Lucy Lang and Peter Roberts – he would never forget them.

Joshua Smith entered, "Sir, ma'am," then he caught sight of Commander Bigship, and did a double take, "Sorry, sirs, ma'am, all the reservists that were able to, have arrived. I just wondered what I should tell them to do next." Ronan was taken aback he'd given no such order.

Commander Most spoke up, "I gave the authorisation, in your absence sir, I hope you don't mind." Commander Strobing smiled, trust Celia.

"Order everyone to the conference room, Josh." Then he enquired, "Are Lisa Bell and Alice Stronglove in."

"I believe they are sir, any reason?" the receptionist asked. Commander Strobing shook his head.

"Just give the order for the commanders, together with their, individual, teams to gather in the conference room, in a quarter of an hour." Joshua Smith nodded and left the office.

*****

Dr Simon Forrestor was aboard the sea fort, just north of Scotland.

The sea fort in question, Simon had never taken that much notice, was a round structure. It was known as *Damancas Fort*, and this was a sea fort which had been built as a result of the 1859 Royal Commission. The fort was located just beyond the Moray Firth, west of Fraserburgh, Scotland.

Work on constructing the fort started in 1861 but was soon halted for a review into the best way to defend the Moray Firth and all other approaches to Scotland. Work was then restarted in 1867 and was completed, eleven years later, in 1878.

The fort's main purpose was to act as a further line of defence for ships that made it too close to the northern coast of

Scotland. It was 162 feet in diameter across at its base, with 1 floor and a basement and armour plating only on the seaward side. It was originally planned to have been armed with nine 10" eighteen ton rifled muzzle loader (RML) guns on the seaward side, and six 7" seven ton RML guns on the landward sides. However, by the time of completion the plan had changed so that the seaward side received nine 12.5-inch muzzle-loading (RML) guns. From 1884 more modern 12-inch breechloading guns were installed and these were in service until after World War I.

In 1898 the role of the fort was changed to defend against light craft and the roof was fitted out with two 4.7" guns and searchlights. In the early 1900s all but three of the original large guns were removed. Minor upgrades to the smaller guns and searchlights continued through the years.

The fort was declared surplus to requirements in 1962 and disposed of by the Ministry of Defence in 1982. The fort was now privately owned, by Floyd Maxwell and his two partners and used to be open as a museum. It had 50 rooms, and had been available for many private functions and had limited accommodation available. However, now it was being used, by *Proagnon*.

*****

Forrestor was in his quarters, at the moment, having a meeting with Dr Paul Santos, head of the *Proagnon* scientists, "I think, as well as our, engineered, virus being airborne, we should also use deodorant body spays to distribute the virus – a fine mist. What do you think?"

"It is a good idea," responded Santos, thinking of the potential impact. "Plus it would maximise the effect, yes?"

"That is correct," confirmed the head of the operation, with a wry smile.

"However, may I remind you, sir, that there are no spray cans on board this fort."

Simon just smiled at the man, crossed to a metal locker and opened it. He removed a, large, box and placed it, on the bed, beside Santos; inside it were approximately a hundred and twenty aerosol spray cans, all had contained deodorant but were now empty. "We do now," he said in triumph.

"Where did you get these from?" Santos enquired suspiciously.

"When I returned, to the mainland, for my few days leave I acquired them at a car boot sale for £8. They were full at the time." Simon paused, "If we need more I have only to let Maxwell know."

"Can we develop our virus into a spray?"

"I'm sure we can fill a hundred and nineteen cans."

"I thought you said you brought ten dozen back with you."

"I did but I've already filled a can, just in case," Forrestor smiled at Santos, his smile was triumphant and evil. "I suggest we get to work." He could see the fear cross the face of Paul Santos; the mighty *Proagnon* had already been double crossed. Paul knew if he breathed a word to the others Forrestor may decide to eliminate them all now.

*****

Hans Schaiffer wandered into the hospital grounds where he spied several CCTV cameras dotted about, and a patrolling security guard. Walking up to the guard he, casually, asked the man, "I see you have CCTV monitoring these grounds. Can you tell me where the monitoring room is?"

"And why the hell do you want to know? Who are you anyway?" Dr Schaiffer calmly produced his HART identity badge and showed it to the guard, whose mood, on seeing the badge, suddenly changed. "It's over that way, sir," he said pointing. "You can't miss it, it's a, small, brick building, shaped like a house."

"Thank you for being so cooperative," Schaiffer responded, setting off in the direction the security guard was pointing. The HART man didn't really like showing his, official, badge to people for security checks, but if it was necessary he would do it.

Opening the door to the monitoring room he found another, older, security guard inside; the walls were covered with shelves of DVD recordings, probably this was an archive.

He noticed that there were three or four DVDs covering each day; therefore the archive was very comprehensive. "Don't worry," announced the security guard as Schaiffer shut the door behind him, "my junior colleague told me, via his radio, you were on the way, Dr Hans Schaiffer of HART isn't it? I'm Richard Scarborough."

"Pleased to meet you," announced HART's medical man. "I'm here as I'm trying to track down a Dr Simon Forrestor, he's an old friend; I believe he vanished a couple of months back."

"I'll just check for you," responded Scarborough, picking up a telephone handset. He dialled a number, "Ah hello, security guard Scarborough here, I'm trying to track down Dr Forrestor." He listened for a moment and then said, "May 30th, right you are, thank you," and he replaced the receiver, in its cradle. All through the exchange Dr Schaiffer had been thinking to himself, *I know Dr Forrestor's vanished so why go through that performance?* Scarborough moved over to the archive, "May 30th, here we are," he handed the four DVDs to Schaiffer. "Here are the right DVDs, the viewing rooms are through there," he pointed through a door to the left.

"Thank you," the German said, "I shall return soon," and with that he disappeared into the viewing room; he sat at the computer terminal, in there, and *booted* the computer up, selecting the final DVD of the day, which covered the final six hours of the day he loaded the disc in its tray, and selected the software he needed to *play* it – generally most criminal activities occurred in the evening, or at night.

Almost immediately he spotted the Renault *Megane* pull into the parking lot, although the footage was only black and white plus a bit grainy, and then a man wandered into shot and removed a box from the car – this man must be Forrestor – as he watched another woman and man joined the first, the man was aiming a pistol at Forrestor's chest, the thing was Dr Schaiffer thought he recognised the man. Suddenly a, civilian, helicopter appeared, the woman indicated that Forrestor should board the helicopter, so gathering a briefcase from his car, and a box he boarded the helicopter; once the door was closed the helicopter flew out of sight. Of the other two figures there was no further sign.

However, it was then that an automobile passed by the camera, he wasn't sure what model it was; anyway, he'd seen enough; the computers at HART would enhance the pictures, removing the graining effect. He closed down the computer and removed the disc he'd been viewing.

He re-entered the monitoring room and asked Mr Scarbourough, "How long would it take to duplicate a disc?"

"Half an hour, give or take," the security man answered. "Which disc do you want copying?" He opened his desk drawer and got out a blank DVD.

"This one," replied the German, handing the disc over. "It contains everything I require."

"Right you are sir," Scarborough said and *booted* up another computer, and then inserted the two discs. Then he activated the *copy* process. "Should be done soon, why don't you take yourself off, see if you can help in the hospital?"

"Yes, I think I will," said Dr Schaiffer, and left the monitoring building.

*****

All the HART personnel, who were on site, apart from the medical staff, were gathered in the main conference room awaiting their commander's entrance. After they had been waiting about five minutes the double doors, at the end of the room, opened and Commander Strobing flanked, on his right, by Commander Most and Commander Bigship, on his left, entered the room. The three of them surveyed the faces around the table before taking their places; Commander Strobing assuming his place at the head of the table. He viewed the expectant faces before him and then stood, "Ladies and gentleman, some of you know and some of you don't but I am Commander Ronan Strobing, with the sad loss of Commander Peter Roberts I am now your overall Commander; as I mentioned to some of you before," he meant the receptionists and the newly promoted commanders, "there will only be minor changes."

"The, initial, conflict with *Proagnon* may be over, and it claimed many lives – on our side and theirs – but I am convinced that the war is not yet over. I think we shall see them again, maybe sooner than later, they will probably be back with a vengeance, and out for revenge."

"Moving on and changing the subject, again as some of you will know, both America and Russia have newly elected presidents. Both of these men, so I'm led to believe, are HART haters, so, therefore, we will never be allowed to operate within their borders again. We must, now, rely, solely, on contributions, such as financial aid and equipment from other countries."

"Finally, as you may have noticed our leading medical expert and psychological profiler, Dr Schaiffer, isn't present. I have been, reliably, informed that he has been called for, to go over to England, by a medical colleague, and is, therefore, currently, engaged on medical business there."

Ronan looked around the sea of faces, "Are there any questions?"

Alice Stronglove spoke up, "Will you be requiring an assistant in your new role sir?" He knew what was on her mind so decided to answer honestly, while at the same time trying to be as tactful as he could

"At the moment, agent Stronglove, Commander Most is acting as my deputy whilst Commander Bigship is acting as my second deputy, so at the moment I must decline." He noticed that her face fell at his answer, as did Lisa Bell's, still he was only being honest. "Right, I'd just like to add my door is always open; for the present time this meeting is over." Everyone filed out the room and headed back to carry on with their everyday duties, the three HART commanders leaving the way they had come.

Once they were back in the commander's office, and had seated themselves at the, wooden, desk Commander Strobing asked Commander Bigship, "What is the status of our sea fleet?"

"As you will recall sir, we lost H-Berlin in our battle with *Proagnon* and H-Newhaven is back at harbour at San Jose, and undergoing repairs to fix the hole in her bow; H-London is still undergoing its refit and H-Moscow is moored off the west coast of Africa. All await further orders," Leon told the commander.

Turning to Commander Most he enquired, "And our air fleet?"

"Again, as you will recall, sir, we lost several fighter aircraft in the conflict, but all in all we are in pretty good shape," replied the air defence liaison.

Ronan then pressed the button on the intercom that would connect him with reception, "Yes sir," Joshua Smith's voice replied.

"Josh, if Gwyneth's there send her through to the office please."

"At once sir," was the reply that came back. About two minutes later there was a knock on the office door.

"Come in," called Commander Strobing. Mrs Jones entered the office, "Mrs Jones, is the overhead satellite still functioning and can we still use it?"

"I believe so sir," the senior receptionist answered.

Commander Strobing first turned to Leon, "Contact H-Moscow and have her travel northwards and dock alongside the coast of Portugal." Next he looked up at Mrs Jones, "Have our overhead satellite monitor the area in and around Iran and Iraq." Finally he turned to Commander Most, "Celia, recall all our fighter planes, the *Blackhawk* UH-60L and a couple of Pave Low IV's, plus all remaining *Apaches*."

"Those are my orders for now."

"At once sir," the other three said and filed from the office. Ronan sat back and relaxed, deep in thought.

*****

On board *Damancas* the team of *Proagnon* scientists, led by Dr Simon Forrestor, were hard at work developing the new version of their virus into an airborne version and a version to go into the remaining spray cans. After refining the infected blood into something similar to a paste type of powder they added a little of this substance and then filled each canister half full with water (mostly collected from outside), added an amount of baking soda (brought in from the mainland, in large containers). Next the scientists shook the mixture up – with the top on – and placed the canister in a cupboard box ready to be taken to the mainland and distributed throughout the population; all they needed was a name for the new product. Paul Santos said that as *Proagnon* scientists had invented the initial virus it should be known as *Proagnon Power*. Of course Forrestor disagreed saying that, "People may associate this new spray with the *Proagnon* terrorist organisation who caused such death and destruction last year."

"And what do you think it should be called?" Santos challenged him.

"Forrestor's Fire!" Simon told him, forcefully.

"No, you only added the final ingredient so we shall call it *Proagnon Power*."

"Forrestor's Fire," the other man said.

Just then a small, balding, scientist stepped forward. "Gentlemen please, why don't we compromise and call it *ProPower*?"

The other two leading scientists considered this, "I like it," announced Forrestor, "subtle but still exercising the power. Well Paul?"

"Agreed," Santos told the assembled scientists. "Now we wait for the next supply ship so we can despatch the spray cans to the mainland. Okay people let's get labelling those cans." As the eager scientists rushed off Simon discreetly exited their workroom and walked, down the corridor, towards his own private quarters.

Once inside he closed and locked the door, *Let those fools have their glory, for now. I will have the last laugh.* He unlocked and opened his wardrobe – which he always kept locked – and produced a wetsuit and a, large, plastic bag filled with, magnetic, underwater mines. Simon changed into the wetsuit, made sure his oxygen tank was full by tapping the readout dial; when it stayed on *full* he knew he hadn't been diddled. Strapping the tanks to his back and inserting the breathing end over his mouth he opened a window and prepared himself.

Simon took hold of the plastic bag, the mines weren't heavy but there were powerful, and then after popping his goggles on he dropped out of the window and into the water below. He then dived, making sure he had the bag well held, and made his way underneath to the far side of the fort; it was there that he reached inside the bag and produced the first mine, this he attached to the underside; once he'd done performed this task he moved on, in a clockwise direction, around the underside of *Damancas* attaching mines at strategic positions – he attached twelve in all.

Once he'd finished his task Forrestor broke the surface of the water and removed the end of the breathing apparatus that was in his mouth – he breathed the fresh air in greedily, before making his way to where his window was to his quarters. Unfortunately a supply ship was moored in the exact spot therefore Simon had to reattach the mouthpiece of the breathing apparatus and dived again. He swum under the fort and waited; luckily after about a minute the supply ship moved off, so Simon was able to re-emerge again and climbed into his room, through the open window.

He peeled the wetsuit off and changed back into his scientist clothes when there came a, loud, knock on his door. "Forrestor!" came a shout, the voice belonged to Paul Santos, "Are you in there?"

"Coming," called back Simon, trying to sound like he'd just woken up; he hastily put the wetsuit back into the wardrobe and locked the door to the metal cabinet. He also closed the window, and then he unlocked and opened the door to Paul Santos.

"Where were you?" he asked with a hint of suspicion, the two men evidently didn't trust each other.

Simon smiled at him, harmlessly, and said calmly, "I was sleeping."

"We've just despatched the initial shipment of twenty nine deodorant spray cans, aboard one of the supply ships. Once the ship reaches Fraserburgh the spray cans will then be distributed to two of Mr Maxwell's people and then they will give them out as freebies to the public." *Excellent,* thought Simon.

"That is good news," he said in a non-committal voice. The mines he'd planted under the fort were there, just in case – he probably would detonate them eventually. The trigger mechanism was hidden in his quarters.

*****

Dr Schaiffer returned to the monitoring building approximately half an hour – forty five minutes after he'd left it. Upon entering the brick building he was greeted by Scarborough, he was just placing Dr Schaiffer's DVD disc in a case for ease of carrying. There you go," Scarborough informed him.

"My thanks to you," the German answered and left the building slipping the case containing the DVD into his pocket. He then took a taxi to Norwich railway station and boarded the train to begin the return journey to Hull; changing trains, again, at Peterborough and Doncaster, the last one was a pity as he'd be returning to Doncaster in another day or two.

The train finally reached its destination approximately four and a half hours after leaving Norwich; when the train had finally come to a halt Dr Schaiffer exited the carriage he'd been travelling in and exited the station, the medical man made his way, on foot, back to Hull Hospital.

Hans entered the hospital and went up, in the lift, to the floor where Dr Lighten's office was situated. Reaching the office Dr Schaiffer knocked and entered when requested to. The first question Schaiffer asked was, "How is the patient in 3A?"

"No better Hans. I hope your trip was a successful one."

"Well maybe not a complete success, I won't know for sure until my eventual return to HART. However, I have a DVD here," he produced the DVD he'd received from the *John Groggins* Hospital's monitoring building, "which may hold a few clues. May I use your computer?"

"But of course," answered Charles. So Dr Schaiffer *booted* the computer up and inserted the DVD into its tray; once the tray was closed the DVD began to play, as Scarborough had incorporated an *Autoplay* feature onto the disc. They both watched in silence.

"That's Dr Forrestor, what's he up to and who are those other two people?" said Dr Lighten.

"I believe I know the man, as I believe I've met him but I'm not sure without the picture being enlarged. If it is who I think it may be I can't understand why he's involved."

"Who is he?" enquired the other medical man. Schaiffer leaned across and whispered in Lighten's ear. "You can't mean that, I will not believe it."

"That's who I think it is, as I say if it is I just can't understand how he's become mixed up in all this," Schaiffer told his friend. "Wait there's more." As the two friends watched the helicopter landed and Forrestor, together with lbriefcase, which they guessed held a laptop computer, and his box of medical instruments, boarded the chopper, and it flew away.

"Whilst I was at *John Groggins* I checked out his car with a compass, and it was facing north. Therefore, as we can see, when the helicopter took off again it headed northwards. Now this footage was captured two months ago, yet you say Dr Forrestor only came to see you about six weeks ago so where was he before that?"

"Scotland or so he said," Lighten told his friend.

Schaiffer looked hard at his colleague, "How do you know what he told you was the truth?"

Lighten looked, slightly, crestfallen. "I don't know it was the truth, yet I'm sure it was."

"Why don't you ring round all the hospitals in Scotland tomorrow, see if there is any trace of him during that two week period?" the German suggested.

Charles looked over at the other medical man, "I've been a fool, a silly old fool, friendship alone is not enough. I will do as you suggest tomorrow."

Charles then invited Hans home with him, the German looked surprised but accepted, so again the two of them left together, and returned to Lighten's country cottage again.

*****

At HART Commander's Bigship and Most were reporting to Commander Strobing. Commander Bigship began, "Sir, I am pleased to report that repairs to the destroyer H-Newhaven are almost complete, H-Moscow has started moving northwards towards the west coast of Portugal. However, the overhaul on H-London has come to a temporary standstill, as the nuclear reactor has become completely wrecked and is having to be totally rebuilt."

Leon paused, "On a more positive note Mrs Jones has realigned the satellite and is requesting it be moved over the Middle East. That is the latest update on both the sea fleet, and the orbital satellite."

Once Commander Bigship had finished Celia spoke up, "All HART fighter planes, be they F-14, -15 or -16 are being recalled, along with the Blackhawk and a couple of Pave Low plus all remaining *Apache* attack helicopters are also withdrawn. That is the current status of our air fleet Commander."

"Thank you both of you," Commander Strobing said to them both, rising from his seat.

*****

In Scotland, the spray cans were being given out by Maxwell's loyal employees to anybody who wanted one.

One of these employees, Grant Pearman, was handing cans out in a shopping centre, when a young man, Phillip Gastron, picked one up from Pearman, the cans were limited to one per person, Gastron couldn't resist a freebie as he was a dockworker. Phillip took the spray, along with a few other items he'd purchased, back home to, his flat in, Turiff, which he shared with his wife, Julie, and his two children, Billy and Susan.

About a week later he got up to get ready for work and decided to try the new *ProPower* deodorant spray; he sprayed it on, aware of his wife standing beside him. There was a hiss and a, fine, mist was ejected, yet it didn't smell of anything; he shook the can and tried it again, still nothing seemed to happen. Shaking his head he found a different deodorant and sprayed that on.

He was pretty certain nothing had happened when he'd sprayed the new *ProPower*, however, what Phillip Gastron, or his wife, didn't know was that the spray had ejected a fine mist containing the virus particles which were, even now, being inhaled by the two adults, mixing with their bloodstream and beginning to infect them, they were now *hosts* to the *Proagnon* virus which would, ultimately, kill them.

By being in such close contact Mr and Mrs Gastron, unknowingly, infected their two children, Billy and Susan. By the end of the day Mr Gastron would have infected everybody who he worked with, Mrs Gastron would have infected her circle of friends, and Billy and Susan would have infected their schoolmates, teachers and everybody else that they came into contact with; plus the Gastron family would've infected their neighbours.

This wasn't an isolated occurrence, all throughout the country people began feeling unwell after using the new spray; they had a slight discomfort in their stomach, for a start, and they put this discomfort down to something they'd, probably, eaten; however, even after going to toilet several times the people still felt no better, so they all sought the help of their GPs, who prescribed some antibiotics. Still people felt unwell, once the more severe symptoms started, sickness, coughing up blood and the thrashing about people started to realise the drugs their GP had described were having no effect at all, everybody rang 999 and were placed in hospital. Again the symptoms got worse with the abscesses developing in and around the mouth. If the patients were not put on saline solution drips about two weeks after they'd admitted themselves they would die.

There were so many outbreaks of this new, mystery, virus that the hospitals were inundated with all these new admissions and, no matter how hard the doctors and nurses worked, the hospitals just couldn't cope.

*****

In Hull, unaware of the panic this new virus was causing, Dr Lighten was busy doing his rounds; whilst Dr Schaiffer was busily ringing every hospital in Scotland to see if Dr Simon

Forrestor had been on their premises during the first two weeks of June; having finished contacting the final one he replaced the handset, with a shrug.

After checking on Mr Stevens, there was no change in his condition, Charles Lighten returned to his office and found Hans Schaiffer deep in thought. "Any luck?" Lighten enquired, sitting down.

"Ah, no, he wasn't seen at any of the hospitals in those two weeks," replied the German doctor. "Tell me is there anything off the north coast of Scotland?" He only asked out of curiosity.

"As far as I recall there is only the old sea fort, *Damancas*, but that isn't a hospital; it's only used for private functions nowadays," responded Charles.

"Who's it owned by?" asked Schaiffer, quickly.

"The Maxwell consortium, which consists of millionaire Floyd Maxwell and his, sleeping, partner," Lighten responded. Hans Schaiffer, still, looked none the wiser at this new information.

"If you don't require my services any further I should like to return to Switzerland."

Charles agreed to this and said, "I will drive you to Doncaster airport, I have a few hours leave owed to me." Lighten and Schaiffer left the hospital and boarded Charles Lighten's Honda *Civic*. "Got everything?" Lighten enquired.

"I believe so," replied Hans Schaiffer feeling his pockets, he had the Vacutainer containing the blood sample in one and the case containing the copied DVD in the other.

Charles drove the red automobile the fifty two and a half mile journey to *Robin Hood* Doncaster-Sheffield airport. Dr Schaiffer exited the vehicle, thanked his English counterpart and then walked into the main terminal building to catch his flight back to *Cointrin* airport, just outside Geneva, Switzerland.

*****

The panic in Scotland wasn't exclusive to that country; in the following weeks many more people both in England and Wales would fall victim to the virus; people would suffer from the same types of symptoms as their northern counterparts. First would come the run down feeling, next would come the sickness and diarrhoea, and then the general feeling of unwellness, next came the inability to control the limbs; eventually the infected people would admit themselves to hospital, where again if they were not attached to a saline solution, via an intravenous drip, they would eventually die. They would suffer the abscesses in and around the mouth and these would, very occasionally, leak a nasty looking, yellow, substance

Hull Hospital started to see its first patients in mid August; that just showed how rapidly this new virus was beginning to spread. Dr Lighten, together with his wife Mary, was enjoying a week's holiday in, the seaside town of, Scarborough. They had left the hotel where they were staying and journeyed to York, for the day.

Upon the couple's return, at 17:30, the receptionist – a tall, slim woman in her forties, informed Charles that the hospital, where he worked, had phoned whilst he'd been out and left the message that Charles was to contact them, immediately, on his return. "Don't worry dear," he told his wife, "probably just need to know where some notes are, you go and get ready for dinner, I'll be up shortly." Reassured Mary got in a vacant lift and journeyed up to their room, on the third floor. Dr Lighten, nor Mary, realised how true his words would be, *I'll be up shortly*.

Dr Lighten dialled the hospital number and requested to speak to Chief Medical Officer Peter Bogg.

That name had caused Peter to be the subject of a few jokes over the years, but he was a well liked, and an easy to get on with, type of, person; Peter and Charles had had their fair share of strange cases over the years.

He was dragged from his reverie by a voice, on the other end of the phone, "Charles, we need you, urgently!"

Noting the urgency in the man's voice but, at the same time, trying to remain calm Charles asked, "Why do you need me, won't somebody else do?"

"No Charles," Peter said then went on to explain. "Since Monday we've had an influx of new cases, you might see nothing wrong in that but all the cases are the same. They all have the same, or extremely similar, symptoms as the gentleman in room 3A, Arnold Stevens."

"What," Dr Lighten replied, totally astonished. "How can that be?"

"Nobody knows," the chief medical officer told him. "But they are the same, or similar. Therefore, we need you to return to the hospital at once, "I wouldn't ask if I didn't think it was absolutely necessary."

"Okay," responded Charles resignedly, "I will return as soon as I can." He then replaced the phone. "Thank you," he said to the receptionist, and then he went to find his wife to tell her the *good* news.

*****

Having arrived back at HART's main headquarters Dr Schaiffer had immediately gone in search of the commander, now commanders and they had viewed the DVD. As they watched Dr Schaiffer pointed out Simon Forrestor, and informed the three commanders that everything they were seeing had occurred at *John Groggins* Hospital in Norwich, on the night of the 31st May. Then the other two people entered the picture, "That's Sandy Tulliver!" exclaimed Commander Strobing, "What is she doing there?" The other two commanders nodded in confirmation as to that's who it was.

"Who's Sandy Tulliver?" enquired the HART medical man.

Commander Strobing looked at his two deputies, in turn, before answering; they both nodded. "She, my dear doctor, is, or was, the second in command of *Proagnon*. However, since the demise of Dr Q or, as he was known to Commander Roberts, Adam Barker, she may, or may not, be the new leader of the terrorist organisation; depending on who this man is and his relevance to the situation."

Hans Schaiffer told the three other members of HART who he thought the man was. "What?" they demanded, as perplexed as the medical man was. Suddenly, a helicopter entered the picture.

Leon suddenly spoke up once the air vehicle could be seen completely, "That, if I'm not mistaken, is a *Hughes* helicopter, one of the MD 500 series, possibly a 500C."

"How far could it travel, on a full tank of fuel?" asked Commander Strobing, pulling up a map of England on his, personal laptop computer. He then turned the computer so it faced Leon.

"If I remember rightly," murmured Commander Bigship, "this type of helicopter can travel a maximum of 375 miles."

Ronan turned to look at Hans Schaiffer again, "And which direction did it head in?" he asked.

Dr Schaiffer looked back, across the desk, at the commander and smiled, "It was headed in a northerly direction. I checked by placing a compass on the bonnet of Dr Forrestor's car."

"Okay Leon, 375 miles north please, assuming it had a full tank of fuel."

Commander Bigship inputted some commands into the computer based on the information Dr Schaiffer had just given them, after a moment or two of performing the calculation requested of it, a cross appeared on the map showing 375 miles from Norwich. "But that's impossible," he said.

"What is it?" asked Commander Strobing.

"There's nothing there but sea," answered his fellow commander.

Ronan looked across at Dr Hans Schaiffer, his eyes boring into the man, "Are you sure?"

"I'm quite sure," Dr Schaiffer said. "Hang on though, there is a sea fort called *Damancas*, owned by the Maxwell consortium, situated in the Moray Firth; perhaps Simon Forrestor is there."

"Hmm," murmured Commander Strobing thoughtfully, "it's possible but why?" He then buzzed through to reception.

Lisa Bell answered the intercom, her voice was bright and cheerful as usual, "Yes Commander."

"Ah Lisa, do we have any aerial photographs of the Moray Firth in Scotland?"

"I'll just check sir. If I find any shall I bring them through?"

"Yes please." Ronan shut off the intercom and dismissed Dr Schaiffer, who, readily, left the office and returned to the medical unit to perform his analysis of Arnold Stevens blood which was contained within the Vacutainer.

*****

Lisa Bell knocked on the office door with her free hand; inside the commanders were discussing a plan of action should Dr Schaiffer's information prove correct, they could attempt to take or destroy the fort – unaware of the mines that had been planted underneath – or they could wait, as it may prove the fort existed but this man, Simon Forrestor, wasn't on board meaning that HART would have destroyed the fort needlessly.

When Lisa knocked on the door their conversation stopped. "Come in," called Ronan. Lisa Bell entered the office.

"Commanders," she said looking around the room. Then she strode up to Commander Strobing's desk and placed the folder, she was carrying, on its surface, "Here you are sir, the aerial shots you requested." With that she saluted the organisation's overall commander, smartly, turned on her heel and left the office.

Once she'd left Commander Strobing removed the photographs from the folder, there were ten of them in all, and started examining each photo for the alleged fort, using a magnifying glass whenever necessary.

When he. Returned to England again he would have to visit his optician and have his eyes tested, as he was convinced his eyesight wasn't what it used to be

It wasn't until he examined the eighth picture that he spotted an object, in the sea, that resembled anything like the type of shape that a sea fort should look like. "There it is," he said with triumph, and then passed the picture around the other two commanders, who were in the office. After examining the area on the picture for themselves they each nodded their heads in confirmation. Commander Strobing circled the area and then called Lisa Bell back in.

When she appeared Ronan passed her the folder containing the other nine pictures back to her. He then handed her the final picture and said, “Can you photocopy the area I’ve circled, maximum magnification please.”

“Yes sir,” she replied and left the office.

Commander Strobing looked at the other two, “Now we think it exists, the magnified picture will either confirm it or not, how do we proceed then?”

“I feel,” started Commander Most, “if my colleague,” indicating Commander Bigship, “is in agreement with me, we should launch a UAV to this area to monitor any activity that occurs in the area around this sea fort, *Damancas* I believe Dr Schaiffer called it. Just monitor it for now until we decide on a course of action.”

“I am in total agreement with my colleague,” said Commander Bigship. “What are your thoughts Commander?”

Commander Strobing thought about this, “I agree that if the magnified picture does contain a sea fort I shall authorise the launch of a UAV, and should it prove necessary I shall authorise HART forces to capture the fort and hold anyone that is aboard it. However, there might just be a bunch of scientists aboard with no links to *Proagnon*. In that case we have no right to hold anybody aboard the fort.”

It was then that the young receptionist entered the office and handed her commander the magnified picture. She then left the office leaving the three commanders to examine the picture. “A regular sea fort – large and round – with a helipad on top, plus a staircase leading down into the main structure, Victorian if I’m not mistaken,” Commander Strobing informed the other two commanders, “now we know it exists.” He handed the picture to the others while he rose from his chair and walled to the drinks cabinet, located on the rear wall, “Drink anyone?” he asked as he poured himself a small whisky.

“Yes please sir,” answered Commander Bigship, “a whisky for me please.”

"A whisky and soda for me," replied Celia. Ronan poured the drinks and then returned, with them, to join his colleagues. He then buzzed through to reception again.

"Yes sir," the cheery voice of Lisa Bell replied.

"Lisa," Ronan started, "will you authorise launch of a, Global Hawk UAV over the northern coast of Scotland. Authorisation code R1."

"Yes sir," she replied. "At once sir."

Commander Strobing looked back at his two colleagues, who had finished examining the picture. He said to them, "We know *Damancas* exists, yet how will we know if this Forrestor's aboard the structure?" They all thought about this.

Commander Bigship suddenly said, "Why not, if the fort is occupied, send Alice Stronglove to Scotland, on an information gathering assignment, she didn't let us down last time," Ronan remembered the ill fated mission to Russia the year before, when he'd lost his two fellow agents Harry Danto and Tammy Smith, plus he too had nearly lost his life. "If the fort is occupied we find out where they are getting their supplies from, and despatch Alice there."

"A very good idea, I agree, and we already have a covert agent, Ralph Williams, over there, so she could liaise with him. However, let's wait and see what the pictures from the UAV show," replied the overall commander. The type of Global Hawk UAV HART used was the RQ-4A model

*****

The Northrop Grumman (formerly Ryan Aeronautical) RQ-4 Global Hawk (known as Tier II+ during development) was an unmanned aerial vehicle (UAV) that had been used by the United States Air Force, and was now used by HART, as a surveillance aircraft.

In role and design, the Global Hawk was similar to the old Lockheed U-2, the venerable 1950s spy plane. It was a theatre commander's asset to both provide a broad overview and systematically target surveillance shortfalls. The Global Hawk air vehicle was able to provide high resolution Synthetic Aperture Radar (SAR)—that could penetrate any cloud-cover and sandstorms—and Electro-Optical/Infrared (EO/IR) imagery at long range with long loiter times over target areas. It could survey as much as 40,000 square miles (100,000 square kilometres) of terrain a day.

Potential missions for the Global Hawk covered the spectrum of intelligence collection capability to support forces in worldwide peace, crisis, and wartime operations. The capabilities of the aircraft would allow more precise targeting of weapons and allow better protection of all forces through superior surveillance capabilities.

The "R" was the USA's Department of Defense's designation for reconnaissance; while the "Q" meant an unmanned aircraft system. The number "4" referred to it being the fourth of a series of these purpose-built unmanned aircraft systems.

The Global Hawk costs about $35 million USD (actual per-aircraft costs; with development costs also included, the per-aircraft cost could rise to $123.2 million USD each).

The RQ-4 was powered by an Allison Rolls-Royce AE3007H turbofan engine with 7,050 lbf (3,200 kgf / 31.4 kN) thrust, and was capable of carrying a payload of 2,000 pounds (900 kilograms). The fuselage was mostly of a conventional aluminium airframe construction, while the wings were made of carbon composite.

The Global Hawk was the first UAV to be certified by the FAA to file its own flight plans and used the civilian air corridors in the United States with no advance notice. This potentially paved the way for a revolution in unmanned flight, including that of remotely piloted cargo or passenger airliners.

The Global Hawk's wings, fuselage, fairings, nacelles, and tails are manufactured from high strength-to-weight composites. The Global Hawk UAV system comprises an air vehicle segment consisting of air vehicles with sensor payloads, avionics, and data links; a ground segment consisting of a Launch and Recovery Element (LRE), and a Mission Control Element (MCE) with embedded ground communications equipment; a support element; and trained personnel.

The Integrated Sensor Suite (ISS) was provided by Raytheon and consisted of synthetic aperture radar (SAR), electro-optical (EO), and infrared (IR) sensors. Either the EO or the IR sensors could operate simultaneously with the SAR. Each of the sensors provided wide area search imagery and a high-resolution spot mode. The SAR had a ground moving target indicator (GMTI) mode, which could provide a text message providing the moving target's position and velocity. Both SAR and EO/IR imagery are processed onboard the aircraft and transmitted to the MCE, at HART headquarters, as individual frames. The MCE could then mosaic these frames into images prior to further dissemination.

Navigation was via inertial navigation with integrated Global Positioning System updates. Global Hawk was intended to operate autonomously and *untethered* using a satellite data link (either Ku or UHF) for sending sensor data from the aircraft to the MCE. The common data link could also be used for direct down link of imagery when the UAV was operating within line-of-sight of users with compatible ground stations.

The ground segment consisted of a Mission Control Element (MCE) and Launch and Recovery Element (LRE), both were provided by Raytheon. The MCE was used for mission planning, command and control, and any image processing and dissemination; an LRE was for controlling launch and recovery; and any associated ground support equipment. (The LRE provided precision differential global positioning system corrections for navigational accuracy during takeoff and landings, while precision coded GPS supplemented with an inertial navigation system was used during mission execution.) By having separable elements in the ground segment, the MCE and the LRE could operate in geographically separate locations, and the MCE could be deployed with the supported command's primary exploitation site. Both ground segments were contained in military shelters with external antennas for line-of-sight and satellite communications with the air vehicles.

The Global Hawk also carried the *Hughes Integrated Surveillance & Reconnaissance (HISAR)* sensor system. HISAR was a lower-cost derivative of the ASARS-2 package that Hughes had already developed for the Lockheed U-2. HISAR was also fitted in the US Army's RC-7B Airborne Reconnaissance Low Multifunction (ARLM) manned surveillance aircraft, and was sold on the international market. HISAR integrates a SAR-MTI system, along with an optical and an infrared imager. All three sensors were controlled and their outputs were filtered by a common processor. The digital sensor data could be transmitted at up to 50 Mbit/s to a ground station in real time, either directly or through a communications satellite link.

The SAR-MTI system operates in the X-band and provided a number of operational modes:

- The wide-area MTI mode could detect moving targets within a radius of 62 miles (100 kilometres).
- The combined SAR-MTI strip mode provided a 20 foot (6 metre) resolution over a swath 23 miles (37 kilometres) wide at ranges from 12.4 to 68 miles (20 to 110 kilometres).
- The SAR spot mode can provide a 6 foot (1.8 metre) resolution over 3.8 square miles (10 square kilometres), as well as provide a sea-surveillance function.

The visible and infrared imagers share the same gimballed sensor package, and use of common optics, providing a telescopic close-up capability. It could be optionally fitted with an auxiliary SIGINT package. To improve survivability, the Global Hawk was fitted with a Raytheon developed AN/ALR-89 self-protection suite consisting of the AN/AVR-3 Laser Warning System, AN/APR-49 Radar Warning Receiver and a jamming system. An ALE-50 towed decoy has also aided in the Global Hawk's deception of enemy air defences.

In July, 2006, the Air Force began testing segments of the improved Global Hawk Block 30 upgrades in the Benefield Anechoic Facility at Edwards AFB. This version incorporated an extremely sensitive SIGINT processor known as the Advanced Signals Intelligence Payload.

In September 2006, testing began on a new specialty radar system, the Multi-Platform Radar Technology Insertion Program, or MP-RTIP, onboard the Scaled Composites Proteus. Once validated, one Global Hawk was modified to carry this new radar set, and the other, larger variant (known as the Wide-Area Surveillance or WAS sensor) was installed on the Air Force E-10 MC2A testbed.

The Global Hawk model 4A's endurance time was 36 hours before having to be refuelled, and it could operate at up to 65,000 ft (19,812 metres).

Suddenly the intercom *beeped* startling the three commanders; Miss Bell's voice was heard, "Apparently there are no usable Global Hawk's at the moment, either they've been destroyed, possibly by sabotage, or are undergoing drastic repairs."

"Thank you Lisa," Commander Strobing told her, and then he turned off the intercom and looked at the other two. "Damn! Trust this to happen now." The others nodded and left the office.

*****

Dr Schaiffer was now back in the medical unit, performing his analysis on the second blood sample taken from Mr Stevens. He drained off the *plasma* in the blood, which just left him with the blood cells and a few of the bigger virus *spores*, he was totally confused at what he saw, the blood cells seemed to be staying at their *natural* size, but the spores seemed to be growing, and swallowing up the blood cells, be they red or white.

He tried injecting the spores, directly, with various antibiotics from his medical stock; however none of them seemed to work, he then tried mixing various antibiotics in turn but nothing seemed to be working. The HART medical man knew he was trying to fight a battle which he would probably lose, in the end. He needed something, a miracle even! The only advice he could give Dr Lighten was to keep the man on the intravenous drip connecting him to the saline solution, and hope that he could come up with a cure soon.

However, what Dr Schaiffer didn't know, couldn't know was that Arnold Stevens condition had deteriorated considerably.

*****

Since the influx of new cases at Hull Hospital, all victims of the mysterious virus, supplies of the saline solution was rapidly running out, the new patients taking priority over the some of the existing cases; thus Arnold Stevens condition had gone from bad to worse. In fact he'd had to be moved to the ICU and had been put on a life support machine.

CHAPTER 4

THE NEXT MOVE!

In the bunker under Iran the *Proagnon* soldiers, along with their, temporary leader – Mitchell Walker, were checking over some attack helicopters that hadn't been used in the conflict with HART forces; these helicopters were the Russian built Mil Mi-28s, developed from the Mil Mi-24 HINDs.

*****

The Mil Mi-28 or *Havoc* is a Russian all weather day and night military tandem two seat anti-armour attack helicopter. It was a dedicated attack helicopter with no intended secondary transport capability, better optimized than the Mil Mi-24 for the anti-tank role. It carried a single gun in an undernose barbette, plus any external loads are carried on pylons beneath its stub wings.

Development on the helicopter began following the completion of the Mi-24 *HIND*, a unique attack helicopter with transport capability, in 1972. This new design had a reduced transport capability (3 troops instead of 8), omitted the cabin, delivering a better overall performance and higher top speed which were important for its intended role fighting against various tanks and enemy helicopters, plus covering helicopter landing operations. Initially, many different designs were considered, including an unconventional project with two main rotors, placed with the engines on the tips of the wings (in a perpendicular layout), and with an additional pusher propeller on the tail. In 1977, a preliminary design was chosen, in a classic single-rotor layout. It then lost its similarity to the Mi-24, and even the canopies were smaller, with flat surfaces.

In 1981, a design and a mock-up were accepted. The prototype was first flown on November 10, 1982, followed by the second prototype, built in 1983. In 1984 it completed the first stage of state trials, but in October 1984 the Soviet Air

Force chose the more advanced Kamov Ka-50 as their new anti-tank helicopter. The Mi-28 development was continued, but was given a lower priority. In December 1987 Mi-28 production in Rosvertol in Rostov on Don was approved.

In January 1988 the first Mi-28A prototype flew. It was fitted with stronger engines and an *X* type tail rotor instead of a standard three-blade variant. This new version debuted at the Paris Air Show in June 1989. In 1991 a second Mi-28A was built. The Mi-28A program was cancelled in 1993 because it was deemed uncompetitive with the Ka-50, and in particular, it was not all-weather capable.

Yet another variant, the Mi-28N, was unveiled in 1995, the N designation meaning *night*. The prototype flew on November 14, 1996. The most significant feature was a radar in a round cover above the main rotor, similar to that of the American AH-64D *Longbow* Apache. It also had improved Tor vision and an aiming device under the nose, including a TV camera and FLIR. Due to certain funding problems, development was interrupted. A second prototype with an improved rotor design was unveiled in March 2004 at Rosvertol.

A changed military situation after the Cold War made specialized anti-tank helicopters, like the Ka-50, less useful. On the other hand, its all-weather two-seater variant the Ka-52 had worse performance due to its increased weight. The advantages of the Mi-28N, like all weather action ability, lower cost, and similarity to the Mi-24, had all become more important. In 2003, a chief of Russian Air Forces stated that the Mi-28N was to become the standard Russian attack helicopter.

The first serial Mi-28N was then passed to the Army. The aircraft joined the two pre-serial machines which were used for army trials. The aircraft then entered service in 2006, along with the similar Ka-50/Ka-52.

*****

The Mi-28 has two heavily armoured cockpits, a nose full with electronic equipments, and a narrow *X* tail rotor. Its engines were two 2,200 hp Isotov TV-3-117VM gas turbines. The *X* type tail rotor (55 deg) had reduced noise characteristics.

While the Mi-28 was not intended for use as a transport, it does, however, have a small passenger compartment capable of carrying up to three people. The planned purpose of this feature was to enable the rescue of downed helicopter crews.

Weapons included on the Mi-28 were 1 chin-mounted 30 mm Shipunov 2A42 cannon with 300 rounds (220° horizontal fire) and up to 2,300 kg (of disposable stores on four hardpoints, including bombs, rockets, missiles, and gunpods).

*****

Each of the Mi-28 helicopters was in fine condition and coupled with the Mi-24 *HIND* helicopters that they would be escorting, would make a formidable force. Once all the attack helicopters had been inspected, and examined, both inside and out, the soldiers made their way back to the conference chamber; on the way back, though, Mitchell Walker walked into the monitoring room and looked around at the technicians, all were diligently working at their computer consoles.

As he approached a younger technician looked up at him, "Sir, I think I've got something on the, orbital, radar."

Walker paused by the technician, his curiosity now aroused, "Show me!" he demanded. The man altered some controls, and activated others; suddenly Mitchell saw it – a small *red* blip appeared on screen, according to the altitude measurement it was approximately 80,000 ft (50,000 metres) up. "I believe it may be a satellite and, by the looks of things, it's monitoring this area."

"Have we any fighters or helicopters that can fly that high up?"

"No sir," answered the technician whose name Mitchell saw was Sam Lowell. "However, I believe our new missile, *Bollinger*, can be launched and will reach that far."

"Okay, is it possible to calculate the firing trajectory from here?" the, temporary, leader asked, happy at the news that something could be done.

Technician Lowell turned - in his chair - and told his superior, "Of course I can calculate a firing trajectory, and then I shall send the coordinates through to the weapons room."

"A simple yes or no would have sufficed," Walker told the man. "Don't be so impertinent in the future." Some of the other technicians had turned, in their chairs, to see what al the commotion was.

Walker then walked from the room, whistling as he went, and set off towards the conference chamber. As he walked down the corridor he smiled to himself, *Who needs that bitch, Tulliver? I'm managing quite alright.*

He entered the conference chamber where several expectant faces looked up at him. "Have you decided on our next target yet?" enquired one of the soldiers.

"Yes, there is a passenger train travelling north-west to east across Iran, from the capital Tehran, eventually terminating in Mashhad; the train will also be carrying some gold coins in enclosed - bomb-proof - compartments; the actual train will consist of the main engine followed by seven carriages, all carrying passengers, and then finally the three box-cars containing the boxes of coins. Once the train has terminated the gold will be transported, in three armoured trucks flanked by motorcycle outriders, northwards to Ashgabat, just over the border with Turkmenistan, from there the convoy will again continue on its journey northwards to the airfield outside Urganch, situated on the border with Uzbekistan."

"They will be using a mixture of main, and track, roads; the convoy of vehicles will be travelling through over rocky slopes and then down onto mainly flat land, .consisting of a heavily wooded area."

"Are you suggesting we attack them?" enquired one of the soldiers.

"But of course," confirmed their, temporary leader, as if the thought had never entered his head. "It'll give us chance to try out the firepower of our Mi-28 attack helicopters, plus the *stinger* laser confusion system (LCS). Is everybody happy with that?" Everybody nodded.

It was then that they all heard a, deep, rumbling sound that seemed to shake the room they were gathered in. Mitchell Walker smiled to himself; that would be *Bollinger* powering its engines up and preparing to lift off; even though the missile was housed in another area of the bunker the soldiers could all hear the rumbling noise and feel the effects as it powered up, in the conference chamber. Suddenly the room shook as the missile took off and flew towards its destination.

******

Mitchell Walker was a youngish man at 32, he had that youthful look which some of the other soldiers resented, plus he was an all out action type of person with his athletic looking body which, again, some of his colleagues resented about him. Even though he was, slightly, older than Sandy Tulliver command had automatically passed to her after Dr Q's sad demise, it was because she was younger than him, plus his boss, and also the fact she was a woman that he disliked her. He would have been happier serving under Tanya Roberts, or *Squeeze* as was her nickname because of how she killed people, as she was, at least or had been, of a similar age to himself. Unfortunately, Dr Q had branded her a traitor, as he thought she had been in league with Abdul Singh - who had turned out to be a traitor - and had, therefore, killed her, or had had her killed.

At least that's what Walker had heard, and as he hadn't seen Miss Roberts for around a year, probably less, the story must have had a ring of truth to it; or one of the leader's bodyguards had killed her. Now he was in charge, albeit temporarily, and so he was making his mark, while he had the chance.

*****

The missile streaked on its journey upwards, into the sky, passing through the thin layer of clouds overhead. Back in the bunker it was being tracked on radar; plus at HART headquarters an emergency transmission had been received, stating that the satellite that was being used had detected a fast incoming projectile, probably a missile travelling straight towards it. They could launch their own missiles from HART, or send up a squad of jet fighters, but neither would reach the satellite in time, unfortunately they were powerless to stop the inevitable. Plus the satellite had no defences.

Bollinger struck the orbiting satellite, exploding on impact and turning the satellite into a giant, orbiting, fireball; debris from the, burning, satellite fell towards the sand below. In the Commander's office the three commanders watched the TV screen, on the back wall, usually this part of wall showed a map of the world but the map had been taken down a few days ago as it was felt this was no longer needed. Commander Strobing watched, in horror, as the missile struck the satellite and caused the resulting fireball, "Damn!" he said sharply.

"What's the matter?" enquired Commander Bigship.

"That's another fifty million pounds worth of satellite gone up in smoke," he complained bitterly. "And we haven't got another to replace it."

"Can't we just buy another?" asked his colleague.

"My dear Commander Bigship, HART simply hasn't got the necessary funds anymore. I shall now have to go, or send one of you two, and see Queen Charlotte of Britain." The other two knew Ronan didn't like to ask people for extra funding but in some cases it couldn't be helped. Suddenly there was a knock on the office door, "Come in," called Ronan, the, wooden, office door was pushed open and Ben Gillespe entered.

"Sir," he said as he walked in, "sorry to trouble you and all that, but that train with the gold coins onboard leaves Tehran in a couple of days." The colour suddenly drained from Commander Strobing's face. "And they've requested a HART escort."

"Thank you for reminding me, I'd completely forgotten," the superior officer told the young receptionist. "Can you round up the four, new, commanders for me, together with Alice Stronglove? However, keep Miss Stronglove in reception until I give you the word to send her in."

"Of course sir, at once sir," responded Mr Gillespe and hurried from the room to perform these tasks.

As the receptionist closed the door Leon said to Ronan, "What do you intend to do now?"

"Well," started Ronan smiling, "as Miss Stronglove isn't one of our, regular, soldiers I intend to allow her to use Miss Lang's, now, empty and disused residence."

Commander Most suddenly said to her superior officer, "What if you then face a mutiny from the other soldiers, after all this may be seen as favouritism."

Ronan peered at her, and then looked at Commander Bigship, "As I am their overall commanding officer they will learn to live with ii, as will you two."

Just followed by the four, new, commanders then entered the office. "You sent for us sir," stated Commander Smith.

"I did indeed," answered Ronan. "Please be seated and I'll explain everything." The four commanders seated themselves on the, plastic, chairs provided. "Now," their superior officer started, "as you may know there is a train leaving Tehran, in a couple of days, carrying some rare gold coins and they have requested a HART escort."

He paused and had a sip of water, "There will only be three box cars carrying the coins, the rest of the train will be made up of carriages carrying passengers. There are six of you, including Commander's Bigship and Most; so each box car will contain two HART personnel, as well as the boxes of coins."

They all digested this information and then Commander Most asked the question they were all thinking. "Who is to guard which box car?"

"Commander's Most and Hunter will take car one, Commander's Cutler and Samuels will be in car two, while Commander's Bigship and Smith will take car three. Are you all clear?" Everyone nodded their heads.

"Where will you be sir?" enquired Leon.

"I shall be visiting Queen Charlotte, to request those extra funds. However, I will tell you, you will be armed with the Beretta M12 submachine gun."

*****

The Beretta Model 12 was a 9x19mm Parabellum calibre submachine gun. It had once been the official submachine gun of the Italian Army and was first introduced in 1959. The

Beretta Model 12 was officially adopted by the Italian government in 1961. It had also been the official submachine gun of some South American and African countries. It was originally made under licence in Brazil by Taurus, and Indonesia by PT Pindad.

In the 1950s, Pietro Beretta Spa., Italy, developed the first Beretta submachine gun prototypes, the models 6–11. The Model 12 was the final production model, and was soon followed by the M12S with differences in the safety and other mechanics.

The Model 12 weighed 3.48 kilograms empty (about 3.820 kg loaded) and was 660 millimetres in its length with the stock extended (418 mm when retracted). Its short length was achieved by the use of a barrel that was recessed into the bolt head, known as a telescoping bolt. This had reduced the length without reducing barrel length or bolt weight. It fired from an open bolt and had a cyclic rate of fire of 550 shots per minute. Its muzzle velocity was 380 metres per second. It was accurate to 200/300 metres.

The barrel and rifling were chromium-plated to prevent fouling. The bolt housing had grooves to allow bolt movement, even in extremely adverse conditions such as exposure to mud, dust, or sand. The exterior surfaces of the firearm were finished with an epoxy resin coating for protection against corrosion and damage. The weapon also had a selective-fire option allowing a choice of single shot or fully automatic fire.

The weapon had three safeties: a manual safety which blocked the trigger; an automatic safety on the rear grip which immobilized the trigger and blocked the bolt in a closed position; and a safety on the cocking handle locking the bolt in case it did not retract sufficiently.

The weapon was provided with a front sight (adjustable for elevation and windage) and a rear sight with a two-position flip aperture (up to 100 metres and up to 200 metres).

The gun was equipped with a side folding stock, but was also seen rarely with a fixed stock. Twenty, thirty, and forty round box magazines were available for the original Model 12, which was chambered for the 9 mm Parabellum cartridge.

The Model 12 was redesigned as the Beretta Model 12S in 1978 and was styled as *the Ultimate Submachine Gun* when it was released. The Model 12S used a 32-round box magazine, and was chambered for the 9 mm x 19 NATO cartridge. It utilized the blowback principle, and was capable of either semi- or full-automatic fire.

A novel feature was the grip safety, which locked both the trigger and the bolt in the closed position, thus safeguarding against accidental firing if the grip was not held firmly or if the gun was dropped. The safety and fire-selector switch, which in the original Model 12 were two separate push-pin button (with the fire-selector being a button that activated single-fire or burst fire whether it was pushed on the right side or the left side) had been re-engineered in a modern lever-type selector with three positions (S for "Sicura" or Safety, 1 for Single-fire, R for "Raffica" or Burst fire). The fixed firing pin on the face of the bolt could strike the primer only when the cartridge was chambered fully, and this also avoided accidental firing, according to its designers.

The PM12S was also designed with easy field-stripping and reassembly in mind, which had been simplified and could be accomplished without use of tools. It could be equipped with a suppressor, but this required a slight modification of the barrel by a competent gunsmith. Minus the suppressor and other optional features, the Beretta PM12S was made up of 84 discrete components.

The current version of the Beretta Model 12, called the PM12-S2, spawned from the adoption of the PM12S by the French Gendarmerie Nationale, to be assembled under licence at the MAS armaments factory in Saint-Etienne from Italian made parts. The Gendarmerie asked for a modification, in the form of a further safety device, which allowed both to keep the bolt of the weapon in the half-cocked position and also acted as an interceptor preventing accidental fire should the bolt or the firing pin suddenly disengage. The so-modified Model 12S were known in the French service as the PM12-SD with SD standing for *Demi-arme*, or *Half-cock*. In the mid-1990s, this modification was implemented in all the Model 12 sub-machineguns manufactured by Beretta as a standard factory feature; and the denomination of the sub-machine gun changed to PM12-S2; this is the only Model 12 variant currently manufactured by Beretta.

*****

The six commanders filed out the office to carry out their superior's orders. Once the door was closed Commander Strobing activated the intercom. "Ben, send in Miss Stronglove please." Whilst he was waiting he got himself another drink from the drinks cabinet. As he re-seated himself there was a knock on the door. "Enter," he called in an authoritative voice.

The door opened and Miss Stronglove entered the room. "Please sit yourself down." She seated herself in the chair, recently, vacated by Commander Celia Most.

Alice Stronglove was of a smallish size, and only 24. Due to her small size her physical attributes were extremely pronounced, and she could often loosen a man's tongue this way; due to the absence of a man in her life she had joined HART as an intelligence gathering operative. She was still a reasonably new HART agent and had been on three previous assignments: the first one in Japan, she'd found the Japanese very accommodating, in both senses of the phrase; her second assignment had been in Germany, and again she'd found this race very accommodating.

Her third, and latest, assignment had been the previous year, in Russia, where she had had to expose certain ministers, these being the foreign minister and the defence minister, as being in league with *Proagnon*. Alice had made a friend in the Russian SVR chairwoman, Svetlana. It was with her assistance that she'd exposed the guilty ministers. She'd nearly been killed when she'd encountered a *Proagnon* agent; when she'd requested help from HART her immediate commander, Leon Bigship, had flown out to be with her. The three of them had gone to a nightclub together, and had almost gotten killed when a group of *Proagnon* soldiers had attacked the nightclub they were at.

Eventually the two of them, Alice and Leon, had escaped while Svetlana, who had assisted them to escape, had - ultimately - been killed when her vehicle had been destroyed in an explosion.

*****

"Yes sir," Alice said once she was seated. "You wanted to see me?"

"Indeed I did, Miss Stronglove, the fact is we may have another intelligence gathering mission coming up, and I feel, in fact Commander Bigship agrees with this, that as you have done this sort of thing before, you would be prepared to go on this mission." He paused to gauge her reaction.

"Yes sir, I would gladly do that."

"Furthermore I feel, and this is my – personal - decision, that as an intelligence gathering operative you shouldn't be sharing quarters with, other, regular soldiers. Therefore, until you are needed for this mission, I propose to install you in the residence, recently, vacated by Commander Lang. If any of the regular soldiers don't like this arrangement they can take it up with me. Is that all okay with you?"

"That is fine by me sir, only thing I want to say is thank you," and she leant forward and gave her superior a big kiss; Ronan was completely taken aback. This from his intelligence gathering operative; he noticed her breasts had become even more noticeable since she'd leant forwards.

As soon as she pulled back Commander Strobing informed her, "You are free to move whatever you require for the duration of your stay into Miss Lang's residence. You are dismissed for now."

"Thank you again sir," Alice said smiling, and left the commander's office.

*****

Once Alice Stonglove had exited the office Commander Strobing gathered, from the filing cabinet to his left, several files that he would need for his upcoming meeting with Queen

Charlotte Pendragon, the latest monarch of Britain; he also placed his Beretta 9000S in his shoulder holster, under his armpit. Then he left his office and walked across to reception; Gwyneth Jones was now seated at the main receptionist's desk.

He said to her, "I will be leaving shortly for my residence, to gather my belongings, and then I shall be leaving for *Cointrin* airport and taking a flight to London's *Heathrow* airport, as I am going to see Queen Charlotte about obtaining extra funding to build another satellite."

"Who'll be in charge while you're away?" she asked.

"Nobody unless either Commander's Bigship or Most return before me; until one of us returns you are in, temporary, charge."

"Thank you sir, it'll be an honour; don't worry I won't let you down." With that she vacated her seat, Joshua Smith became main receptionist, and strode over towards the commander's office, to take temporary charge. Ronan smiled to himself, everything was safe in her hands.

Commander Strobing then left the fourth floor, and took the elevator down to the ground floor; he then exited the main building, passing the guards on duty as he went outside.

The commander made his way over to his, own, residence, and noticed Alice carrying a suitcase across to the empty residence which had once housed Lucy Lang. Being the gentleman he was he offered to carry Miss Stronglove's case over to her new abode. Alice accepted his offer and so, with his files under one arm – he'd only needed two - in the end – and the suitcase in his other hand, he made his way over to the residence and took the suitcase inside, putting it down in the kitchen. "Don't leave it there," Alice told him. "Will you take it up to the bedroom, for me, please?"

So Ronan placed the files he was carrying on one of the side units, and with a *grunt* hoisted the suitcase up again and started up the stairs with it; he was aware of Alice following him. He entered the main bedroom and dumped the, heavy, case on the bed, he hadn't really noticed how heavy it was before; Alice undid the suitcase, totally unashamed, and threw back the lid – revealing several sets of underwear, and certain pieces of other clothing.

Since she'd returned from Russia, the year before, Alice had invested in many sets of underwear, deciding that she'd, probably, revealed too much of herself before. Ronan was aghast, here he was – overall commander of HART – being shown the interior and contents of Miss Stronglove's suitcase; he made his excuses and left. He wandered over to his, own, residence, went inside and packed, and then returned downstairs, placed his suitcase into the boot of his *Apollo II* automobile and drove to *Cointrin* airport.

*****

London *Heathrow* Airport was located 14 miles (22 kilometres) west of Central London, near to the southern end of the London Borough of Hillingdon, it was also the largest and busiest airport located in the United Kingdom. It was the world's second busiest airport in terms of total passenger traffic and it handled more international passengers than any other airport in the world. It was also the busiest airport in the European Union in terms of passenger traffic and the second busiest in terms of traffic movement. The airport was owned and operated by BAA, which also owned and operated five other UK airports, and was itself owned by ADI Limited, an international consortium, which included Caisse de dépôt et placement du Québec and GIC Special Investments, that was led by the Spanish Ferrovial Group. *Heathrow* was the primary hub for BMI, British Airways and Virgin Atlantic Airways.

Heathrow was designed to have six runways in three pairs but now has two parallel main runways running east-west and five operational terminals. The site covered 12.14 square kilometres (4.69 sq mi). Terminal 5, which was the latest terminal, was officially opened by Queen Elizabeth II, grandmother of the present queen, on 14 March 2008 and opened to passengers on 27 March 2008. The construction of a new Terminal 2 complex to replace the original terminal building and adjacent Queen's Building began in 2009; the first phase is expected to open in 2014. Beginning in 2007 and completed in 2009, Terminals 3 and 4 have both undergone major refurbishments. In November 2007 a consultation process began for the building of a new third runway and this was controversially approved on 15 January 2009 by UK Government ministers.

Heathrow Airport has a CAA Public Use Aerodrome Licence (Number P527) that allows flights for the public transport of passengers or for flying instruction.

*****

About an hour earlier the other six commanders had been in the airport and boarded a Gulfstream *G550* executive business jet, and had started their journey to Tehran's *Imam Khomeini* airport – a journey that would take approximately four hours and nineteen minutes – the personnel had left *Cointrin* at 16.20 and would land at the airport in Iran, including the time difference plus journey time, at about 23.10; then they had to get to the hotel they had been booked into for the night, ready for the next day's guard duty; the train they would be aboard was due to leave at 15.00 (local time).

When the HART personnel arrived at 23.20, ten minutes late, the air outside was warm and humid (21 centigrade) and a light drizzle had begun to fall. The commanders made their way through the main building, and outside. They boarded three, separate, taxis and instructed their drivers to take them to the hotel they'd been booked into, the *Majestic*, which had a total of one thousand rooms over fifty floors.

They entered the main reception area and showed the receptionist, on duty, their HART passes. "Ah, our visitors from Geneva, I have put you in rooms 314, 315 and 316, all are double rooms."

Celia looked alarmed, "I'm not sharing my bed."

"No ma'am, you misunderstand me; I meant there are two single beds in each room," responded the hotel's receptionist. Celia muttered an apology to the man; the six HART employees then gathered up their suitcases, and walked over to the elevators – they stepped inside the two elevators and went up to the third floor.

The six of them found their rooms fairly easily, went inside and went straight to bed – they had a long couple of days ahead of them.

*****

Proagnon soldiers, led by Mitchell Walker, boarded the two Mi-24 helicopters, plus the three Mi-28 attack helicopters, ready for the day ahead. Aboard the two HIND helicopters were the pilot, weapons system officer and a technician, plus eight soldiers; aboard the three *HAVOC* helicopters were the vehicle's pilot, and the weapons officer, plus three soldiers; therefore, in all, twenty-five *Proagnon* soldiers would be used, of course Walker was going along to lead them.

Each of the soldiers would be armed with the Russian made AK-47 assault rifles – not many of them had gotten used to the AK-74, two gas and two smoke grenades, plus a knife for close combat.

When everyone was ready they boarded the five aerial combat vehicles, once every soldier, and their leader, was aboard the pilots started the engines and the five top rotor blades began turning on each machine, and then the tail rotors (three on the *HIND*, and four on the *HAVOC*) started turning. Once the engines were at their full power the air vehicles emerged from the bunker, and rose, vertically, into the sky; when they had reached an operating height of 2,500 metres (8200 feet) the helicopters travelled, in convoy, to an area south of the railway line that would be carrying the passenger train, which would include the three box cars containing the cases of gold coins; the first *HIND*, plus one of the *HAVOC*'s, landed and disgorged the soldiers they were carrying, and then the two helicopters flew further away and landed in a, heavily, wooded area. The remaining three helicopters carried on and the next two (*HAVOC* and *HIND*) landed north east of Asgabat, in Turkmenistan. The final *HAVOC* carried on northwards and landed at the airfield outside Urgench, in Uzbekistan, (this *HAVOC* was to be used as back-up).

The first group set up the *stinger* LCS; once that was done everything was ready.

*****

The next morning the six personnel from HART rose and made their way to the restaurant, where they all had a simple Iranian meal and something to drink. Afterwards each of them returned to one room for a quick conference on what they would do if an attack took place.

"Apparently," remarked Commander Mike Hunter, "the box cars are bomb proof, so no one should be able to get at any of us."

"However," continued Commander Leon Bigship opening an extra suitcase, "in the event of an attack, if it happens, we will all be armed with our Beretta M12's," he lifted the weapons out the suitcase and handed them round. "Also each of us will be carrying our new pistol, the Beretta 8000."

*****

The Beretta 8000 (*Cougar*) series pistols were, again, manufactured by Beretta of Italy; and were recoil operated, locked breech semi-automatic pistols. These pistols used a relatively rare rotating barrel locking system, in which the barrel rotated on recoil to unlock itself from the slide. The rotating motion of the barrel was controlled by the stud on its bottom, which followed the cam track in the steel frame insert. To decrease peak recoil and stress to the frame, the insert was mounted on the recoil spring and was buffered.

The frame of the weapon was made from lightweight aluminium alloy. The basic version of the *Cougar* pistol was the F model, with a double action trigger with an exposed hammer, and ambidextrous safety/decocker levers, located on the slide. The alternative being the D version, which was double action only and so had a spur less hammer and no safety/decocker levers. *Cougar* pistols use double-stack magazines in 9 mm, .357 SIG and .40 calibre models, and single stack magazines in .45 calibre models.

The pistol first appeared on the market in 1994 as a more compact alternative to the full-sized Beretta 92 service pistol in order to offer a compromise between conceal ability, ease of carry, accuracy and firepower.

It was originally developed for the .40S&W cartridge, which was a new cartridge at the time. It was later also manufactured for other calibres, such as 9 x 19 mm, .357 SIG and .45 ACP. These pistols are suitable for use by the police and for civilian self-defence.

The 8045 Beretta *Cougar* was produced between the years of 1998 and 2004 in the D and F configuration. A Mini 8045 Cougar was also produced in the same configurations. No factory 8045 *Cougar*s were produced in the "G" configuration. The G specification was a DA/SA variant with *decock* only feature. It features an exposed hammer with ambidextrous decocking levers (on the slide). There is no safety on this model.

In 1999, Beretta USA offered 2000 special edition kits to accompany the 8045F *Cougar*. Accompanying the basic 8045F was a kit comprising of a special edition case, lapel pin and charcoal laminate grips with inlaid cougar medallions. Several kits were sold but the number of kits is unconfirmed. With 2000 units initially projected, it was believed the total number sold to be far less than that. There was no specific serial number run for these as the kits were sold with the standard pistol as they were ordered. Typically, the Cat Pak cougars had a date code of BM for 1999.

*****

He handed the, lightweight, 9mm pistols around the group. "Finally, we shall all be carrying knives, just in case," Leon handed these round to his comrades, plus several extra magazines of 9mm ammunition for their weapons. "Now I suggest we all put on our body armour and have some lunch before the mission begins."

"One more thing before we depart," Commander Most said. "I think, now we all know what weapons we'll be using, we ought to just go over the plans of the train," she then produced several drawings and photos – some of the box cars, some of the carriages, and some of the full train. "As you can plainly see," Celia began, "the box cars are exactly that, basic box shapes; however, there are grilles in the tops of the cars – two each side – to provide ventilation. The doors between the cars will be unlocked, in case any of us need a jimmy." They all then studied the layouts of each of the passenger carriages, locating the exits, toilets, as the ten hour journey would be a long one, etc. "Oh and don't forget the TAC-SAT," Commander Most reminded them.

Four of them then left for their separate rooms and put on their *Kevlar (Mark II)* body armour, the *Kevlar* armour had been improved since the last conflict. By the end of the morning all six of them were ready for action, each of them would be boarding the train as an ordinary citizen, but had been requested to arrive early and show the guard their passes so he would know which car to let them into; only the train's guard would have the keys to unlock each door thus letting them into the cars. Would they have to deal with any type of attack, none of them knew.

*****

The plane carrying the overall commander of HART, a Gulfstream *G550*, landed at *Heathrow* a little under an hour after leaving *Cointrin*. However, due to the hour's time difference the plane landed at, practically, the same time it had taken off; once Ronan had gathered his cases together he walked through the airport building and outside, it was still fairly warm but there was also a, light, breeze blowing. He climbed aboard an empty taxi and instructed the driver to drive him to Buckingham Palace. The taxi set off and, an hour later, after much muttering and swearing from the driver – it was rush hour, after all - the taxi, finally, pulled up outside the gates of Buckingham Palace; the HART commander paid the driver, entered the grounds and then walked up the, long, drive to the building, he was shown inside – Gwyneth must've phoned ahead – and asked what his business was.

He explained he was on HART business and needed to see the queen about acquiring extra funding. When the receptionist was fully satisfied he was who he said he was she requested one of the palace servants take him to the White Drawing Room. The servant entered the room and announced him. He stepped into the room, "Queen Charlotte Pendragon, ma'am, pleased to meet you." The servant withdrew discreetly.

"You are Commander Strobing of HART," she said as he seated himself. "Tell me, where is Mr Roberts?"

"Unfortunately, ma'am, he was killed in action, in our final battle in the Iraqi desert, with *Proagnon*."

"I am sorry. And what became of the head of that terrorist organisation?"

"He was killed also," replied Ronan. "In fact many people, both HART and *Proagnon*, lost their lives that day, some months back. Of course there were survivors, as well, I survived along with a couple of my fellow commanders, plus about twenty HART soldiers survived. As for *Proagnon* I believe some of their personnel also survived."

"Do you believe they still pose a potential threat?" enquired the young queen, looking straight at Commander Strobing.

"I believe they may do," he answered, "one of them was spotted in Norwich, with we believe, your consort, Gareth Andrews," he turned to look at the man, to see if he made any reaction, there was none.

"I'm sorry Mr Strobing but my consort is totally innocent, he has been away visiting one of his relations, his brother I believe. You must have made a mistake," Ronan took a photo out of the folder he was carrying.

"This image was produced from a DVD that was taken by one of the CCTV cameras overlooking the parking lot at *John Groggins* Hospital in Norwich." He passed the image over.

Queen Charlotte peered at it then looked up at Mr Andrews, "A most remarkable resemblance, a doppelganger perhaps; but I still don't believe it, it must be somebody else."

"Okay," replied Ronan, "I trust your judgement. Now I need to ask you something else."

"Ask away Mr Strobing," the queen told him.

Commander Strobing considered a moment and then asked, "We have just lost our orbiting satellite over Iran and were wondering, as this country seems to be the friendliest towards our organisation, if it would be possible to secure further funding to build a new one?"

"No!" snapped Miss Pendragon fiercely. "First of all you come in here and, practically accuse my consort, and boyfriend, of being mixed up with this *Proagnon* organisation, and then you have the audacity to ask for extra funding. If you can prove me wrong please do, but until then HART gets absolutely no extra funding."

Ronan was taken aback by the queen's sharp retort but decided to ask anyway, "I presume, Miss Pendragon that I cannot stay here for the duration of my stay."

"Certainly not at the moment," was Queen Charlotte's answer. Therefore Commander Strobing picked up his briefcase, rose from his seat and left the room, the bodyguard following him all the way.

At reception he picked up his suitcase and left the building. Walking down the drive he thought to himself, *Dr Schaiffer identified the man in the photo, he seemed so certain. Was he mistaken?*

*****

In Tehran the six other commanders of HART were on their way to the railway station; they were travelling on a bus full of Iranians – some young, some old – it was extremely hot, humid and dusty outside. Once the bus reached its destination the six operatives got off and entered the, relative, coolness of the station building.

They each showed their, official, passes to the guard standing on the platform, and were allowed to board the box car they'd been allocated; the cars were absolutely full of boxes containing the coins. The six of them settled themselves in for the, long, journey that lay ahead of them.

*****

At about 15:20 the train pulled out of the station to begin its ten hour journey to Mashhad, from there a further 250 miles would be travelled to Asgabat; finally another 450 miles to the airfield outside Urgench, this part of the journey would be made along – relatively - unmade roads.

Everything was going smoothly until…

*****

Commander Strobing hailed another taxi outside the palace gates and asked to be taken to the, *Ritz*, hotel in Piccadily, overlooking Green Park, London. Ronan exited the taxi outside the luxury hotel; carrying his case, he walked up the stone steps that led into the building and passed through the door, which was held open by the doorman, on duty.

The commander of HART entered the main foyer area and booked himself into one of the hotel's 133 rooms. He then walked across to the main notice which contained the history of the *Ritz* hotel, as well as other information.

*****

Famed Swiss hotelier César Ritz opened the hotel on May 24, 1906. The building was neoclassical in the Louis XVI manner, built during the Belle Époque to resemble a stylish Parisian block of flats, over arcades that consciously evoked the Rue de Rivoli. Its architects were Charles Mewès, who had previously designed Ritz's Hôtel Ritz Paris, and Arthur Davis, with engineering collaboration by the Swedish engineer Sven Bylander. It was the first substantial steel-frame structure in London.

Ritz personally managed much of the hotel's operation for many years. He hired world-famous chef Auguste Escoffier to provide cuisine to match the opulence of the hotel's decorations; he placed a special bell in the entryway by which the doorman could notify the staff of the impending arrival of royalty. The high standards to which he held his staff and the ultimate luxury which he provided his guests had been entirely foreign to Victorian Londoners, and the sensation he caused in the hotel industry precipitated a dramatic shift in that industry's focus.

The hotel was owned for some time by the Bracewell-Smith family who also had significant stakes in the nearby Park Lane Hotel. However the oil crisis in the early 1970s affected business and prompted the family to sell their stake to Trafalgar House in 1976 for £2.75m.

David and Frederick Barclay purchased the ailing hotel for £80 Million from Trafalgar House, in October 1995, through their company Ellerman Investments. They spent a further eight years and £40 Million restoring it to its former grandeur.

The *Ritz*'s most famous facility was the Palm Court, an opulently decorated cream-colored Louis XVI setting for the world-famous institution that is *Tea at the Ritz*, (though, strictly speaking, Tea at the Savoy is the original version) once frequented by King Edward VII, Charlie Chaplin, Daniel Altwasser, Sir Winston Churchill, Charles de Gaulle, Noel Coward, Judy Garland, Gary Glitter, Ryan Parasmo, Evelyn Waugh, Jonathan Crook and Queen Elizabeth, the Queen Mother. The *Rivoli* Bar, built in the Art Deco style, was designed in 2001 by interior designer Tessa Kennedy, to look like a bar on the Orient Express. A table at the Restaurant still needs to be booked weeks in advance. The hotel had six private dining rooms, the Karl Betts Suite, a popular venue for noise band GAZE and the rooms within the William Kent House.

In 2006 the William Kent House was opened as an extension of The *Ritz*. The William Kent House had been converted into a complete Function area with the Burlington Room, the Queen Elizabeth Room and the most ostentatious William Kent room. The William Kent House also accommodates three of The *Ritz*'s top suites: The Arlington Suite, the Royal Suite as well as the Prince of Wales Suite.

The *Ritz* Club was a casino in the basement of the *Ritz* Hotel in London. The casino was open from 2pm to 6am, seven days a week. However, unlike most casinos, it required a fee to enter. The games are considered *high stakes* in that the minimum bet was usually very high. They offered roulette, black jack, baccarat, and poker, as well as some slot machines.

On 27 January 2007 around 300 people were evacuated to the nearby May Fair Hotel following a fire alarm in the hotel. No one was hurt in the blaze, which started in the basement *Ritz* Club casino kitchens extraction vents. The *Ritz* casino only suffered *minor damage*. The blaze happened at around 14.20 on that day and fire-fighters were present in the building for two hours before allowing the guests and staff to return.

*****

Interesting, thought Commander Strobing as he made his way through the foyer and lobby, and on to the lift; his room was located on the second floor. He journeyed up, in the lift, and exited the vertical moving compartment once it had, finally, come to a halt. He found his room, 25, unlocked the door and walked inside; the room was the same as most hotel rooms nowadays; bed, a table & chairs, TV, internet access, tea making facilities etc. Therefore he unpacked his suitcase, almost wishing his wife, Mandy, were still alive; he had a big double bed, yet nobody to share it with.

Once he'd unpacked everything he went down to the *Rivoli* bar, and ordered himself a tumbler of whisky; as he was sipping his drink he looked around, most of the tables in the bar were occupied, mainly by older people, but there were a few, younger, business looking people about. He spotted a young woman seated at a table, in the corner, on her own; he made his way over and asked, "May I sit down?"

The woman looked up at him; she couldn't have been older than twenty – probably younger, "What? Oh yes, please do join me, sir." So Ronan seated himself opposite her. Suddenly alarm bells began to ring in his head – Ronan wasn't sure why so just ignored them.

"What is your name," Commander Strobing said, "And what are you doing here?"

"My name sir is Maria Sanchez, I am Italian-American – my father, Don, is Italian, while my mother, Annie, is American; however, my mother ran out on my father and myself when I was aged five." Ronan, even though he hadn't asked for her life story, was, actually, enjoying it, "Now my father owns a block of apartments near Washington and I stay with him nowadays as he is an old man, however, I am over here at my father's request."

"Your business?" the HART commander prompted.

"I am here to try and, how you say, promote my father's business."

"I hope you succeed," Ronan told her. "Unfortunately, I have to return to my own room now." He got up from his place and left the bar.

What he didn't notice was Miss Sanchez get up and start to follow him. He made his way over to the two lifts – both were on the ground floor – observed by the young woman. He stepped inside the lift, on the left, and began the journey to the second floor; as soon as the lift doors had closed Maria had darted, nimbly, over to the lift on the right, and pressed the *hold* button. Once his lift had stopped, on the second floor and showed no further sign of moving Maria got, fully, in the right lift and pressed the button that would take the lift to floor *2*.

Upon exiting the lift Miss Sanchez observed Mr Strobing, she wasn't sure of his name yet but did it matter to her?, going into a room mid-way down the hall; once he was inside she smiled to herself and walked over to see which room it was, 25. She grinned and then wandered back to the lifts and left floor *2*. She and Mr Strobing would meet again; the young woman would make sure of it.

*****

Maria Sanchez left the hotel, took off the high heeled shoes she was wearing, and walked a few streets away to a small, dilapidated looking, shop – which was now boarded up – the young woman located the entrance she'd made, in the brick structure, she entered and undressed out of her business clothes, in reality she'd managed to borrow these from a cousin.

Once she was in her jeans and T-shirt again, she sat on the floor. What she'd told the man was partly the truth; the only couple of things she'd lied about were the apartments – in reality they were just old, run down, flats; plus she wasn't here to promote her father's business – in reality she'd run away from home. Still a couple of lies wouldn't hurt, would they?

Then her thoughts, strangely enough, turned to the Russian, Sergey Satov, who she'd encountered the previous year. Where was he now?

*****

The Iranian passenger train, along the three box cars had stopped approximately two hours into its journey, Commander Mike Hunter couldn't understand why they'd Come to a sudden halt, there were no other stations on the route so he queried Commander Most on why she thought the train had stopped. "Probably to let a farmer and his livestock across."

Then the train began on its journey again, "See, I told you it was nothing," Celia assured Mike. However, little did Commander Celia Most know what was waiting around the corner for the train.

*****

At the *Ritz* hotel Ronan Strobing changed into more casual, but smart, clothes and went down to the restaurant, the time was 21:00, so he was just in time to get a meal; he sat at a table and ate, slowly. Looking around he saw many people, as there had been in the bar, but he couldn't see Maria Sanchez anywhere, however, did he want to see her? Maybe they'd bump into each other again, maybe not; he wasn't that bothered either way.

Finishing his meal he got up, from his seat and exited the restaurant; he then exited the hotel and wandered through the streets, Ronan noticed a small, boarded up, shop, he thought he saw something move inside but dismissed it as nothing. Therefore, he carried on walking on his return journey towards the hotel. Upon his return Mr Strobing went up to his room and retired to bed.

*****

The *Proagnon* soldiers had set up the *stinger* on its tripod mount opposite a railway signal. The operator pressed the trigger on the, gun shaped, device, and the signal which was green turned to red, the passenger train pulled up at the *red* signal and halted; the signal was located at the top of a hill – the track followed the hill downwards while at the bottom was a turn to the left, just beyond was a deep ravine.

Mitchell Walker, who had changed into a senior railway workers uniform, went over just to reassure the driver that everything would be done in a minute. Another two *Proagnon* soldiers were hard at work, fixing the train; one was uncoupling the three box cars, whilst the other was cutting through the engine's brake fluid pipe. As they were both well drilled this part of their mission didn't take long.

"What's happening?" Commander Smith asked Commander Bigship, Commander Hunter was now in car two as Commander's Samuels and Cutler had both gone to the toilet.

"Probably nothing lad," Commander Bigship assured his younger partner, they had been travelling for five hours now. Outside both *Proagnon* soldiers gave the thumbs up to Walker.

Upon receiving the signal he told the driver of the, diesel, engine, "You're free to go now mate, sorry about the delay, have a good trip." The engine powered up and started to move, slowly, towards the brow of the hill; the signal was *green* now.

*****

Commander Cutler emerged from the toilet, in the seventh carriage and began to move through the rows of passengers towards the interconnecting door, meanwhile Commander Samuels emerged from the sixth carriage and joined his comrade, the train was still. Suddenly the train began moving, slowly, and then quite suddenly it started going faster and faster. They were moving down a slope but why were they moving so fast? Quite suddenly the two commanders realised, the train wasn't braking.

The driver, in his cab, pressed his foot down on the brake pedal but nothing happened. Aware of the carriages behind him, with all their passengers onboard, and knowing the speed they were travelling at would throw the whole train over the edge and into the ravine below. There was no way he could prevent the tragedy that was about to happen.

The two HART commanders also knew what was about to happen and rushed to the interconnecting door in a desperate bid to warn their colleagues. However, when they burst through the door all they saw was the lead box car moving backwards from them, so they hurled themselves outside and rolled when they hit the ground. They would've liked to save the train's passengers but, at the speed the train was now travelling at, that would prove an impossible task.

Meanwhile the four personnel wondered what was happening so Commander Bigship gave Commander Smith a, quick, bunk up so he could see through the ventilation grille. "The train's gone!" he cried.

"What?" demanded Leon.

"I can't see the train anywhere sir," his fellow commander replied.

"Right," Leon said, "I'd better inform the others." He moved off towards the door connecting the box car with the one in front. "Stay here Ben."

"Yes sir," Ben Smith responded. Leon informed Mike Hunter of the situation, and had just entered the car with Celia Most in when they heard it.

*****

Unable to stop or slow down the train, with the passengers on board, flew straight on at the bend and down into the ravine below. There was a loud crash and an explosion as the train smashed into the floor of the ravine, killing everybody onboard outright.

*****

Outside Commander's Samuels and Cutler were crawling, slowly up the slope of the hill, when Lloyd Samuels noticed a man carrying an AK-47 assault rifle, he had to be *Proagnon*. As if sensing he was being observed the man, suddenly, turned and fired off a rapid burst from his weapon – the 7.62x39mm cartridges striking the, sandy, ground in front of the two HART men and throwing up little clouds of sand, "Oh shit!" exclaimed Samuels to his companion. "Have you got your M12 on you?"

"No," responded Cutler, "I left it in the box car. By the way where's yours?"

"Same place as yours," admitted Lloyd shamefacedly. "I didn't think I'd need it in the khazi. However, I assume you've got you *Cougar* on you."

"I have,"" answered his fellow commander, drawing the weapon from his shoulder holster. At a word from Samuels they, both, charged up the slope and towards the lone gunman, firing 9mm cartridges as they went. The man from *Proagnon* simply spun and fired off some more ammunition, the gas powered action pumping the cartridges out in quick succession; both HART commanders were caught by the bullets and were killed instantly, the bullets finding *chinks* in the body armour.

It was then that Commander Most emerged from box car one and fired her M12 at the group of enemy soldiers – in fact two of the other three HART commanders, except Mike Hunter who had the TAC-SAT, emerged and began firing their weapons, as well. A fierce firefight ensued.

Commander Hunter tried to radio headquarters but couldn't hear a thing, of course, he suddenly realised he was surrounded by metal, lead lined, walls, probably the roof was made from the same material, so he needed to get outside to get a, good, signal. Carefully he made his way to the interconnecting door, carrying the remaining three M12's; as he reached the door he peered out and was greeted by the sight of Commander's Most, Bigship and Smith firing their 9mm cartridges at the enemy, and then, as he watched Commander Smith went down, blood coming from a wound in his stomach.

Mike knew he had to get a message out, but he was transfixed at the scene around him. It was, at that moment, a *slug* hit Commander Most and she fell.

CHAPTER 5

CASUALTIES & CAPTIVES!

Commander Bigship saw Celia fall and yelled, "Bastards!" and fired his M12, indiscriminately, at the terrorists. He managed to shoot and kill six of the *Proagnon* soldiers, and then he heard a helicopter behind him; he turned and looked up where he saw three choppers, one he recognised as a Mil Mi-24 *HIND*, yet the other two were of a, slightly, different design; yet they were the same type as each other. "Falcons," he shouted, hoping that if Commander Mike Hunter were nearby he'd hear Leon and understand.

Just then the two Mil Mi-28 *HAVOC*'s 30mm Shipunov 2A42 cannons opened fire, raking the, sandy, ground in front of Leon; once the sand dust had died down the HART commander noticed, on its wingtips four rockets (two on either wingtip) and under the small, stubby, wing was, what looked like a bomb. Suddenly he felt a gun press into his back and a voice whispered menacingly, "One false move and you're dead." Commander Bigship sighed, he was now a prisoner. He was forced at gunpoint towards one of the, newer looking helicopters which had landed.

Aboard the box car Commander Hunter had heard Leon shout but had been unable to fathom what he had meant at first, yet when he'd seen the helicopters he had realised, he tried contacting headquarters again and got through to the duty officer, George Burnett. "Yes."

"George, this is Commander Mike Hunter here," he said in a low voice, "please radio, I believe its, H-Moscow, and request assistance from a squad of F-16 *Falcon* fighter aircraft. We're about five hours east out of Tehran; I guess that's 250 miles."

"Will do," replied Mr Burnett. "What is the situation there?"

"We have four, possibly five, commanders down," responded Mike simply. Just then he saw the *HIND* land, "Sorry George, got to go."

"Okay, I'll get air support to your position as quick as I can, in the meantime sit tight." Mr Burnett then contacted H-Moscow and requested that a squad of F-16C *Falcons* be sent to the position he'd been given, but was informed there was only one of these aircraft left aboard now.

The order was given, anyway, and the pilot raced to his aircraft, once he was, safely, aboard and had done the checks he powered up the aircraft and took off to begin their 1,750 mile journey at a speed of 1,500 miles per hour; the aircraft was armed with the standard 20 mm (0.787 in) M61 Vulcan gatling gun, which could fire up to 511 rounds, 4× LAU-61/LAU-68 rocket pods (each with 19× /7× Hydra 70 mm rockets, respectively), 6× Python-4 air-to-air missiles, 4× AGM-88 HARM air-to-ground missiles. The aircraft was also carrying 4× Mark 84 general-purpose bombs, plus SUU-42A/A Flares/Infrared decoys, just in case.

*****

In the desert the *Proagnon* men from the *HIND* helicopter were boarding the box cars and removing the crates of rare coins, and then each would carry a crate back and load it aboard the Mi-24 helicopter; as there was only the two pilots to carry the crates it would take a while; suddenly, from the corner of his eye, Commander Hunter thought he saw movement, there it was again, he looked over – from his hiding place behind a large boulder – and saw the movement had come from Commander Most, so she wasn't dead. She was now laid on her front, slowly sliding her M12 out from underneath her body – her movements were so slow that none of the *Proagnon* men had noticed her – she brought the weapon to bear on one of the enemy pilots and fired a quick burst; one of the pilots fell dead, he dropped his crate of coins which emptied all over. Then she saw a third man and fired at him, unfortunately her shots fell short. The man turned to her position, brought his AK-47 to bear, grinned, evilly, at her, and aimed the assault rifle.

*****

Suddenly there was an almighty *boom* causing the two remaining *Proagnon* men to clutch their ears and fall to their knees; as everyone looked up, again, they saw an F-16C *Falcon* fighter aircraft.

The pilot engaged his radar and detecting the two enemies, he unleashed a spray of 20mm bullets from the gatling gun; the shots sprayed the ground and one caught the other pilot of the *HIND* and he fell, dropping the crate he was carrying. The second Mi-28 then reappeared and fired on the *Falcon* whilst the first *HAVOC* emerged and collected Mr Walker and then flew south towards the bunker.

The *Falcon* turned and seemed to flee deploying some of the flares/decoys to confuse any following missiles. The *HAVOC*, the pilot assuming the *Falcon* had fled back to its base, fired a stream of 30mm ammunition from its chin mounted cannon. However, unknown to the HAVOC's pilot the F-16 hadn't fled; it had just fled beyond the helicopter's radar coverage and then travelled in a wide arc until it was behind the enemy air machine. The Mi-28's radar detected the aircraft once it entered coverage, but by then it was too late; the HART fighter launched three of its Python-4 air-to-air missiles, these missiles streaked towards the helicopter, and as soon as they hit the air machine exploded creating a huge fireball, and debris rained down.

Suddenly the other three *HAVOC* helicopters, who had been alerted by the Mi-28 that had escaped, appeared and started launching missiles at the F-16. Deploying more decoys the *Falcon* dived downwards and, again, appeared behind the enemy air vehicles. It launched its final three Python-4 air-to-air-missiles which destroyed two of the air machines, creating further fireballs. The third *HAVOC* held back and the pilot watched the destruction of his two fellows; facing the F-16 the pilot launched his missiles which streaked towards the *Falcon*. The pilot, aboard the jet, knew he had run out of decoys and air-to-air missiles, all he had left were his air-to-ground missiles and the general purpose bombs; plus the 20mm gatling gun; he operated his cannon and fired on the missiles, each was hit and exploded – this operation had used up a further 100 rounds, leaving him with 361. It was then that the second *HIND* reappeared and noticing the absence of activity from the first *HIND*, landed beside it, the F-16 had backed away, out of sight.

Once the Mi-24 had landed the F-16 made its reappearance, and before the *Proagnon* soldiers could disembark the pilot of the *Falcon* launched his 4× AGM-88 HARM air-to-ground missiles. These struck the *HIND* and it exploded in flames, and scattered debris. Unfortunately, one of the pieces of debris hit Commander Hunter, killing him outright. By the time this happened the F-16C *Falcon* had turned eastwards, and started on its journey back to H-Moscow.

*****

In London Commander Strobing awoke in his hotel room and looked over at the clock, 10:00, being commander of HART did have its perks. He climbed out the double bed and went through to the bathroom, where he showered and dressed in his T-shirt and jeans. Exiting the room he took the lift to the ground floor, and exited the hotel; he decided to go for a walk in a similar direction to the one he'd taken the previous evening.

He popped into a café and had a, full, cooked breakfast; as he was eating he was looking out, of the main window, at the people passing by, he was just drinking his mug of tea when he spotted Miss Sanchez, or was it someone who looked very similar? As Ronan wasn't sure he, quickly, finished his tea, paid the woman behind the counter and exited the café. She was just in sight, and seemed to be heading towards the small, boarded up, shop; suddenly a noise startled him and he turned towards it, it was just a bin lid that had rattled, turning back to observe the woman he was following he saw she'd somehow disappeared, where had she gone? Undeterred Ronan carried on walking, past the boarded up building and onwards into the Piccadilly area of the city.

*****

Piccadilly was a major London street, which ran from Hyde Park Corner in the west to Piccadilly Circus in the east. It was located completely within the city of Westminster. The street was part of the A4 road, London's second most important western artery. St. James's lay to the south of the eastern section of the street, while the western section was built up only on the northern side and overlooked Green Park. The area to the north was Mayfair.

It was the location of Fortnum & Mason, the Royal Academy, The *Ritz* Hotel and *Hatchards* book shop. *Simpsons*, once amongst the United Kingdom's leading clothing stores, opened on Piccadilly in the 1930s. The store closed in 1999 and the site was now the flagship shop of the booksellers *Waterstone's*. The area was also home to a number of popular nightclubs ranging from the exclusive *Paper* Nightclub on Regent Street to the tourist-friendly *Sound* in Leicester Square.

*****

Commander Strobing thought to himself *While I'm here, I may as well buy one or two things.* With that he wandered into *Hatchards* and purchased a couple of *mystery* books for himself, and a copy of the *Sherlock Holmes* book *The Hound of the Baskervilles* for Simon, as his son seemed to have developed a liking for these types of books; he wasn't sure if Simon had that particular book, but if he had he had. Ronan paid for all four of the books for twenty pound, slightly more than he wanted to pay but, hopefully, it'd be worth it.

Once he'd paid he continued to look around the books, just to see if there was anything else he was interested in. As he was perusing one of the shelves of *Tom Clancy* novels a hand touched his shoulder, "Hello," said a female voice.

Ronan turned, standing behind him was Maria Sanchez, dressed similar to him, in jeans and T-shirt – he didn't think she was wearing a bra though – still, that was up to her, "Hello Miss Sanchez, not working today?"

"No," she answered, "I've got a few days off. I was just passing when I noticed you in here and I thought I'd make your acquaintance again."

"I'm glad you did," the commander of HART replied. "I thought I saw you outside earlier but I think I must've been mistaken."

"Shall we go for a walk?" Maria suggested, taking his hand; he looked down at the young woman. She, suddenly, didn't seem like the businesswoman she'd told him she was the previous evening.

"Yes," Ronan answered, "I'd like that." So they exited the shop together and headed towards Green Park, Ronan admiring the sights around him, and Maria with a, big, smile on her face.

*****

Green Park was one of the Royal Parks of London. Covering 19 hectares (47 acres), it lay between London's Hyde Park and St. James's Park. Together with Kensington Gardens and the gardens of Buckingham Palace, these parks formed an almost unbroken stretch of open land reaching from Whitehall and Victoria station to Kensington and Notting Hill.

By contrast with its neighbours, Green Park has no lakes, no buildings and very few monuments, having only the *Canada Memorial* by Pierre Granche and the Constance Fund Fountain. The park consisted entirely of wooded meadows. The park was bounded on the south by Constitution Hill, on the east by the pedestrian Queen's Walk, and on the north by Piccadilly. It met St. James's Park at Queen's Gardens with the Victoria Memorial at its centre, opposite the entrance to Buckingham Palace. To the south was the ceremonial avenue of The Mall, and the buildings of St James's Palace and Clarence House overlooked the park to the east. Green Park tube station was a major interchange located on Piccadilly, Victoria and Jubilee lines near the north end of Queen's Walk.

*****

They entered the park and walked through several of the wooded areas and they jogged across meadows before the two of them sat down on one of the park benches; Miss Sanchez looked at Mr Strobing and enquired, "You never told me your name last night, what is it?"

"Oh, Ronan Strobing," he told her absently, placing the plastic, carrier, bag on the ground beside the bench.

"And what do you do Mr Strobing?"

"I'm in the property business," he lied. He didn't want everyone to know what he really did. "I mainly buy property nowadays, as there seems to be so much on the market."

"That's true," replied the young woman beside him. "Daddy's always looking out for something new to invest in, that's why he sent me over here."

"That explains a great deal," the HART man murmured, more to himself than to anyone else. The alarm bells had been ringing again since their encounter in *Hatchards* earlier; he was still unsure why, but it must have something to do with his choice of female companion. He then moved the carrier bag and placed it between them, on the ground, for some reason Miss Sanchez's eyes seemed to develop a mischievous look to them; Ronan wondered why.

Suddenly, Maria grabbed the bag and ran off; Ronan gave chase, wondering what had come over her, why did she want a bag of books? She zigzagged through the trees, probably trying to shake her pursuer off. Once or twice Ronan almost missed his footing, but he stayed upright, slowly, ever so slowly, he began to gain on her; when he deemed himself close enough behind her he leapt forward, he didn't want to hurt this woman, just stop her and reclaim his property.

As he launched himself at her she tripped on a, sticking up, tree root and fell, the bag flew from her hand and skidded along the grass. Unable to stop himself the commander of HART landed on top of her. "Oof," she grunted and tried to wriggle free from under him.

"Sorry," he apologised; he then noticed that Maria wasn't trying to wriggle free, she was trying to turn onto her back. He tried to rise but she held him in place, "Maria! What are you doing?"

"Just this," she responded, reached up and kissed him.

Ronan was shocked, he looked at her and said angrily, "No, stop this at once; I thought we were friends." He managed to disentangle himself from her grip, and rose to his feet again. Ronan then went and fetched the carrier bag, which had landed on the grass spewing the four books he'd bought, on the ground. He became aware of somebody standing behind him, probably Miss Sanchez.

"I'm sorry," the apologetic voice behind him said, "I meant no harm. Of course we're friends." Mr Strobing turned, slowly, to face her, and saw her – properly – for the first time, "Come and sit with me, again, and I'll explain all."

Reluctantly Commander Strobing followed her back over to the bench where they'd been seated about ten minutes earlier. Once they were both seated Maria turned to face him, "Here is the truth my father's apartment block is just a, basic, block of flats – most are run-down. Plus I'm not here to promote my father's business I have run away from home, I'm only seventeen."

"Thank you for being honest with me, that business suit I saw you in, that's not yours is it?"

"No it isn't, it belongs to my cousin; I borrowed it – no I pinched it," she told him.

He turned, looked at her and then asked, "What is your own then?"

There were tears forming in her eyes, now, "Only the clothes you see me in; the trainers aren't mine though – I pinched those from a shop. As to how I got here I stowed away on a ship that was bound for these shores. Finally I live in that boarded up shop." It was then that she broke down in floods of tears.

"Don't cry, the commander of HART told her, in a gentle voice; and then, he was unsure why but, he held her to him. "I'm glad you've been honest with me. I'll help you."

She, suddenly, peered into his, gentle looking, face, "You will?" she asked in disbelief. Here was a man who wanted to help her; since she'd arrived in England many men she'd met had, simply, taken advantage of her as she was so young.

Ronan smiled at her, "Of course I will, I'm not an ogre," and he kissed her, on the forehead. He then looked at his *Rolex* watch, a present from his, now deceased, wife. "Shall we go for some lunch?"

"Okay," Maria answered and took her trainers off, she had, lovely, slender feet. She then popped the trainers in the carrier bag and got up from the bench; to Ronan she simply said, Catch me if you can," and then Miss Sanchez ran off in the direction from which they'd just come.

As he watched her run Ronan thought to himself *I wonder what she'd look like with no clothes on*, then he reprimanded himself for even thinking such a thought he got up and, steadily, followed her.

*****

In the Iranian desert Commander Most climbed to her feet, the wreckage of the second *HIND* still burning fiercely, the final *HAVOC* helicopter seemed to have gone; she wandered over to the, dead, bodies of Commander's Cutler and Samuels and removed their Beretta *Cougar* weapons, she then did the same to Commander Smith, also relieving him of his M12; finally she made her way over to Commander Hunter's body, relieving him of his Beretta semi-automatic pistol but the three M12s he'd been carrying were wrecked. She also relieved him of the pack on his back, which contained the TAC-SAT. Of Leon there was no sign.

Hopefully, as the back-pack was reinforced with *Kevlar* armour, the TAC-SAT would have suffered only minimal damage, if any. Again like Commander Hunter before her Celia first contacted HART headquarters where Dan Manto was now the duty officer; she explained the situation, as best she could, and requested he contact H-Moscow and request that a *Pave Low IV* be sent to the same position as the *Falcon* had earlier, with a couple of extra pilots on board that could fly a *HIND* helicopter – she told him why.

"I'll get onto it right away," he informed the commander. "However, as it's now 01:00 the helicopter you've requested won't be with you until approximately 10:00, possibly a little later, and that'll be travelling at maximum speed."

"That'll be fine," Commander Most answered, "I'll leave it to you." She knew she could rely on Dan. Once she'd finished speaking to him, Celia figured she might as well get some rest, so she dug a hole and buried the weapons and then went to sleep herself, on the cold, sandy, floor of the desert.

The next day, Celia rose from her makeshift bed, and went over to one of the box cars to wait. She knew each crate of coins weighed 500kg and there were forty of them, a total weight of 20,000kg; as the HART helicopter was able to transport 21,000kg all the crates should fit aboard the *Pave Low*. Then all the HART commanders bodies, with the exception of Commander Hunter – who was in several pieces,, along with the weapons, both HART and *Proagnon*, plus the TAC-SAT, would fit aboard the *HIND*. Producing her own *Cougar* Commander Most stood guard.

At about 12:15 the *Pave Low IV* arrived, the aircraft was piloted by Colonel Sebastian *Seb* Mcintyre, with his co-pilot Lieutenant Alice *Ali* Havers. The helicopter hovered, its whirling rotors throwing up clouds of sand, the closer it got to the ground the quicker the sand whipped about; Celia Most could feel the downdraft created by the whirling blades. Finally the helicopter landed and came to rest. Once it had stopped Alice Havers appeared in the doorway.

"Where's everybody else?" she enquired of Commander Most.

"Everybody else is dead, apart from – I think – Commander Leon Bigship, who I think has been captured. Anyway, we need to transport these crates of rare, gold, coins, to the airfield outside Urgench."

The lieutenant nodded and stepped from the aircraft; before she stepped outside she called over to her superior, "Colonel, set the *board* up."

The *boar*d was a long flat board, type device, with another board on top with castors on that could be pushed from one end to the other. Alice joined Commander Most at the box car and carried the first crate over to the *board* and set it on the board with castors on; once both women were sure it was safe they sent the crate along the *board*. At the other end the colonel and one of the extra pilots lifted it off; slowly, each crate made its way into the *Pave Low*, eventually all the crates were stacked, safely, aboard the aircraft.

Once this task was finished Alice Havers re-boarded the helicopter, the two extra pilots, both were men, climbed out and joined Commander Most on the desert floor, closing the, sliding, door to the HART air machine behind them. The helicopter, with its 20.000kg cargo on board, lifted off into the sky overhead, and then began its seven hundred mile journey north eastward.

The three remaining HART personnel loaded the weapons, equipment, and all the intact bodies, plus Commander Hunter's nametag, identity card and dog-tag, aboard the undamaged *HIND*. Once all this had been done they boarded the Mi-24 helicopter and started up the twin Isotov TV3-117 turbine engines, hoping neither had clogged with sand; luckily neither had so the helicopter was able to rise, vertically, into the sky.

*****

The two Mi-28s descended, and landed, in *Proagnon's* underground bunker; once both had landed the armed *Proagnon* soldier pushed Commander Leon Bigship along the corridor, Mitchell Walker following behind. "Take him to the interrogation room, I'll be along shortly, and secure him" he called to the soldier.

The soldier called back to his superior, "Yes sir," then to Leon he simply said, "move." To emphasise his point he pushed the barrel of the assault rifle into the man's back. Wearily Commander Bigship trudged forwards; eventually he was ordered to stop outside a guarded door. The *Proagnon* guard opened the door and followed the two other men inside, they seated Leon in one of the wooden chairs – while the first soldier kept his weapon aimed at the HART commander, the other tied him to the chair, tightly.

A few moments later Mr Walker entered the room with a variety of torture devices. These devices included: a cattle prod, a box of matches, two electrodes attached to a battery, and some knuckle dusters. Once he'd set these items down, on the table, between the two of them he casually looked up at the second guard – who was a big, burly, looking man – and simply said, in an orderly and authoritative tone of voice, "Strip him."

The soldier just said, "Yes sir," and proceeded to undress Commander Bigship. Once he was undressed all three *Proagnon* men looked at the HART commander's, naked, body and laughed. Leon just had to sit there, he felt completely embarrassed.

Walker dismissed the two guards and stared at his captive, "You will tell me what I want to know or I will use these implements on you." Leon Bigship just sat there, staring at the *Proagnon* man with contempt. "Now," he studied Leon's identity card, "Commander Leon Bigship, where is the HART aircraft carrier located?"

Commander Bigship just stared at his torturer, not saying a word. "Tell me!" demanded Mitchell.

"No," Leon told him. "You can torture me all you want, I will never tell you."

"You're either very brave or very stupid," his torturer said to him, attaching the clamps that held the electrodes to the HART man's nipples; he then turned the dial on the battery and an electrical current jolted Leon's body. "Now tell me and the pain will stop, refuse to tell me and I move onto the next level; this is only level 1, there are a total of 5 levels."

"I thought it wasn't working," remarked the HART commander conversationally. Mitchell twisted the dial, on the battery, and a more powerful current jolted Leon's body. Again Walker demanded to know, again Leon refused so level 3 was used.

"You are exceedingly stubborn," remarked the *Proagnon* deputy leader. "I can see I'm going to have to use different tactics, he picked up the cattle prod and pressed it, lightly, into Leon's lower body. Commander Bigship howled in pain, and slumped back in the chair.

"Okay, torture time over for now, but you will *crack* in the end" Walker announced and then called the guards in. "Take him to one of the cells," he ordered. Then to Commander Bigship he said quietly, but menacingly, "Take this time to consider your options, old man, we shall meet again soon, and, in the end, you will plead for your life."

Leon just said nothing andt let the guards untie him and drag him from the room.

*****

In Piccadilly Ronan had caught up with Miss Sanchez, at the Piccadilly entrance to Green Park, and handed her, borrowed, trainers back to her, he didn't judge her as a bad person – just maybe slightly misguided, and they walked off, in the direction of the little café Commander Strobing had been to earlier, hand in hand; it felt strange to Mr Strobing to be walking, down the street, with a woman twenty years younger than himself, people they passed would stare at them but make no comment.

The two of them entered the café, selected a table by the window, and they both ordered Scampi & Chips; as they ate they talked, Ronan happened to mention he was single, following the unfortunate and untimely death of his wife – but he had a son aged nine. "I like children," Maria enthused, "tell me Mr Strobing, is there anyone special in your life, apart from your son, at the moment?"

"Not at the moment," he responded honestly – well as honest as he could, he, suddenly, thought he saw Miss Sanchez's eyes light up at this bit of information; Ronan could tell what she was thinking, yet she was way too young to have a relationship with him. They then talked about her upbringing in America, but then she mentioned that the previous year a Russian had rented a room for the night. Ronan asked her what the Russian's name had been, he was interested – for some unknown reason; Miss Sanchez told him, his name had been Sergey Satov; she'd tried to seduce him but he hadn't been remotely interested.

Commander Strobing was shocked at her admission; so her father, plus her, had harboured a terrorist for one night. Did he tell her the Russian was now dead, still Ronan thought it was unimportant now and decided not to tell her.

They finished their meal, drank their drinks of tea, paid up and departed. Leaving the café Ronan led Maria to the hotel and took her inside. She sat on one of the chairs, in the foyer, while her companion enquired, at the reception, of the quickest and cheapest way to travel to Doncaster. He was informed that it would, probably be quicker by aeroplane; yet it may prove cheaper to travel by train. He thanked the receptionist, led Maria out and they walked back to the entrance with Green Park.

As there had been a, light, rain shower while they'd been in the café the air around them felt damp. "C'mon," Maria urged him, removing her trainers again, "live dangerously," and she ran off again across the meadows.

If only you knew he thought and set off after her, walking more slowly. Upon reaching a set of trees he came across a T-shirt hanging from one of the branches – it looked like hers but he wasn't sure – and further on he found a pair of jeans. *Oh God, she hasn't has she?* Commander Strobing wondered, as he placed the, discarded, garments in the plastic bag. Eventually he found her rolling about, naked as he'd thought, on the grass. "Get some clothes on," he growled, tossing her T-shirt and jeans at her; though even he had to admit she was quite attractive.

Reluctantly, or so it seemed, she put the garments back on and then apologised to him. "No harm done," he told her and then asked curiously, "why did you do it?"

"I guess I wanted you to take more notice of me," she answered, "plus I quite like you. You're different from the other men I've met; you didn't try to take advantage of me just now like some people would have done."

"You certainly achieved your first goal," Ronan responded to the young woman standing in front of him. "As for the second thing, yes, I admit I like you, but nothing will ever come of it, I'm twenty years older than you. The reason I'm different from other men is, probably, partly due to the age difference between us, I've already been married and have a son; so, therefore, I have a greater respect for women." He then took her hand and led her over to a bench, where they seated themselves and just chatted for most of the afternoon, Ronan found he was beginning to like this young woman more, but if he did involve himself with Miss Sanchez would it be a wrong move? Should he just send her back to America?

At about 16:00 Maria took Ronan's hand and they walked back to the *Ritz* hotel; as they parted at the bottom of the stone steps Maria leaned up and kissed him, he didn't object this time. Once their lips had parted Ronan said to Maria, "Maria, I'm thinking of going home tomorrow. Would you care to join me?"

He could tell by the look on her face that she was thinking; he waited with bated breath, finally she announced, "Yes! I think I would like to come to your home and meet your son." She paused and then continued, "Book it and we'll discuss it more a bit later on. Meet me in the bar at 20:00." With that they parted company, Ronan Strobing walked inside the hotel, and went up to his room; he had about an hour and a half before the hotel served dinner at 18:00.

*****

Over at HART headquarters, in Switzerland, Commander Celia Most had returned to find the chief receptionist seated in the, overall, commander's office. "Where's Commander Strobing?" Mrs Most asked, apparently shocked by his absence.

Gwyneth Jones looked up at her superior, "He's had to travel to England for a few days, so he asked me if I would take, temporary, command until either Commander Bigship, you or he returned. I'm surprised he didn't tell you of his plans."

Celia, who didn't want to get on the wrong side of Gwyneth, or Ronan for that matter, simply said, "I seem to remember he mentioned something about going to England, but I didn't think he meant right now."

Gwyneth rose from the chair of command and Commander Most took her place. She had resumed, overall, command again.

*****

In the *Proagnon* bunker Commander Leon Bigship's naked body, together with the suit he'd been wearing, had been tossed, casually, into one of the cells.

The cell he'd been thrown into was a, small, boxlike, cell with a heavy, metal, door. Like most, old, prison cells it had just basic facilities: there was a hole in the floor that acted as a toilet, and a straw, covered, mattress that acted as a bed; the only window was in the door, there was no window to the outside; probably as the prison cell was underground.

Viewing his surroundings and seeing no immediate way out and knowing, even if he did find a way out, the bunker would be crawling with the blue uniformed soldiers so Leon redressed in the business suit he'd been wearing when he'd been captured; he knew his Beretta would've been confiscated, plus any other weapons that he'd had on him. Resignedly he sighed and seated himself on the makeshift bed, Leon's chest and groin hurt from the mild torture; his torturer, he'd recognised the man, he'd said he'd return for Commander Bigship so, at the moment, Leon had no other option than to wait and get some rest, if he could.

*****

The next day, in London, Ronan packed his suitcase and left the *Ritz* hotel at about 10:40; he met Maria Sanchez outside, she was wearing the same clothes as the day before, they'd arranged to meet the previous evening, and walked off together – holding hands – in the direction of Piccadilly Circus tube station.

Ronan explained that the *Tube* was similar to the American *Metro* system, but it was mainly confined to big cities; they finally reached their destination a while later and walked down the steps into the, well lit, underground area. Commander Strobing booked them two tickets – one for him and one for his young, female, travelling companion – for the 11:30 train direct to London's King's Cross; from there they would board a train at the railway station, this would take them direct to Doncaster railway station.

The underground train arrived a minute or two late; the two companions boarded, along with quite a few other commuters, the doors slid shut and the train set off. The *tube* train arrived at the station, at King's Cross, at around 11:45 and everyone got off. Mr Strobing, together with Miss Sanchez and ascended the stairs to the open air; crossing a few streets they reached the main railway station and Commander Strobing purchased two tickets for the 17:00 train from London King's Cross to Doncaster station – the journey should take approximately an hour and thirty five minutes.

As it was nearly time for lunch the two companions had a lunch of steak pie, potatoes, vegetables and gravy for lunch – Maria had two helpings, Ronan was surprised at this, this was followed by a dessert of apple pie & custard. Afterwards they left the restaurant and exited the railway station, the two of them wandered around the surrounding streets, just killing time until the train arrived at five.

Thankfully the high speed, *Intercity*, train arrived, but it arrived about half an hour late; Ronan and Maria climbed aboard the carriage numbered five, loaded the suitcase in the luggage compartment, and then found their seats.

Approximately ten minutes later the train set off on its 170 mile journey and, finally, arrived at its destination of Doncaster railway station at 19:05. Both people, along with quite a few others, got off the carriage they were in and exited the station; finding a taxi they travelled the final 7 miles to *Robin Hood* airport. "Why are we here?" asked the young woman as she saw where they were. "You're not thinking of sending me back home are you?"

"No, of course not," Mr Strobing answered, taking his case from the driver. "As for why we're here you'll see." He then paid the driver the £15 fare. The taxi driver thanked the HART commander, climbed into the taxi and drove away.

Ronan led Maria inside the building as it had started to drizzle. He then walked over to one of the security personnel, and flashed his HART pass at the man; instantly he was rewarded with a smile, and the guard hurried into another room, Mr Strobing followed him.

Ronan reappeared a moment later brandishing a set of keys, he was followed by a different man; the two men followed by Miss Sanchez left the building and crossed to some garages, where Commander Strobing walked inside, once the garage was unlocked, and reappeared about five minutes later driving his *red* 4 x 4. Stopping beside Maria he helped her load the suitcase in the boot, and then she climbed in the passenger seat of the vehicle; her, male, companion got in the driver's seat and drove the automobile from the airport.

He then drove his vehicle the 56 mile journey to his hometown of Hull; the journey took just under an hour. "I've got to make a couple of calls first, before we go home."

"Okay," Maria said from the passenger seat. "Where to first?"

"Firstly I've got to visit my mother-in-law, and then I've got to visit my sister-in-law and pick up my son. I will be dropping you off at my mother-in-law's; I thought you could keep her company for a while."

"Okay," Miss Sanchez sighed, not sounding entirely happy, "I thought the plan was to collect your son and go to your house, be a family."

"Give it a day or two, I've got to get Simon used to the idea first."

"I understand that," she announced, "but, surely, the final decision is yours," she looked at Ronan.

"It is," he answered, pulling up outside a house, "but I've got Simon's feelings to consider." They, both got out his vehicle and walked to the front door, Ronan knocked; the door was answered, after a moment, by Elle Stevens.

When she saw who it was she said, "Hello Ronan, it's lovely to see you, who's your friend?"

"This," answered her son-in-law, indicating Maria; "is Miss Maria Sanchez. If it is okay with you I'd like to leave her here, keep you company while Arnold's incapacitated. By the way how is he?"

"Unfortunately Arnold has had to be moved to the intensive care unit as his condition's worsened, that happened while you were away. I would be glad to have some company, at this time, Melissa's always busy with her latest man and Simon wants to do the complete opposite of what I want to do. So I'll be glad of some female company," Mrs Stevens told him.

"Thank you," said her son-in-law, and then left to let the two women get acquainted. He climbed into the 4 x 4 and drove round to see his son. Once he reached the house belonging to Melissa Stevens he parked up, got out, and went and knocked on the door; there was a blue *Toyota* pickup in the drive, he was sure it wasn't Isaac's.

The door was answered a minute or two later by Melissa, she was wearing only a towel, "Hello," Ronan said, "I've come for Simon."

"He's in the front room, watching TV," she answered. It was then that a different black man descended the stairs, like Melissa he was only wearing a towel. "Ronan, this is Eric, my latest boyfriend. Eric, this is Ronan, my brother-in-law."

"Hello," Ronan greeted him cheerfully.

"Hello," growled Eric in response.

"Be a love and fetch my dressing gown," Melissa told Eric. "I just want a quick word with Ronan." Eric turned and Melissa patted his towel covered backside, "Don't worry I'll be up in a moment." One he was out of earshot the young woman turned to her brother-in-law, "Isaac, you remember him," Ronan nodded, "caught this flu like bug, similar to Dad, and so he felt he ought to leave – he didn't want to pass it on to, either, Simon or me. As I didn't hear from him for a week I took on Eric, unfortunately though, he's a married man and so I don't think it'll last; Isaac was good to me but I haven't heard from him since he left, that was a month back." Melissa lowered her voice as she said the next bit, "If you ever want to see me again, anytime, you've got my number, you know, just as friends."

Ronan simply nodded, "Can I take Simon home?" He knew she wouldn't have any objection, as Simon was his son.

"Of course, I think he's enjoyed his stay here, but he has been a little quiet since Isaac left."

"I suppose you've heard the latest on your father," Mr Strobing said to Miss Stevens as Eric reappeared with her dressing gown.

"No I haven't," she replied, slipping into the gown, "what's happened?"

"Just that he's been moved to the intensive care unit," her brother-in-law answered conversationally. "Apparently he's in a bad way." Melissa's face as she digested this new information was a picture.

"I'll go and see him tomorrow," she quickly answered, and then let Ronan past to fetch his son. Simon, who seemed not to have heard a thing, was overjoyed to see his father, "Where have you been?" the youngster asked; he had a slight runny nose, and complained of stomach pains.

"I'll tell you at home," Commander Strobing said. Simon collected what he'd brought with him and he, together with his father bid Melissa and Eric farewell and, left the house and climbed aboard the 4 x 4. Ronan noticed his son sniffing the air inside the *Hyundai*, "Dad, have you had a woman in here?" Simon seemed very perceptive nowadays.

At least his son had come straight to the point, so Ronan would be honest with him, "Yes I have. I brought somebody to stay with Gran, while Granddad is in hospital. Actually, I need to talk to you about her at home."

They drove the few streets to their house; it did seem empty without Mandy and Zoe. As soon as they entered Simon had to dash upstairs, to the bathroom, while Ronan took his suitcase into his bedroom and began to unpack. About a quarter of an hour later Simon emerged from the bathroom and descended the stairs; Ronan followed about ten minutes afterwards, and joined his son in the front room; he seated himself beside his son and said to him, "I've been, on business, in London. I've got you a present." Mr Strobing handed his son a rectangular, shaped, object – which made it slightly obvious it was a book – wrapped in Christmas wrapping paper. "That was all I could find," the boy's father told him, indicating the wrapping paper.

Simon tore open the paper to reveal *The Hound of the Baskervilles*, the full unedited edition. "Thanks Dad, I'll treasure it forever." Placing the book beside him Simon then said to his father, "I believe you were going to tell me about this new woman."

"Ah that," Ronan answered. "Where to begin; I met her in London and I think she's taken quite a liking to me although..." he paused, unsure how to say the next bit.

"Go on," Simon prompted.

Ronan realised that Simon deserved the truth, "To be honest with you Maria, that's her name is more like a big sister to you as she's only seventeen, twenty years younger than me. Now I want your opinion, with her being that age, would you want her as your new Mum?" He looked into his son's blue eyes trying to read his thoughts.

After a moments pause Simon announced, "No I wouldn't. However, it's up to you." Although they were father and son Ronan treated Simon as an equal, never dictating unless it was absolutely necessary.

"I'll be bringing her here tomorrow, just for a day, to get your full opinion of her," the commander of HART told his son.

"Okay," the boy responded. "But Dad, why don't you marry Aunt Melissa? I like her, plus she's more your age."

"She's with Eric at the moment, and anyway would you want me to?"

"Of course I would, but it's up to you," was the answer. Ronan said he'd think about it, and then told his son he was just going into the study. Once he was in the study Ronan dusted off the STU-8, picked up the handset and dialled an international number

*****

Celia Most picked up the receiver in the HART commander's office. "Hello."

"Celia, how are you?" He was happy to hear her voice again and didn't mind showing it. "How did the operation in Iran go?"

Ronan noticed her pause before she answered, "I'm fine thank you Commander Strobing." He noticed her answer seemed a bit guarded. "As for the operation it was a complete disaster."

Curiously Commander Strobing enquired, "Why? What went wrong?"

"*Proagnon* forces attacked us, we lost all four of our new commanders plus Commander Bigship was captured. That is everything sir." Now he knew why Celia's response had had seemed guarded. "What do we do now?"

Commander Strobing considered the options before replying, "We have to mount a rescue mission somehow. Before the satellite was destroyed see if it got a fix on where that missile was launched from, if it did that's where Leon will be. Choose a small squad, Dan Anco, Theresa Robins, Shinto Howell and one other – your choice, and deploy them to that area. Got all that?"

"Yes sir," was the deputy commander's response. "Anything else you'd like me to do?"

"Ah yes," was the reply, "see if there's anything, in our archives, concerning a Don or Maria Sanchez, if they have links to *Proagnon*, as they harboured our Russian friend, Sergey Satov, for a night last year. Probably it's totally innocent but I just want you to run a check for me."

"I'll see to it straight away," was the reply. "Did you manage to secure any further funding?"

"No I didn't," was the truthful reply. "Queen Charlotte seemed most obstinate, maybe it had something to do with that picture I showed her, of her consort collaborating with Sandy Tulliver and, therefore, having links with *Proagnon*. However, on my return home I learnt that, you remember that virus," Celia confirmed she did, "apparently it's reached Hull, my sister-in-law's boyfriend caught it and not wanting to risk her catching it he left. She hasn't seen or heard from him since he left."

The deputy commander of HART listened to this with interest, "I think I'd best contact Mike, see how he is, as for that other stuff you want I'll contact you as soon as any link has been confirmed or not. By the way how's Simon?"

Ronan's voice sounded like he was close to tears. "I think he's got the virus, and I'm afraid I'll lose him too. I can't lose him as well." Celia, although she was hundreds of miles away, knew exactly how her superior felt.

*****

Commander Most, good as her word, first contacted reception. Lisa Bell was on duty. "Yes ma'am," she said.

"Lisa, can you see if we have any information concerning a Don or Maria Sanchez, and any possible links to *Proagnon*, then report back to me."

"I'll see to it at once ma'am." Commander Most then dialled her own home; the phone rang several times before her son answered.

"Hello," he said as he picked the receiver up.

"Mike," his mother replied. "There's a new virus been unleashed in Hull, so be careful." She then thought she heard a, female, giggle in the background. "Have you got a girl with you?"

Her son knew the game was up, "Yes I have mother, her name's Maria, we met earlier today."

He knew his mother didn't approve by what she said next, "What would your father say? Is he even there?" Her tone of voice told him she didn't approve and, probably, knew what he'd been up to.

"I haven't seen Dad for weeks," her son responded.

"What?" Celia nearly shouted. She knew the longest Peter Most had been out of contact was a week. It was most unlike him. "If you hear from him let me know."

"Yes Mum," and he rang off.

Celia was now frustrated, had her husband contacted this mystery virus? Suddenly the STU-8 warbled; she picked up the handset, "Yes," she said, not angrily but not cheerfully.

"Ma'am," Lisa Bell's cheerful voice said, "I've run those checks on Don and Maria Sanchez, and there are no links between either and *Proagnon*."

"Thank you Miss Bell," Commander Most replied, regaining her composure. "That'll be all." Mrs Most then rang off and then rang Commander Strobing at home. When he picked up she told him, "I've had the archives checked and there is no connection between Don, or Maria, Sanchez and *Proagnon*. On a different note I've contacted my son, he's been entertaining a girl named Maria – but that's beside the point, anyway he hasn't heard from my husband for a few weeks now."

"Thanks for the information Celia; I'll do a bit of checking myself."

"Okay, see you soon Commander Strobing," and she rang off

*****

At the *Proagnon* bunker Mitchell Walker had given orders that the HART commander, Leon Bigship, was to be brought to the interrogation room again; two *Proagnon* soldiers went and dragged Leon, from his cell, to the interrogation room, when they arrived Walker was waiting for them. He'd selected, for today's torture, the electrodes, again, the matches which hadn't been used last time, plus some kind of stick.

As on the previous occasion Leon was tied to the chair using strong rope, "Strip his top half," demanded Walker, "let's see if he'll talk this time." The men stripped Commander Bigship as their leader had requested, and then quietly left the room.

"Pigs," Leon shouted after them, and then Mitchell Walker walked over and attached the electrodes to Leon's nipples again. "I'll never talk to you, you bastard pig."

"We'll see about that shall we Commander Bigship of HART?" Walker remarked, smiling evilly. He then asked his first question, "What is the strength of the HART forces?"

"I thought you'd know that," Leon said, almost, conversationally. Suddenly his body was wracked with pain as an electric current coursed through his body; Mitchell smiled in satisfaction.

"That's level three," he told Leon. "There are only two further levels to go, my friend, nobody's ever been to level five, I wonder if you will. All you have to do to make the pain stop is tell me what I want to know."

"Never!" Commander Bigship retorted fiercely. "I will never tell you anything under torture."

"Oh well," sighed the deputy leader of *Proagnon*. "Guards," he opened the interrogation room door and called.

Two guards entered the room, "Remove his shoes and socks;" Mitchell then, not too kindly, removed the electrodes from Leon's exposed chest. "What is about to happen next won't hurt, much," Walker announced, removing twenty one matches from the pack, on the table.

He then instructed the two *Proagnon* soldiers to place each match in between Commander Bigship's nail and the skin, on his fingers and toes, but not to be too gentle when they placed the matches in. Leon winced, a little, as the matches were inserted. Once they'd performed their task the guards left the room. "Now then," announced Walker as he struck the other match, on the wall, thus lighting it, "we'll see what sort of man you really are."

As he watched the match being lit and then Mr Walker started advancing towards him the colour drained from Commander Bigship's face; he hoped the man was bluffing, though part of him told him he wasn't. Walker lit the other twenty matches – in turn - and then retired from the room. "Now we'll let the fun begin," he said as he reached the door, and then he was gone. Leon looked at the burning matches knowing he, probably, couldn't extinguish all of them in the few minutes he had, but he knew the pain would probably be excruciating.

He couldn't let this man, Walker, win; he did consider making fists with his hands but surely then the matches would push further into his skin. Then, quite suddenly, the match that was lodged in his right thumb fell out and onto the floor. Quickly Leon, using his right thumb, extracted and flicked the other matches from his right hand; extracting a pair of tweezers from his trouser pocket, lucky they hadn't thought to search him, and plucked the matches from his left hand.

He then brought his feet up, as far as he could manage, bent forward and plucked the matches from his toes. He figured he was safe now, his torturer, though, would, probably, have other ideas.

About five minutes after he'd left Mitchell Walker entered the room and saw Leon Bigship of HART, smiling up at him, "Sorry, the plan didn't work," Leon had managed to untie his bonds, but made it appear as if he were still securely tied up. Slowly Walker picked up the stick that was on the table, and advanced towards the HART operative, once he was near enough Leon lashed out with his feet, managing to kick and knock Mr Walker off his feet. As he fell backwards, onto the floor, Commander Bigship jumped to his feet and darted for the door.

"You'll never get out," Mitchell told him, as he got, unsteadily, to his feet again. "There are guards everywhere."

"Let me worry about that," the HART commander said. All of a sudden Leon felt a sharp pain, across his back, as Mitchell hit him with the stick, and he fell unconscious.

"Back to the cells for you," announced Walker triumphantly. "Guards!"

*****

In Switzerland, after she'd come off the phone with Commander Strobing Commander Most had enquired if the satellite had detected where the missile had come from that had destroyed it; she'd been rewarded with some positive answers for a change. Once the data had been assessed and the location of the *Proagnon* underground bunker had been pinpointed Commander Most, using her wrist communicator – these weren't that widely used now – contacted, in turn, Major Shinto Howell, Sergeant Dan Anco – who was also the HART explosives expert, Captain Theresa Robins, and new recruit Private James Shearman.

Once all four of them arrived – in the office and were seated - Celia outlined the situation, and the events that had led up to this point, plus the operation the four of them were required for. "Any questions?" she asked once she'd finished.

"What sort of gear will we be using?" enquired Theresa Robins.

"As well as wearing black, commando style, uniforms – along with gas masks, you will be wearing the new *Kevlar* mark II body armour. As for the *gear* you'll be taking you'll all be carrying your, standard, Beretta semi-automatic pistols, gas, plus smoke, grenades, a couple of *flashbang* grenades, a TAC-SAT in a *Kevlar* lined backpack, and of course an M16A2 rifle.

*****

The development of the M16A2 rifle was originally requested by the United States Marine Corps as a result of the USMC's combat experience in Vietnam with the XM16E1 and M16A1. The Marines were the first branch of the U.S. Armed Forces to adopt the M16A2 in the early/mid 1980s with the United States Army following suit in the late 1980s. Modifications to the M16A2 were extensive. In addition to the new rifling, the barrel had been made with a greater thickness in front of the front sight post to resist bending in the field and to allow a longer period of sustained fire without the barrel overheating. The rest of the barrel was maintained at the original thickness to enable the M203 grenade launcher to be attached. The front sight was now a square post with 4 detent positions; this was adjustable for vertical zeroing by using a cartridge, nail or special tool. A new adjustable rear sight was added, allowing the rear sight to be dialled in for specific range settings between 300 and 800 metres to take full advantage of the ballistic characteristics of the new SS109 rounds and to allow windage adjustments without the need of a tool or cartridge. The flash suppressor was again modified, this time to be closed on the bottom so it would not kick up dirt or snow when being fired from the prone position, and acting as a recoil compensator. The front grip was modified from the original triangular shape to a round one, which better fitted smaller hands and could be fitted to older models of the M16. The new handguards were also made symmetrical so that the armouries needn't separate left and right spares. The handguard retention ring was tapered to make it easier to install and uninstall. The pistol grip added a notch for the middle finger and more texture to enhance the grip. The buttstock was lengthened by 5/8 inch (16 mm). The new buttstock became ten times stronger than the original due to advances in polymer technology since the early 1960s. Original M16 stocks were made from fibreglass impregnated resin; the newer stocks were engineered from DuPont Zytel glass-filled thermoset polymers. The new stock included a fully textured polymer buttplate for better grip on the shoulder, and it also retained a panel for accessing a small compartment inside the stock, often used for storing a basic cleaning kit. The heavier bullet reduced muzzle velocity from 3,200 feet (980 m) per second (975 m/s), to about 3,050 feet (930 m) per second (930 m/s). The A2 also used a faster twist rifling to allow the use of a trajectory-matched tracer round. A spent case deflector was incorporated into the upper receiver immediately behind the ejection port to prevent cases from striking left-handed users.

The action was also modified, replacing the fully-automatic setting with a three-round burst setting. When using a fully-automatic weapon, poorly trained troops often held down the trigger and *spray* when under fire. The U.S. Army concluded that three-shot groups provided an optimum combination of ammunition conservation, accuracy and firepower. There were mechanical flaws in the M16A2 burst mechanism. The trigger group did not reset when the trigger was released. If the user released the trigger between the second and third round of the burst, for example, the next trigger pull would only result in a single shot. Even in semi-automatic mode, the trigger group mechanism affected weapon handling. With each round fired, the trigger group cycled through one of the three stages of the burst mechanism. Worse, the trigger pull at each of these stages could vary as much as 6 lbf (27 N) in pressure differential, detracting from accuracy.

All together, the M16A2s new features added weight and complexity to the M16 series. Critics also pointed out that neither of the rear sight apertures was ideally sized. The smaller aperture was described as being too small, making quick acquisition of the front sight post difficult; and the larger aperture was described as being too large, resulting in decreased accuracy. To make matters worse, the rear sight apertures were not machined to be on the same plane. In other words, the point of impact changed when the user changed from one aperture to the other. The rear sight's range adjustment feature was rarely used in combat as soldiers tended to leave the rear sight on its lowest range setting of 300 metres. This distance was seen by many as an excessively long range for the minimum setting, given that most engagements take place at significantly shorter ranges. Despite this criticism, a new rifle was needed both to comply with NATO standardization of the SS109 (M855) and to replace aging Vietnam era weapons in the inventory.

Since the introduction of the SS109 rifle had been brought in HART had managed to obtain the aged M16A2 rifles, which had been adjusted to HART specifications by the organisation's technicians.

CHAPTER 6

RESCUE & THE VIRUS SPREADS!

"Are there any more questions?" enquired Commander Celia Most looking around at the four other members of HART.

"What transport will we be using?" Theresa enquired of her superior.

"You will be transported from here to the H-Moscow aircraft carrier, which is, presently, docked off the west coast of Africa, Mauritania I believe, by a *Pave Low* helicopter; from there you will travel aboard a *HIND* helicopter into Iran, and the bunker of our enemies, where, hopefully, you will be able to rescue Commander Bigship." Commander Most looked over at Dan Anco, "Sergeant Anco, take any explosives you feel may be needed," next she turned to Shinto Howell, "Major Howell, you will be carrying the backpack containing the TAC-SAT, to make your mission report afterwards – hopefully your mission will be a very successful one."

"I think that's everything, now you may go and ready yourselves. Dismissed!" and the team of four left the office to return to their quarters – which was located in team C's barracks. Once they'd all left Celia sat back and thought to herself *I just hope we're not too late and Proagnon haven't already killed Leon.*

She felt rather sorry for Private James Shearman as he'd only joined HART a couple of months back; yet here he was, going on this, commando style, mission to rescue one of their own, she sort of wished he hadn't volunteered as he was only young – just 26 – and hadn't been on any other military manoeuvre before; unlike the other three who had been involved in the mission to rescue Dr Hans Schaiffer the year before.

Still Private Shearman knew the risks and had still volunteered.

*****

Over in Hull the weather had started to turn more autumnal, the wind had started to gust – admittedly not all the time – and it had started to rain quite often. Commander Ronan Strobing of Human Alliance for the Retaliation against Terrorism (HART) had booked an appointment with the Strobing family GP, Dr Kazaski, to have his son Simon checked over, and to see if there was any further way he could help his son. Later, that afternoon, he had told Miss Sanchez that he would collect her from Mrs Stevens's house.

They arrived at the GP's surgery at 11:00 for Simon's 11:15 appointment. As they entered Ronan was surprised to see so many other people there, all of them seemed to have the same, or similar, symptoms: runny nose, and an upset stomach, basic flu like symptoms, although it was obvious that some people's noses had bled. Ronan took an appointment number, number 69, and led Simon over to a corner seat, trying to put as much distance between them and the other patients; suddenly, a man started coughing, in fact he started to cough so violently he, actually, shot a stream of blood across the room which hit the wall and made a dark *red* stain.

Eventually, twenty minutes late, Simon's appointment number flashed up on screen; his father took him through to see Dr Kawaski, who diagnosed Simon as having *normal* flu and prescribed him some mild antibiotics; however, to be on the safe side the doctor also advised that that Simon attend the hospital, to undergo a, full, body scan, Simon looked very scared at this but the doctor explained to, both, son and father what this procedure involved.

More reassured Ronan and Simon left the office and made their way through the main reception; as Ronan glanced at the waiting patients he noticed a familiar face, Mike Most. What was Celia's son doing there?

Casually wandering over Mr Strobing asked Mike why he was there; Mike told his mother's work colleague that somebody had been giving out a, new, body spray called *ProPower*, he'd used it a day ago but nothing had happened. Thinking it was faulty he intended to take it back, however, for some reason he'd suddenly started with an upset stomach and a runny nose, although his nasal discharge had – for some reason – been black.

Ronan quickly retreated wishing the young man well, and led Simon out to his red *Hyundai*. He then drove them home and they had some lunch of Fish fingers & Chips. At around 14:00 they boarded Mr Strobing's vehicle and drove to the Chemist's to collect Simon's prescription. The chemist told Ronan that the prescription, for these types of antibiotics, would be ready in about half an hour, so he could either wait or call back later.

Knowing he had also arranged to collect Maria he told the chemist he would call back in a while, so he left and drove to Elle Stevens, Simon had to travel in the back seat, and picked up Maria Sanchez. She hopped in the passenger seat and hugged Ronan fiercely; it was only when she'd stopped that he noticed she was wearing some of Melissa's old clothes, at least they were more respectable than what she wore nowadays.

"What are you looking at me like that for?" she enquired. Ronan just smiled at her.

"It's just that you're wearing some of my sister-in-laws clothing, from her younger days," he replied. Once she was, safely, strapped in Ronan proceeded to drive away, back to the Chemist's, he collected Simon's antibiotics and then resumed the journey home.

Later that evening once Simon had gone to bed Maria snuggled up to his father and put her arm round him, "Ronan," she began.

"Yes Maria," he answered her, thinking he knew what she was about to say. As they were sat there, on the sofa, Miss Sanchez kissed him, lightly, on the cheek.

"Tonight," the young woman said to him, "what are the sleeping arrangements going to be?"

"Well," he began, considering what his answer would be. "I suppose we could share my bed, on one condition." He looked hard, at her.

"And what's that?" she enquired innocently yet with a casual air.

"Absolutely nothing is to happen between us," he informed her; she smiled, sweetly, at him.

"Okay then," Maria Sanchez responded. However, Ronan was sure she was lying to him, but how could he be certain? The only way was to share his bed with this young woman.

A couple of hours later Ronan and Maria ascended the staircase, and he told her he was going to change in his, now deceased, daughter's room; when he returned, a towel wrapped round his waist, Maria was already in bed, although she was sitting up she had the covers pulled up – covering her young body. Commander Strobing climbed in the other side and removed the towel. They lay next to each other and slept.

*****

Next day they both woke and dressed; after breakfast Miss Sanchez offered to tidy up while Ronan took his son out for the morning.

As soon as they'd been gone a couple of minutes Maria Sanchez stopped her tidying up, found the house phone and dialled a number. Once the receiver, at the other end was picked up, all she said was, "Thanks for the other day." She then replaced the receiver, picked it up again and dialled an international number. Once somebody answered, at the other end, she simply said, "Can I come and join you now?"

"Yes, of course," responded the voice at the other end, it was a male voice belonging to a youngish man.

*****

The *Pave Low* helicopter, carrying the four HART commandos, had landed on the H-Moscow; the sliding, left, side door slid open and the four commandos left the MH-53M helicopter to board the waiting Mi-24 *HIND*-D aircraft to travel the next 2400 miles of their journey. Once the HART personnel had strapped themselves in and the pre-flight checks had been completed, the main pilot started the five bladed rotor head and the three bladed tail rotor; once the two IsotovTV3-117 turbine engines had achieved full power the aircraft began to ascend into the sky, up to a service ceiling of 14,000 feet.

The helicopter then began its journey to the *Proagnon* bunker, travelling at its maximum speed of 208 miles per hour it would reach the bunker in about 12 hours, hopefully then they would be able to rescue Commander Bigship.

*****

Several hours into their flight the *HIND*-D attack and transport helicopter was detected, on the radar, in the bunker. One of the radar operators rushed to inform Mr Walker; he knocked on his superior's, office, door and entered when he was requested to. He seated himself, in the chair that he was offered by his superior; once the radar operator was seated Mitchell Walker fixed him with his steely, steady, gaze. "Yes," he said.

"Sir, our *lost HIND* helicopter has just come into our field of radar detection, but it seems to be approaching from the west, as if it's been somewhere else," the young radar operator, named Adam Chambers, reported to his leader. Mitchell Walker considered what the man had told him before issuing a reply.

Finally he said, "Maybe it flew westwards, after the attack to initiate repairs somewhere, probably it's nothing." He was still thinking and wondering why as Adam left the office. He was probably right; still they'd know more when the aircraft landed.

Proagnon scientists had recently invented a truth serum that would loosen any stubborn captive's tongue, at least that's what he'd been told. Mitchell Walker intended to test this claim by injecting Commander Leon Bigship of HART; then he would, hopefully, reveal plenty of information connected with the antiterrorist organisation.

He ordered a couple of guards to bring Leon to the interrogation room, whilst he fetched the truth serum and a hypodermic needle; also the Mi-24 helicopter was due to land in the next couple of minutes.

*****

A hatch slid open, in the desert floor, giving access to the bunker. The helicopter descended into the earth below, and landed on the floor inside the underground base. The side door then slid open and four people dressed in black jumped out.

Seeing they were armed the *Proagnon* soldiers brought their AK-47 assault rifles to bear on the four intruders. The assault rifles spat bullets that connected with the HART personnel, but as the commando squad were all wearing their *Kevlar* body armour not one of them fell.

The four members of the squad then threw their *flashbang* grenades which, as the name suggested, exploded with a flash and a bang disorientating the enemy soldiers; as soon as the, initial, smoke had cleared the M16A2's chattered away firing their, standard issue, 5.56x45mm cartridges, in, rapid, three shot bursts. Many of the shots connected with the enemy and, as they weren't wearing body armour, they fell – red spots appearing on different areas of their chests; for those that managed to survive and got too close the HART operatives soon despatched these men with their Beretta's.

Suddenly a familiar figure came into view, dragged along as he was by two further *Proagnon* soldiers. "Commander Bigship," shouted Theresa, he looked up at her and smiled weakly. She darted forward, the others unable to prevent her doing this, and firing a, quick, three round burst from her assault rifle; the slugs hit the enemy, one man fell – fatally wounded, however, the other man brought his weapon to bear on the, female, HART captain's head. Before he could fire, though, Leon – who had regained some of his strength – managed to lash out with his arm and knocked the assault rifle off aim, and the shot went wide. Theresa, however, fired three more shots – at point blank range – at the man and he fell backwards, a red stain developing on his uniform.

Mitchell Walker, who had been observing proceedings from the shadows, extracted Leon's Beretta *Cougar* 9mm pistol and stepped from his hiding place, he raised the pistol and aimed it at the, two, fleeing figures.

Sergeant Dan Anco saw this movement and shouted out, "Theresa, Leon, behind you." It was then that Mitchell Walker fired.

*****

Over in England Ronan Strobing had made an appointment at the opticians for that afternoon. When he and Simon arrived home they found Maria making a start on lunch; "Ronan," Maria said when she saw them, she looked a bit down Ronan thought, "I have some bad news."

Curious Mr Strobing enquired, "What is it?"

Sadly she responded, "I have to return to America as my father is ill." Ronan could tell Miss Sanchez was lying, if her father was that ill she would've gone already. Even if she was telling the truth then she was showing good manners by letting him know, although Ronan still doubted it was the truth.

*****

So after lunch he took Simon to Melissa's again. Eric answered the door and Mr Strobing said to him, "Can Simon stay with you this afternoon, as I have a few jobs to attend to?" Commander Strobing noticed a scowl cross the married man's face and thought he was going to refuse.

However, Eric looked over his shoulder and back down the corridor, "Melissa!" he called, "Your brother-in-law would like us to look after his son again. Do I say yes?"

"Of course," she shouted back. So the black men turned back to father and son and simply nodded.

"Thanks," Mr Strobing said, and then he looked at Simon, "I'll be back as soon as I can," he kissed his son, on the forehead, and then returned to his 4 x 4. He climbed into the driver's seat and looked over at Maria, "I suppose we'd better get you t *Robin Hood* airport, see when the next flight leaves for *Dulles* airport, just outside your home city of Washington, I believe." Mr Strobing drove over to *Robin Hood* airport; the vehicle arrived at the compound at about 14:00.

Exiting the vehicle the two of them walked inside the main terminal building and looked up at the *departures* board; the next, outward, flight to *Dulles* left the next morning at 11:00. Seeing this Ronan, casually, wandered over to the *Help* desk and enquired if there were any vacant seats left on the flight. He was told, by the assistant, that there was one single seat left and would he like to book it. Informing her that he would he gave his companion's details and paid the £500 for the allocation of the seat, on the 11:00 *American Airlines* flight, the next morning; the plane for the journey would be a Boeing 747-8.

*****

The 747-8 was a development of the Boeing 747, which took advantage of many improvements in technology and aerodynamics. The two variants of the 747-8 were launched in 2005, and, as of 2006, featured a fuselage stretch of 18.3 ft (5.6 m) over the 747-400, bringing the total length of the aircraft to 250 ft 2½ in (76.264 m). The 747-8 was the world's longest passenger airliner, surpassing the Airbus A340-600 by 3.6 ft (1.1 m). With a maximum take-off weight of 975,000 lb (442,000 kg), the 747-8 was the heaviest aircraft, commercial or military, that had been manufactured in the United States.

Compared to the 747-400, the main technical changes were on the wing of the aircraft, which had undergone a complete design overhaul. The sweep and basic structure were kept to contain costs, but the wing was thicker and deeper, with the aerodynamics recalculated. The pressure distribution and bending moments were different, with the new wing for the passenger version had been planned to hold 64,225 US gal (243,120 L) of jet fuel, and the cargo aircraft 60,925 US gal (230,630 L). The new wing had single-slotted outboard flaps and double-slotted inboard flaps. Raked wingtips, similar to the used on the 777-200LR, and 777-300ER models, were used on the new 747 variant instead of the winglets that were used on the 747-400. These wingtip structures helped to reduce the wingtip vortices at the lateral edges of the wings, decreasing wake turbulence and drag, and thereby increasing the aircraft's fuel efficiency.

The extra fuel capacity in the redesigned wing compared to the 747-400 obviated the need to radically change the horizontal tail unit to accommodate any auxiliary tanks, further saving costs. Nonetheless, the vertical tail unit had been raised slightly to 64 feet 2 inches (19.56 m) on the 747-8. Some carbon fibre-reinforced plastic was used as part of the 747-8's airframe to reduce the weight. However, structural changes were mostly evolutionary, rather than revolutionary with respect to the 747-400.

The General Electric GEnx, which was one of the two powerplant choices offered for the Boeing 787, this was the only engine available for the 747-8. However, the 747 variant had been adapted to provide bleed air for conventional aircraft systems and featured a smaller diameter to fit on the 747 wing. The flight tests of the GEnx 2b engine that was fitted to a Boeing 747-100 aircraft at the left inner engine occurred in March 2009.

*****

The 747 has proven to be a very popular freighter, carrying around half of the world's air freight. In an effort to maintain this dominant position, Boeing has designed a freight variant of the 747-8, dubbed *747-8 Freighter* or *747-8F*. The 747-8F had been the initial model to see entry into service (EIS). As on the 747-400F, the upper deck was shorter than on the passenger models; the 18 feet 3½ inches (5.575 m) stretch is just before and just aft of the wing. With a 975,000 lb (442,000 kg) maximum take-off weight, it had a total payload capability of 308,000 lb (140,000 kg) and a range of 4,390 nmi (8,130 km). Four extra pallet spaces were created on the main deck, with either two extra containers and two extra pallets, or three extra pallets, on the lower deck.

The 747-8F was expected to achieve a 16% lower ton-mile operating cost than the 747-400F and offer a slightly greater range. The 747-8F had more payload capacity but had less range than the current 747-400ERF. When Boeing launched the -400ERF, all of the 35,000 lb (16,000 kg) increase in MTOW over the 747-400F 875,000–910,000 lb (397,000–413,000 kg)) allowed airlines to take off with more fuel, burn it during flight, and then land at the same weight as the regular 747-400F. This had increased the range of the 747-400ERF compared to the 747-400F. Cargo carriers often moved machinery or indivisible loads that required a plane with a higher payload and landing capability. As was common with cargo planes, range was given with the maximum payload, not fuel. The 747-8's 65,000 lb

(29,000 kg) MTOW increase had been directed exclusively to its Zero-Fuel weight or payload capacity. If taking off at the maximum payload, the 747-8 takes off with its tanks not full. On trips where the payload was not at maximum, the plane could take on more fuel and, therefore, extend its range.

Cargolux and Nippon Cargo Airlines first ordered the 747-8 with orders for the freighter variant coming in November 2005. Cargolux was to receive the first -8F.

The passenger version, dubbed *747-8 Intercontinental* or *747-8I*, was capable of carrying up to 467 passengers in a 3-class configuration over 9,315 miles at Mach 0.855. The 747-8I could carry 51 further passengers and two more freight pallets with 26% more cargo volume than the 747-400. Despite the initial plans for a shorter stretch than the freighter model, the two variants were of the same length, increasing its passenger capacity and allowing for easier modification of the 747-8I to freighter use, if required. The upper deck had been lengthened on the -8I. New engine technology and aerodynamic modifications allowed for a longer range.

For the 747-8, Boeing proposed making some changes to the interior layout of the aircraft. Most noticeable was the curved stairway to the upper deck and a more spacious main passenger entrance. The 747-8's main cabin used an interior that was similar to that of the 787. The overhead bins were curved, and the centre row was designed to look as though it was attached to the curved ceiling, rather than integrated into the ceiling's curve like on the 777. The windows were also of a similar size to the type used on the 777, which were 8% larger than those on the 747-400s. The 747-8 featured a new solid-state light-emitting diode (LED) lighting system, which could create mood lighting; LED technology also offered improved reliability and lower maintenance costs.

Further down the aircraft, it had been proposed to place cabin-accessible facilities in the *crown* area (the space above the passenger cabin, used for air-conditioning ducts and wiring). The wiring and ducts were moved to the side to create extra space; as a consequence, they did not have windows. This added space was used for galleys and crew rest areas, freeing up main deck space for additional passenger seating. During the initial 747-8 marketing phase, Boeing also proposed creating a revenue-generating *SkyLoft* passenger facility in the crown space. This facility included *SkySuites*, which were small individual compartments with sliding doors or curtains, featuring beds, seating, and entertainment or business equipment. A common lounge area was also provided. Boeing also provided smaller, more modest *SkyBunks*. Access to the crown area was now via a separate stairway at the rear of the aircraft. Passengers using the *SkySuites*, which were sold at a premium price, would sit in regular economy class seats for take-off and landing, and move to the crown area during the flight.

However, in pricing feasibility studies the *SkyLoft* concept was found to be difficult to justify. Therefore, in 2007, Boeing had dropped the *SkyLoft* concept in favour of further upper-deck galley storage options, which were favoured by the airlines.

*****

In the bunker, under Iran, the 9mm cartridge struck the back of Theresa's head, forcing her to let go of Leon and she pitched forwards; falling to the floor of the bunker, a small *red* mark had developed in the back of her head and thin rivulets of blood were leaking from the wound and beginning to mix with her *blonde*, shoulder length, hair. As soon as he felt her body start to crumple Commander Bigship grabbed the two grenades, she still had, from her belt; he selected the one he wanted and casually tossed it back over his shoulder, hoping to catch the man who'd killed Miss Robins and throw his aim.

The *smoke* grenade exploded, throwing out, horrible, *black* smoke; upon seeing their companion fall the other three, male, members of the team were, momentarily, stunned into inaction. Quickly recovering his wits James Shearman rushed forward and grabbed Commander Bigship, by the arm, and dragged him away from any further, immediate, danger whilst Sergeant Anco and Major Howell provided covering fire, from their M16A2's.

James dragged Leon back to the safety of the *HIND* helicopter and climbed inside; the other two personnel followed. The bullets from the enemy's AK-47 assault rifles bounced – harmlessly – off the vehicle's armoured plating. All the HART personnel strapped themselves in except for Major Shinto Howell who lifted the TAC-SAT handset and dialled the number for headquarters. He was just about to press the *connect* button when Commander Bigship stopped him. "Gentleman I believe it's time to despatch our *gas* grenades and then get the hell out of here!" Then he said authoritatively to the pilots, "Begin the take off procedure."

"Yes sir, "they responded in unison and started the, five bladed, rotor head, and the, three bladed, tail rotor turning. Suddenly, the side door was slid open and the three commandos, plus their commander threw their *gas* grenades into the bunker and then Dan Anco, who was nearest the door, slid it shut – re-sealing the hold.

As the Mi-24 helicopter ascended - vertically – the pilots operated the controls that would fire the machine's weapons. The helicopter's twin 7.62mm GshG cannons, located under the nose of the machine opened up; *Proagnon* soldiers who were running toward the helicopter were easily cut down. The top hatch, to the bunker, was still open so the *HIND* had a free run up into the sunny, mid-morning, sky. The *Proagnon* personnel – below – couldn't, really, close the hatch due to the gas.

Thankfully the pilots had refuelled the aircraft – including its external tanks – whilst the *rescue* team had been rescuing Commander Leon Bigship – so the aircraft was full of fuel for the 2400 mile journey back to their base on H-Moscow. As they were travelling the four men, in the cargo compartment were mourning the loss of their friend and comrade, Theresa Robins. Finally Leon broke the silence. "I think I speak for us all when I say Miss Robins was a good friend and trusted comrade;" he turned to James Shearman, "admittedly some of us didn't know her as well as others but I'm sure we will all miss her."

"She died doing the job she was trained for; maybe she was a bit hasty – in her decision – to rush forward and rescue me from those two soldiers. As I say she knew the risks when she joined HART; but there is no excuse for such foolhardy behaviour."

"Anyway," he was still looking at Mr Shearman, "I believe I owe you my thanks – if you hadn't pulled me away, when you did, that man would've probably killed me as well, so thank you…"

"Shearman, James Shearman."

"Thank you Mr Shearman. I am Leon Bigship, as I'm sure you know," Leon said. Then he looked across at Shinto Howell, "Major Howell, please contact headquarters now and inform them of the situation, plus of the, sad, death of Captain Theresa Robins."

"Yes sir," the Japanese man answered, and lifted the TAC-SAT handset and dialled the number for headquarters; he pressed the *connect* button which would scramble the signal.

*****

At HART headquarters Commander Most was just finishing up for the day when the STU-8, on the desk, started to chirrup and warble. Sighing she picked the receiver up, "Hello," she said.

"Ma'am," Major Shinto Howell's voice came back loud and clear. The next two words answered her unasked question, "Mission completed most satisfactorily."

"Were there any casualties?" Mrs Most asked, curious now she knew the outcome. She was afraid of the answer that she was about to receive.

Shinto Howell's voice tone changed slightly, "Unfortunately we lost Captain Theresa Robins. Apart from that we're all okay; we've rescued Commander Bigship and are on the return journey to the aircraft carrier H-Moscow."

"Thank you for letting me know the outcome," Commander Most responded and then replaced the receiver. No sooner had she done that than the STU started warbling again. "Who is it now?" Celia asked herself. Hastily she picked the receiver up, "Hello," she said again.

"Celia," responded Commander Strobing, "I took Simon to see our family doctor the other day and, apparently, he's just got *normal* flu. However, when I came out I saw your son waiting to go in; he seemed to have the same symptoms everyone else – who gets this virus – develops, a runny nose and upset stomach, basically flu like symptoms. It's probably nothing, however, your son did tell me that a couple of days before he'd been given a can of some new body spray, *ProPower* I think it was called – he used it once but said it didn't smell of anything. Like I said it's probably nothing."

"You're probably right," Celia replied, "probably just a bug he's picked up. Onto some other news – that's happened in your absence - I sent a squad to the *Proagnon* bunker in, Iran, to rescue Commander Bigship – as you suggested – and I have just received news that the operation was a complete success; however," Ronan noticed a change in his long time friend's tone, "we lost Theresa Robins in the attempt."

The silence that greeted Commander Most was very audible in the office. Finally, after what seemed an eternity, her superior spoke, sadness in his voice, "Please send my condolences to her family in Scotland. I shall be staying on here for the next day or two then I will be returning to Geneva."

"That's fine Ronan. I look forward to your imminent return." Celia replaced the STU's handset and left the office to return to her residence for the evening and overnight. Informing the receptionist, Joshua Smith, of her whereabouts – in case anything else should happen – she left the reception area, and made her way out the main building.

*****

Maria Sanchez waited for Commander Strobing to fall asleep, on the sofa, and then she made her way – stealthily, her bare feet making no sound on the carpeted floor – into the hallway; she, quietly, made her way to the house phone – she didn't know about the STU-8 – and dialled the same international number she'd used earlier that day, she just hoped that the person she wanted hadn't gone to bed yet, or wasn't out.

The phone was answered at the other end. "Hello," he said.

"Marco, it's Maria," she responded trying to keep her voice quiet. "I am afraid that the next flight to *Dulles* leaves

Robin Hood at 11:00 (local time) tomorrow. Therefore, I shall have to stay here tonight – with him – and fly home to you tomorrow. I should arrive at *Dulles* at around 16:30; you can pick me up then."

The young man then said something further. Miss Sanchez smiled. "Oh yes, I'll give him a night to remember." Then she replaced the receiver and made her way back to the commander of HART's side. Suddenly Mr Strobing yawned and awoke – to see the young woman gazing affectionately at him.

"Sorry," he murmured as way of apology, "must've dropped off; probably starting to feel my age a bit." He reassured her with a smile but he still felt sadness inside, since he'd become overall commander of HART he'd nearly died in a crash landing, five of the personnel had been killed in action, plus his father-in-law lay in intensive care. What misfortune would happen next?

Maria looked over at him and said casually, "Come to bed. We've got a long day ahead of us tomorrow." Ronan knew she was right.

He'd managed to arrange it so that Simon could stay overnight at his aunt's house; admittedly Ronan didn't like the thought of this Eric person being in the same house as his son – the sooner Melissa found Isaac again and kicked Eric back to his wife the better.

Both the young woman and her older companion ascended the staircase, to the upper floor, where they went through the same routine as the evening before – Ronan changed in the bathroom, while Maria changed in the bedroom and climbed into the double bed; Ronan came back into the room and climbed in beside her.

*****

The helicopter carrying the commando group, together with Commander Leon Bigship landed on the deck of the H-Moscow at around 13:00. The group had eaten what food rations they'd found - in one of the overhead storage lockers – aboard the *HIND*; however, they were still remarkably hungry as the group of four disembarked from the helicopter and went below decks to the crew's mess room where they all had a, warm, meal; as soon as the Mi-24 helicopter was parked up and made secure the two pilots joined them in the mess room.

*****

Next morning, in Hull, both Ronan Strobing and Maria Sanchez were up at 06:30, ready for the day ahead. Neither had got that much sleep - the previous night – as they'd been rather busy. By 07:45 they were up, washed, dressed, had eaten a breakfast of porridge and had a cup of tea, and other *normal* parts of the morning routine. About five minutes later Ronan'd loaded Miss Sanchez's, meagre, possessions aboard his red *Hyundai*; he'd told Maria she could keep some of Melissa's clothes, well he didn't think she'd be wanting them again.

So at around 07:55 Ronan drove his automobile with his young passenger aboard towards *Robin Hood* airport so she could check-in for her flight to America's *Dulles* airport; Ronan was permitted – by the airport staff, who knew him – to accompany his young companion, and stay with her until her departure time – which was 11:00. Normally he wouldn't have been allowed to do this but because of his HART credentials he was.

Again normally Maria wouldn't have been permitted to travel on a civilian flight due to how she'd arrived; however, Ronan's credentials had helped there as well. At 11:00 Maria kissed Commander Strobing and thanked him for everything – he became slightly embarrassed as this woman – twenty years his junior – kissed him in front of all the other passengers.

Then the Boeing 747-8I airliner drew alongside the airside lounge and the 467 passengers were requested to board the aircraft. As he turned to leave the airside lounge Maria called back to him, "Thanks for last night, it was great!" He looked back, she waved at him and then she was gone

*****

Commander Strobing drove to Melissa Stevens house and was, again, greeted by Eric; he told the man he'd come for his son. "Simon," Eric called somewhat gruffly, "your father's here."

Suddenly Simon Strobing came, hurtling, down the stairs, "Dad!" his son cried when he saw his father standing at the door. Melissa followed her nephew at a more sedate pace – and helped him on with his coat, hat, and scarf.

Once she'd done this she looked up at her brother-in-law, a serious look on her face, "He had a touch of diarrhoea last night so I cleaned him as best I could, still no harm done."

"Simon's got a hospital appointment this afternoon that should show if it's just *normal* flu – a bug."

"Let's hope it is and nothing more serious," Melissa replied to this, Eric just grunted. "I just hope it's nothing like what my father's got."

"We can but hope," responded Mr Strobing as he led the boy to his vehicle. Once inside Ronan reassured the boy, "I believe Dr Kawaski was right, you'll be better in a couple of days. So don't worry about this afternoon." With that the boy's father pulled away from the kerb.

"Dad," Simon suddenly said.

"Yes," announced Ronan, trying to keep his eyes on the road. "What is it?"

His son came out with, "I don't want to stay at Aunt Melissa's anymore, at least not while Eric's there. I just don't like him." The boy went quiet and Ronan pulled over.

"What's the matter? Has he harmed you in any way?" his father asked him, now becoming very concerned. Ronan had heard stories of mental, physical, even sexual, abuse towards children; but surely if Eric was like that Melissa wouldn't have got involved with him unless, of course she didn't know. Then there were his own children – after all he was married – did his wife know, did anyone know?

Then again it might just be nothing – he stopped the vehicle so he could divert his full attention to his son. Simon looked up at him, "No," he started, "he hasn't harmed me at all. It's just..." his son paused.

"Go on," his father said to him.

Simon simply said, "I just think he's a bit creepy, I wish Isaac was back."

"Is that it?" enquired the elder Strobing somewhat confused now.

"Yes, that's it," the young boy told his father. Looking somewhat irritated Mr Strobing restarted the vehicle they were in and carried on towards home.

*****

On the H-Moscow the ship's captain, Peter Johnson, joined the members the HART personnel in the mess room. "Sir," all the men said and saluted the vessel's commanding officer.

"At ease men," Johnson responded - and then - placing a hand on Commander Bigship's shoulder he said, to the man, somewhat gruffly, "On your feet dog, and show your captain some respect." The men were about to protest but Leon simply smiled at them.

"Sorry sir," he remarked, standing but not saluting, and then turning so the captain could see who he was. As he had thought the captain suddenly went, very, red with embarrassment.

"Begging your pardon sir," and he saluted the superior officer. "I didn't know you were aboard this vessel."

"No need to apologise Captain Johnson, an easy mistake to make especially if all the information isn't passed on." Leon beamed jovially at the man.

The captain relaxed somewhat. "I just came to inform you, gentleman that the *Pave Low* helicopter is standing by, up on deck, to take you the final 1,100 miles to headquarters in Geneva."

"Thank you captain and thank you for your hospitality," Commander Bigship said to the aircraft carrier's commanding officer. Every man except the two pilots, who were to stay behind, shook hand's with the captain of H-Moscow; gathered the equipment they'd brought with them and made their way up the steps to their waiting transport.

The Sikorsky MH-53M *Pave Low IV* helicopter was waiting for the HART group – on deck – the six blades on its rotor head, and the three blades on its tail rotor, were turning; the three commandos and their commander rushed over to the door – in the aircraft's *port* side, Major Howell opened the sliding door and the four personnel boarded. Once they were all in and the door was slid shut – the four men buckled themselves into the seats they'd been designated – the air crew performed the *final* pre-flight checks the chopper rose – vertically – into the sky; all along the journey back to headquarters – a journey that would take approximately six hours – the helicopter would be shadowed by an MC-130P *tanker* aircraft for in-flight refuelling – which would happen once, as the helicopter could only travel approximately 623 miles on a *full* tank of fuel.

After arriving back at the main HART compound at around 20:00 (local time) all four men went into the main building and up to the fourth floor, and walked into the commander's office. "Greetings Commander Most," Leon announced with enthusiasm. "We're back."

Commander Celia Most looked up at the four newly-arrived personnel standing in front of the desk; she'd been alerted to their – imminent – arrival by the man on reception and had decided to greet them personally. "Welcome back, all of you. Please pull up a seat and tell me everything that happened." They each brought a chair forward and sat down. "Now who's going to start?"

"I suppose I will," Sergeant Anco said. "Well it was a basic helicopter flight there for the four members of our team – Theresa Robins, Shinto Howell, James Shearman and myself – aboard the, captured, Mi-24 *HIND* helicopter – nobody tried to blow us out the sky. Anyway about twelve hours later we arrived at our destination – thankfully with it being a *Proagnon* helicopter we were allowed to land in the bunker – no questions asked; we landed, exited the chopper and, immediately, ran into *Proagnon* soldiers – there was rather a large firefight and we threw our *flashbangs* which disorientated the enemy – thus making them easier targets. Then two soldiers began dragging a prisoner forward – this turned out to be Commander Bigship."

Commander Bigship took up the story, "Theresa Robins – seeing my predicament – rushed forward from the group and managed to kill one of my escorts with her M16A2 rifle; the other man brought his AK-47 assault rifle to bear on her – but upon seeing this I lashed out – knocking the soldier's arm so the bullet went wide. Captain Robins shot the other soldier and then started to lead me away; suddenly a shot rang out behind us and Captain Robins crumpled and fell to the floor. I – more or less recovered by that time – grabbed Theresa's remaining grenades and tossed the *smoke* grenade behind me; it exploded and threw up a cloud of *black* smoke. James Shearman then rushed forward and pulled me out of harm's way."

James Shearman took up the story then, "I didn't do much – I just saw Captain Robins begin to fall and knew somebody had to pull Commander Bigship to safety, so I darted forward, grabbed the commander's arm and pulled him away from any further danger – whilst Sergeant Anco and Major Howell provided covering fire."

Major Howell finished the story, "Then the four of us boarded the *HIND* helicopter and it started to ascend – the *Proagnon* soldiers firing at the chopper. When we were high enough Commander Bigship ordered us – all – to toss our remaining *gas* grenades at the soldiers down below. Once we'd done this and the aircraft was free of the bunker I contacted headquarters."

"Interesting," murmured Commander Most and turned to Commander Leon Bigship, "Leon, what was your assessment of this rescue mission?"

"I would say that it was well organised, well executed, and resulted in my – successful – extraction." He paused and began to look serious, "However, the only aspect that I thought was a little wrong was the – somewhat – hasty behaviour on Captain Theresa Robins' part. Admittedly, she – probably – only did what she did as she thought it was the right thing to do, at the time."

"I agree with you there – it was rather reckless – but as you say she, probably, felt it was her duty." Commander Most dismissed the other three men, with a wave of her hand, and then turned her attention back to Leon.

"Commander Bigship," she started, "tomorrow I would like you to take command from me – if you feel up to it – as I wish to travel to England; check on Mike as I can't seem to get him on the phone – it just rings and rings. I've tried to contact his mobile phone but get the same result – I just hope nothing's happened to him; first Peter disappears and now Mike seems to have vanished, whatever next?" The two HART commanders then left the office together.

*****

Over in England several men – all Floyd Maxwell's business associates – had each received several consignments of the spray cans containing *ProPower* with some instructions stating that each man was to travel – by civilian jet liner – to various main shopping centres in the capital cities of different countries and spray the substance in each can into the air conditioning system; armed with these instructions the men journeyed to their nearest airports and took flights to Paris in France, Madrid in Spain, Lisbon in Portugal, Berlin in Germany, Rome in Italy, Brussels in Belgium and Athens in Greece.

Mr Maxwell's agents all booked themselves into hotels for a few days – they didn't see that any problems should arise, in their mission, and were hoping to have a few days relaxation afterwards. So it was that each of the men simply went to the main shopping centre in the, relevant, city – found and removed a ventilation grille, put a gas mask on – just in case, and sprayed the contents of one of the spray cans into the air conditioning system.

The agent in Spain, Robert Davis, was spotted by one of the shopping centres, uniformed, security guards. "What are you doing?" demanded the guard – who had produced his gun.

Robert lifted the mask from his face and hid it in his pocket, "Sorry sir I thought I spotted a bird – somehow fly in through this grille. I was just checking for it – as I can't see anything I can only assume my eyes were playing tricks on me."

"I see," remarked the guard re-holstering his pistol, he wasn't sure whether to believe this man but was prepared to give him the benefit of the doubt. "I notice you have a new spray," he said eyeing the boxes, "are you giving them away?"

Mr Davis suddenly had a thought – he had intended something different for them but this opportunity was too good to miss; "Indeed I am," he replied. "Would you like one?"

"I'll take the lot off you – I'm sure everyone at headquarters will appreciate this kind gesture from," he read the label on the top of the box, "the Maxwell consortium." Robert Davis handed the consignment of four boxes over, turned, and left the centre – whistling as he went. What he didn't realise was he too had become infected – by removing his gas mask too soon – and before the day was over he would infect many more.

In the other countries the agents had all performed their – individual – tasks and were now looking forward to their remaining days of rest and relaxation.

*****

The next day at the HART compound Leon and Celia – who was still on site until later that day – were standing at the HART garden of remembrance surveying he row upon row of, simple, wooden crosses that were used whenever a member of personnel was killed in conflict. There were crosses marking the fallen that had been killed in the last conflict with *Proagnon*; there were four crosses to mark the passing of the four, newly promoted, commanders, Leon moved into the enclosure and planted a new cross to mark the passing of Theresa Robins.

Every HART member had an individual cross – so if they were killed in action they could be remembered; these crosses were stored – in a box – in the Commander's office, along with a box of duplicate dog tags – if a member of the medical staff or a receptionist was killed the commander, at that time, would simply write the fallen's name on the cross.

Once he'd positioned the cross in the ground Commander Bigship rejoined Commander Most at the entrance to the garden and said, solemnly, to her, "Another one gone, that's five in a matter of months. I wonder if there'll be anyone else."

"Who knows," Celia responded quietly and now more worried about the two men in her life. "I shall be leaving for home after lunch – although you may take command now as I have some packing to do." They then stood there - for a minute - in quiet contemplation looking at the rows of crosses – there were over a hundred of them, all of them had dog tags on.

Leon finally broke the silence, "I will take command now," he told her, "you go and do your packing, I can only guess how worried you must be." He then tried to reassure his - female – counterpart, "I'm sure everything's fine." They then walked back towards the main building; Leon entered the building while Celia carried on past – on her way to her residence.

*****

That afternoon Commander Ronan Strobing took his son to Hull hospital – for his scan - as had been advised by Dr Kawaski. They entered the building, Simon was nervous, and Ronan enquired at the main reception desk as to where they should go; the nurse on duty informed him that he needed to take his son up to the third floor where the scanning department was. Thanking the woman Mr Strobing led his son over to the lifts and they ascended to the third floor.

Upon reaching their destination Ronan led Simon down the corridors to the right department where he handed the appointment card to the receptionist seated at the desk, he was told by the woman to take a seat. Both father and son seated themselves to await Simon's appointment time of 14:00; as with most hospitals they weren't seen on time, Simon was eventually called in at 15:00.

The younger Strobing was then injected with some fluid that the doctor, Dr Shamus, assured his father was just a dye that would help improve the clarity of the pictures, but wouldn't harm the boy in any way – Simon was then asked to remove his clothing and any jewellery, watches, he was wearing; Simon stripped down but was a bit reluctant when it came to his underwear – Dr Shamus informed the boy that if he didn't want to remove his underwear it didn't matter too much. The scanning machine that Simon was to go through looked very similar to a – giant – washing machine.

Once his son was settled Ronan told the doctor he was just going outside to phone somebody to collect Simon as he had an optician's appointment at 16:00. He wandered outside and produced his mobile phone and dialled Melissa's number – he was reluctant to phone her but knew his mother-in-law had no transport whereas Eric did. After a few rings the phone was answered, "Hello lover," Melissa's bubbly voice said.

"Hello, Melissa" Mr Strobing replied. "Expecting someone else?"

Melissa was a bit taken aback, "No, of course not. What can I do you for?"

Ronan tried to ignore the sexual innuendo in her voice. "Could you and Eric come over to Hull hospital and stop with Simon; once he's finished having his scan could you take him to your house for a while as I have an optician's appointment?"

"Of course we will, we'll be over as soon as we can."

"You know where we are?" Ronan enquired.

Melissa paused, "Oh yes – third floor – Dad had a scan the other week. See you soon."

"See you," Mr Strobing said and ended the call. He returned to the scanning room to be with his son until his aunt arrived. She arrived with Eric at approximately 15:30 – Ronan greeted both of them and gave his sister-in-law a quick kiss on the cheek – and waited with them until 15:35 and then told them both he'd have to leave. So he left the room – Simon was about halfway through his scan, maybe a little more – and walked out to his *Hyundai* vehicle which he climbed aboard, and then drove out the hospital car park and made his way into the centre of Hull.

*****

In the *Proagnon* bunker Mitchell Walker was surveying the scene of carnage as the remainder of the soldiers cleared the dead bodies away; many men had been killed and they'd lost their prisoner, but – on the plus side they'd managed to kill one of the HART soldiers – a woman no less. If she ever found out Sandy Tulliver wouldn't like the fact that he'd endangered the soldiers in this way – much less the fact that many had been killed, Mr Walker would face a demotion for this – so he had to execute an operation that would *rock* their enemies.

He then retired to his office and thought about it – he knew HART had a smaller, less well guarded, headquarters in Turkey; if he could find a way to infiltrate and kill the personnel inside surely that would put him in her good books again. How could he achieve this though?

*****

A Gulfstream *G550* – carrying Commander Celia Most took off from Geneva's *Cointrin* airport, at 16:30, and flew in a north westerly direction towards England – it touched down at *Robin Hood* airport approximately an hour and a quarter after it had left *Cointrin*, however – as usual – due to the time difference it only seemed like a quarter of an hour.

Celia exited the executive business jet and, once she had collected her luggage, she made her way through the terminal building – once outside she hailed a taxi – the car was an old, blue, Ford Mondeo – the taxi driver helped her load her luggage in the boot of the car and then she climbed in the, rear, passenger seat. The driver got in and asked her, "Where you going Miss?"

Celia gave her address in Hull – and the automobile drove off and travelled on its journey to the city of Hull. After another hour the vehicle pulled up outside the house where the Most family lived.

Mrs Most paid the driver his fare and unlocked the door to her house so the driver – of the taxi – could place her suitcase in the hallway; once he'd gone Celia closed the door and relocked it then called, "Mike," no answer. "Mike," she called again, louder this time, still no answer; "Don't make me come and get you," and then – fearing he may be in bed with some, young, tart she marched up the stairs and noticed both of the bedroom doors were shut, yet she could hear no noise.

First she opened her son's bedroom door and found…nothing – except an untidy bedroom, as usual – Celia exited the room and flung open her, own, bedroom door where again she found…nothing. Where was her son? Returning downstairs and feeling very alone – now – Celia spent the next half an hour ringing her son's friends – well the ones she knew about but nobody had seen him for the past day.

Resigning herself to the fact that her son had vanished, like her husband before him – calming herself she rang Commander Strobing and told him that Mike had vanished now, like Peter. Ronan told her that, perhaps, he'd gone to a friend's house – one his mother didn't know about – and would probably be back soon.

Commander Most told him he was probably right, and then she went and made herself a light meal of *Cheese on Toast* and ate it while watching the TV – it was now 19:02.

*****

At his own home Ronan Strobing was now perplexed regarding the disappearances of Peter Most and now Mike Most. At least when his wife had been in hospital he'd known where she was, but this not knowing must be very frustrating for his colleague; he was – almost tempted – to take Simon and offer to go over and join her.

Things seemed to be going from bad to worse for Commander Celia Most. *Oh well,* he thought and settled down – on the sofa – next to his son and watched the TV with him, as per usual Simon had put a cartoon channel on and they were currently watching an old episode of *Wacky Races*. "Do we have to watch this?"

Reluctantly Simon handed the remote control to his father who changed the channel to BBC1 therefore Simon told his father that he was going up to his room to read – the time was now 19:02.

*****

Sandy Tulliver and Floyd Maxwell were sitting in the main room – of his south London house – with the TV switched on and tuned into BBC1 – the time was 19:02.

*****

Commander Leon Bigship was sitting – in the Commander's office, relaxing; he viewed the screens connected to each –

individual – monitoring camera, around the compound; none of them showed anything out of place so he – idly – flicked the TV – in the office – and switched it onto the Swiss equivalent of BBC1. The time, according to the office clock, was 20:02.

*****

The same thing was happening in the *Proagnon* bunker – in Iran – in Mitchell Walker's office. The time there was approximately 22:32.

*****

Suddenly a *newsflash* came on screen – everyone of the six people watching, be they HART or *Proagnon*, immediately turned the volume up. "Reports are coming in from Spain, Portugal, France, Germany, Belgium and Greece of a new, mystery, virus that has affected many of those countries citizens; the virus has all the symptoms of flu and is said to have originated in Britain. Thankfully the virus hasn't spread any further around the world yet. This reporter is signing off now," and then he sneezed.

CHAPTER 7

REALISATION DAWNS!

Commanders Strobing, Most and Bigship – although in different locations – were now horrified, they'd initially figured this virus wouldn't affect anybody beyond the shores of the United Kingdom; however, now it seemed otherwise.

Ronan Strobing was rather shocked – how could the virus that had put his father-in-law's life in danger have spread from Hull into these other countries? Plus how many people had it affected? Was there a cure? He knew Dr Hans Schaiffer had visited Dr Lighten – the doctor who was overseeing the treatment of Arnold Stevens. Was there a connection, if so what was it? Plus HART had detected *Proagnon* activity aboard an old sea fort just north of the coast of Scotland, and then a second helicopter had been detected in the same area – had it transported an extra person onto the sea fort? Oh so many questions – probably the answers were simple enough but what were they? He sat there thinking about this but could find no answers.

Suddenly he was dragged back to reality by the phone ringing; he wandered into the hallway and answered it. "Hello."

"Ronan, did you see the *newsflash*?" Melissa's voice asked from the other end of the phone line. "Isn't that virus similar to what Dad's got?"

Ronan knew that answer but he phrased his answer carefully, "I did see the *newsflash* – and yes, I believe this virus is similar to the one that's affected your father – but I think, I may be wrong, that as your father's seems more progressed it may be a more concentrated version. Plus I believe that's why Isaac left – he developed the less concentrated version and decided that instead of risking infecting you, or Simon, he upped and left." Ronan hated to admit it but he was starting to warm to his sister-in-law, after all these years.

Melissa then said to him, "Ronan, Eric's gone as his wife found out about me so, if you want to feel free to come over."

"No thank you Melissa – I appreciate the offer though, just not at the moment."

"Okay Ronan, see you," and she replaced the receiver as did he.

The next phone call he received was from, a distraught, Celia Most. She told him that with the news that the virus was spreading she was becoming more and more convinced that this was the reason Peter had disappeared – plus Ronan'd told her that when he'd been at the doctor's with Simon Mike had been there. Had he also succumbed to this virus? Judging by the past outbreak – in Scotland – anything was possible.

Commander Strobing sympathised with his fellow commander but told her not to give up hope as her husband and son may return any day – but even he admitted anything was possible. They then said their good-byes and replaced their – individual – handsets. Mr Strobing walked back into the main room – he then heard the toilet flush, evidently Simon as there was nobody else in the house.

As he was just about to settle himself down – on the sofa – again the STU, in the study, started to chirrup and warble; Ronan hurried over and entered the – small – study and picked up the handset on the STU-8 – which was located on his desk.

He usually did his writings at his desk, unless he was acting as a HART operative – he'd already had three books published and was working on a fourth; that was – until he'd been called away the previous year, to join in the fight against *Proagnon* – originally led by Dr Q, later revealed to be Adam Barker, the son of a man called Richard Barker. The original HART commander – Peter Roberts - had helped send the older Barker to prison when he'd served as a policeman, and his son had sought revenge on Roberts.

That was in the past – coming back to the present he answered the STU-8, "HART Commander Strobing."

"I know who you are," Leon Bigship's voice said, jokingly. It was a good thing the two men knew each other well, "I've just seen the news. It doesn't look good does it?"

"Admittedly it doesn't," replied his colleague. "I reckon it's a similar strain of virus as that which my father-in-law, Arnold Stevens, caught. That's the man Dr Schaiffer's friend, Dr Lighten, is treating."

"Is that why Dr Schaiffer was in England?" asked Ronan's older colleague.

"Yes it was," responded Commander Strobing in confirmation.

*****

In his south London residence Floyd Maxwell was having a drink with his partner. "Here's to a very successful operation," he said.

"Hmm yes, very successful indeed, cheers," and she clinked glasses with him. "Our plan seems to be progressing well," the woman he knew as Miss Carol Turner remarked, "admittedly the virus isn't spreading throughout Britain as rapidly as we'd anticipated but I'm sure it will – given time." Miss Turner had a quick sip of her wine, "As we – also – saw – on the news about two weeks ago *Proagnon* forces, led by my deputy, attempted to steal three train box car loads of gold coins; HART forces intervened but couldn't stop the runaway passenger train, killing all three hundred people on board – plus the driver – and five of the six HART personnel sent to guard the coins. I think they captured the sixth, I'll have to check on that."

Floyd looked over at her youthful face, topped with her blonde hair – which was shoulder length. "Don't forget it was my business contacts who distributed the virus for us."

Before she'd joined the terrorist organisation, *Proagnon*, Carol had joined the Maxwell consortium – figuring that if she ever left *Proagnon* she'd have something to fall back on; initially Miss Turner had thought she'd just be a sleeping partner, as there were nine others – in the group – including Maxwell himself.

Things had gone a bit wrong with the initial organisation led by Dr Q, but now she was in command of *Proagnon* things would be done her way.

She had been a sleeping partner in the consortium, but now she had now – actually - become Maxwell's sleeping, as well as business, partner.

Carol looked over at the man known as Floyd Maxwell, "Ah yes, you're such a love," and she leant over and kissed him. A couple more hours passed and they ascended the stairs to bed.

*****

Mitchell Walker – who had also seen the news – was beginning to wonder if that's what the *Proagnon* scientists had been working on before, whilst Dr Q had been in charge. Had Sandy Tulliver being planning – like Abdul Singh before her, and, possibly, Tanya Roberts – to overthrow Dr Q? If so, how safe was his position and should he take precautions against this type of thing happening again? Probably his mind was playing tricks on him and he was safe – he could easily stand up to her and dispose of Miss Tulliver easily.

*****

Commander Strobing had packed ready for his return trip to Geneva he had asked Melissa, a little reluctantly, if Simon could stay with her and her new man, Lloyd Edwards – he was approximately twenty years younger than her, immediately she'd said it was okay.

Commander Strobing informed Simon that he would be staying with his aunt until a week before Christmas – which was about eight weeks away – and then his father would return home.

After loading his luggage he drove his red *Hyundai* 4 x 4 to the school where Simon Strobing was a pupil – and then he carried on with his journey to *Robin Hood* airport; as he was driving past a car showroom – on the outskirts of Doncaster – he noticed a SAAB 9-4X Crossover Utility Vehicle (CUV)

*****

The Saab 9-4X was a mid size crossover SUV that had been released by the Swedish automaker Saab Automobile. It had been based on the premium GM Theta platform which it shared with the 2010 Cadillac SRX, previewed by the Cadillac Provoq concept at the 2008 Consumer Electronics Show. The 9-4X had begun production in 2010 and was built at Ramos Arizpe, Mexico. The main challenge, according to Svante Kinell at the marketing department at Saab, had been to find the right Diesel engines for the European market.

The focus of the 9-4X took shape once the Saab 9-6X project was cancelled, after the divestment by General Motors of its holding in Subaru. The 9-4X had been to replace the larger U.S. built Saab 9-7X SUV, production of which had had ceased in December 2008. The 9-4X concept had made its initial debut at the 2008 North American International Auto Show.

The Saab 9-4x crossover had entered production at General Motors' Ramos Arizpe, Mexico plant. 147 examples of the 9-4x were produced, 49 of which occurred the week of January 23, 2010. The production crossover car was almost identical to the concept on the exterior and was similar to the 2010 second generation Saab 9-5 on the inside.

*****

Ronan pulled over and walked into the showroom – he still had a bit of time before he was due to check in – he asked the salesman the if he could take the silver automobile for a test drive; the salesman told him he could and handed the keys over. Mr Strobing eagerly boarded the 2.8L Turbo V6 vehicle and started it up – and then he drove it, slowly, from the forecourt – selecting the front wheel drive option he drove onto a section of deserted dual carriageway, he built up the speed to about 70mph – the vehicle handled easily, and there was plenty of room in the car.

Realising that time was pressing he took the car back to its base, thanked the salesman and handed the keys back, and then re-boarded his own vehicle and carried on to the airport.

*****

Mitchell Walker sat – in his office – and pondered the best way to strike at HART, he could just give the order to blow up something close to HART or kidnap somebody, something like that. However, he could wait until he'd heard from the *Proagnon* operative over in England, agent Edwards. Edwards was a – fairly – new recruit; he had joined around the same time Sandy Tulliver had – due to his young age it had been decided to leave him in England until he was needed.

*****

Robert Davis - Floyd Maxwell's man in Spain – had begun to feel ill with the symptoms of flu; dismissing it as just *normal* flu he dressed for the day and went down to the restaurant of the hotel he was staying in, as he wasn't feeling that brilliant so he just had some cereals and milk – followed by a cup of coffee. Once he'd finished he felt a slight pain in his stomach but – again – dismissed it as a slight twinge of indigestion; he left the restaurant and made his way back up to his room.

He entered his hotel room and was just getting changed into his T-shirt and shorts – ready for a day of sunbathing – when he suddenly felt the need to visit the toilet, very urgently. Unfortunately, his trousers were round his ankles and he had to struggle out of them before he could move – properly – again. He rushed to the bathroom but just before he got there he heard a little *purp*, it was then he thought he had – possibly – a touch of diarrhoea; upon reaching the toilet he removed his underwear and saw the evidence he had *soiled* himself, he still sat on the toilet – just in case. About ten minutes later he cleaned himself up and continued getting changed.

He sort of knew then that if this happened when he was at the beach he wouldn't be able to get back to any toilet in time – certainly there were no public toilets – so he just resigned himself to a day of sunbathing on the terrace.

*****

In Hull, England the virus was now spreading like wildfire affecting many people; in fact every hospital in the city was full to bursting point – many operations had had to be cancelled – some patients were being placed in corridors until beds became free. Some patients – like Arnold Stevens – had been placed in the intensive care unit as their symptoms seemed more severe than other, newer, patients.

Of course, every new patient had the same, or very similar, symptoms, runny nose and diarrhoea – yet the mucus wasn't its usual colour, it was red – practically the colour of blood. Every so often the symptoms would prove severe and the patients would develop small growths on the face and body, even inside the mouth – every so often these growths would leak pus and blood – and there was also the, violent, shaking to contend with. However much the medical staff tried to restrain the patient, they failed in this task; therefore many other injuries could result – the only person that seemed to be in a stable condition was Arnold Stevens. Eventually, after about four weeks the patient would die.

There seemed to be no stopping this *killer* virus. Dr Charles Lighten was as baffled as the rest of his colleagues; if only the HART doctor, and his close friend, Dr Hans Schaiffer would hurry up and find a cure then everything would be okay – still, his German friend was doing his best. Plus what had happened to Dr Simon Forrestor – he'd just seemed to have vanished.

*****

Lloyd Edwards and Melissa Stevens collected Simon Strobing from the Hull Church of England primary school at about three thirty. The school was a - reasonably – large one, boasting nearly three hundred pupils. Ronan and Melissa's sister, Mandy, had enrolled him at the school four years previously – in 2009.

However, as Commander Strobing had had to return overseas to attend to business Melissa had agreed to look after his son – with her new partner – until he returned, just before Christmas. So it was that when Simon exited the school gates his aunt met him and led him over to the green Ford Mondeo and helped him inside the vehicle. Seeing the – young – man in the driver's seat Simon piped up, "Hello."

"Hello Simon," the black man responded in a friendly voice, "your aunt's told me a great deal about you. My name's Lloyd." He shook Simon's hand. Melissa then climbed into the passenger seat, beside Mr Edwards, and strapped herself in; once the younger Strobing had put his seat belt on the green automobile pulled away and they began the journey to Melissa's house.

Once they'd pulled into the drive and the vehicle had come to a complete halt the two adults, together with the youngster, got out and entered the semi detached house. Simon then walked upstairs to check on the bedroom he'd be staying in while he was there – it was the usual bedroom he slept in so nothing had changed. He then nipped over to the bathroom – about five minutes later he ventured downstairs.

*****

Over at HART headquarters – in the medical centre – Dr Hans Schaiffer was still experimenting with various antibiotics – in his attempt to find a cure for this new *mystery* virus; he'd already tried many different combinations but found that none of these had worked. He was frustrated – he was supposed to be one of the finest doctors in the world - that was one reason HART had recruited him – yet he couldn't find a cure for this virus.

He decided to take a break – for the moment – and have a wander round to clear his head. He'd made a list - on his notepad – of the different combinations of antibiotics he'd used so far.

Dr Schaiffer wandered through the medical centre checking on the patients – in there – as he went; he pushed open the swing, double, doors and walked down numerous corridors – most had windows in with corridors leading off to join up with other corridors in the building. After a good ten minutes of walking he entered the main part of HART headquarters where the offices, conference rooms, and main reception were located; the medical man knocked on the, main, Commander's office door and he waited until he was requested to enter.

Inside was seated Commander Strobing – who had taken over from Commander Bigship a few hours earlier. It was no secret that the previous year Dr Schaiffer had – in a way – arranged for Ronan's close call with death, and other – numerous – occurrences. However, all that had been resolved and the two men were now good friends again.

The HART medical man, and psychological profiler, seated himself in the chair across from HART's latest commander, due to the death of the previous commander earlier that year.

"Dr Schaiffer," Commander Strobing said to his – medical – colleague. "Have you found a cure for this *mystery* virus yet?" Ronan leant back in the chair of command.

Dr Schaiffer responded, sadly, "Alas, I have not yet. However, after much thinking, what I really need is a blood sample from somebody who has been exposed to this virus – but not realised it – in other words somebody who has come into contact with an infected person but is still healthy."

Ronan thought of Simon – he'd been to the doctors but he'd just had *normal* flu. Then he remembered meeting Mike Most on the way out – he'd had the symptoms of flu, had he been infected? "Would I do doctor?" he enquired.

"Yes you would be perfect, but have you come into contact with an infected person?"

"I believe I have," and Ronan explained to his German colleague about Simon's appointment at the doctors, and then meeting Commander Most's son. "I'll have to contact Commander Most to see if she's heard from Mike since I last had contact with her, a couple of days back;" he pressed the speakerphone button on the STU-8 and dialled Celia Most's home number.

The phone rang a couple of times and then Celia answered, "Hello."

Ronan then explained why he was ringing and then asked if she'd heard from her son – the answer she gave was a negative one; Ronan thanked her and then switched the speakerphone off. "There you are Dr Schaiffer. I'm your perfect guinea pig."

"If you're sure Commander Strobing, please follow me." The, overall, commander of HART rose from his chair – behind the desk – and followed his German colleague from the office and down the – numerous – corridors to the medical centre;

where Dr Hans Schaiffer took a blood sample from his superior to aid him in finding a cure for this virus.

Commander Strobing was then given a cup of tea and a couple of biscuits - to boost his energy levels back to normal again – by a fairly young nurse called Angela Diamond, she was very pretty, Ronan thanked her. "Well?" enquired Commander Strobing of the chief medical man.

"I can't see any difference yet," the doctor replied truthfully.

Meanwhile the commander of HART finished off his tea and biscuits, and then said to the German, "I'll be in my office when there are any results."

The doctor looked up momentarily, "I'll notify you of any results as soon as I have any sir." Commander Strobing got up and left the medical centre.

*****

In Hull Melissa Stevens and her nephew – Simon Strobing – were out shopping, they had caught a bus into the centre of Hull, leaving Lloyd Edwards at Melissa's house; when all was clear he made his way back inside and dialled an international number from the phone – in the hallway – when the person picked up at the other end Lloyd simply said, "I have found out the information you require."

"I shall send an agent, along with a group of twenty soldiers, to meet you at *Humberside* airport. They should be on the 14:30 flight from Iran's *Imam Khomeini* airport. See that you are there to meet them when the aircraft – carrying them – lands at 16:00 – your time; do not fail the cause," the voice at the other end told Edwards and then replaced the receiver.

Of course I won't fail, thought Lloyd angrily, *what do you take me for?* He knew his employer could be harsh, even cruel, at times but that was life wasn't it? Realising this was for real, now, he ascended the staircase and walked into the bedroom he shared with Melissa; he crossed to the wardrobe, opened it and reached into the back, where he produced a case containing the separate components that made up his MAC-11 machine pistol.

*****

The Ingram MAC-11 (Military Armament Corporation Model 11) was a machine pistol that was developed by American gun designer Gordon Ingram at the Military Armament Corporation (MAC) during the 1970s. The weapon was a sub-compact version of the Model 10 (MAC-10), and had been chambered to fire the smaller .380 ACP round.

This weapon was sometimes confused with the Sylvia & Wayne Daniels M-11/9 or the Vulcan M-11-9, both of which were later variants of the MAC which were chambered for 9 mm Luger Parabellum cartridge.

A specific suppressor was developed for the MAC-11, which used wipes as baffles, instead of the reflex baffles that Mitchell Werbell III had created for the MAC-10. Though these wipes were less durable than reflex baffles, they had the advantage of proving quieter for the MAC-11.

The rate of fire of the M-11A1 was listed as approximately 900 rpm (rounds per minute), though in reality, it was closer to 1,200 rpm. At this incredibly high rate of fire, the weapon was difficult to control while on full-auto, but short bursts could be accurate at ranges of up to about 30 yards (27 m); because of the low penetration of the .380 ACP round, the M-11 found uses in situations where a more powerful round could pass though a wall. The M-11 was used by some security forces and by special task forces around the world during in-vehicle operations such as aboard airliners, because of the low penetration of the .380 round.

The M-11 was the least-common version in the MAC family of firearms. This was mostly due to the .380 ACP round, which had a muzzle velocity of approximately 950 ft/s (290 m/s) and 200 ft·lbf (270 J) of energy, and was widely considered to have insufficient stopping power. At the MAC-11's high cyclic rate, extreme trigger discipline was required to discharge any short bursts, which were required for combat expediency. Without proper training, the natural tendency of the inexperienced shooter was to hold down the trigger, discharging the entire magazine in little more than a second, often with poor accuracy due to the recoil.

Like the larger M-10, the M-11 had open sights with the rear pinhole sight welded to the receiver. These sights were for use with the folding stock, as using them without the stock was nearly useless because of the initial jump of the weapon due to its heavy, open-bolt design. The M-11A1 also had two safety features which were also found on the Model 10A1. The charging handle rotated to 90 degrees to lock the bolt in the forward position thus preventing the weapon from being cocked. The second safety was a slider which could be pushed forward to lock the trigger, which in turn pinned the bolt to the rear (cocked) position. This action prevented the weapon from discharging even when dropped, which was a typical problem with the open-bolt design.

*****

Edwards checked over the weapon and then checked the 32 round box magazine to make sure it was full – just in case he needed to use it, though he hoped he wouldn't – with .380 ACP cartridges; he did have the choice of using 16 round box magazines instead but Edwards – actually – preferred the 32 round box magazine. However, he checked the 16 round magazines as well – he wouldn't, hopefully, need them.

*****

Commander Ronan Strobing was seated in his fourth floor office, sorting through some documents, when there was a knock on the door. Ronan stopped what he was doing and called for whoever it was to enter; the door opened and Dr Hans Schaiffer followed by Commander Leon Bigship entered the office – they both pulled up a chair and seated themselves across the desk from their superior. "Gentlemen," the overall commander greeted them. "What can I do for you?"

Dr Schaiffer began first, "I have compared your blood sample to the one I took from Mr Stevens – when I was in Hull – and there is a difference, although to the untrained eye there would be no difference."

"And this difference is?" enquired the commanding officer as calmly as he could, but he was slightly irritated that Dr

Schaiffer hadn't come to the point – and told them what the difference was – straight away.

"It turns out sir," the medical man said, "your blood seems to be a great deal clearer so the solution to this problem now seems clearer. Basically all that is needed is to take an amount of blood off the infected person and then to put clean blood back into the body; plus put the patient on a course of combined antibiotics; therefore giving the white blood cells – that make up the immune system - the boost they need to help them fight off the infection "

He paused to allow the two commanders to digest what he'd just told them before he continued, "Admittedly we won't be able to cure everyone who's been infected, but we should still be able to cure a great deal."

"That's so simple," remarked Commander Strobing to the others, "I wonder why nobody's thought of it before."

"Possibly everyone's been trying to cure it with antibiotics, as they treat most viruses."

"You're probably right, Commander Strobing stated, Commander Bigship nodded as if he agreed which he did. Then the commander of HART turned to his other colleague, "What brings you here Leon?"

Dr Schaiffer didn't leave as Ronan had expected him to, he must want something else – still he could wait until after Ronan had dealt with whatever Leon wanted.

Commander Bigship looked across at his superior, "Sir, as you will know we lost the four newly promoted commanders in the Iran episode, do you feel the time is now right to replace them?"

"You're right my old friend – I had forgotten all about that – however, I have drawn up a short list for the new team leaders, they won't be known as commanders; here are the four I have come up with. For team A their new team leader will be Dave Newbend, team B will be led by Samantha Goldsmith, team C will be led by Larry Sanders, and team D will be led by Mary Bishop. Are these choices okay with you?"

"Yes fine, responded Ronan's fellow commander, "I shall implement your instructions straight away." He took the list and left the office.

"Now Dr Schaiffer, you – evidently – stayed behind for another reason; what is it?"

"Well," began the German, "as you know I do psychological profiling as well; and I believe the attack in Iran was mounted in an effort to find a weakness in HART."

"You're point being?" asked Ronan out of curiosity.

"I believe that whoever is in charge of *Proagnon*, at the moment, isn't accustomed to being in command and is trying to prove themselves - personally I think Sandy Tulliver is still in England, hidden somewhere – also I think that *Proagnon* will keep making these – somewhat – random attacks to find a weakness in our armour; can you think of anything that might be seen as a weakness?"

Ronan leant back – in his swivel chair, thinking, "Nothing springs to mind at the moment. Anyway why would they?"

"Think sir," the medical man replied; "they've already tried to bring down HART from the inside. So what is to stop them finding something or somebody – on the outside – and threatening them or it thus finding a weakness and exploiting that weakness."

"True, Dr Schaiffer, very true but I still can't think of anything that might prove to be a weakness to us." Commander Strobing and Dr Schaiffer then had a drink together, and then the HART medical officer left his superior's office, to return to his medical business.

*****

In Hull Lloyd Edwards informed his partner that he was going out to see a friend of his – Melissa told him not to be too long – he assured her he wouldn't and then exited the house and started up his Mondeo, he drove away to see his friend.

Whilst he was out Melissa and Simon played a short game of tennis – on the back lawn – Melissa told her nephew that afterwards – if he wanted – they would go into Hull, on the bus, to the local swimming baths. Simon told his aunt he would like to go as with his father being so busy nowadays he couldn't take his son. Finishing off their game of tennis the two of them wandered back inside and went upstairs; about ten minutes later both aunt and nephew re-emerged onto the landing, both of them holding rolled up towels. "Got everything?" the boy's aunt enquired.

"I think so," Simon replied, "let's see, towel and clean underwear. Is that everything?"

"I believe it is," Melissa told him, "I'll need some money though – for our entrance fee and the bus." Once she'd got her money Melissa and Simon left the house, Melissa locking the door behind them. "I wonder how Lloyd's getting on," she mused to herself.

*****

The man in question had driven to a disused garage and swapped his green Mondeo, albeit temporarily, for an old, battered, blue *Transit* minibus – capable of seating 22 people, including the driver. He then made the journey to *Humberside* airport, a journey of 12 miles yet it took nearly half an hour in the bus; he arrived at a little before 16:30.

He parked up and made his way through the airport to the arrivals gate for the flight that would be bringing in the twenty *Proagnon* soldiers plus someone in authority over them, all would be dressed in business suits and they would each be carrying an attaché case containing the different components that made up their AK-47 assault rifles. Lloyd spotted them among the crowds and saw that they were all youngish men; then he saw the figure who was to be in charge of the mission, Lloyd held up the placard/sign he was carrying and the businessmen moved through the remainder of the new arrivals towards him.

When they were all together the man in charge introduced them to the black man, "Greetings, my name is Mitchell Walker and I will be in charge of this mission. These fine men," he said gesturing to the twenty others, "are my soldiers; you must be agent Edwards."

"Indeed I am," replied Lloyd, "your transport is outside so if you and your colleagues would follow me we shall board and I will drive you to your destination."

As they were all walking back towards the main entrance doors Walker said to Edwards, almost conversationally, "Have you picked out a target?"

"Indeed I have," answered Edwards, "I will brief you on our journey back to Hull." All 22 people exited the airport terminal and boarded the blue *Transit* minibus; once everyone was aboard – Mitchell Walker in the passenger seat while his colleagues sat in the rear area of the vehicle – Lloyd Edwards started the minibus up and drove it from the airport compound and northwards towards Hull.

"Tell me about the target you have selected," Walker said prompting Edwards. As they were travelling through a countryside area plus the windows were shut, however the skylight was partially open, Edwards felt he could talk freely now.

"The target I have selected is a young boy named Simon Strobing, he is a relation to Ronan Strobing. The boy goes to Hull's church of England primary school which has approximately 300 pupils and staff."

"Just a moment," interrupted the man in charge, "did you say Ronan Strobing?" Lloyd nodded in confirmation. "He is one of the accursed HART commanders, you have selected well – he could've been any child but a relation to Commander Ronan Strobing. I believe if we take him hostage, as well as everyone else in the school we shall have HART knocking on our door trying to mount a rescue attempt, they will never succeed as my men are hand picked."

Lloyd digested what had just been said and started to wonder then if he'd done the right thing and would Melissa ever forgive him; did she have to know anyway? He drove on, over the Humber Bridge, and on to Hull. Upon entering Hull he drove the vehicle towards the centre of the city, stopping in front of the Portland Hotel.

*****

The Portland Hotel was the first and only AA four star Hotel in Hull. It was centrally located next to the City Hall and within walking distance to St Stephens and Princess Quay shopping centres. Waterstones, Hammonds, Debenhams, M&S, Starbucks, Pizza Hut, Toni & Guy and other brand names were just steps away. It was also located within walking distance of all the major tourist attractions including The BBC, Hull's historic old town, the theatres, the law courts, museums, galleries, the Queen's gardens and the marina. The KC Stadium and The Deep are also within a 15 minute walk.

The Portland Hotel offered the latest wireless technology to enable its residents to tap in to a total communications network, with secure high-speed Internet access, wherever you happened to be in the hotel. The Portland Hotel also offered complimentary car parking.

Finally there were 126 bedrooms and suites as well as a selection of restaurants, bars and meeting rooms.

*****

Of course none of the shops or other tourist attractions interested the *Proagnon* soldiers – they had a mission to carry out. Once they were all signed in and had been allocated rooms Lloyd and Mitchell went to the bar and ordered themselves drinks whilst the other men went up in the lifts to check over the equipment they'd brought with them; the two men, in the bar, found a corner table and seated themselves at it. Each sipped at their drinks and Lloyd said, "Here's to a successful mission and a positive outcome."

"Let's hope so," replied Mitchell and then enquired, "what time will you be picking us up tomorrow?"

"Oh," answered Edwards, "about 9.00, don't want to arouse any unwanted attention. If anyone does ask I'll tell them you're all businessmen working for an electronics firm and I'm taking you all to a meeting."

"A brilliant deception my friend," replied Walker and sipped at his drink; once both men had finished their drinks they parted company, both knowing tomorrow would be a long and big day.

*****

Lloyd Edwards drove the minibus back to the house he shared with Melissa Stevens, and, at the moment, Simon Strobing. As he parked in the driveway he noticed Melissa peer out from behind the front room curtains; he couldn't blame her, the *old* minibus did sound very different from his Mondeo. He smiled at her, turned off the engine and exited the vehicle. Once he had entered the house Miss Stevens enquired, "Why have you got that thing?"

The black man knew she meant the minibus, he couldn't tell her the truth in case she forewarned Simon or had some way of contacting Ronan so he just said, "I've got a job tomorrow transporting some businessmen to a meeting. The firm I'll be working for wanted me to get used to the vehicle."

"Oh Lloyd that's great news," and she kissed him.

"Unfortunately, as I have to be with the businessmen at 9.00 it means I won't be able to do the school run with you," he confessed. Melissa Stevens looked at her, latest, man friend thoughtfully.

"I suppose if you've got to work you've got to work, Simon and I will take one of the regular buses," she said to him. "It won't do any harm."

Over the evening meal of fish fingers & chips Miss Stevens told her nephew about the following day and why Lloyd wouldn't be able to take them to school. Simon just seemed to accept this, as his aunt had told him the regular bus was their only, real, alternative.

Later, whilst he was laid in bed next to Miss Stevens, Lloyd was troubled by thoughts that he was doing the wrong thing but, hopefully, casualties – if there were any – would be kept to a minimum. If anything were to go wrong Lloyd could simply escape and even if he was picked up and questioned, by HART or the police, he would protest his innocence. However, this Mitchell Walker seemed to be trained well enough to execute this operation himself, why did he need Edwards? Perhaps it was because only Lloyd knew what Simon looked like; if that were so then if things went dramatically wrong

Lloyd could turn the tables on his *Proagnon* paymasters and escape with Simon as his hostage and leave Walker to take the flak, but would Walker let him go?

With these thoughts going round in his mind he rolled over and tried to sleep.

CHAPTER 8

THE SCHOOL SIEGE!

The twenty *Proagnon* soldiers, along with Mitchell Walker, all armed with AK-47 assault rifles and knives, plus an assortment of grenades, left the hotel to rendezvous with the minibus driven by Lloyd Edwards armed with his MAC-11 semiautomatic hand pistol; the soldiers boarded the vehicle, found a vacant seat and seated themselves - Mitchell Walker sat in the, front, passenger seat alongside Lloyd Edwards who would be taking them to their ultimate destination. Edwards looked across at the leader of he soldiers and asked, in a voice slightly tinged with worry, "Are you sure we're doing the right thing?"

Walker looked over at the young, black, man and replied, in an annoyed tone, "Of course it's the right thing to do. As with everything, my friend, there is a certain element of risk; but this attack, and subsequent hostage taking, should draw HART forces to us." After another two minutes of driving the *Transit* minibus pulled up outside the gates of the Hull church of England primary school; the twenty-one armed *Proagnon* men disembarked, Lloyd informed Walker that he would take the minibus and dispose of it. Mitchell said to him, "Don't be too long," and then he, followed by his men, casually walked through the empty playground and onward into the main school building; as it was only 09.10 everyone - except the schools secretary - was still in the main hall for morning assembly. Walker dispatched one of the *Proagnon* soldiers to deal with the woman, the soldier entered the office - his AK-47 at the ready just in case; as expected the secretary gave a sharp cry of surprise and would've probably screamed her head off but as soon as she saw that the assault rifle was levelled at her she decided to do the sensible thing and keep quiet.

"What do you want?" demanded the startled young woman as Mitchell Walker walked into the office brandishing his Glock pistol The *Proagnon* leader, although he was only really the deputy leader, answered her question, "We merely require your silence." He then turned to look at the soldier and ordered, "Tie her up" so the man did as he had been ordered, "And then join the rest of us in the hall."

"But there are children in there," she protested.

"We know," Walker said, "so stop your prattling;" and then as an afterthought said to the soldier, "and gag her." Then, not waiting for an answer, he strode from the room. He rejoined the other, remaining, soldiers in the corridor outside and led them forwards towards the hall where there could be heard the lyrics from *All things bright and beautiful* accompanied by the sound of a piano. The soldiers, along with the two other men, crashed through the door and pointed their weapons at the staff and pupils; when they all saw the men in blue carrying their fearsome looking assault rifles every one of the 300 staff and pupils screamed. Even the head teacher, who was conducting the assembly, had turned white and looked very scared. "Shut up!" snapped Walker pointing his Glock pistol at the head teacher; everyone immediately fell silent. "Lloyd," called Mitchell. Edwards had returned at about 9.20, "you know what the one we seek looks like, find them." Lloyd, who had been standing idly by, looked up as he was shouted; he nodded his understanding then moved among the rows of children. one of the female teachers then decided to make a break for it, she started down the corridor; "Stop her," Walker shouted, one of the soldiers quickly turned, levelled his ak-47 at her retreating back and fired; he watched as she crumpled and fell.

Lloyd Edwards found the pupil he wanted, Simon Strobing, and pointed his MAC-11 pistol at the boy; the other children - in the same row - recoiled, in fear, at the sight of the weapon. "Come with me," he said to the boy, in a tone that told Simon he'd be shot if he refused to obey; obediently he stood up and followed the black man from the hall and down the corridor, on their journey they passed the *Proagnon* soldier who had tied up, and gagged, the secretary. The boy was led into the head teacher's office, which was opposite the main office, and instructed to sit down. Simon sat down and stared up at his aunt's boyfriend - he looked very afraid; "My leader will be with us shortly."

Suddenly the door was thrown open and Mitchell Walker strode in; he smiled - evilly - at the young boy and seated himself in the chair opposite Simon. He looked over at Edwards, "Has he said anything yet?" he said

"No," was the immediate reply. "Look at him, he's terrified," Lloyd told his superior.

"He will," Walker informed the other man. "Now return to the hall." Edwards nodded and left the office. Walker removed his Glock pistol and placed it on the desk - out of reach of the boy. "Now then young man, we know you are related to Commander Strobing of HART, whether you are his son or nephew I am not entirely certain, Lloyd reckons you are his son. Therefore I am hoping you will tell me."

"Never!" retorted the young Strobing.

"Ah," said the man behind the desk, "you have just given yourself away, you are his son. So we have the famous Commander Strobing's son as our hostage;" the man smiled again at the boy.

*****

Celia Most was sitting, by the phone, at home awaiting any news of her husband or son; though she knew - in her heart of hearts - that there would be none. She walked into the sitting room and, idly, switched the TV on, she normally didn't pay much attention to the news but one item caught her attention 'We have just learned that Hull Church of England primary school has been invaded by terrorists. These terrorists, we believe, are members connected to the Proagnon organisation; the same organisation who waged a worldwide terror campaign last year. All the staff and pupils have been taken hostage.'

She watched the news report just for something to do, and then suddenly remembered that Ronan Strobing's son went to the school; realising the young boy may be in danger she bolted out the room and dialled the number on her STU that would connect her to HART headquarters. The STU at the other end rang approximately three times before it was answered, "Hello," announced Ronan's clear crisp tones, "Commander Strobing speaking."

"Ronan," answered his female counterpart rapidly, "there's just been a newsflash on the TV saying that *Proagnon* forces have invaded the primary school where your son is a pupil. Armed police have surrounded the school and a cordon has been set up. I thought you should know."

"What?" exclaimed Ronan in disbelief, "join the people at the cordon, I will bring a team in and join you shortly."

"Understood, I await your arrival," Celia responded and replaced the STU-8's handset. She then went to her, blue, Honda *Civic*, car and made the journey to the school. She approached the cordon that the police had set up and flashed her pass at the policeman who she took to be in charge, "HART," she announced authoritatively, "what's the situation?"

The policeman lifted the tape to let her through, much to the gathered parent'sannoyance; Mrs Most noticed Ronan's sister-in-law among the crowd, she'd only seen the woman in a few photos but – instantly – recognised her in the flesh.

"Well ma'am," announced the policeman, an Inspector, "it appears that a group of terrorists, *Proagnon* we believe, invaded the school at around 9.20 and are now holding the staff and pupils in the hall – at gunpoint. We also believe another man, a local, is assisting them in this operation as this school seems to have been purposely targeted."

"Have any shots been fired?" Commander Most demanded to know.

"None from my men although, again, we believe a shot was fired inside, earlier."

"HART forces are on their way, I have been in contact with their leader."

*****

At headquarters Commander Strobing summoned Commander Bigship and Dr Schaiffer to the office and informed them of the news he'd just received from Commander Most. "We will be taking a group of twenty soldiers with us to retake the school, and rescue my son. Leon, you will be in charge of picking the soldiers we will be taking with us."

"Yes sir," responded Leon, saluted and then left the room.

"Why do you want me along?" enquired Dr Schaiffer curiously.

"Because," replied Commander Strobing, "you are HART's psychological profiler so I think your assistance may be required."

Commander Strobing then contacted the hangar where the MC-130H *Combat Talon II* was stored and requested it be made ready for lift off in approximately ten minutes. Once he'd done that he took the German doctor to the armoury, unlocked it and handed the man a Beretta 8000 *Cougar*, "Just for your protection," he said, handing over the weapon. Ronan was armed with his usual Beretta 9000 and had his combat uniform, including the *Kevlar II* body armour. Then the two of them went to join Commander Bigship, together with the waiting twenty soldiers – all were armed with the M16A2 rifle fitted with target tracers, at the aircraft that had been chosen. Everyone climbed aboard and sat down in the seats aboard the aircraft. As well as the M16A2 rifles most of the men also carried a *Cougar* semiautomatic pistol; also they'd brought along the TAC-SAT, which Major Shinto Howell was carrying, some *flashbangs* as well as, ordinary, smoke grenades.

Once everyone was aboard the tail ramp was raised and closed, and the four Allison T-56-A-15 turboprop engines were started; Ronan saw that the aircraft was piloted by the legendary Colonel Mcintyre, while alongside him sat a new recruit named Sam Weston, plus there were five other crew members. As the machine rose, steadily, into the air Mcintyre asked, "Everyone okay back there?" Of course he had to shout to make himself heard above the noise the engines were generating.

Commander Strobing looked around him, everyone seemed to be fine, so he shouted back, "Yes we're all okay," then he shouted, "colonel what is our estimated time of arrival (ETA) in the UK?"

"At our present speed I would guess between four and five hours sir." Ronan did a quick calculation in his head; they would arrive in the United Kingdom at approximately 15:30 (local time) but 14:30 (British time). Adequate but not ideal. "Parachutes are under your seats," called back Mcintyre. "I daren't land this *bird* too close to our target."

"That is understood colonel," responded the commander.

At around 14:15 (British time) Commander Strobing called to the other twenty two on board, "Parachutes on, we shall soon be approaching our final destination." Everyone removed their parachute, from under their seat, and fitted them on. Major Howell was the only one who had a slight problem as he was wearing the backpack that contained the TAC-SAT.

About ten minutes later the tail ramp was lowered and the men formed into a single line ready to jump. "Go! Go! Go!" called Ronan, aware his son's life may be in extreme danger. Each man jumped and once down far enough pulled on their ripcords to unfurl their parachutes; every one of the twenty three HART personnel landed in a sports field located behind the school. They watched as the aircraft flew on.

Once they'd all gathered their parachutes up the soldiers made their way, stealthily, to the police cordon. Commander Strobing located Commander Most and asked quickly, "What's the situation?"

"Apparently," she began as Commander Bigship and Dr Hans Schaiffer joined them, "*Proagnon* soldiers, aided by a local man, invaded the school at approximately 9.20 and have taken all members of staff, and pupils, hostage; they are currently being held in the main hall."

"Have there been any shots fired?"

"This man," Celia said introducing Mr Hubert; "was passing this way at 9.25 and believes he heard one shot ring out and a woman's strangulated scream, though he can't be certain."

"At least it wasn't Simon," said the concerned father. Turning to Mr Hubert he shook the man, warmly, by the hand, "Pleased to meet you sir."

*****

Of course the activity outside had gone unnoticed by the *Proagnon* soldiers as their HART enemies had ducked down when they'd passed the windows. Mitchell Walker was still holding Simon Strobing hostage, in the head teacher's office, while Lloyd Edwards and the other *Proagnon* soldiers were keeping everyone else hostage in the main hall, thankfully all the hostages had brought in packed lunches that day so nobody had gone hungry; some of the staff and pupils had shared their lunch with the terrorists, in the vain hope of being released but the men had their orders.

The terrorists then set about, under the guidance of Lloyd, the barricading of windows and both entrances. Once this task was completed every one of the 298 members of staff, along with the pupils, were persuaded to sit themselves on the wooden hall floor. The pianist was also persuaded to keep playing, to keep the other people's spirits up.

*****

Outside Commander Strobing was deep in consultation with the Inspector in charge, "I notice there are a portable cabin in the playground," he indicated a long, green, shed like building situated apart from the main building, "I assume that is an extra classroom."

"Yes sir. May I ask why you appear so interested in it?" the Inspector replied.

"With your permission, though I don't really need it, I intend to commandeer that building and place my men inside there," was the answer Ronan gave.

"In that case sir you have full authority here; however, my men will remain in place as long as you need them."

"Thank you Inspector," and then he looked up at his men. It was then that he noticed his sister-in-law, Melissa Stevens, standing at the cordon with the other – worried – parents, "Melissa," he called to her, "with us."

Melissa Stevens had been shocked to discover her brother-in-law was the head of HART; no wonder he didn't talk about his job, it must be very dangerous work. She was still shocked but, gradually, coming to terms with this new realisation.

Miss Stevens made her way over and joined the HART team, there were many admiring glances from some of the younger members of the HART team as Melissa had a bright pink T-shirt on; her, luckily she was also wearing a black polo-neck jumper over the top, blue, short skirt; a pair of stockings and her blue high heeled shoes; Ronan shook his head, he felt embarrassed to admit to being her brother-in-law while Commander Most just viewed her with a certain air of disgust. "Follow me," said Ronan to his men and led them, quietly, over to the extra classroom. They all made their way up the steps and into the extra classroom and sat at the tables where, usually, the pupils worked

Commander Strobing picked up some chalk and summarised the situation, "We have about twenty two armed and dangerous men over in the main building with about 300 innocent civilians – mainly schoolchildren. I have absolutely no idea whether my son, who is a pupil at this school, is still in the main hall with the others or if he has been singled out and moved to a different room." Every soldier looked shocked when their commander made the admission that his own son was a pupil here; up to then they'd all thought this was a simple rescue mission – which it, in essence, still was – but with a, very, minor – or it could be described as a major - complication.

"We could just storm the building and hope none of the innocent civilians get hurt, but that's an extremely long shot; also we know a local man is helping *Proagnon*, somebody who knows Simon's related to me." He turned to Melissa and looked directly at her, "Have you any idea who it could be?"

"No I don't," she answered, "it could be any one of a number of people."

"What about Lloyd Edwards?"

"It can't be Lloyd," she responded, shocked that he would even think such a thing. "He informed me, last night that he's busy chauffeuring some businessmen about today."

"Would he be driving a blue *Transit* minibus?"

"I believe so, anyway why all these sudden questions about Lloyd?" Miss Stevens was angry that her brother-in-law could even think her latest boyfriend could be involved in some way. Lloyd was a good man and definitely no terrorist.

"Show her Commander Bigship." Leon produced his mobile phone and selected a picture; he showed the picture to Melissa, it showed a burnt out blue *Transit* minibus. A look of horror crossed her usually smooth features. "Is that the minibus?" demanded Ronan.

"Yes it is," Miss Stevens answered, now realising how little she had really known about Mr Edwards. "You mean he's involved in some way?"

"Unfortunately we do."

"So you believe he's the one that made the connection?" she asked in disbelief.

"I'm certain he did." Melissa looked very angry now, Ronan knew, as she now realised, that she'd been used. The question was, was Lloyd being used by his *Proagnon* paymasters? All he could concentrate on, now, was the safety of his son.

"Hans Schaiffer," the German looked up.

"Yes sir," he answered.

"As you're our psychological profiler what do you think our next move should be?"

"Try to establish contact with the hostage takers, see if they have any further demands or if we can negotiate with them," the man replied.

The commander looked around the group, "See if we can get a telephone in here and – someone – get me the phone number of the school."

"Sir," announced Major Howell, "why not use the TAC-SAT."

Commander Strobing looked over at the little Japanese soldier, "An excellent idea, I wonder why I didn't think of that."

Shinto Howell produced the TAC-SAT phone. "Somebody get me the phone number."

"It's okay Ronan," replied his sister-in-law, "I know it."

"Commander Strobing, I am in my official role," Ronan snapped at her.

"Sorry Commander Strobing," she apologised.

The commander of HART then dialled the number on the handset, attached to the TAC-SAT, and waited.

*****

Inside the head teacher's office the phone started to ring. Mitchell Walker let it ring five times before he answered it. Of course he let the other person speak first. "Hello," said the voice at the other end, "may I know whom I'm talking to."

"My name is Mitchell Walker and I am the deputy commander of *Proagnon*. Now may I know who I am speaking with."

"You are speaking to Commander Strobing of HART."

"Ah, Commander Strobing, it is a great honour to speak to you, at last."

"Cut the bull Walker, is my son safe?" enquired Ronan, concern in his voice.

"Oh yes," Mitchell said, "he's quite safe and will remain that way as long as you follow my instructions." Walker smiled across at the, now, bound and gagged boy.

"What do you want?" demanded the commander of HART.

"A million pounds," the terrorist leader replied coolly, "And safe passage out of here. The money is to be delivered to the main office by daybreak, by you Commander Strobing – unarmed – and no tricks. Do I make myself clear?"

The HART commander thought before he answered, "Yes, as clear as crystal, but a million pounds is a huge amount of money, it may take a bit longer to get it all."

"Get it by daybreak or your boy gets it," there was real menace in his voice.

"I'll do my best," Ronan told the terrorist commander.

"You'd better," snarled Walker and hung up. "There," he announced to his captive, "I believe I've ruffled a few feathers. Well, anything to say," he lowered Simon's gag.

"My father will never accept your demands; he'll do everything he can to stop you and rescue me."

"Oh such faith in one so young," remarked Walker and re-gagged the boy.

*****

Commander Strobing replaced the TAC-SAT handset, as the speakerphone had been activated as well everyone in the room had listened to the conversation. "A million pounds," the commander exclaimed standing up and looking around him. "Where are we going to find that sort of money?"

"You are forgetting the golden rule commander," said Schaiffer, "HART never submit to the demands of a terrorist. Even if it appears that they hold all the cards."

"So what do we do?" Ronan asked the man, "and what about my son?"

Hans Schaiffer had obviously considered this eventuality, most terrorists demanded money or the freedom of prisoners; *Proagnon* evidently fell into the first category of terrorists, as he looked up at his commander and said simply, "We play the long game, sit it out, and call their bluff if necessary." Schaiffer then considered Commander Strobing's second question, "As for your son, sir, he should be okay unless they decide to start executing the hostages; though I believe they'll wait until tomorrow."

"Thank you for your assessment Dr Schaiffer," responded Ronan. He then consulted his watch, "Well ladies and gentlemen," he began, "it is now 17.30, I believe we should carry out a brief reconnaissance of the area. Leon and two soldiers with me," and they left the command post and crossed the playground to the main building. "Now we assume they're holding the staff and children in the main hall so the other classrooms should be deserted; there are twenty four of us, if you include Melissa, and several empty classrooms."

They continued with their reconnaissance, but never going too near the hall, even though the windows in the doors had boards over them.

*****

Back at the command post Commander Most had been left in charge; she knew from what Ronan had sometimes, inadvertently, told her that his sister-in-law was a bit of a tart, now Celia could see for herself that there was a great deal of truth in his words. There she was, dressed – Celia thought – like an amateur prostitute; she'd be surprised if Miss Stevens was wearing any underwear, and she seemed to be flirting with many of the younger soldiers.

Melissa happened to notice Mrs Most's gaze and knew immediately what she thought of her; so just to wind Celia up she said to the older woman, "He's not interested in you any more, Ronan's mine, accept it you bitch."

Celia Most began to walk, slowly, towards Melissa Stevens and shot back, "Ronan and I go way back, you do know he once proposed to me." Miss Stevens just stood her ground.

"Yes I know and you turned him down, that was a great move on your part," Melissa told the older woman, "because then he married my sister, as well as meeting me, and had children with her. However, he's always wanted me."

Commander Most snapped at the younger woman, "You two bit whore, is that why he entered my bed when we were in Iran."

Most of the soldiers just looked at each other, those who'd been in Iran the year before had never known about that, how could they?

"Ladies please!" shouted Dr Schaiffer angrily. "This isn't helping anything; there are people being held hostage in there," he indicated the main building, including Commander Strobing's son, and all you two can do is argue over Mr Strobing." Nobody had ever heard Hans Schaiffer raise his voice to anybody before, let alone a woman, everyone was equally as shocked as everyone else.

After another minute Commander's Strobing and Bigship, along with the other two soldiers re-entered the command post, to complete silence; the HART soldiers were looking out the windows, Dr Schaiffer was writing out different scenarios they might face and the resulting consequences, and Celia and Melissa were just seated at opposite ends of the room – glaring at each other.

"Okay," remarked Ronan to nobody and everybody, "what's going on?"

Dr Schaiffer stood up, "Well commander, whilst you've been away we've had something of a catfight," he looked at the two women, "over you."

"Oh yes, there's no need to explain further Hans; I'll take it from here." He looked at both of them then announced, "I will have no internal fighting among the members of this party, whatever squabbles you have can wait until we've completed the mission here. Is that understood?"

"Yes sir," they both responded. Melissa had accepted, now, that she was – obviously – part of this team and so she ought to obey without question. Being Ronan's sister-in-law came second at the moment.

"Good," the commander replied, "now while you were busy squabbling, like schoolchildren Commander Bigship and I have been exploring the inside of the main building; we found seven empty classrooms – we didn't venture too close to the hall, just in case – and two cloakrooms, one situated at either end of the building. So basically, it means we could position soldiers in any classroom – say three in each room or seven in three rooms – leaving Dr Schaiffer plus Melissa Stevens here."

"I'm coming with you," Melissa protested. "I'm not missing out on the chance of being part of the team that rescues my nephew."

Commander Strobing turned to face her and said to his sister-in-law, "Melissa, this is a highly dangerous situation. You aren't trained for this, plus you could easily get shot – fatally I might add."

Again Miss Stevens stood her ground, "I can shoot a pistol; I'm good at hand to hand combat. Just give me a gun and take me with you."

Ronan looked at his fellow commanders Leon shook his head whilst Celia nodded. It was Dr Schaiffer who made the decision, "Take her with you I'll be okay on my own, take my gun as well," and he handed his weapon over.

"It appears that, by a majority of two to one, you are in – remember though you must follow my orders at all times. No going off on your own."

"That is all understood Commander Strobing," Miss Stevens replied, with a new respect for her brother-in-law.

"Okay people, as we're playing the long game might I suggest that we break out the rations, it looks like we'll be sleeping here tonight. I've indicated where the washrooms/toilets are. We'll stay on duty until 22.30 and then bed down for the night, but we'll leave a commander on duty overnight – in fact we'll have a rota system. Leon you're on first watch from 23.00-02.00, I'll relieve you at 02.00 and take watch until 05.00 and Celia you'll take third watch from 05.00-08.00."

They ate some of the rations they'd brought with them – not exactly five star luxury accommodation but it would have to do, for now. After they'd eaten Commander Strobing looked from one to the other of his two equals and asked, "Where would we get a million pound from anyway?"

"We don't need to sir," answered a soldier who'd, evidently, overheard his superior's question, "you simply cut some paper the same size as notes of money, and then add a few forged notes, put them in a briefcase or two and hand them over."

"That's as maybe," responded the man in charge of the mission. "But where do I get hold of forged notes before daybreak?"

Again the soldier spoke, "If I remember rightly my brother runs off forged documents, sometimes money. I'm sure he'll assist us if we needed him to."

"Admittedly this is highly irregular," announced the commander, "however, it might get us out of this situation. Tell me how do we contact your brother, plus why hasn't he been caught yet?"

"I could contact him using the TAC-SAT; he only lives a few miles away. As for why he's never been caught he's also chairman of a legitimate business; a few people know about the extra services he offers but not that many."

"Including us now, as I say it is highly irregular but it may just work. I'll tell you what if you're brother will do this and Walker thinks the notes are real then I won't report him; if however Mr Walker realises the notes are forgeries I have no option but to turn your brother in to the authorities. Is that understood?"

"Perfectly sir," replied the soldier crossing the room and dialling the number on the TAC-SAT handset. He left the speakerphone *on* so everyone gathered in the room could listen to the conversation. The soldier's brother agreed to assist but wasn't too keen on the conditions, that was understandable of course. Once he'd heard everything that was needed he promised he'd deliver by 23.00. The HART soldier thanked him and replaced the handset. "Don't worry sir we'll get your boy back."

Ronan smiled weakly as he digested the words the soldier had said. The HART soldiers, along with their commanders, as it was only 18.20 wandered outside into the cool November air. They performed another perimeter patrol on the playground; Commander Strobing then exited the playground and examined the surrounding houses, looking for suitable places to house marksmen – should they be needed. He spotted a few ideal locations and then he hurried back through the playground whilst the others continued with their patrol.

He found the Inspector, leant against a patrol car, smoking a cigarette as there seemed to be nothing he could do – at the moment – the parents had all returned to their homes. The commander of the HART forces said to the Inspector, "Could you get me ten of your best police marksmen to take up positions in these buildings that surround the school?" He then produced a rough sketch he'd made and showed it to the Inspector.

The Inspector studied the rough sketch – by torchlight as the light was fading - and, after a few moments, replied, "I think this could be achieved as most of these houses are now deserted. Those that aren't we'll have to obtain the owner's permission. I shall contact police headquarters and request that they send ten highly trained marksmen to rendezvous at this position."

"Request that they arrive in an unmarked van, I don't want the *Proagnon* terrorists getting jumpy and trigger happy," said the HART commander.

"Of course not sir," the police Inspector answered, "I will pass along all your instructions to my headquarters." Commander Strobing thanked the man and returned to rejoin his comrades, while the police Inspector crossed to one of the, now, vacant police cars and spoke into the radio.

Pleased with the way things were turning out Ronan returned to the command centre to find twenty three expectant faces looking at him. "What have you been up to?" Leon asked.

"I've been requesting some outside assistance," announced the superior office smiling at them all, "in case we should need it." The HART soldiers watched the main building for any signs of movement, however small and significant. Unfortunately there were none. By 22.00 many of the HART personnel were growing bored and some looked tired; even Ronan's sister-in-law looked rather worn out. The only member of the team who still looked fully alert and ready for action was Commander Most.

The soldier whose brother was bringing the forged money had been despatched to the front gate to meet him, even though he wasn't due for another hour the soldier would be there should his relation be early. With many of his personnel looking weary Commander Ronan Strobing, reluctantly, gave in and sent the other soldiers, along with Commander Bigship, Dr Schaiffer and Melissa Stevens across to the main building to wash and change should they need it; Miss Stevens hung back and said, “No, I’ll wait until you go over.”

Her brother-in-law said nothing in response, he just grunted, although he did notice Melissa glance across at the female HART operative and smile innocently. There was no response forthcoming from Celia. About twenty minutes later Leon and the rest of the group returned, the man all looked refreshed; most had stripped down to their T-shirt’s which had meant having to remove their body armour, this could easily be put back on in the morning.

Commander Bigship said to his immediate superior, “Your turn now sir. I’ll watch for any activity from inside.”

“Okay,” murmured the commander of HART and then, reluctantly and knowing there was nothing else he could do – at the moment, he crossed over to the main building for a refreshing wash, Melissa followed him after giving Commander Most a two fingered salute behind her back; Celia followed them both but at a disceet distance.

Upon entering the building Ronan moved over to the washrooms/toilets, selecting the male ones he nipped inside; his sister-in-law carried on to the other side of the facilities and went about her business. Commander Most arrived about a minute later and walked calmly into the same side as Miss Stevens.

*****

In the main hall most of the schoolchildren – watched over by the *Proagnon* soldiers – had curled up on the wooden floor and were asleep or close to sleep; even some of the adults were beginning to nod off, the only people who were still wide awake and alert, or so it seemed, were the hostage takers.

Lloyd Edwards wandered out into the main corridor and walked to the main entrance. he opened the door and walked into an area that was in shadow – he removed a packet of cigarettes from one of his pockets while from another he produced a lighter; the black man was just about to light one of the cigarettes when he saw the armed HART man carrying two deep briefcases. Lloyd could guess what was in the cases as he and Mitchell Walker had discussed this part of the *Proagnon* plan beforehand, how much they should ask for; the black man knew he could probably take this other man easily and relieve him of his burden, and then make a break for it. He considered this idea but decided against it and let the soldier carry on to his eventual destination, he then checked for any other signs of activity, and seeing none ducked back into shelter and lit the cigarette. Once the cigarette was finished Lloyd walked over to the toilets, used one, and then returned to rejoin his terrorist comrades.

In the head teacher's office Simon Strobing had fallen asleep; Mitchell Walker watched the boy, he looked so peaceful, and then took his gun and exited the small office, locked the door behind him and crossed to the main office. He looked at the secretary and pointed the pistol at her, "No trouble or you get it. Is that understood?" The secretary nodded so Walker lowered her gag and then untied her, one hand firmly clamped on her shoulder, "There, now we're going for a little stroll."

"Where are we going?" The, young, blonde haired woman asked him.

"I don't know about you but I'm going to use the facilities. So lead on but remember my pistol aimed at your back."

"I think I'll remember," she said and led the way out the office and turned left, she led the way along the corridor – down a flight of three stone steps – past a couple of classrooms and to the area where the facilities were, these were the same ones the HART team had used less than an hour ago. "Boys this side, girls that," she said helpfully; Walker prodded her – with his *Glock* pistol - into the female toilets.

He shoved her into a stall and said to her, "Now go!"

"What? With you watching me?" she responded.

"You think I'm gonna leave you? Of course I'll be watching your every move."

"Oh okay," she answered and pulled down her underwear and urinated. Even though he was watching Walker wasn't bothered what she looked like. She finished, cleaned herself up, and re-dressed.

"Right, up against the wall and no tricks;" keeping one eye on his captive – as best he could – he urinated in the toilet. Once he was all finished he leered at her, "See that was easy." He was so close to her now she was afraid that he was going to rape her, but as if reading her thoughts he laughed and said menacingly, "Back the way we came and no tricks."

The secretary nodded and walked, resignedly, back to the office. Mitchell bound and gagged her again and then crossed and, quietly, unlocked the head teacher's office. He entered to find Simon was still fast asleep.

*****

Dawn broke over the area and the three HART commanders stood outside, breathing in the air. "Oh well," Commander Strobing muttered once his watch showed 08.00, "time for me to make my phone call," and he walked back inside the command centre, many of the personnel were still laid on the floor sleeping – those that were awake, including his sister-in-law, looked refreshed and alert. Ronan made his way over to the TAC-SAT and dialled the school's number.

*****

The phone in the office started ringing startling Simon into full wakefulness. Mitchell lifted the receiver. "Greetings," he announced cheerfully.

"Walker."

"Correctly guessed Commander Strobing. Have you got my money?"

"Yes, I await your instructions on where you want it bringing."

"Bring it into the main building, I trust you've set up in the portable cabin, turn right and up the three steps, and leave the cases outside the office, and then leave. No tricks and come alone, unarmed of course. After five minutes contact me again and I will release your son, as well as the other hostages; and I want your assurance that my soldiers, as well as myself, are given safe passage to leave. Any tricks and my men will kill the hostages. Goodbye Commander Strobing," and he replaced the receiver

*****

Over in the command centre everyone was now fully awake and they'd all listened to the conversation and, subsequent, instructions. "Leon, Celia," the commander of the mission said, "I want each of you to take seven soldiers with each of you and set up in classes three and four; both are at the far end. Dr Schaiffer, take the remainder and Melissa with you and set up in class two. I want our men in place in case things go drastically wrong. I will join you all as soon as I can."

Everyone left the command centre - the HART soldiers were all fully armed with their M16A2 rifles with target spotters, grenades, plus a Beretta semiautomatic pistol – and crossed to the other end of the main building. Commander Strobing, however, carried the briefcases across to the main building and followed Mitchell Walker's instructions to the letter; once he had deposited the cases outside the office he turned and wandered back the way he'd come. He was unaware that the terrorist was, even now, aiming his *Glock* pistol at the retreating commander's back – having left the office to retrieve the cases which were full of money.

The HART commander crossed the playground back to the command centre – it was raining; he entered and crossed to the TAC-SAT and dialled the school phone number, as soon as Walker answered Ronan said, "Well satisfied?"

Walker held a note up to the light then another and another; it was then he answered, "These are forgeries, I told you no tricks, now I shall order my men to start executing the prisoners – one by miserable one," and he slammed the receiver down. The HART commander, knowing he'd got about five minutes, produced a radio handset from inside his tunic.

He'd given the other two commanders a radio each, should they need to start without him. Pressing the *transmit* button he spoke quickly, he said just three words, "Go! Go! Go!"

Inside the classrooms Commander's Bigship and Most ordered their soldiers in. The men burst into the main hall and threw *fllashbangs* to disorientate their *Proagnon* enemies and started firing – using the target spotters to aim their shots.

Commander Strobing joined his men after about two minutes; as soon as the HART soldiers had kicked the double doors in and burst in the hall many of the children had run out. The adults, who had been kept hostage as well, tried to help the HART personnel but were quickly cut down by the terrorists; a fierce gun battle ensued. Commander Strobing ran across the hall, managing not to get caught in the crossfire, and threw himself down the far corridor.

He could guess where Mr Walker was and tapped on the door, "Come in Commander Ronan Strobing," announced a voice from inside. Ronan entered the room and saw Mitchell Walker using Simon Strobing as a human shield, the *Glock* pressed against the side of the boy's temple. "Now you are here to bear witness I shall execute your son," Mitchell smiled at the HART commander cruelly.

Commander Strobing studied Mitchell Walker, he was dressed much the same as the other *Proagnon* soldiers – blue uniform, black boots and black gloves; although he wasn't wearing a helmet, he had short cut jet black hair. "This whole place is surrounded, you'll never get away alive," the HART commander informed the terrorist's leader.

"Okay," sneered Walker, "I admit my life may be forfeit, but what is my life compared to that of your son?"

"Give me my boy Walker."

"On one condition," was the response.

"I want safe passage out of here you have till the count of three to decide. One," Ronan considered shooting the man but daren't endanger Simon. "Two," Ronan knew he'd regret his decision but, very reluctantly, found himself agreeing; "Don't go back on your word," Walker warned. Ronan thought that once he'd agreed Simon might be released but Walker clamped his hand on the boy's shoulder and held him tight.

*****

In classroom number two Melissa Stevens and Dr Hans Schaiffer were patiently waiting until all gunfire ceased.

Once the gunfire seemed to have stopped Miss Stevens turned to Dr Schaiffer and said, "I'll just check it's safe." The

German man nodded and she walked out into the corridor where she came face to face with, of all people, Lloyd Edwards; the black man stopped when he saw her and then sauntered up to her, casually and calmly.

"Hey what's up?" he asked her, in that drawl of his, as he saw the gun she held was pointed at his chest. Outside they could hear sirens which indicated that ambulances had arrived, and the paramedics were now on standby.

"You know what's up," she retorted. "You betrayed Ronan, you betrayed Simon, but what really hurts is the fact that you betrayed me. Why?"

"When I was approached by a *Proagnon* officer a year or two back I didn't realise how much my life would change; admittedly it didn't change that much until I met you, and then Simon and Ronan appeared. When I found out what their surname was I reported back to my paymasters who informed me I had to trap the boy somehow as somebody, probably Mitchell Walker, at the main bunker had correctly guessed that there was a link between the two of them."

Melissa stood her ground. "Admittedly I didn't know they had this sort of operation planned; if I'd known I'd have tried to persuade them to call the whole operation off and let me take Simon hostage. Please you have to believe me," Edwards protested as Dr Schaiffer appeared.

"I am trying to believe you," Miss Stevens told the man who had been in league with these terrorists. "That is why I'm not going to kill you," Lloyd visibly relaxed. "No, I'm not going to kill you, just do this," she lowered the weapon but before she'd lowered it fully she pulled the trigger and fired.

"You bitch!" spat Edwards as he looked down and saw where he'd been hit; he hadn't felt any pain straight away.

The 9 x 19mm cartridge had struck Lloyd in the groin, probably causing irreparable damage. "There," Melissa snarled at him as blood started to ooze from the wound – the rich, red, coloured liquid dripped onto the floor of the corridor, "you tried to take away a boy from his father, now I've taken away any hope you have of becoming a father."

Dr Schaiffer just stood there – a tight smile on his face – before he said, “I, honestly, don’t know if you should have done that,” Edwards limped past, his features creased in pain, once he had managed to limp out of sight Hans continued, “but it sure was funny what you said afterwards.”

As the gunfire from the hall seemed to have ceased the two people in the corridor made their way – slowly – towards the doors. Suddenly the double doors burst open and Commander Most stood, framed, in the doorway, “Dr Schaiffer.” The older man pushed past the woman ahead of him and hurried into the hall; when he saw the bodies laid on the wooden floor he gasped in utter shock, there were five murdered adults and about twenty shot pupils, as some of the older boys had tried to assist the adults in their fight against the blue uniformed men – probably they hadn’t realised the full extent of the danger but the adults should have known better, and made sure every child had vacated the room.

Dr Schaiffer walked amongst the fallen bodies; ten of the HART personnel had fallen as well and checked each one for a pulse; when he finally stood up again he sadly shook his head. Melissa then burst into the hall, “Okay, where’s the …,” then she stopped as she surveyed the scene, of carnage, that greeted her; most of the dead children looked no older than eleven, twelve at the outside, they looked so angelic and peaceful - as if there were asleep.

Miss Stevens then broke down in floods of tears as she, suddenly, realised that Simon could have been among those who’d been slaughtered by these bastard terrorists; Commander Most left the group of HART personnel and walked over to her; she knelt by Melissa and placed a comforting arm round her shoulders, and then spoke soothingly to her.

*****

Commander Strobing, meanwhile, watched, with some regret, as Mitchell Walker pulled Simon along – using him as a human shield; the only time he turned round was to negotiate the three stone steps. Once he had walked down the steps – dragging the boy with him – Walker, and his hostage, turned the corner and disappeared from view.

Leon watched the scene, knowing the tough decision his commander had had to make. Suddenly Ronan turned and bolted back through the building; as he rushed across the width of the hall; in his haste he nearly tripped over the body of a young girl. Undeterred by the scene around him he charged on down the corridor and out the other end, he knew he only had moments to spare; the HART commander emerged from the entrance and raced towards the gate. "Inspector," he shouted, "tell your men to hold their fire. He's got my son;" as Ronan reached the gate the Inspector nodded that he'd heard and produced a hand radio. He spoke into it and waited, once he'd received acknowledgement from all the marksmen he gave the thumbs up sign to Commander Strobing who breathed a huge sigh of relief.

As he walked back towards the building he came across the fallen body of Lloyd Edwards; Edwards looked up, "Please Ronan, I'm so sorry." The commander of HART looked down into the face of the black man there was a patch of dried blood under the man. Commander Strobing said nothing, just produced his Beretta 9000S and pointed it at the other man.

"I don't think you are," the HART commander said. "You were in league with these terrorists, you led them here; they have killed 25 teachers, as well as pupils – one of them could've been my boy – so I am sorry Lloyd," and he pulled the trigger. The 9mm cartridge struck the man in the head and he his head fell, face down. Ronan looked at the dead man and said, "Truly I'm sorry."

It was then that he heard a car start up, so he ran – full pelt – towards the other end of the playground; he covered the distance in about eight seconds. The man bolted out the gate and watched as a green *Mondeo*, he registered it as the one that had belonged to – the now deceased – Lloyd Edwards, pulled away from the kerb and drove away. Commander Strobing had committed the registration to memory and sauntered back to his men. "Celia," he said to her, "I notice your car is parked outside the front, hand over the keys please."

Commander Most thought about questioning the reason behind her superior's request but decided against it, she handed the keys over and said quietly, "Not a scratch," Ronan nodded and left the building. He got into his female counterpart's vehicle and started it up, as the engine powered up he noticed that many of the ambulances had vacated the vicinity – the crews had obviously heard that they wouldn't be needed after all. Commander Strobing drove through the streets of Hull and followed the M62 towards the junction with the M18. Once he drove onto the M18 – he guessed Walker would be heading for *Robin Hood* airport to make his escape, he followed the green *Mondeo* closely.

The reason Commander Strobing, in Commander Most's vehicle, had caught Mitchell Walker so easily was because Walker had needed to stop at the AA hotel to collect his belongings; even though this task only took five to ten minutes it had given Ronan time to get on his tail.

Now the HART commander was only one car behind the *Mondeo*; however, once the car in between them – a white *Hyundai* – turned off onto a slip road off the motorway the blue Honda *Civic* speeded up until it was right behind the green *Mondeo*. Mitchell overtook a lorry in front, and then a couple of minutes later he was joined by the blue car, following close behind; the *Proagnon* leader had the thought that he was being followed so sped up again – he overtook a red *Fiesta* and was soon followed by Commander Strobing; it was at this time that the commander of HART wished he was driving his SAAB *9-4X*. The two cars were both now travelling at 85 mph.

Mitchell Walker was now convinced that the Honda *Civic* was following him, and there was only one person it could be; he did have Simon Strobing tied up in the front passenger seat. He built up speed again, up to 110 mph, and began to weave in and out of the other motorway traffic – closely followed by the other vehicle; Mitchell had to slow as they were approaching a roundabout, once past it though he accelerated away but the other vehicle was soon behind him again.

Three, slower moving, coaches loomed up and the *Mondeo* had to reduce speed down to 65 mph, the driver assumed that the car carrying Commander Strobing would shoot past; however, Ronan had already spotted the three coaches and was – at this moment – reducing his speed to keep up with the vehicle he was following.

Once past the coaches both cars sped up and began the chase again. However hard Walker tried he couldn't shake off his tail; Ronan was pretty sure he knew where Walker was going and was rewarded by a sign for *Robin Hood* airport. Mitchell followed closely by Ronan pulled into the airport car park; the *Proagnon* leader jumped from the *Mondeo*, pulled Simon – still tied up – from the vehicle and – again – used him as a human shield. Ronan had to park the Honda *Civic* three rows behind the *Mondeo* and climbed out the automobile, locking the car up after him, and brandishing his Beretta moved slowly forward. Having got his bags and cases from the vehicle Walker pushed the boy forward and hissed, "Do as I say, boy, or I shall kill you without any hesitation." Simon could feel Mitchell's pistol pressing into his back so obeyed without question; Ronan followed them both – maintaining about a car's length between him and his target.

Once he was within easy running distance of the main airport entrance Walker suddenly removed his pistol from the boy's back and he shoved Simon into the road. "Simon," shouted the boy's father as he saw his son fall in the middle of the road. Fearing he'd been shot Ronan dashed over and pushed the boy onto the path as one of the coaches was now approaching; he was just in time and managed to save his son.

The coach pulled over a few hundred yards up and the driver got out, "Sorry mate," he apologised, "I never saw him."

"No harm done;" answered Commander Strobing as he untied his son – Simon hugged his father furiously. Resigning himself to the fact that Mr Walker had – probably – got away he put his Beretta away, turned and led Simon back o the Honda *Civic*. They travelled at a more sedately pace back to Hull and the primary school. "How's the mop up going?" he asked Commander Bigship who he met in the school corridor.

"Well sir," answered his fellow commander, "we lost a total of ten soldiers, all the *Proagnon* soldiers were killed as well as six teachers and a total of twenty pupils. Having said that everyone else seems to be in pretty good shape, sir," and Leon saluted his superior.

Once he'd finished Commander Strobing simply said with sadness and regret in his voice, "If only we could've got everybody out in time."

"I know how you feel sir, but the fact is we couldn't and none of us could have predicted how things turned out. I guess we'll just have to live with the consequences."

"I suppose you're right," murmured Ronan just as Commander Most appeared followed by everyone, in the HART team, who was left. "Let's move out," said Commander Strobing as he led everyone outside. Then he saw the Inspector walking towards them, "Inspector," Ronan greeted him, "I request your help again."

"Gladly," said the man, "what can I do for you?"

"Can you lay on some transport for my men?"

"Of course," he replied, "where would they like to go?"

Ronan gave the Inspector the address of the AA hotel that the *Proagnon* soldiers had recently stayed in, though he was unaware of this fact. The Inspector, whose name was Daniel Fitzgerald – according to his name card, went and radioed his headquarters and about five to ten minutes later a, large, police van pulled up. "Okay men, all aboard, you'll be staying at the AA hotel at this address."

Commander Strobing then addressed the most superior soldier, Lieutenant Bill Sutton, and told him to tell the hotel's staff to bill HART headquarters. With that done the soldiers boarded the van and it pulled away from the kerb.

"Now for us," said Commander Strobing addressing the small group that was left; the group was made up of Commander's Bigship and Most, Melissa Stevens, Dr Hans Schaiffer, plus himself. "Celia," he began, "do you think we'll all fit in your car?"

Commander Most looked round at them before she replied. "Let's see," she began, "there are five of us, plus Simon. Yes I should think it could be done." The police personnel were just leaving when the five remaining members of the HART team crossed to Celia's blue Honda *Civic*. As she drove away she asked her superior, "Where are we all going?"

Ronan looked across and answered, "You can drop Melissa, Simon and me at my house. I was wondering if you could put up Leon and Hans, just for tonight."

"That's a big ask, but the house feels empty without Peter and Mike, so yes I will – the company will be good for me." Commander Most carried on with her journey and dropped Ronan, Melissa and Simon off then pulled away and carried on to her own house. Commander Strobing opened the front door, using the spare key, and while Melissa and Simon walked to the main sitting room Ronan picked up the post, most was junk mail but there was a letter from America.

At Celia Most's residence Celia was picking up the post; among the letters was one addressed to Mike, from America.

CHAPTER 9

THE LETTER AND CONSEQUENCES!

Celia Most and Ronan Strobing opened the letter from America at the same time, although neither of them knew it; Celia didn't like prying into her son's affairs but she assumed, as she hadn't heard from him for weeks that he'd caught this new virus and had died. The letter in question read:

35 Madison Avenue
Crisfield
New York
NY58

During my stay in England I met you; we spent time together and slept together. Since my arrival back in my home country of America I have discovered I am pregnant, and since I have never slept with my boyfriend I can, safely, assume it isn't his; I am not the sort of girl who gets her kicks, or whatever the phrase is, by sleeping around. Therefore I assume that you are the father of my unborn child.

I never intend to return to England again, well not in the near future anyway, so if you wish to play a part in your child's life then I request that you come over to America and join us; the address is at the top of this letter. However, if I hear nothing from you in the next month my boyfriend and I will bring up the child, as our own, once it is born.

Yours truly,

Maria Sanchez

Celia read the letter over and over again, she just couldn't believe it. Here was a letter from this Maria Sanchez, whoever she was – probably some tart - a bit like that Stevens woman, informing her son that he might be a father. When had he met this girl, indeed did he even know her? Commander Most's mind drifted back as she searched her memories for any type of clue.

Then she remembered a conversation she'd had with him, on the telephone, a couple of months back – there had been a woman or girl in the background. Could it have been her? Next she wondered if this woman was telling the truth – or the whole thing was made up. Plus if it was the truth why would her son take such a risk. She could, at this moment, gladly throttle Mike but only after she had got the answers to her questions, but Mike was dead wasn't he? Or had he already gone to join her.

*****

Similar thoughts were occurring to Commander Strobing once he'd read his copy of this same letter. Had anyone else received a similar letter? No of course not. Okay he'd had to leave her – temporarily – with Elle Stevens, but other than that she'd never left him.

He pondered what his best option was; should he go a join her in America? He had too many responsibilities at HART and anyway Simon was happy at Hull's Church of England primary school; okay the last couple of days had been a bit rough on the boy but he'd – eventually – been reunited with his father. So he couldn't really up sticks and leave him.

He stuffed the letter in his pocket and then walked solemnly into the sitting room and seated himself at the side of his sister-in-law on the settee. Melissa sensed that something was invading her brother-in-law's thoughts and enquired, "What's up?"

"I'll tell you later," he responded darkly, and then got up again and poured them each a drink; Simon had a drink of milk and some biscuits and then – as it was 20.30 Ronan took him upstairs to bed, leaving Melissa downstairs on her own.

Once Ronan had taken the boy up she tried to raised her skirt – it was only short she, maybe, raised it a further centimetre but that was all she could manage – she then undid a couple of buttons – on her blouse – revealing a little bit of flesh but not too much, then lay back down on the settee. Her brother-in-law would want her now!

After about fifteen minutes Commander Strobing descended the stairs and walked into the room; the first thing he said when he saw her was, "Sit up Melissa. Anyone would think you were waiting for something." Once she'd sat up Ronan sat next to her but not too close. "And do yourself up you look like a common tart."

"Okay," she replied – sounding disappointed - and did one button up but left the final one undone. "Now what's wrong?"

"This," he answered, producing the, now crumpled, letter from his trouser pocket; his sister-in-law un-crumpled the letter and read it, in fact she had to read it twice.

First thing she said to him was, "Is it true?"

"Yes," he answered, ashamed of himself now.

"But why did you do it?"

"I, honestly, don't know," she knew from his tone of voice that h now regretted it.

"Tell me the full story," Miss Stevens demanded.

Okay, it all started when I came to London. We met, in the bar of the Ritz hotel – she told me she was over here to promote her father's business - if my memory serves. That turned out to be a lie; but I enjoyed her company and she seemed to enjoy mine. Anyway we met the next day, she seemed to be following me; a few days later I returned to Hull and brought her up here with me. To cut a long story short we did spend a night together and then she returned to her home in America."

Melissa looked over at Ronan and said, seriously, to him, "I think, dear brother-in-law, that this letter is a deliberate hoax. Are you sure she didn't have the opportunity to sleep with anyone else?"

"Pretty sure," admitted Commander Strobing and then he thought and added, "I admit I left her with your mother for an hour, maybe two, as I had a few jobs to do in town so I guess she could've slipped out, while your mother wasn't looking, or was busy, and met up with someone else. She might even have had time to sleep with them."

"How old was she?" was Melissa's next question.

"Seventeen," he answered.

"Of all the stupid things to do!" she said angrily. "Fancy going with a girl twenty years younger than yourself; you know I've always liked you so why didn't you come to me?"

"If I remember rightly you had your hands full with Lloyd, or was it Eric, at the time?" he retorted.

"Whoever it was wouldn't have come between us, you only needed to say the word."

Ronan considered what his sister-in-law had just said then he – lazily – put his arm round her, "Now you know what my job entails, do you still want to have a relationship with me or will you worry about me too much and want me to resign?"

"Oh no," she responded and kissed him, gently, on the cheek, he could tell she wanted more; "I don't want you to resign. If you think you ought to I won't stand in your way. Yes, I still want a relationship with you I always have."

The man of the house looked up at the clock above the fireplace, 22.30 – where had the time gone? Melissa got up and walked over to the drinks cabinet, Mr Strobing's eyes following her every move, where she poured a drink for them each and then handed one to her brother-in-law, though he was really her ex brother-in-law. "A night cap and then off to bed," she said. "Here's to a well executed rescue mission, Cheers," and she raised her glass to him.

"Cheers." He responded, raised his glass and then they drunk the contents of their glasses. "Time for bed I believe," the commander of HART announced once their glasses were empty. The two of them exited the room together, ascended the staircase and then disappeared into the main bedroom.

*****

At Commander Most's house Celia had decided to keep the contents of the letter that Mike had received to herself for the time being; she couldn't bring herself to tell the two men in her sitting room, so she refolded the letter, put it back in it's envelope and pushed the envelope under the phone directory. She could just make out the men chatting quietly to each other.

She wandered through to join them, fixed each of them a drink, including herself, and seated herself in a separate chair. Once they'd all finished their drinks of Scotch Mrs Most looked at them both and said, in an authoritative tone of voice – she was the highest ranking person in the room, "Sleeping arrangements are as follows: Leon, you will sleep in Mike's, old room while Dr Schaiffer, you will take the couch." She had expected them to protest at these arrangements but both men simply nodded; Celia had made herself a promise now Peter had gone, she didn't think he was still alive, that no other man – whoever it was – would ever join her between the sheets again.

She'd also informed the men that there was a lock on her door, in case either of them was tempted to try any funny business. At about 22.45 they all retired to their different sleeping quarters. At about 02.17, Celia was awoken by a strange hammering noise; groggily she raised her head, "What the hell's that noise?" she asked herself - puzzled, she stepped out of bed and fastened a, pink, dressing gown around her – grabbed her firearm off the side table where she'd put it – and slowly unbolted her bedroom door and Celia Most made her way – cautiously – down the staircase.

She did think that it may have been one of the two men possibly waking up suddenly and blundering about but the door to the room where Leon was sleeping was closed, and Dr Schaiffer was still asleep on her settee – snoring. Then it came again, this time the noise sounded like it was coming from the front door – Celia wondered if she was imagining it but the noise, it sounded more like a knocking that was now becoming more insistent; how Commander Most wished she had Commander Bigship with her but then she thought, *No, this is my house, I should be the one to defend it*. So with her Beretta 92 in her left hand she held the key in her right and unlocked the door; cautiously again she drew back the two bolts and opened the door slowly, prepared to shoot whoever it was and ask questions later should the person outside prove to be hostile.

Celia opened the door fully and a, shabby looking, figure fell inside – the person fell face down on the on the floor and Celia slammed the door shut to keep out the bitter wind. With as much menace in her voice as she could muster she pointed her weapon at the human person, it was the figure of a young man, and said, "I will not hesitate to use this gun if I have to, so raise your hands above your head and get up – slowly."

"Mum, it's me," replied the figure of the young man as he got up and looked into the face of the female HART commander.

Celia was shocked as she came face to face with her son Mike again; he looked bloody awful, his hair had grown and was very untidy, his face was covered in muck and grime, his clothes were untidy – dirty – and totally dishevelled; all in all he just didn't look like the son she knew and loved. He looked as though he'd been sleeping rough – Hull was full of tramps and vagrants who slept on park benches or anywhere else they could find – "Mike is that you?" his mother enquired, still a little dubious.

"Of course it's me Mum, I've come home."

"Oh Mike it is you, come here," and mother and son embraced. Commander Most said tearfully, "It is you. What's happened to you, where have you been?"

"Its a long story," Mike said to her simply.

"Come into the kitchen. We can't go in the sitting room, there's a man asleep in there and one upstairs in your room, and before you jump to the wrong conclusion they're just work colleagues." Celia and Mike seated themselves on two, wooden, chairs in the kitchen, "Now tell me all," she said. She wasn't bothered about the timing of his arrival.

"Well," began Mike, "it all started when I went to the doctors – I met Ronan and his son, Simon, there."

"I know, Celia said to him, "he told me."

Mike carried on, "When I'd left there, the doctor said I just had a mild dose of *normal* flu, I came straight home and relaxed a bit and had a bath; afterwards I went out again – just for some air – and I met a girl named Maria. I brought her home and one thing led to another – that was when you rung – and we ended up in bed together." Celia didn't comment, just let her son carry on, "Anyway I thought she'd really taken a liking to me but she seems to have disappeared."

"I walked her to a nearby park and after we'd parted I began to walk back when this gang jumped me; there were four of them – they were all wearing hoods – one was short, big and thick set, one was tall and thin – he seemed to be their leader, whilst the other two were of average height and build. Anyway they beat me up and then left me in a ditch; when I came to I discovered they'd robbed me and taken my mobile phone and what money I had on me, plus I couldn't remember anything."

"I've lived rough for the past two months – nearly three, no-one has even bothered with me; thankfully my memory's been coming back, slowly, and when I heard about the siege at Hull Church of England primary school and HART being called in I knew you'd be involved, therefore I knew the time was right to come home."

His mother listened to his tale without any comment and didn't interrupt. "Wait there," she told him and then added mysteriously, "I've got something for you." His mother left the kitchen and went and retrieved the letter from America. "This came for you, I don't know when – probably yesterday," Commander Most told him. "Read it."

Mike Most produced the letter from the opened envelope, unfolded it and read it; he had to read it again to make sure he'd read it correctly, afterwards he just looked blankly at his mother and breathed, "It can't be true," and then he asked Celia, "what do you think Mum?"

Celia considered what these implications may have on her son's future. "Well, I know what you did was wrong but you did and so you must consider this. She states that she slept with you which you have admitted yourself but," his mother paused, how do you know what she's saying is true, she might be pregnant but if she is how do you know it's yours? You don't. She states that she's not the sort of person who sleeps around. How do we know this? It could be anyone's, just because you slept together doesn't automatically mean the baby, if there is one, is yours."

Just then Dr Schaiffer appeared and said to Commander Most, "I thought I heard voices." He yawned and then enquired of the lady of the house, "Who is this person anyway?" he indicated Mike.

"This Dr Schaiffer," she announced proudly as he poured himself a glass of water, "is my son Mike, and he's got himself into a, slight, spot of bother, which we are endeavouring to sort out."

"Can I be of any assistance?" he asked his superior as he drank the water.

Celia considered telling him but instead said, "We'll all discuss it later this morning because I, and I'm sure Mike would, would appreciate yours and Leon's views on this matter."

"What matter?" enquired a new voice, Commander Most turned and saw Commander Bigship standing in the doorway; he was wearing his boxer shorts.

"A small matter concerning a, slight, spot of bother my son, here has got himself into," she responded. "Let's all go back to bed for now."

"Where am I going to sleep, if I can?" Mike asked his mother.

"You can sleep on my bedroom floor; I'll provide you with a pillow and a cover." They all, except Dr Schaiffer – who was sleeping on the settee walked upstairs and disappeared into different rooms.

At about 09.00 in the morning everyone congregated in the kitchen for a full English breakfast. As the two HART men ate Mike introduced himself properly to them and they – likewise – introduced themselves. Once all four of them had finished eating Celia cleared the table of breakfast pots and Mike showed the two men the letter he had received.

They each took it in turn to read it and then offered their opinion and advice; Dr Hans Schaiffer began by enquiring, "Is it true that you slept together?"

"It is," the young man confirmed shamefacedly.

"And you had sex with her?"

"My memory's a bit hazy on that one," he replied. "I might have done."

"Let us suppose you did and what she's saying is true, what do you intend to do about it?" he asked calmly. He knew that probably Mrs Most could have easily throttled her son for his irrational actions therefore he was trying to defuse the situation by talking to the boy calmly. He knew he wasn't the boy's father but he was a medical doctor.

"Well," answered Mike thinking. "Supposing she is pregnant, with my child, she has requested that I go over there to join her, yet I don't want to leave Mum until we know if anything's happened to Dad."

"Most admirable my boy, spoken like a true Englishman," remarked Leon with a smile.

"Now as I'm sure your mother has said this baby, if indeed there is one, could be anybody's; never mind what she says. So I'm advising you just to write back and ask her how she can be so sure it's yours; however, if just – let's say – it is true but you don't want to leave your mother just tell her, I'm sure she'll understand. Plus how do you know she's from America? She could just be living a couple of miles away and had a relation of hers write to you."

All through this exchange Leon had been nodding and murmuring. Commander Most looked at the clock, it read 09.50.

*****

Over at the Strobing household Melissa Stevens woke up and looked at the man lying next to her, she couldn't believe her luck – she'd finally got him. Once Ronan awoke they both got out the bed and dressed; Commander Strobing then said to Miss Stevens, "Check on Simon will you?" then he added, "Thanks for last night, it was fun."

"Don't forget you've got that letter to think about, I gave you my opinion last night." Hull Church of England primary school was closed – following the siege by armed gunmen – until the following Monday; still today was Thursday so Simon had four days to recover. Of course some pupils wouldn't return on the Monday as they'd probably be traumatised so they'd need counselling, others would never be returning.

Even though Commander Strobing had seen people killed before, usually adults – just the thought of those children lying dead in that hall was a thought that would haunt him for the rest of his time as HART commander, and probably afterwards.

*****

One person who had heard about the siege and seen the pictures on TV was the *Proagnon* leader – Sandy Tulliver – along with her business partner – though he meant much more to her than that now – the man she knew as Floyd Maxwell; she had cursed Mitchell Walker for this totally irrational behaviour, still he was probably trying to assert his command and possibly turn the soldiers against her, so when she rejoined the main group in the Iranian bunker she would face a revolution by forces from her own side and Walker would then depose her and, possibly, dispose of her.

Sandy then realised she could just stay in England with Maxwell and watch as the *Proagnon* terrorist organisation was, hopefully, destroyed by HART forces. That is what she would do – she finally decided.

There hadn't been that much on the news lately about the virus, maybe all the initial panic was over, but she was sure the panic would resurface in a few weeks once the *flu* season started.

*****

Later that day, at about 14.20, every HART soldier, along with the three commanders and Dr Schaiffer, rendezvoused at Doncaster's *Robin Hood* airport; Commander Ronan Strobing arrived in his Saab *9-4X,* Commander's Most and Bigship plus Dr Hans Schaiffer arrived in Celia's Honda *Civic*, whilst the soldiers arrived in a Ford *Transit* police van.

Once they'd all bypassed the check in desk, much to the annoyance of the other waiting passengers, they were shown to a more private lounge - by a member of airport security - to await their transport back to Switzerland. As they were sitting there they all began to swap stories about the part they'd played in the resulting gun battle. Many were saddened that children's lives had been lost and expressed their feelings. The thirteen men, who were left, and one woman all boarded the Gulfstream *G550* jet and the personnel all stowed their equipment in the aeroplane's overhead lockers and then found a seat and strapped themselves in.

The bodies of the other ten HART soldiers who had been killed in the gun battle at the school were being flown back aboard the C-130 *Hercules* that had brought them all in, once all the bodies had been identified and the HART personnel had said a proper farewell to their fallen comrades the bodies would be flown home to their, native, countries where a family funeral could take place; their passing would be marked with a, new, cross in the garden of remembrance. As the HART members felt partly responsible for the deaths at the school Commander Strobing had felt it might be wise to fly back to Switzerland, and not to attend the funerals.

Once the clock had reached 15.20 the business jet powered up the two Rolls Royce BR710 turbofan engines, once the engines were at full power the aircraft began to roll down the runway on it's, standard, three sets of wheels. When the plane had achieved its maximum speed the jet ascended into the air at a forty five degree angle; once at an altitude of 40,000 feet the plane levelled off and flew at a cruising speed of 904 kilometres per hour. The journey distance to their destination of Geneva's *Cointrin* International Airport was 951 kilometres so the jet would land in just over an hour; however, as there was an hour's time difference the time when they landed would be a further hour ahead.

Once the jet had levelled off the HART personnel moved about the interior of the aircraft and chatted to each other, some off them also read the latest newspapers; Leon read *The Sun*, Celia read *The Telegraph* and Ronan read *The Independent*. When Commander Strobing had finished reading he requested the Major Howell hand him the TAC-SAT phone, he contacted the main headquarters just outside Geneva and requested that both of the *Apollo II* cars plus both Land Cruisers be at the airport to meet them, the aircraft's Estimated Time of Arrival (ETA) of landing was 17.30 (local time).

Joshua Smith, who was on reception, acknowledged this request and passed the order on to the garages where the vehicles were stored.

Once the executive business jet landed in Switzerland, at *Cointrin* airport all the fourteen HART personnel disembarked and walked over to their transport back to headquarters; eight of the personnel (soldiers) boarded the two Land Cruisers – four in each – while the remaining six personnel (commanders, soldiers and Dr Schaiffer, boarded the two *Apollo II* cars and then the convoy of four vehicles left the airport compound and began their journey back to headquarters.

As they were travelling along nobody took much notice of the silver Mercedes *Sprinter* van following them; as the convoy reached a section of the road that was dual carriageway the van started to overtake the Land Cruiser at the back of the convoy of HART vehicles, once it had drawn alongside the sliding side door flew open and two gunmen fired their AK-47 assault rifles at the Land Cruiser. The bullets raked the side of the 4 x 4 vehicle but as the vehicle being fired at was fitted with bullet proof armour the bullets fired didn't penetrate the armour; seeing the bullets bounce harmlessly off the armoured vehicle the gunmen fired at the tyres instead.

Meanwhile the drivers of the other three vehicles – in the convoy – had seen what was happening behind them and increased their speed, hoping to pull away before the Mercedes *Sprinter* van caught up with them.

The Land Cruiser, whose tyres had been punctured by the bullets, started to swerve about dangerously; the silver van closed its side door and accelerated away at full speed. Meanwhile the vehicle with the punctured tyres swerved about and then hit a pothole – in the road – this caused it to swerve about even more, narrowly missing a bus full of passengers. It was then that the Land Cruiser swerved off the road, crashed through the barriers and carried on down the hillside; suddenly a clump of trees appeared – of course these were visible from the road – the soldiers aboard figured that they would be okay because the vehicle was moving more slowly now, "Brake," ordered the soldier who was sitting in the passenger seat.

"Okay," replied the driver, slightly annoyed; he knew he had to brake, didn't this soldier realise this? The driver pressed what he thought was the brake pedal but the vehicle accelerated, he'd got the wrong pedal.

"Stop!" they all shouted as the clump of trees suddenly loomed up larger than ever. The Land Cruiser suddenly sped forward and hit a tree root; it was suddenly thrown up into the air and crashed back down to earth, and then the engine exploded killing the five occupants aboard.

The silver Mercedes *Sprinter* van easily caught up with the three remaining HART vehicles and overtook the remaining Land Cruiser, thanks to the customisation it had undergone, slotting back in between it and the leading cars.

When the driver of the van judged the vehicle was far enough past he gave an order to the men in the back and the rear doors of the van flew open revealing an object on a tripod covered by a sheet. At another command the sheet was pulled away to reveal a mortar!

The driver of the black Land Cruiser tried to swerve out the way but he had no chance. The mortar shell smashed into the following vehicle, penetrating the front grille and the – outer – engine casing. Inside the engine it exploded causing a huge fireball that completely engulfed the vehicle and one or two following cars, by this time the silver van had sped off again, leaving the burning Land Cruiser behind, and bore down on the two *Apollo II* automobiles.

The driver of the chasing van swung out and overtook both cars easily, even though the HART vehicles were travelling at around 80mph. As the Mercedes *Sprinter* swung across in front of the cars, the driver of the vehicle and the three commanders watched as the van's rear doors were opened again, and the mortar was revealed, again. All aboard the car knew that as this was a second generation *Apollo* automobile it was protected by the bullet-proof doors and windows, while the front of the vehicle, where the engine was, plus the roof and the boot were also mortar proof. Plus they also had the added advantage that the windows were now all made of tinted glass, enabling the occupants to see out, but no one could see inside.

As the van started to pass them Commander Strobing said to the driver, in a pretty urgent tone, "Contact the other car and request that Dr Schaiffer jump out, and then take evasive action."

"Roger sir," and the driver did as requested. The mortar fired its second shell straight at the second, which had now become the lead, automobile. Commander Strobing watched with interest as the shell struck the HART vehicle; as with the Land Cruiser before it, exploded in a large plume of flame and smoke. "Bastards!" Ronan swore, "That's another thirteen personnel dead, ten soldiers and three drivers. My command isn't going well."

"Don't worry sir," answered Leon, "most new commanders have to deal with many losses. At least Dr Schaiffer's safe,"

"Hmm, yes, there is that. Where is Dr Schaiffer?"

*****

As soon as the order for Dr Hans Schaiffer to *jump* had been received and acknowledged the medical man had exited the vehicle he was travelling aboard and rolled down a grassy embankment. Suddenly he'd heard a loud explosion and peered upwards – while laying flat on his stomach; he couldn't see much except a huge ball of flame and horrid black smoke rising from it.

Therefore, Schaiffer judged from the position of the explosion, the *Apollo II* he'd been travelling in had met a fiery and – distinctly – nasty end. Covering his head to protect it from any falling debris; he'd lay there about a minute and then rose to a standing position and walked back up the embankment to find the remaining *Apollo II*.

The car, in question, had pulled over to the outside of the road and come to a halt with its *hazard* lights going. Hans ran to the car and climbed into the back seat between Commander's

Most and Bigship as the back door had been opened for him to climb in.

Once the man was aboard and strapped in the *Apollo II* pulled away and carried on with its journey towards the HART compound, and headquarters; of the silver Mercedes *Sprinter* van there was no sign. Eventually the vehicle reached its destination and drove through the gates; the four passengers exited the *Apollo II* car and walked – somewhat gloomily – towards their main headquarters building.

Once on the fourth floor Dr Schaiffer wandered away from the other three towards the medical centre, whilst Commander's Strobing, Most and Bigship walked off to their separate offices. As they entered reception the other two separated from Commander Strobing and entered their offices. Before the overall HART commander entered his own office he looked over at Lisa Bell, who was doing her shift on reception, and asked, "Can I have a list of names of the twenty personnel who went with us to England, and the names of the drivers of *Apollo IIB* and the two Land Cruisers, and files on those personnel; soon as you can."

"Right away sir," Lisa replied and as Ronan moved across to enter his own office Miss Bell removed the keys to the various filing cabinets – from a drawer in the desk – and walked over to the cabinets. Locating which ones she wanted the young receptionist unlocked them and got the twenty three files out that she'd need.

About a quarter of an hour after Ronan had issued his instructions there came a knock on the wooden door, "Enter," he called. The door opened and Lisa Bell entered pushing a small trolley with twenty three files on it; some were extremely thin whilst others were more average sized as they contained more paperwork. She placed the files on the commander's desk, "Take a seat Miss Bell," so she seated herself on the other side of the desk.

Lisa could tell from the way he looked that something was bothering him, but why should he want to tell her - if indeed he did, she was – after all - the most junior receptionist. "What's wrong sir?"

"All these men are dead Lisa, dead because they followed me. Maybe I'm not fit to lead HART after all." There was real doubt and sorrow in his voice then he added, "Maybe command should have passed to Leon – after all he is older and, probably, wiser. What do you think Lisa?"

"Sir, with all due respect shouldn't you be having this conversation with someone more senior?" She leaned on her elbows, while looking into his face to gauge his reaction.

Commander Strobing pondered her words for a moment before issuing his response, "I could have this conversation with someone more senior but I would like your opinion," suddenly their eyes locked.

"Okay," said Miss Bell, "here's my opinion. "You are fit to lead HART – there is no doubt in my mind – you are the youngest of the three commanders whereas Leon, pardon me for saying this, is old and stale. If we chose him over you things would go back to the way of how Mr Roberts led, and, I know I shouldn't say this but, I actually prefer you." Then she added, "Okay you've got off to a shaky start and it's thrown your confidence a bit, but you'll regain that confidence – I believe in you."

"Thank you for putting my mind at ease," he said to her and then asked the young woman seated opposite, "drink?"

"Don't mind if I do, an orange juice please sir?" Ronan broke her gaze, got up from his seat and got two drinks; he poured himself a whisky and got her an orange juice, "There you go," he said, sitting back down and placing the drink in front of her. "Cheers!"

They both drank their drinks and chatted awhile; once they'd drained their glasses Commander Strobing said to Miss Bell in a bit of a sad voice, "I suppose I'd better get my reports up-to-date and fill in the HART condolence letters informing the families of these soldiers that they died in the line of duty."

"Right you are sir," and Lisa suddenly leaned forward and kissed her superior. Ronan was taken totally by surprise and a slight tinge of anger rose up inside him; sensing his uneasiness over the situation the young receptionist quickly added, in way of apology, “Sorry sir. I don’t know what came over me, but you must know I like you commander and always have.”

The commander looked hard, across the desk, at her and replied, “I suppose I knew you felt something for me, but this is beyond belief. I’m sorry to disappoint you but you know the rules, no relationships between any of the HART personnel. I ought to dismiss you - here and now - for your actions, but you are still young and I see you have a great career, at HART, ahead of you; therefore we will forget what just happened.” Then he said, more pleasantly, “Would you care to be my guest tonight and join me at the *L’Entrecote Couronne*? I have a table booked – for two – at 20.00.”

“I’d be delighted to sir,” Miss Bell eagerly responded, with a smile developed on her face. “Thing is I’m meant to be on reception.”

Her superior consulted the reception rota computer file, on his laptop; a paper copy of the rota was also kept in one of the desk’s drawers – just in case the computer broke down or – for whatever reason – the file happened to get deleted. “I see Ben Gillesie is due to take over from you at 22.00. I’ll see if he’s prepared to come in a couple of hours earlier.” So whilst she was still in the office Commander Strobing dialled Mr Gillespe’s home number and requested the young man come in a couple of hours earlier; he didn’t tell him why, just that Miss Bell needed to leave two hours earlier than usual.

Ben must have agreed because when the commander replaced the handset he looked up at the young woman standing before him – a broad smile on his face – and said to her, “That’s that settled; he’ll come in early.”

Pleased Lisa Bell left the commander to his other work. Once he’d finished writing the letters of condolence, and signing each one personally, he produced another twenty-three of the small wooden crosses and went out to place them in the HART garden of remembrance.

It was cold outside – well winter was on its way – plus it was raining which made it feel even colder, his watch thermometer told him the temperature was about six degrees centigrade, and the rain wasn't just a light drizzle it was a full rain shower.

*****

The silver Mercedes *Sprinter* van, the occupants happy with their work of dealing another blow to the HART organisation, had been driven to a – rented – garage on the Av. Picttet de-Rochemont where it had been put to prevent it from being seen by the prying eyes of a passer by. The four *Proagnon* agents climbed out the vehicle; once the mortar weapon together with the shells had been unloaded from the back compartment two of the men walked through into a room at the back of the garage, whilst the other two men both set to work customising the van's engine – again - to give it more power for the next mission when it would need to be used.

The mortar weapon was covered by a tarpaulin, just in case somebody managed to break into the garage, and then the other two men went and joined the first two in the back room where they all had something to eat and drink. Suddenly the radio, on the table, crackled into life and a voice said, "You did well earlier but keep monitoring their radio transmissions." The leader of the four agents, also the driver of the van, acknowledged that the order had been received and understood.

As there was nothing they could do, at the moment, the men placed the radio transmission monitoring device in the centre of the table and began playing a game of cards.

*****

Commander Strobing finished his task and went back inside. He took the elevator to the fourth floor and walked – steadily – back to his personal office, once back inside his cosy office he took the coat off and hung it on the coat stand then sat back down at his desk and began typing reports on his computer; this device was attached, via cable, to a printer so once Ronan had finished typing a report he would print it out and file it away, plus save the computer file containing the report to his hard drive.

Therefore again, if the computer broke down or the report file – accidentally – got deleted HART would have a copy in the files. HART commanders were allowed to save reports for a month then they were permitted to delete the computer files, however all personnel lists were kept for an unlimited period of time, but as these files contained sensitive information they were advised to be encrypted and only accessible with a case sensitive password – the present password was *Buffalo* - although this password was changed on a monthly basis.

Presently Lisa Bell brought a cup of tea through and placed it in front of him; he'd ordered it as he was passing through reception. "There you are sir," she said pleasantly. It was then that Commander Most walked into the office.

Seeing Miss Bell leaning forward, over the desk, the deputy commander said, "Sorry to disturb you sir, ah I see you're busy so I'll come back later."

"Wait Celia, Miss Bell was just leaving, I've actually got a letter for you to look at," her superior hastily said then added, "thank you for the tea Miss Bell perhaps you'd be kind enough to fetch Commander Most a cup."

"Certainly sir," Lisa answered, sounding a bit disgruntled but she went anyway. Ronan watched her as she walked away, so young and inexperienced yet he had to admit she was rather pretty with her long blonde hair, pale blue eyes and a figure that any woman would die for; she was fairly tall, about five foot seven, and not thin yet not fat – average build. She took Commander Most's order and then left.

Celia sat down opposite Ronan and looked at him then said, "I noticed you looking, no gazing, at Lisa. Are you contemplating starting a relationship with her? If so I strongly advise against it."

Her superior suddenly asked, "Why?"

"She's much too young and immature for you and, well, she's not exactly brilliant."

"Your concern is duly noted Commander Most," Ronan replied. "However, my personal life is my responsibility and if I make mistakes I will admit to them. Now the subject is closed."

"Yes sir," answered his deputy knowing he would do what he wanted anyway – he was headstrong and obstinate in that way. "Now sir I believe you said you had a letter to show me," she sat back as Commander Strobing fished the document from out one of the desk drawers; he produced a neatly folded document.

"Now before I read it I just want you to know that I found it on my doormat when we were back in England, yesterday." He then proceeded to unfold the letter and began reading; Celia Most listened attentively as he read it.

Once he'd finished she said to him, "My son, Mike, received exactly the same letter in the post that is interesting."

"I fail to see how," her superior snorted.

"One child with two possible fathers, that's if she is pregnant." Then she proceeded to ask Ronan the same, or similar questions that Melissa had; he informed her he'd known the girl, had only let her out his sight once when he'd had to place her with his mother-in-law, however, the two of them had slept together that night.

"Sorry Celia," he apologised, getting up from his chair. "I have a dinner date tonight and I need to go and get changed."

"As indeed I do," she answered, also rising from her seat. "We'll finish this conversation some other time, perhaps tomorrow." Her superior agreed and they left the office, and the building. The weather had cleared up and the temperature was now – Commander Strobing consulted his watch/thermometer – eight degrees centigrade. They parted company outside the HART residences and went their separate ways.

*****

Ronan Strobing went inside, had a quick shower and then changed into a dinner suit of black trousers, white shirt etc. He then returned outside and climbed into his personal *Apollo II* vehicle; he did notice Commander Bigship's had gone as well, where could he have gone? The commander had no time to worry about that now, he drove slowly round to some bungalows, at the rear of the compound – these were used by the medical, and reception, staff; he drove to number four and pressed his horn.

The front door of the bungalow opened and Lisa Bell walked out, Ronan looked at what she was wearing – as if he were inspecting her – she was wearing a white blouse – that was okay – but what might have been more suitable attire for a disco was the short denim skirt she was wearing, along with the white knee high boots. Miss Bell, who didn't know how her superior felt about her choice of clothing climbed into the passenger seat, fastened her seat belt, and then Ronan drove slowly away. "You look lovely Lisa," he commented as they moved off.

"You really think so?"

"Yes I do."

Miss Bell then sighed, "I wish I'd had the foresight to put some trousers on; it's a bit nippy out there." *So do I,* thought the commander, once the soldiers – those on duty at least – saw the pair of them together speculation would be rife.

The vehicle headed towards the main gate which was always guarded; as if on cue a sentry appeared and Ronan wound down his window. "I'm going off site for a while, if an emergency arises," he prayed it would so he could leave the inappropriately dressed Lisa Bell – at least for a while, "contact Ben Gillespe and inform him, he'll contact me."

"Taking Miss Bell too?" the sentry enquired. Lisa just giggled as the vehicle left the compound if he'd looked back Ronan would have seen a big grin cross the other man's face. The car drove south down Route de Lausanne until it led into Rue de Lausanne then turned left and drove down Rue Rothschild and finally turned right – at the bottom – onto Rue des Paquis. Ronan found the restaurant and parked the HART vehicle in the parking area of the eating establishment.

He escorted his dining companion into the restaurant where the maitre'd escorted them to the table Commander Strobing had reserved earlier; once they were both seated the maitre'd took their drinks order and retreated, Ronan looked around – it wasn't that often he came here, especially not with a young woman as his companion – he was a bit astonished to see Commander Bigship seated at a table with Commander Most.

Both seemed to be enjoying the food and each other's company. Suddenly his mind was dragged back to the present by the reappearance of a waiter brandishing a bottle of wine, although it was Swiss it was one Ronan had had before, many years ago, and had found had an excellent taste to it – not too sharp – would Lisa Bell agree with his choice? Her face – as she tasted the wine, told him he'd made the right choice.

"Not many here tonight Alfonso," commented Ronan as the maitre'd appeared to take their order.

"Unfortunately not sir," Alfonso replied, there were only four tables full. "I blame that new restaurant, the *Al-Ken*, which has opened. However, our loss is their gain," such a philosophical man; "Getting back to the matter at hand what would sir, madam, like to eat?"

"What would you like Lisa?" the HART commander enquired of his, young, female companion.

Lisa looked up at the, waiting, maitre'd, "I think I'll have a medium to rare steak, chips and peas please." The man wrote her order down.

"And for you sir? He asked, turning to Commander Strobing.

"I think I'll have the same please." The maitre'd hurried off in the direction of the kitchens. When he returned one couple paid their bill and left.

"Please call again," Alfonso called after them.

*****

Whilst they were waiting Ronan asked Lisa, "Do you like it here?"

"Yes sir," she answered with calmness in her voice that her superior had never noticed before. It was then that Ronan realised she was gazing at him again, like she had in his office back at headquarters a little earlier, with her – baby – blue eyes.

"Please call me Ronan for tonight," the commander said. "Sir sounds a little too formal."

"Okay Ronan," she replied and gave a slight giggle. Before the commander could ask what she was giggling at their food arrived; the food looked extremely well done and was well presented. As they ate, steadily, the two of them chatted away about this and that.

Later on Ronan paid the bill for two steak dinners, two desserts, a bottle of wine and two cups of tea. Leon Bigship and Celia Most had already left the restaurant to return to the HART compound where Commander Most would assume, temporary, command until Commander Strobing returned; the man in question assumed they'd spotted him with Lisa Bell and he could imagine the sort of conversation they'd be having on the journey back.

Once he'd paid Ronan escorted Lisa back to his *Apollo II* vehicle, when they were both seated inside he radioed headquarters to inform them he would be back in, roughly, an hour; he spoke to Ben Gillespe. When he'd done that the commander turned to his female companion and asked, "How about going for a stroll in the Parc des Bastions before we return to the compound?"

"A wonderful idea," commented Miss Bell, "a perfect end to a perfect evening." Again Ronan radioed headquarters and informed Ben of this, slight, change of plan; Ben informed the duty officer, Simon Beresford, and then went for his break. Back at the restaurant parking lot Ronan drove the HART vehicle out and turned right onto Rue des Paquis and journeyed southward.

*****

In the back room behind the garage the radio, suddenly, crackled into life, a voice said, "He has just left the restaurant and is now proceeding to Parc des Bastions. Get moving."

"Message received and understood;" the four *Proagnon* agents walked back through to the area where the van and mortar were stored. Two of the men loaded the mortar weapon, into the back, and then joined the others in the van, pulled out the garage – which was located on Rue de Berne – drove to the junction with Rue des Alpes and parked at the corner, awaiting their quarry.

A short while later, probably just a few minutes, the white *Apollo II* came within sight and turned to the left to connect - after a few hundred yards - with Quai du Mont-Blanc. At the junction the car turned right and carried on southward - the Mercedes *Sprinter* van followed a moment later; at the junction with Pont du Mont-Blanc the target vehicle turned left.

Meanwhile the pursuing vehicle drove past this turning, to avoid suspicion, and turned left down Pont des Bergues and onto Quai general Guisan; the driver drove down the connecting road onto Rue du Rhone. The van speeded up to beat the slower moving HART car and turned onto a street that connected with Rue de la Croix-D'or. After passing down four or five more streets they reached their destination; a few moments the four men situated, in the Mercedes *Sprinter*, watched as the white HART car parked up and the two people inside it got out Two men, armed with the usual AK-47s, then emerged from the van into the trees that lined the park, following their quarry at a safe distance.

*****

The two HART people, Commander Ronan Strobing and Miss Lisa Bell - it was evident, to the *Proagnon* agents, he was quite a bit older than her, entered the tree lined park and stopped to read a sign that gave them information about the park they were now entering.

*****

Parc des Bastions was built in the year 1817 and initially covered an area of 10,000 square metres. It was originally built in order to provide the citizens of Geneva with some space to stroll around and thus was Geneva's favourite park used by students, families, tourists and locals – in fact people from all walks of life came here, just to chill out. This was the first ever strolling ground in the city of Geneva. Formerly it was a garden surrounded by trees, springs and memorials, and it was very refreshing to take a walk along its shadowy alleys. The place was surrounded by 50 different types of trees that encroached upon the roads. In later years the area expanded with the filling up of the ditches around the park. Presently the area of the park was 64,968 square metres.

Parc des Bastions owes its names to the bastions, which formed part of the fortifications. The Reformers' Wall today stands on the site of the former city walls. Built between 1909 and 1917, it depicts the main protagonists and events of the Reformation. Opposite the Reformers' Wall is one of the University buildings - "Uni Bastions" – this was built between 1868 and 1873

The park used to be Geneva's first botanical garden until the end of the 19th century and it was still an extremely popular place. If you take the slightest interest in Geneva's history, you can admire the Reformation wall, a rather impressive monument, erected in the year 1909 in honour of the founders of Protestantism.

The park contained a giant chess board which is worth a watch. Visitors could also play chess on the board. There is a restaurant right next to the chess board – however, people could also bring your own food and drink and have a picnic or enjoy the terrace of the pavilion-restaurant. The life-sized chess and checker games which are located at the main entrance are a popular meeting place all the year round and those who are travelling with a laptop may appreciate the wireless hotspot of the park.

*****

Interesting, thought Ronan as he placed an arm round Lisa and led her away, and further, into the park. The two of them strolled amongst the trees and then they walked into an open area of the park; there were one or two people wandering around – just as the couple from HART were doing.

Suddenly a gunshot rang out and a 7.62x39mm cartridge whizzed over Ronan's left shoulder. "Down," he called to the young receptionist, trying to pull her flat; Miss Bell, evidently disorientated stayed standing up, Ronan tried again, "Down," the urgency in his voice was unmistakable. There was no response from his female companion; it was as though she was in a trance. "Lisa!" he shouted at her, "Get down, for God's sake!" He felt her quiver and another shot rang out, it was then that she fell – a patch of crimson developing and spreading on her stomach area – evidence, if any were needed that she'd been shot. "God No!" Commander Strobing shouted and then more urgently, "Lisa, talk to me."

She opened her eyes and looked up into his face. "Is this the end?" she asked him.

"Not if I can help it!" her superior answered, "I'm going to get the first aid kit from the car, but I need you to do two things for me."

"Which are?"

"I need you to keep your eyes open, no matter how bad the pain gets."

"And number two?"

The commander ripped a piece from his shirt, partly undid Miss Bell's top and located the wound; he then passed her the material he'd torn off and said urgently, "I need you to press this on your wound, try and stop the flow of blood."

"Right you are Ronan," she replied from her position, on the ground. Once she was firmly grasping the material her superior had given her Commander Strobing raced off – in the direction of the *Apollo II* vehicle to fetch the first aid kit.

While he was there he radioed headquarters and informed them of the situation and requested one of the nearby hospitals be contacted and an ambulance be deployed to their position. Then grabbing the green first aid kit he turned and raced back to where Lisa lay.

Back at headquarters Commander Strobing's message was passed, by Ben Gillespe, to Commander Most – it was, naturally, assumed that she would contact the emergency services herself; once Ben had passed on the message the young man retreated from the office.

Back at the park Ronan had arrived back at the spot where Miss Bell had been earlier but found she wasn't there; however, there was a trail of blood, just patches really, leading off to a darkened area of trees. Ronan followed the trail of blood, his Beretta 9000S – which he'd taken from the glove compartment

– in his hand. Commander Strobing found Miss Bell's body where the trail of blood ended, she'd evidently been dragged to this point and then shot in the head; as there was a pool of blood surrounding her head. Ronan was physically sick at the sight.

"Come on you bastards! I know it's me you want," he shouted once he'd recovered, "why take it out on an innocent young woman. She had nothing to do with any of this." As if in answer a bullet whizzed past his head. "Show yourself or are you scared as well as stupid?"

"We are not stupid," answered a voice from behind, Commander Strobing turned, slowly, to find himself staring at an AK-47 assault rifle; this was held by a man, obviously a *Proagnon* agent judging by the blue uniform, "Your female companion," the man added, a smile on his face, "was killed, and dragged here, as a lure." Now we have you." Suddenly Ronan heard the unmistakable sound of another weapon being cocked, ready for use, behind him.

"You have indeed," the commander of HART told them, smiling; then, in the distance came the wail of sirens announcing the imminent arrival of an ambulance and, perhaps, a police cruiser or two. Ronan could see the look of panic cross each man's face.

"We could kill you here and now – another dead body doesn't matter to us one way or the other – but we have decided to let you live, for now. There will be a reckoning one day." Then the *Proagnon* agent said to his companion, his voice betraying some urgency, "Back into the bushes." They both withdrew leaving Commander Strobing to inform the paramedics and police personnel that his female companion, Lisa Bell, was now dead, he even led them to her body and she was pronounced dead.

Commander Strobing walked wearily back to his vehicle and drove away from the area – he was sure there'd been a slight delay before the emergency vehicles got there, he'd query them back at headquarters when he got back. He decided to take a different route back and cross the river Rhone using the bridge on the Pont de la Machine. This bridge was only single file but there wasn't that much traffic around.

As he came to the bridge he could see a silver Mercedes *Sprinter* van waiting to cross from the northern half of the city, Ronan had driven about halfway across when the van suddenly revved up and came hurtling towards the HART car.

CHAPTER 10

CASUALTIES!

The two vehicles collided, head on, and the customised van pushed the HART *Apollo II* – still with Commander Strobing inside – slowly off the edge of the bridge where it fell into the water below; acting as if nothing had happened the van drove on its way.

*****

As the HART vehicle hit the water it made a loud *splash* and started to sink – front end going down first; Commander Strobing – still saddened by the untimely death of Miss Lisa Bell - had to put those thoughts to the back of his mind and act quickly if he wanted to stay alive.

Thankfully the seat belts in the *Apollo* cars, whether generation one or two – as well as having the standard buckle devices – also had a *Velcro* fastening about halfway up the strap to allow for an easy escape, in just such emergencies. Ronan tore open the *Velcro* fastening, as well as unbuckling the belt, he then, once free had to escape from the sinking vehicle - he did attempt to open the driver's door but the water's pressure on the door was too great so that wasn't really an option; then he considered kicking out a window but remembered that every door window was made of reinforced glass – his only escape would be by breaking enough glass on one of the windows that wasn't reinforced.

Time for him was running out, as the air in the vehicle would be – sooner or later, thankfully he still had his Beretta pistol in his jacket pocket. Holding it in one hand and shielding his eyes with the other he smashed the butt of the semiautomatic weapon against the glass – the HART commander heard a *crump* as the glass broke but didn't fully shatter; he risked a quick peek between his fingers, water was now cascading in; he knew then it was all or nothing. Perching himself on the seat, in a crouch – and shielding his eyes again Commander Strobing kicked out at the window repeatedly and heard it *smash*; finally after five times he judged, as he peeked through his fingers again, that the gap created was now large enough to get through.

Holding his, trusty, Beretta he launched himself through the hole where the windscreen used to be and let himself be carried back up to the surface of the water; his lungs were close to bursting at this point. Ronan, carried on by the upward surge of water, finally broke the surface after a few minutes and exhaled deeply and then gulped in deep breaths of fresh air – thank God he was still alive – he wasn't that far off shore either; his clothes, though, were absolutely wet through, and that biting wind didn't help matters either. He looked at his pistol which was, again, wet through – the HART commander tried firing it – just into the air – but it wouldn't fire; knowing it was, probably, now useless he tossed it into the water, as it hit it made a resounding *plop*. A little more happily he swam to the shoreline and climbed up an old ladder to reach the side of the road, the ladder looked as though it had seen better days and creaked – dangerously – as Ronan neared the top, with a final effort he climbed the last few steps and swung himself over the concrete reservation onto the grass.

Standing upright he looked in both directions but there were no vehicles about, Ronan sighed – it was going to be a long walk back, he wasn't even sure which direction to go in – then spotting a very faint light, to his right, he turned and started walking towards it.

*****

Meanwhile, at HART headquarters everyone, even the other two commanders, were beginning to worry over the *prolonged* absence of Commander Strobing, as well as Lisa Bell. Commander Most was the most worried over the situation, and she felt a little guilty, as it had been her that had been in command when Ronan had radioed in about Lisa; after all Celia Most hadn't particularly liked Lisa Bell as she seemed too young for the job of receptionist, plus – in the last couple of months she'd tried to get into the affections of Celia's superior and Mrs Most hadn't liked that.

In fact that was probably why Commander Most had delayed contacting the emergency services for a minute or two, but what if something had happened to Commander Strobing? What if he was dead? If something had happened to him Celia would never forgive herself; on the other hand if nothing had happened to him – she prayed nothing had – then he'd be looking for answers.

*****

Back in England the *flu* season had begun, people were being immunised against seasonal strains of the virus but – still in some areas – the new killer virus – which was similar to *flu* was being reported in counties such as: Northamptonshire, Essex, Oxfordshire, Wiltshire, Surrey and West Sussex; this was mainly due to people not realising they'd got this virus and travelling between counties thus infecting more people, soon the hospitals in these areas were full up – none of the medical staff had been trained to handle more than a handful of cases at once.

Slowly the great city of London was gradually being surrounded by this new killer virus.

*****

One day a man, Richard Carcroft, had to make a journey from his home which was located in Tiptree, Essex to the city of London – just to catch up with an old friend or so he said – but his wife knew better, a journey of approximately 57 miles. Carcroft left his house at 14.00 and made the journey in his, aged, Honda *Civic*; after approximately one hour and forty five minutes he arrived at his destination. He parked down a side street, he knew this area well, and walked nonchalantly to his ultimate destination – a little café/restaurant known as *Macallroy's* She was waiting at a table, in the corner, for him; as Carcroft approached she stood up. "Hello," she said, "it's good to see you again."

"And you Debbie," her full name was Debbie Linden. "Shall we eat or get straight down to business?"

"Hmm," she considered his question. "Let's eat first and conduct our business later." They both ordered Lasagne, as they ate Debbie asked how Mrs Carcroft was; the reason being even though Richard wore a wedding band every time he met his mistress – Debbie assumed that's what he saw her as – he never mentioned his wife.

Richard was shocked; he'd never mentioned his wife and had gone to great lengths to try and hide his wedding band but he knew she'd noticed. "She's fine," he answered, a bit pathetically.

"What's her name again?"

Before realising he blurted out, "Julia."

"Perhaps I should tell Julia about us," she said to him calmly.

"Are you crazy? She'd probably either kill me or divorce me."

"Don't worry, sweetie, I'm only teasing. I'd never tell anyone," Debbie told him, "now eat up, like a good boy, it'll make you big and strong."

"Patronising bitch," Richard muttered under his breath. Miss Linden made no comment, either she didn't hear him or she wasn't that bothered.

Once they'd both finished their meal Mr Carcroft paid the bill and then the two of them left the café/restaurant, hand in hand, as they'd done on previous occasions – and walked a few streets to a block of flats. Debbie and Richard went into her, small, flat – located on the fourth floor – and through to the bedroom; they quickly undressed and fell into her bed where they made love, not for the first time.

Richard, unaware he was carrying the virus as he was showing no outward symptoms, sneezed and immediately said, "Sorry."

"Don't be darling," Miss Linden told him, "I'm enjoying myself." Little did Mr Carcroft know that those exact words would be repeated later; plus little did he know he'd just infected his mistress.

After they'd finished the two of them redressed and Richard left to return home; he was surprised, upon reaching his car, that it was only 18.00. Why was he leaving so early? Then he remembered, well it was obvious from the snow that had fallen, that his journey may be longer than expected due to the snow and ice; plus it would soon be Christmas, and he was expected to spend time with his family.

Richard Carcroft was around forty five years of age and had had a couple of sons with his wife, Julia, and one of his daughters-in-law was expecting her first child in a few months time.

Richard was one of three sons to his father, John, and his mother, Mary, he also had two sisters, Alice and Christine. John (senior), as one of Richard's brothers was called John, had been a lawyer but was retried now – being sixty seven; Mary, his mother, had been a till operator for a supermarket chain but was, again, retired as she was sixty three.

Richard and his brothers, John and Charles, had all married and had given their parents two grandchildren apiece; even the daughter's had not disappointed – also bestowing on their parents at least one grandchild each. Christine, or Chrissie as she liked to be known, was expecting a second child at the age of thirty five.

Richard was employed as a used car salesman for Honda and was paid handsomely, in fact Julia and himself lived in a country cottage which was reasonably large with four bedrooms, kitchen/diner, living quarters etc; in fact two of the bedrooms were en suite, as well as all four being doubles.

Dragging himself back to the present he drove along at a moderate speed, not wanting to have any undue accidents – the *Civic* was a good vehicle but as it was very aged he felt he ought to change it, someday, for a more up to date model. As he rounded a corner he saw that a car up ahead had crashed into an oncoming bus; the emergency services were on the scene trying to free the driver of the red automobile, the car in question was a *Kia*. Richard cursed, this would have to happen; thankfully there was a policeman guiding traffic round the two vehicles, as he drove slowly past he looked at the entwined vehicles, the car was a complete write off – having had its front end completely destroyed - the driver seemed unconscious as he was slumped forward – the fire crew was having to cut him out, the bus – however – still looked driveable but would require some attention to its front; once past the crashed vehicles Mr Carcroft drove on towards his home in Tiptree.

Back in the city Carcroft had left just an hour beforehand Miss Linden was entertaining another guest in her flat, but there was one difference – this guest was a woman; eventually when Debbie and her other lover parted the lover was infected as well. So it went on, women infecting men, men infecting other women; people infecting their relatives etc.

Eventually as one after another was hospitalised there was wide spread hysteria and panic among London's citizens. Buckingham Palace was immediately sealed off and Queen Charlotte wasn't allowed outside, the weekly food deliveries were made by men in radiation suits – complete with helmets which were fastened to their collar; Charlotte knew this precaution was necessary – after all she was the Queen of England – however of her consort, Gareth Andrews, there was no sign. During the shutdown only the most necessary staff was allowed to carry on with their duties and all were found bedrooms within the palace. During the following months Charlotte became very nervous and, visibly, jumped whenever anyone sneezed who was standing near her.

Many of the hospital's of the city became overcrowded and the medical staff were run off their feet, most wore face masks to protect the nose and mouth while some also wore goggles as well to protect their eyes.

*****

Overseas was fairing no better either. In every country Floyd Maxwell's agents had been in people were dying – those people that weren't dead or dying had shuttered themselves in their homes. Traffic had halted altogether, shops had closed; beaches were deserted in holiday resorts, everything had just stopped.

Tourists had fled in their droves from hotels, hostels and anywhere else they were staying, they'd made their way to the airports – some not caring if they had the virus, they just wanted to get away before they died.

Most of the outward bound flights were already full but still people tried to get on a flight home; those that were turned away spent the night sleeping on chairs, in the airport, hoping for a quick getaway in the morning but still more tourists came, determined to get home. Soon violence broke out as people fought over tickets; security was called but they couldn't do anything – the men just got caught up in the violence.

In the mass panic one old man, who was wandering along, minding his own business and trying to keep away from the violence around him, was suddenly struck from behind by a young woman, Stupid old fool!" she almost shouted at him, "Get out the way;" as the man fell his glasses slipped from his nose and smashed on the floor, he lay still – his walking cane lying by his side; the man's nose started to bleed.

"My glasses," he mumbled and felt around – on the floor – for them. "I'm blind without them." A middle aged man had separated from the crowd and was striding, purposefully, over.

The younger men smiled at the woman and picked up the old man's cane. "Bugger off woman," and he swung the stick at her, it connected with her side knocking the breath from her. As she watched the man raised the stick then swung it again at her; the cane connected with the side of her head and she fell, blood started to pool around her as she lay there. He then turned his attention back to the, helpless, old man, "Now," he snarled, "give me your ticket or I shall kill you."

"Please take it," said the white haired man, "just don't kill me." He knew the younger man probably would anyway; but after all, he thought, *I'll probably die soon anyway – I am 80 after all.* As if to prove him right the other man raised the cane and was just about to bring it down on the back of the old man's skull when a shot rang out.

Everybody looked round and saw three men standing there, all of them were dressed in black and wore face masks with respirators built in; they were all carrying Beretta pistols, this was one of HART's rapid assistance teams (RATs).

*****

HART had received a panicked call about an hour ago from this and, numerous, other airports; each of the rapid response teams, mainly made up of three personnel, was put aboard a plane and sent to these trouble spots, even the commanders went on occasions if there wasn't enough soldiers. On the flight to their destination each of the team leaders was briefed and brought up to speed on the situation that awaited them, they then changed into their combat gear for the mission; whilst onboard.

Usually these men were flown in at night but some did operate in the daytime, they were dropped – attached to parachutes – into trouble spots. However it had been seen, at this airport – as in many others – that the men were needed now; therefore a member of the security forces had contacted HART headquarters using the red *panic* button in the security building, and this was linked to a wall console in the main reception area.

Joshua Smith, who was on duty, immediately informed the commander on duty – this happened to be Commander Ronan Strobing – who was now fit for duty again after his close call with death. Commander Strobing ordered the RATs into action as it had been noted that this hadn't been the only flashing light. The soldiers in each team grabbed their individual combat gear black commando uniform, Beretta *Cheetah* pistols – all semiautomatic, and any other equipment they may require for this operation. They then boarded the waiting *Hercules*; once everyone was aboard, the rear tail ramp was raised and the four large Allison T56-A-15 turboprop propeller driven engines were started, each engine was capable of putting out 4,910 shaft horsepower.

Once the transport plane was at maximum speed it rolled down the runway and lifted off, when it reached an altitude of 30,000 feet it levelled off and carried on at its cruising speed of 300 miles per hour – throttling back to just 100 miles per hour when it reached each different destination; then the ramp was lowered and the three team members would parachute to the ground and the *Hercules* would fly on.

Each man, or woman – depending who was available, would disentangle themselves from their *chutes* and make their way, on foot, to their ultimate destination; each would now be dressed in their combat uniforms, including *Kevlar II* body armour.

*****

Commander Strobing had made his way to the light he had seen – the glow had turned out to be coming from an old, rundown, farmhouse type building – this probably wasn't a farmhouse at all as it was too near Lake Geneva; maybe it was, or had been at one time, a fisherman's house. Ronan had knocked, politely, on the door which was eventually answered by a young looking – though she was probably much older – woman in a dressing gown and some nightwear; as soon as she saw him standing there, in his wet clothes, she'd demanded, "Who are you? What do you want?"

Commander Strobing had to admit she looked rather scared, terrified maybe, and she had every right – it probably wasn't often that she received gentleman callers at this late hour "Dear lady," he began, "I mean you no harm, my name is Ronan Strobing, I work," he still had his dinner suit on, "for a firm of lawyers in Geneva. I simply ask that I be allowed into your home to dry off and warm up."

"Why? What has happened?"

"My car decided to take itself off one of the bridges, and I got rather wet," he responded to her question, it wasn't exactly the truth but she seemed to accept his explanation. The lady of the house invited him in, she was probably still a little suspicious of him and she had the right to be – after all he could be anyone. "By the way what is your name?" Commander Strobing asked her.

"Ruth, Ruth Langford," answered the woman as they made their way through the hallway and on into the main room; she then found some old newspapers and placed them on a chair for Ronan to sit on. "You're lucky to have found me up; usually I'd be in bed but something made me stay up a little later tonight – call it some sixth sense. Anyhow, I'll make you a fire up so you can get warm and I'll get you some towels to help you dry off; them clothes'll have to come off as well." Miss Langford, the HART commander hadn't seen any evidence of a wedding ring, then made a fire up as promised, and then she went upstairs to fetch him some towels.

Hesitantly Ronan started unbuttoning his shirt, "Don't worry, you haven't got anything I haven't seen before," she said to him before she left; reassured he undressed completely and felt the warmth – from the fire – on his body. He turned once his rear half was warmed up and had his back facing the door to the staircase when he heard it open. "Oh my!" he heard a woman's voice exclaim in surprise.

Instantly he swung round – giving Ruth a full frontal view – she gasped. "Erm sorry," he apologised and tried to cover himself up quickly.

"Here," she told him, handing him a towel, "please use this to cover yourself up. I know I said you hadn't got anything I hadn't seen before but I didn't expect you to flaunt yourself in front of me." Ronan took the offered towel and wrapped it round himself, covering himself up. "That's better," murmured Miss Langford and moved his wet clothes into, what Ronan assumed to be, the kitchen. A minute later he heard a washing machine start up.

Ruth came back through and removed the – now wet – papers from the chair, "Sit down, please, and tell me the full story"; Ronan seated himself.

She sat in a chair opposite his and listened, without interruption, as he told her about having taken his work colleague, Lisa Bell, to the restaurant *L'Entrecote Couronnee*; he told her about the trip around Parc des Bastions over the river; he neglected to tell her about the *Proagnon* terrorists or who he really was, he felt that if he told Miss Langford she would only panic and worry.

Finally Commander Strobing informed his host of the car journey back, in short they'd been travelling over one of the three bridges that connected north and south Geneva when their vehicle had left the road and fallen into the water below; he'd managed to escape but of his companion there was no sign, it was then Ronan feared that Lisa hadn't escaped and had drowned. He had then climbed up on to the bank and called Lisa's name but there had been no response; so the HART commander had made his way to this house.

The lady of the house listened without comment, once he'd finished she said, "Could this Lisa Bell have escaped and made her way to the south shore? Are you certain that she's dead?"

"I'm pretty sure, no definitely certain, she's dead," he announced with firmness in his voice, Miss Langford noted the firmness in his voice which seemed to tell her not to argue with him. "Miss Langford," he began, "may I use your toilet?"

"You may," she told him, "follow me." She led the way upstairs and down a long corridor to a door at the end, as they were walking along the corridor Ronan admired the pictures of boats – on the walls. Upon reaching the end of the line of pictures he noticed a door off to his left. "That's the spare bedroom," Ruth informed him. "Once you've used the toilet if you want a rest you may rest in there." She then opened the door to the bathroom and he proceeded inside. "I'm going to get some rest myself now, and," she held up her right hand in a *stop* gesture, "don't think of following me." Ronan used the toilet, and then went into the spare bedroom for a lay down.

He consulted his watch, luckily this hadn't stopped working, he was surprised to find it was already 02.30; he pulled the towel away and collapsed onto the bed, aware of his nakedness, but unashamed of it, and fell sound asleep.

Later that morning, at around what his watch said was 10.00 he got up, wrapped the towel back round himself and proceeded to descend the stairs. At the bottom, in the main room he found Miss Langford waiting for him, the table laden with breakfast pots and a steaming pot of tea. "Come and sit down," she told him. "Your clothes are all ironed and pressed, ready for you to wear again." Ruth must have been up for hours, realised Ronan, yet she still looked as if she'd just got up herself.

When they'd finished eating HART Commander Strobing asked, "May I have a shower this morning, just to freshen up?"

"Of course you may," Ruth answered, "you know where the bathroom is. There is a curtain that can be pulled round for privacy; when you go back upstairs take your clothes with you as you look a, little, ridiculous in that towel." Then she added good-humouredly, "What will the neighbours think, me entertaining a naked man?" Ronan laughed at this, it was the first time he'd laughed, properly, since he'd been at the restaurant the previous evening.

Commander Strobing went back upstairs at around 10.30 to get showered; he switched the shower on and felt the warm water cascading down on his body, refreshing him. Halfway through he heard the lady of the house coming upstairs, *probably wants to use the toilet*, he thought resignedly, so he pulled the two shower curtains around him. He was correct in his assumption as she did use the toilet, a minute later he heard her call to him, "Ronan. I've put clean towels out for you and laid your clothes on top of the toilet." Ronan called back his thanks; she then left the room.

A minute or so later Ronan switched the shower off and stepped out to dry himself off, he felt refreshed, once he'd finished drying himself he put his clothes back on; next, he decided, would be to contact headquarters and arrange for some transport to come and collect him. Even though he'd thoroughly enjoyed Miss Langford's company he felt he should return to duty at HART.

He then descended the stairs into the main room and casually asked his host, "Have you a telephone I could use to contact the rest of my colleagues, and possibly arrange transport? By the way what number is this place?"

"I do have a telephone you can use it is in the entrance hall, you probably noticed it last night. As for your other question we are at number 6 Rue des Quai," Ruth answered helpfully.

Commander Strobing walked into the entrance hall and located the telephone; it was a red cordless phone. Ronan carefully dialled the number for the headquarters at HART, shielding the keypad – as best he could – while he dialled.

After a couple of rings the phone, on reception, was answered by Gwyneth Jones, "Hello," she said.

"Gwyneth, it's Commander Strobing here."

"So good to hear your voice sir," said the woman from Wales. "Where are you sir? How's Miss Bell? What happened?"

"It's a long story Gwyneth but in answer to your questions, I'm at 6 Rue des Quai, Lisa Bell's dead, and we were ambushed by *Proagnon* agents."

"Are you sure Lisa's dead?" Mrs Jones enquired. Lisa had seemed such a lively young woman.

Ronan said into the receiver, "I'm quite sure. I held her while she was dying, it wasn't pleasant; by the way, who was the *acting* commander last night?"

He heard a rustle; the senior receptionist must be looking back through the duty sheets. Finally she told him, "It was Commander Most, she took over when she returned with Commander Bigship."

Commander Strobing was almost certain that the answer, before Gwyneth confirmed it, was Commander Celia Most – after all, the two women had never exactly hit it off; Ronan would be having words with his immediate deputy, maybe even demoting her though he, secretly, hoped he wouldn't have the need to. Next he said to the Welsh HART receptionist, "Could you arrange for some transport to be sent to my present location and return me to headquarters?"

"Of course sir, I'm afraid it'll have to be the *Range Rover* as Commander Bigship is out, on patrol, in the *MegaCruiser*. I shall instruct the driver to collect you at 15.00."

"Thank you Mrs Jones," Commander Strobing answered. "I look forward to returning to my seat of command. Bye for now."

"Goodbye Commander, thank goodness you're alive," Gwyneth Jones then replaced the receiver; as soon as he heard the *click* at the other end Commander Strobing terminated the call at his end and replaced the phone's handset, it was then he noticed that he'd forgotten to close the door to the main room. *Damn!* Miss Langford may have heard everything, as he wandered back into the room he saw Ruth was sitting by the fireplace, a raging fire was burning in the hearth – thankfully there was a fireguard in place.

"Ruth," he began, she looked up, "I am returning to work this afternoon. That's who I was on the phone to; someone's coming for me at three." If she had heard the conversation she seemed very calm, she may not have heard he didn't know either way.

"I know Commander Strobing," she replied. She seemed totally unafraid of the situation she now found herself in.

"Aren't you in the least bit afraid for your own safety?" the HART commander enquired. She stood up and faced him.

"Not in the least, after all if anyone was after you they'd be here by now plus I was safe before so I'll be safe again. Plus I'm sure you'll look after me."

Was she hinting that he should take her back with him? Quickly he told her, "Ruth if you're thinking I should take you with me I think your life could be in more danger than if you stayed here."

"Hmm," she murmured and pondered his words, after a minute she responded, "I guess you're right, I reckon your job is dangerous, perhaps I should stay here." A quick afterthought occurred and she added, "However, you told me your companion, Lisa wasn't it?" Ronan nodded, "Had been killed, so surely you must need someone to replace her."

He sighed, "I guess we will do, are you offering yourself up as her replacement?"

"Yes," was the simple answer, he then proceeded to explain what Miss Bell's duties had been; Miss Ruth Langford nodded an affirmative each time he asked her if she could fulfil each duty Lisa had performed.

Once he'd finished questioning her, there was only one sticky patch – when Commander Strobing mentioned she'd have to live onsite but she agreed, he announced, "I reckon the job is yours." Ronan didn't really like employing new people from outside the organisation – that was one difference between Commander Peter Roberts (now deceased) and himself - but, after all, she'd provided him with a roof over his head, a place to warm up, to freshen up, sleep, plus he'd been provided with food; so he guessed she could be trusted and make an ideal employee.

Over lunch and into the, early, afternoon Ruth and Ronan talked about their lives in general; Ruth, Ronan learned, had had a husband called Brian but he'd died in a traffic accident about five years earlier, so that was why she didn't wear a wedding ring anymore – there were no children though; Ronan, Ruth learned, had had a wife called Mandy who had been killed by terrorists a year earlier – they had had two children, one of which had been killed along with Mandy, the other was back in England with his aunt.

Ruth then confessed to Ronan, she had never spoken – to anyone – about this before though she found she liked this man – that she wouldn't mind having children now, if the right person came along.

At around 14.50 there was a knock at the door, Miss Langford got up from her chair and answered it. Outside stood a man in military uniform and parked, further back, was a black *Range Rover*, "Please come in," the lady of the house said. "You must be soaked." It was raining outside, plus there was a new covering of snow on the ground.

The military man nodded his thanks and stepped inside the house to keep dry. "Is Commander Strobing ready ma'am?" he asked politely.

"I believe he is," she answered then called, "Ronan your transport's here." The HART commander then appeared in the doorway.

"Thank you Ruth," he said, "in fact thanks for everything," and he kissed her on the cheek. It was then he added, "I'll send transport to fetch you tomorrow;" suddenly he remembered he hadn't got her phone number.

As if reading his mind Ruth placed a piece of paper in his hand, "My phone number," she told him; he pocketed the paper, thanked her again for her hospitality and then left with his driver. They quickly boarded the *Range Rover* and set off back to headquarters.

As the vehicle drove on its journey Commander Strobing turned to the driver and enquired, "Has any new emergency arisen today?"

Without taking his eyes off the road the soldier replied, "The only thing worth mentioning is a panic at the airport, that's why Commander Bigship's got the *MegaCruiser* – he's gone to sort it out."

"And Commander Most?" he asked.

"At headquarters, as far as I know, sir; she's sitting in for you." Eventually, after about half an hour's drive – the driver had to steer the vehicle they were in steadily as the roads were slippery in some places, the soldier manoeuvred the 4 x 4 vehicle through the gates of the HART compound and up to the residences of the commanders. His passenger climbed out and walked over to his residence while the *Range Rover* was driven back round to the garages at the rear of the main building.

Commander Ronan Strobing entered the house type building and ascended the staircase, where he stripped off and had a further shower. Afterwards he went and changed into a fresh set of clothes as well as a clean uniform; once he was dressed again he left his residence and bumped into, of all people, Alice Stronglove. "Hello Alice," he said, "I thought you'd be in Scotland by now."

"I should be sir but, unfortunately, my aunt's been very ill so I've been looking after her. I do, however, aim to go over as soon as I can – admittedly you may have to find a, temporary, replacement for me to go over there until my aunt is fully fit," she told her commander as they walked towards headquarters together. Just before they reached the main building, though, Alice turned left and entered a smaller building which was used for target practice – it was run by quartermaster Mark Jacobs who was a veteran of the second Gulf War, the one that had seen the capture and, eventual, execution of Saddam Hussein.

Ronan, however, entered the main building and went up, in the elevator, to the floor where his office was situated. He walked calmly much calmer than he felt, through reception and on towards his office. He flung the door open and snapped at Commander Most, who was seated in his chair, "Get out the fucking command seat NOW!"

Celia was most taken aback by the ferocity in her superior's tone, hesitantly she said, "What's wrong with you Commander Strobing?"

The HART commander, who had by now regained his composure, replied, "I apologise for my untimely outburst but I need to talk with you. May I have my seat back?"

"Certainly sir, but next time please don't shout at me like that;" she then she moved to the chair on the other side of the desk, once they were both seated, facing each other, Celia asked him again, "What's wrong sir?"

"Lisa Bell's dead."

"Dead, Are you sure?" she asked, had she played a part in the young woman's demise?

"Yes. She was shot by *Proagnon* agents; I radioed this information in but it took at least eight minutes for the emergency services to reach our position, and then I find out that you were the officer on duty that night and it was your duty to contact the emergency services. Why did you delay?"

Ronan's immediate deputy knew the game was up so she might as well explain, perhaps even cover herself. "I didn't delay, sir, I admit I couldn't get through for about half a minute, but that is all. Maybe there was some other reason like a traffic hold-up somewhere."

"Perhaps you're right," the commander muttered. "It's just so convenient that you could have turned the situation to your advantage. I mean you two didn't always see eye to eye."

"I know that but do you, honestly, think I'd want her to die unnecessarily? Anyway what happened to you?"

Ronan explained everything that had occurred the previous evening. When he'd finished his story all Commander Most said was, "So this Ruth Langford, what was she like?"

"You'll have your own chance to judge tomorrow, as I've decided to employ her as Miss Bell's replacement," he told his deputy.

He was then asked, "Does she have all the necessary skills?"

"Oh yes," her superior responded. "Now as it is only a week until Christmas I intend to get Miss Langford settled in and then Leon, yourself and I will return home. Admittedly if Commander Bigship does not wish to return home with us I shall respect that decision."

"Very good commander." Celia saluted and was about to get up and leave when the office door opened and Commander Leon Bigship walked in and, without being told to, found a chair and sat in it.

"Commander Bigship what a pleasant surprise. What news do you bring us?"

"Well sir, Commander Most. It appears from what contact we've had, that the rapid assistance teams or RATs have succeeded in quelling the panic at the airports." Suddenly there was a knock on the outer door.

"Enter," called Commander Strobing authoritatively. The door opened and Gwyneth Jones entered the office, carrying a tray with tea things on it. She came over and set the tray down on the desk; Ronan noticed there was also a sheet of paper on the tray, it seemed to be a report of some sort, so he picked it up and read it. After he'd read it, twice, he uttered two words, "Oh fuck!"

"What is it commander?" his two deputies asked seemingly concerned. Mrs Jones discreetly withdrew from the office after pouring them each a drink of tea.

"The virus has entered London it would seem, Hospitals are reporting massive overcrowding, even Queen Charlotte has been confined to the Palace." Commander Strobing handed the report over so that both his deputies could read it for themselves. "The sooner we get someone placed in Scotland, as that seems to be where it all started, the better."

"But sir" Leon reminded him, "Alice Stronglove has her aunt to look after, and won't be clear to go until, at least, next year." It seemed like there was no other alternative until Commander Bigship said, "I wonder and it's a long shot if Shinto Howell's daughter could help? After all she does want to be a HART agent."

"An excellent idea," the man in charge told him, "get me Major Howell and his daughter."

*****

A short while later there was a knock on the office door, "Come in," called Commander Strobing, the other two commanders had left earlier for their own offices.

Leon had refused his superior's offer of spend Christmas at home saying that he had no-one to spend it with; on the one hand Ronan felt sympathetic yet on the other he respected Leon's decision, if he wanted to forego leave at Christmas then so be it – his commander wasn't going to argue.

The door opened and Major Shinto Howell entered followed by a younger woman – Ronan assumed she was his daughter. "Greetings Commander Strobing," the major said. The woman stepped forward, there certainly was no denying it – this Japanese girl was a beauty. "Allow me to introduce my daughter Suki."

The two of them shook hands, "Now Suki," began Ronan, "your father informs me that you wish to become a member of HART," he leaned back and waited for a response.

"That is correct sir," she answered matter-of-factly.

"You understand the dangers involved in this job?"

"I do indeed sir."

"How would you feel about performing an intelligence gathering mission? We need someone to go to Scotland and gather information on the Maxwell consortium as well as their sea-fort which is situated in the Moray Firth." He leaned back again – in his chair – and waited for her answer. Suki answered with a question.

"Yes I'll go and gather whatever information I can, however what methods am I authorised to use?"

"You are authorised to use any methods you see fit to use and I mean any methods."

"Understood Commander Strobing," responded the young raven haired Japanese woman. "When do I leave?"

The commander filled in some paperwork and handed her a HART badge, "As soon as you are ready, show these," he handed Miss Howell the paperwork and badge, "show these to the airport staff - at check-in – and you will be fast tracked to the airside lounge where a plane will arrive, a business class Gulfstream or Learjet aircraft to take you to Inverness airport. You will be met by one of our agents over there who will transport you to a suitable hotel or other accommodation; the agent's name will be Ralph Williams."

"He will also brief you on the situation over there. Are there any further questions you wish to ask me?" There was a shake of the head from Miss Suki Howell. She saluted the commander again, turned on her heel and walked towards the office door – Ronan watching her every move.

"Coming dad?" called Suki over her shoulder.

"In a moment dear, I just want a few words with the commander," he replied and then waited until she shut the door. The Japanese man placed his hands – palms down – on the wooden desk. "Do you realise commander," he began, "that you're placing my only daughter in extreme danger."

Commander Strobing looked up at the little man, "Yes I do Major," he said, "and believe me if there was another way I'd take it."

"Couldn't you postpone this operation until after Christmas?" he looked imploringly into his superior's face.

The HART commander thought for a moment before replying, "I understand your concern Major Howell. Speaking as a father myself, Shinto, I can see you're very worried."

"Damn right I'm worried!"

"There is a solution though."

"And that would be?" enquired the concerned father.

"I feel we could place your daughter over there – over the Christmas period and for the month of January; then we could despatch Alice Stronglove and bring your daughter, Suki, back to Geneva. Are we in agreement?"

"Yes sir," responded the little Japanese man. With a quick salute and a word of thanks he turned and left the room. Ronan smiled to himself.

*****

About half an hour later Suki Howell was packed and ready to leave the compound for *Cointrin* airport. He father offered to take her in an unmarked Renault *Megane*.

As they drove, on the journey, towards the airport Major Howell explained to his daughter his concerns and what Commander Strobing had suggested; Suki agreed that it was the best option if her father was that worried. They finally reached their destination at 19.45, the Japanese woman – assisted by her father – carried her suitcases inside where the young woman found a trolley and, again with assistance from Major Howell, placed her cases onto the trolley.

Suki then joined the queue for the Inverness flight; while her father exited the building, just before they parted he kissed her – on the cheek – and said, "Look after yourself."

"I will try dad, and you look after yourself," and then she turned and joined the queue. Once she reached the head of the line she reached into her handbag and produced the paperwork – signed by Commander Strobing – and the HART badge. As soon as the check-in operator saw these items Suki was led to one side by a security officer and led away to – as Ronan had told her – the airside lounge; presently, at 20.30, a Learjet *60*.rolled up to take her on the journey to Inverness.

Suki Howell climbed aboard the business class jet and seated herself, once her luggage was aboard - and she was strapped in – the plane taxied to the top of the runway to await a vacant slot; the journey, she had been informed, would take approximately 2 hours. Miss Howell sat back and waited.

At around 20.48 the business jet was cleared for take-off and started rolling down the runway, reaching its maximum speed of 534 mph the plane began its ascent into the sky above; when it reached an altitude of about 44,000 ft the plane levelled off and began its 2 hour flight to Scotland. The plane flew in a north-westerly direction.

After only an hour and a half the Learjet *60* began the descent into Inverness airport, she cried out as the cabin returned to its normal pressure; eventually the jet landed and sped along the runway, slowing down as the pilot applied reverse thrust. Once the plane had come to a full halt, at 21.40 (local time) did the pilot lower the built in staircase, as Suki Howell walked down the staircase a car drove over to the plane; as the car first approached the Japanese woman – instinctively - stepped back, afraid the man driving the vehicle might want to kill her – she needn't have worried though.

As the automobile drew to a halt, beside the plane, a man dressed in a brown suit got out and said, "Hello, I'm Ralph Williams; you must be Suki Howell," she walked over to him and they shook hands. "Now where's your luggage?" he asked; as if on cue a side compartment towards the rear of the business jet opened up, "Ah there it is."

He loaded her cases and bags into the boot of the car he was driving, and then the two of them climbed inside, fastened their seatbelts and proceeded to drive away (at about 21.55). "I've booked you into the local pub in the village of Ardernseir, as they had no room at the hotel."

*****

As Ralph was driving the vehicle he informed Miss Howell that parts of the land in and about Ardersier were originally owned by the order of the Knights Templar. These lands were often referred to as: Temple Land, Temple Cruik, Temple Bank, Bogschand. These were located between Connage and the sea, and between Flemington and the sea. The Temple lands of Ardersier were held by Davidsons and Mackays as portioners. They were acquired by Cawdor in 1626.

A charter granted at Nairn refers to the *locus trialis* at Ardersier, and according to the historian George Bain, this may have been an ancient place of trial by wager of battle.

*****

He also told Suki the history of Ardersier. Church lands of Ardersier owned by the Bishop of Ross and Delnies had passed into the hands of the Leslies of Ardersier, and they sold them on to Cawdor in the year 1574, *having consideration of the great and intolerable damage, injury, and skaith done to them by Lachlan Mackintosh and others of the Clan Chattan, in harrying, destroying, and making hardships upon the said hail lands of Ardersier and fishings thereof* and no apparent hope of reparation for the "customary enormities of the *said Clan Chattan.*" It is charged against the Mackintoshes that they depauperised the tenants, debarred them from fishing at the stell of Ardersier, breaking their boats and cutting their nets. The Laird of Cawdor was not allowed to have peaceable possession, and he raised an action against Lachlan Mackintosh and his clansmen for the slaughter of several of his servants and tenants. In 1581, Lachlan renounced all claim to the Ardersier lands and to Wester and Easter Delnies, and the legal proceedings were dropped.

After the Jacobite rising of 1745, there was a fear of further French-supported risings, especially of the possibility of a naval assault quickly landing a large number of rebels. The fort provided the facility to house an increased number of soldiers (compared to the original Fort George built elsewhere in 1727) and its position on the coast both guarded the Firth at its narrowest point, and allowed for supplies to be brought in by sea in the event of a land siege.

The requirement for the fort to be built opposite Chanonry Point where the firth narrowed considerably, this meant that the population of Blacktown, a small fishing hamlet, had to resettle about a mile away on the shores of the Moray Firth. Here were founded two different communities, separated by land ownership and religion. The narrow strip of land on which Stewart-town was built belonged to the Earl of Moray and fell within the parish of Petty. Literally across the road, the householders of Campbell-town worshipped in the church of Ardersier, This land belonging to the Earl of Cawdor (of *Macbeth* fame), a Campbell. Collectively these two settlements were later referred to as Ardersier, but it was not officially known as such until the late 1970s, thus preventing confusion on postal deliveries to the other Campbeltown in Argyll.

*****

Suki looked slightly bored at having to listen to the history of the place so Mr Williams decided to *jump* to the present day. The village remained a popular tourist spot due to the pleasant views, the shore, and the proximity to Fort George, which remained an active base for the British Army. Although there were only two shops, a hotel, a pub and a post office left in the village, it is now predominantly a commuter base for nearby Nairn and Inverness.

Local residents, though, were active in regenerating Ardersier being keen to see it once again a thriving village. They formed their own community company ARDCO in December 2009 to take over local community buildings to create a Community Hub.

"Now as you are probably already aware you are to gather any information you can regarding both the Maxwell consortium and the sea fort they own in the Moray Firth," he said and then produced a radio from his inside pocket and handed it over. "That, my dear, is linked to my radio so that when you feel you have gathered sufficient information you can pass it along to me; also," the man said to her handing over a brooch, "there is a tiny radio transmitter in here, a bug if you like, that will record all conversations. So wear it all the time, are we clear on everything so far?"

The Japanese woman confirmed that she'd understood everything with a nod of her head. "Finally," Ralph informed her, "there is a *Sterling* sub-machine pistol, in the glove compartment, which is for you to take for your own protection. Ah here we are." He drove up the main street of Arderseir and turned into the public house car park. The time was 22.09.

Suki placed the sub-machine pistol down the back of the blouse she was wearing and into the top of her underwear, the pistol was held in this position by the waistband of her trousers; Mr Williams helped her inside with her luggage and carried it up to her room, luckily she only had one suitcase and it wasn't particularly large. They reached the top of the stairs and walked down the corridor to room 2A, the room was of an average size but quite plain with a single bed, a wooden wardrobe, one chair – also wooden – and a sink with a mirror above it; however the pipe work was exposed, there was also a single electric socket with a lamp plugged in. Once he'd deposited her luggage in the room Ralph said to her, "Don't worry Miss Howell, the bill's been taken care of." He then departed without another word, leaving her to unpack.

Suki Howell unpacked and sorted her clothes out, finally at around 22.40 she climbed into bed, exhausted.

*****

Back at HART headquarters, in Switzerland, a communication was received from Ralph Williams – informing them that Miss Howell was in place and he would contact them again when he had some further information.

Joshua Smith, who was working the night duty took the message and told their British agent that he would inform Commander Strobing in the morning. Although all three of the commanders were on-site, asleep in their residences, they were only usually disturbed if an emergency arose. Thus it was felt by the receptionist that this particular message could wait until morning.

Morning arrived and there had been fresh snowfall overnight; the three commanders trudged through snow to headquarters and made their way to their separate offices, as they walked through reception a note was handed to Commander Ronan Strobing, the message was that of the phone conversation between Joshua Smith and Ralph Williams; Ronan smiled as he read it, at last they had an intelligence gathering operative in England. The reason they hadn't used Mr Williams was because he had been trained more for a soldier's role, plus Ronan found women better suited for the role.

Later that morning he contacted Ruth Langford but she explained she'd thought about it and decided against taking the job as receptionist, the HART commander told her he understood, they exchanged pleasantries and then rang off. The commander had been slightly taken aback by her decision but didn't show it.

He walked briskly over to Commander Bigship's office, knocked on the door and entered without waiting to be asked to. Leon was doing some paperwork, but looked up as his superior entered, "Yes sir," he said.

The overall commander decided to come straight to the point, "Leon, you informed me that you weren't that bothered about a Christmas break."

"No sir I'm not."

"In that case you shall remain in command until Commander Most and I return from our vacation."

"Very good sir," Commander Bigship responded. With that Ronan left the office and knocked on Celia Most's office door; again he entered without waiting and informed her they would be returning home that afternoon.

Mrs Most got up from behind her desk and said to her superior, "As I've finished all my report writing may I be allowed to go and pack?" The way she asked, though, reminded Commander Strobing of a child asking for their parents, or teacher's, permission to do something.

He answered, "Certainly Celia, I'm going to head that way myself once I've checked up on Dr Schaiffer's progress." He strode out of her office and down to the medical unit to check in with Hans, while Commander Most left for her residence.

Ronan entered the double doors, as he couldn't see the German anywhere so he crossed to Dr Schaiffer's office and knocked on the door. "Come in," called the doctor.

As this was the medical unit and therefore Dr Schaiffer's *kingdom* Ronan couldn't just *barge* into the office as he had done in the main headquarters; the commander saw at least fifteen Petri dishes on the doctor's worktable, each had a drop of blood in it. On another worktable were another fifteen dishes with spots of blood in. Dr Schaiffer looked up, "Ah Commander Strobing what brings you here?"

"I came to see if there was any progress in finding a cure for this *mystery* virus."

"The Petri dishes you see on table 'A'", he'd marked the tables 'A' and 'B', "are ones with the blood I took from Arnold Stevens whereas the dishes on table 'B' contain the blood I took from you. I was just about to start treating those on 'A' with a mixture of antibiotics, sometimes combining two or three, to see if I can find the right combination that when added to Mr Stevens blood, turns it more similar to yours."

"Thank you for the progress report doctor. Commander Most and I are returning to England for the Christmas break, but will return in ten days; however, if you get a breakthrough while we're away Commander Bigship is remaining onsite, so you're to report it to him."

"Understood commander, I hope you and Commander Most have a most pleasant time." The HART commander nodded and left the medical unit, and then the main building; however as he made his way through reception he issued instructions that while he was away all messages were to be dealt with by Commander Leon Bigship. Satisfied that Leon was more than capable of running the shop for the next ten days he left for his own residence.

*****

In the deserts of Iran *Proagnon* computer operators were building a virus which they would attach, when finished, to an email and send it to commander@hart.com; they only knew this email address as their agent, who was now dead – Sergey Satov – had seen this address on some correspondence from FBI headquarters to HART headquarters, passed this information on Lon Hwan, who had radioed it to Abdul Singh or someone within the *Proagnon* organisation, before he'd been killed himself by Sergey.

This information had remained on file but had never been used; now Mitchell Walker was back in command he thought if a virus was attached to the email it may disrupt, but not destroy, HART from within. He wanted to show that bitch, Tulliver, that he should be in charge and not her.

*****

South of the Thames, in England, Floyd Maxwell was also developing a way to enable him to *hack* into major roadway network systems computers and create some mayhem of his own. Miss Carol Turner was sitting next to him, watching; admittedly she knew how to use a computer – most people did nowadays – but she'd never really used one to its full capacity, now though she would be able to.

Floyd made one final keystroke, pressed the *Return* key and sat back in anticipation.

*****

In Iran the computer operator who had added the finishing touches to the computer virus attached it to the email he'd written, just random letters and numbers, which he'd put the subject as 'Good Day' and clicked the *send* button. The virus would activate on opening; as well as disrupting the HART systems it would also duplicate their computer screens, therefore *Proagnon* would see what HART saw. There was a way to get rid of the virus, but that would mean HART technicians would have to *completely* cleanse their systems – start from scratch, so to speak – and anyway, how long would it be before they noticed?

*****

In a London street, the traffic lights at the crossroads turned to green and so the bus – full of passengers - approaching kept going; little did the driver know that the lights at the other junctions were also on green and there was a petrol tanker approaching the junction, on his right, therefore both vehicles were heading for disaster.

CHAPTER 11

MORE CASUALTIES!

The bus driver, totally oblivious to the danger that awaited him, pressed on. He wanted to be back at the depot before evening and was already half an hour behind – the reason being he had had to assist a young mum with getting her child's *buggy* aboard, he knew he shouldn't have but he had a kind heart and when it came to children – especially young children, as he was a father too - he had a soft spot.

The petrol tanker driver – too – was behind schedule – it having taken longer to unload the last load of petrol than expected, therefore he was rushing to return to the depot as the driver knew he had several more deliveries to make that day. He was also oblivious of the danger approaching him.

One vehicle was full whilst the other was empty; slowing down – fractionally - as the two of them approached, they started across the junction.

CRASH!

The tanker driver hadn't seen the bus and the lights were green anyway. The four wheeled tanker ploughed into the right hand side of the London bus, killing the driver of the vehicle almost instantly – pushing him against the left hand side window of his compartment.

Such was the force of the tanker's impact that the bus's radiator burst and it careered onto its side, the passengers were trapped – some managed to break windows and climb out onto the side of the vehicle, many were covered in bloodstains. The woman with the child had been injured in the crash and was crawling about – as best she could – trying to locate her missing child; she found him at last – he'd been thrown out his *buggy* and been thrown across the aisle of the bus hitting his head on the side wall. There was blood everywhere, it seemed as though the child was dead!

Upon finding the child's body his mother started to cry uncontrollably – such a young life, cruelly snatched away – and then she started to scream.

The passengers who'd made it outside saw the tanker that had smashed into them, the front was bent inwards and there was the tiniest hint of a flame underneath. With a dramatic realisation that the vehicle could *blow* at any moment they knew they had to get off the bus and as far away as possible before the two automobiles exploded.

Suddenly the small flame became a raging inferno, licking at the sides of the tanker – as well as the underneath. The bus passengers, although they knew they were in danger, watched this spectacle in fascination; finally the flames – somehow – managed to enter the body of the tanker.

BOOM!

The two joined vehicles exploded killing all on board and any passers by – cars flew up in the air and crashed down onto the ground, shop fronts had their windows shattered and in some cases even the whole shop front was blown away or set alight.

*****

HART Commanders Most and Strobing were, at that moment, heading for Geneva's *Cointrin* airport to begin their journey home; they were being driven there in the black HART *Range Rover*; once they'd been deposited, along with their luggage, at the airport's main building the driver – of the vehicle – wished them both a safe journey home and an enjoyable break. Then he climbed back aboard the black *Range Rover* and drove away.

The two HART operatives entered the main building and, after showing a member of security their passes, were – like Miss Howell the day before – fast tracked to an airside lounge; as they were waiting Celia leaned over and placed her head on her superior's shoulder, "Isn't it great to be alone at last?"

Ronan was shocked at her impromptu question, he raised her head then turned to face her, "Why now?" he demanded.

"Don't tell me you don't feel the same way," she said to him. "You've lost your wife, I've lost my husband."

"You think you have," Ronan corrected his deputy.

"No I'm certain I have, so it would make sense for us to get back together." Before Commander Strobing could tell her he had feelings for somebody else, but he still cared about her, their plane rolled up alongside the lounge – it was the same Learjet *60* that had been used to transport the young Japanese woman to Scotland, though neither Ronan nor Celia knew that.

They ascended the staircase into the aircraft, found a couple of seats and seated themselves and strapped themselves in; both of the pilots – they also acted as the cabin crew nowadays, meanwhile, loaded their suitcases in the hold – assisted by a security officer from the airport. Once everything was safely stowed away the pilots returned inside and informed the two commanders from HART that the journey to *Robin Hood* Doncaster-Sheffield airport would take about an hour and twenty minutes. They then entered the cockpit area and seated themselves at the controls; the executive business jet taxied to the top of the main runway at Geneva's *Cointrin* airport to await a vacant slot.

Once a vacant slot had been found the two pilots powered up the twin Pratt & Whitney 305A engines – each capable of providing the aircraft with 4,600 pounds of force building the engines up to their full speed of 534 mph, when they had built up enough speed the aircraft ascended into the dark sky. Once the plane reached 33,000 feet – though it could go another 18,000 feet higher if required – it levelled off and flew at its cruising speed across the North Sea and onward over England; at about 16.20 (local time) the Learjet began its descent into *Robin Hood* airport, again as the cabin area returned to normal pressure both commanders felt pain in their ears. Once the business jet had landed, safely, on the concrete runway it started – not immediately – to slow down as reverse thrust was applied to the engines. Once the jet had drawn to a full standstill the staircase was lowered and the built-in luggage compartment was opened.

Ronan and his deputy un-strapped their seat belts and descended the steps onto the tarmac below – the air was cold; they then unloaded their suitcases and other bags from the luggage compartment, and then proceeded to walk into the main terminal. They, again, showed their HART passes to a security guard, on duty, and he led the two commanders out the building and across to the garages; which he unlocked to reveal Ronan's silver Saab *9-4X* and Celia's blue Honda *Civic*. Each commander loaded their luggage into the *boots* of their individual automobiles; once this was done they boarded the two vehicles and drove, slowly and in convoy, from the airport compound – Commander Strobing leading the way.

As the two vehicles journeyed towards their ultimate destination of Hull Ronan Strobing hoped his sister-in-law, Melissa Stevens, and his young son were okay. In the following car Celia's thoughts turned to her son and she wondered if he was the father of this American woman's child. Then she wondered if her husband was still alive, as Ronan had told her; if not would she ever have another relationship with another man? Putting those thoughts aside for the moment she followed Commander Strobing's car towards home. As they drove through the outskirts of Hull they both saw people – in anoraks or heavy coats, all of them fastened up – hurrying towards their homes.

Upon reaching his home Ronan pulled into his snow covered driveway; as he pulled in Commander Most carried on past – Ronan watched as the Honda disappeared down to the end of the street and turned right; sighing to himself the HART commander retrieved his luggage from the boot of the Saab, walked up to his front door and unlocked it, and then entered his property.

He set his suitcases and bags down, in the entrance hall, and walked down the corridor and on into the main room; Melissa looked up from her place on the settee, "Hello Ronan," she greeted him, "I'm glad your home," and then she got up – her long blonde hair was now tied back – walked over to him and kissed him, quite passionately. Simon looked up at this scene – his aunt kissing his father – and immediately looked away.

"Dad!" he cried, trying hard to pretend he'd only just realised his father was home.

"Hello Simon," said Ronan and kissed his son on the head, "how are you?"

"I'm okay," his son replied, "Aunt Melissa has been looking after me well."

"Oh yes," Ronan's sister-in-law said suddenly, "Simon's doing very well at school – since it reopened – I've got his half yearly report card upstairs, I'll just go and fetch it." She walked from the room, wandered down the corridor and began to ascend the stairs; Ronan's eyes following her every move. He then turned, thoughtfully, and looked across at his son, "You saw us kissing didn't you?" he said.

Simon sat up straighter; he looked – slightly – embarrassed as he replied, "Yes I did."

"And do you mind?"

"No," the younger Strobing responded. "If Aunt Melissa makes you happy I don't mind at all." Just then Melissa re-entered the room, carrying Simon's report card.

She seated herself next to her brother-in-law and passed him the report card, "Here you go." He took the card and read it; he congratulated his son once he'd read it thoroughly. "I nearly forgot," the blonde woman said, "This arrived the day after you'd returned overseas," and she handed him a card; it was from the optician's informing him that his glasses were ready for collection.

"I'll pick them up tomorrow," Mr Strobing said, for now he just wanted to relax. Later on he told the others he was going for a hot relaxing bath; Miss Stevens offered to scrub Ronan's back but he refused knowing where it would lead and he didn't need that distraction, at the moment.

After his father had had his bath Simon decided to go to bed, he didn't have to but he wanted to give the two adults some time by themselves, so up he went. Once he'd gone Ronan went and got them some drinks – a whisky for himself and a gin and tonic for his sister-in-law; once Commander Strobing had seated himself next to Melissa she proposed a toast, to future happiness. The HART commander was unsure what the toast actually meant but he had a pretty good idea.

The two of them then drained their glasses, of liquid, and went off to bed.

*****

Commander Most drove on, through the meandering streets, to the house she now shared with her only son – even though she had another two daughters neither of them knew of their father's status of missing; Celia had felt it would be unwise to worry them in case he did turn up safe and sound, though she had the feeling that Peter Most had become another victim of this *mysterious*, and *deadly*, virus. The Honda *Civic* was driven down the drive and parked in the garage at the end. Commander Most turned off the engine, got out and locked up and then unlocked the boot and got her luggage out – the suitcases were pink – relocked the boot and carried her bags inside the house.

"Mike!" she called once she'd put her luggage down; there was no answer. "Mike!" she called again. A figure then appeared at the top of the stairs.

"Mum," the figure said, as if not recognising her straight away. Then with more confidence he called, "Mum, you're home." With full recognition now he flew down the stairs, nearly falling over twice, and hugged his mother furiously; finally letting her go they walked into the kitchen – had a quick snack and a hot drink – and then went through to the main living room. Celia and her son then sat down and told each other what had happened to each of them since they'd parted company a little under two months ago.

Mike then said to his mother, "You remember that letter I received from America?"

"Indeed I do, go on Mike," she urged him, thinking he was about to reveal to her that he was – actually – the father, and therefore wished to join this Maria Sanchez over in America.

Her son simply said, "I still can't work it out, why tell me I may be the father when I don't recall sleeping with her?"

"Maybe she was simply looking for someone to blame, you know Commander Strobing received a similar letter stating he may be the father, so I just think she's looking for someone to blame. I wonder, though, if anyone else received similar letters and if so how many?"

"Who knows?" her son replied. For the rest of the afternoon and into the early evening the two of them, mother and son, just chatted about this and that, watched a little TV, etc.

Finally at about 22.30 both of them decided to go to bed. Mike helped his mother carry her suitcases and bags upstairs.

*****

In London emergency services were at the scene of the accident, firemen were now extinguishing the fire that had been raging. Once the area had been damped down and the fire had been put out members of the police force and paramedics started to sort through the wreckage, all fearing the worst but knowing that they may – just by pure chance – find somebody alive in the wreckage, and be able to help them; but all that was discovered – relatively unscathed as it had been thrown from the bus – was a child's *buggy*.

After concluding, wrongly, that this accident had been caused by the slippery conditions – the traffic lights at one junction were now back at red – the emergency services left the scene leaving the two wrecked vehicles to be collected by tow trucks, or low loaders, from various repair garages.

Unknown to anyone – who had been at the scene of the accident one of the policemen, a constable called James Andon, had contracted the new virus and was now sneezing heavily. "Are you okay James?" asked his partner and long time friend, Officer Gareth Masters.

"Oh what, sorry, yes I'll be fine; I just need a good night's rest." However what he didn't know was his partner, Sandra Kensindale, was the one who was having the affair with Miss Linden and had become infected during the previous week. She had passed the virus on to James in a night of passion but it had lain dormant for a few days; now it had risen to the surface and James had, unknowingly, just infected Gareth.

James Andon did not return to work the next day or the day after, in fact he didn't return after a week.

*****

Over in Geneva, at HART headquarters Commander Bigship switched on the commander's computer machine and immediately checked HART.net, the organisation's own space on the internet, for any new, or unread, emails; there was about 6 awaiting the attention of the superior officer – whoever it may be, he noticed the one whose subject was *Good Day*. He was tempted to open it but then noticed the others had come from various heads of State and required his attention first; he'd answered 3 and had opened the fourth which was an invitation from the latest president of India's office, the latest president being Ali-Akhbar, inviting the key personnel – this meant the commanders - of HART to a formal dinner. He would also be making a key speech in Agra – a city in the north of the country of India, Leon was surprised that the speech wasn't to be made in the capital city of New Delhi - earlier in the day and requested a HART presence for his protection; the personnel and the security soldiers would be housed in rooms at the Taj Mahal, located at Agra.

*****

The Taj Mahal was a mausoleum (tomb) located in Agra, India; it had been built by Mughal emperor Shah Jahan in memory of his favourite wife, Mumtaz Mahal. The Taj Mahal (also known as the *Taj*) is considered to be the finest example of Mughal architecture, a style which combined elements from Persian, Indian, and Islamic architectural styles. In 1983, the Taj Mahal became a UNESCO World Heritage Site and was cited as *the jewel of Muslim art in India and one of the universally admired masterpieces of the world's heritage.*

While the white domed marble mausoleum was its most familiar component, the Taj Mahal was actually an integrated complex of structures. Building began around 1632 and was completed around 1653, and employed thousands of artisans and craftsmen. The construction of the Taj Mahal was entrusted to a board of architects under imperial supervision including Abd ul-

Karim Ma'mur Khan, Makramat Khan, and Ustad Ahmad Lahauri. Lahauri was generally considered to be the principal designer.

The base of the structure was essentially a large, multi-chambered cube with chamfered corners, forming an unequal octagon that was approximately 55 metres (180 ft) on each of the four long sides. On each of these sides, a massive *pishtaq*, or vaulted archway, frames the iwan (an arch-shaped doorway) with two similarly, shaped, arched balconies stacked on either side. This motif of stacked pishtaqs was replicated on the chamfered corner areas, making the design completely symmetrical on all sides of the building. Four minarets frame the tomb, one at each corner of the plinth facing the chamfered corners. The main chamber houses the false sarcophagi of Mumtaz Mahal and Shah Jahan; the actual graves are at a lower level.

The marble dome that surmounted the tomb was the most spectacular feature. Its height of around 35 metres (115 ft) was about the same as the length of the base, and was accentuated as it sat on a cylindrical *drum* which was roughly 7 metres (23 ft) high. Because of its shape, the dome was often called an onion dome or *amrud* (guava dome). The top was decorated with a lotus design, which also served to accentuate its height. The shape of the dome was emphasised by four smaller domed *chattris* (kiosks) placed at its corners, which replicate the onion shape of the main dome. Their columned bases open through the roof of the tomb and provide light to the interior. Tall decorative spires (*guldastas*) extend from the edges of the structures base walls, and provide visual emphasis to the height of the dome. The lotus motif was repeated on both the chattris and guldastas. The dome and chattris were both topped by a gilded finial, which mixed traditional Persian and Hindu decorative elements.

The main finial was originally made of gold but was replaced by a copy made of gilded bronze in the early 19th century. This feature provided a clear example of integration of traditional Persian and Hindu decorative elements. The finial was topped by a moon, a typical Islamic motif whose horns point heavenward. Because of its placement on the main spire, the horns of the moon and the finial point combined to create a trident shape, reminiscent of traditional Hindu symbols of Shiva.

The minarets, which were each more than 40 metres (130 ft) tall, display the designer's penchant for symmetry. They were designed as working minarets — a traditional element of mosques, used by the muezzin to call the Islamic faithful to prayer. Each minaret was effectively divided into three equal parts by two working balconies that ring the tower. At the top of the tower was a final balcony surmounted by a chattri that mirrors the design of those on the tomb. The chattris all share the same decorative elements of a lotus design that was topped by a gilded finial. The minarets were constructed slightly outside of the plinth so that, in the event of collapse, (a typical occurrence with many tall constructions of the period) the material from the towers would tend to fall away from the tomb.

The exterior decorations of the Taj Mahal were among the finest to be found in Mughal architecture. As the surface area changed the decorations were refined proportionally. The decorative elements were created by applying paint, stucco, stone inlays, or carvings. In line with the Islamic prohibition against the use of anthropomorphic forms, the decorative elements can be grouped into either calligraphy, abstract forms or vegetative motifs.

Throughout the complex, passages from the Qur'an are used as decorative elements. Recent scholarship suggests that the passages were chosen by Amanat Khan. The calligraphy on the Great Gate read, *O Soul, thou art at rest. Return to the Lord at peace with Him, and He at peace with you.*

The calligraphy was created by the Persian calligrapher Abd ul-Haq, who came to India from Shiraz, Iran, in 1609. Shah Jahan conferred the title of "Amanat Khan" upon him as a reward for his *dazzling virtuosity*. Near the lines from the Qur'an at the base of the interior dome is the inscription, *Written by the insignificant being, Amanat Khan Shirazi*. Much of the calligraphy was composed of florid thuluth script, made of jasper or black marble, and inlaid in white marble panels.

Higher panels were written in slightly larger script to reduce the skewing effect when viewed from below. The calligraphy found on the marble cenotaphs in the tomb was particularly detailed and delicate.

Abstract forms were used throughout, especially in the plinth, minarets, gateway, mosque, jawab and, to a lesser extent, on the surfaces of the tomb. The domes and vaults of the sandstone buildings are worked with tracery of incised painting to create elaborate geometric forms. Herringbone inlays define the space between many of the adjoining elements. White inlays were used in sandstone buildings, and dark or black inlays on the white marbles. Mortared areas of the marble buildings have been stained or painted in a contrasting colour, creating geometric patterns of considerable complexity. Floors and walkways used contrasting tiles or blocks in tessellation patterns.

On the lower walls of the tomb there are white marble dados that had been sculpted with realistic bas relief depictions of flowers and vines. The marble had also been polished to emphasise the exquisite detailing of the carvings and the dado frames and archway spandrels had been decorated with pietra dura inlays of highly stylised, almost geometric vines, flowers and fruits. The inlay stones were of yellow marble, jasper and jade, polished and levelled to the surface of the walls.

The interior chamber of the Taj Mahal stepped far beyond traditional decorative elements. Here, the inlay work was not pietra dura but lapidary of precious and semiprecious gemstones. The inner chamber was an octagon with the design allowing for entry from each face, although only the south garden-facing door was used. The interior walls were about 25 metres (82 ft) high and topped by a *false* interior dome which was decorated with a sun motif. Eight pishtaq arches define the space at ground level and, as with the exterior each lower pishtaq was crowned by a second pishtaq about midway up the wall. The four central upper arches formed balconies or viewing areas, and each balcony's exterior window had an intricate screen or *jali* cut from marble. In addition to the light from the balcony screens, light entered through roof openings which were covered by chattris at the corners. Each chamber wall has been highly decorated with dado bas relief, intricate lapidary inlay and refined calligraphy panels, reflecting in miniature detail the design elements seen throughout the exterior of the complex. The octagonal marble screen or *jali* which bordered the cenotaphs was made from eight marble panels which had been carved through with intricate pierce work. The remaining surfaces had been inlaid in extremely delicate detail with semiprecious stones forming twining vines, fruits and flowers.

Muslim tradition forbids elaborate decoration of graves and hence Mumtaz and Shah Jahan were laid in a relatively plain crypt beneath the inner chamber with their faces turned right and towards Mecca. Mumtaz Mahal's cenotaph was placed at the precise centre of the inner chamber on a rectangular marble base of 1.5 metres (4 ft 11 in) by 2.5 metres (8 ft 2 in). Both the base and the casket were elaborately inlaid with precious and semiprecious gems. Calligraphic inscriptions on the casket identify and praise Mumtaz. On the lid of the casket was a raised rectangular lozenge meant to suggest a writing tablet. Shah Jahan's cenotaph was beside Mumtaz's to the western side and was the only visible asymmetric element in the entire complex. His cenotaph was bigger than his wife's, but reflected the same elements: a larger casket on a, slightly, taller base, again decorated with astonishing precision with lapidary and calligraphy that identified him. On the lid of this casket was a traditional sculpture of a small pen box. The pen box and writing tablet were traditional Mughal funerary icons decorating men's and women's caskets respectively. The Ninety Nine Names of God were to be found as calligraphic inscriptions on the sides of the actual tomb of Mumtaz Mahal, in the crypt including *"O Noble, O Magnificent, O Majestic, O Unique, O Eternal, O Glorious...."*. The tomb of Shah Jahan bore a calligraphic inscription that reads; *"He travelled from this world to the banquet-hall of Eternity on the night of the twenty-sixth of the month of Rajab, in the year 1076 Hiri."*

The complex was set around a large 300-metre (980 ft) square *charbagh* or Mughal garden. The garden used raised pathways that divided each of the four quarters of the garden into 16 sunken parterres or flowerbeds. A raised marble water tank at the centre of the garden, halfway between the tomb and gateway with a reflecting pool on a north-south axis, reflected the image of the mausoleum. The raised marble water tank is called *al Hawd al-Kawthar*, in reference to the *Tank of Abundance* promised to Muhammad. Elsewhere, the garden is laid out with avenues of trees and fountains. The charbagh garden, a design inspired by Persian gardens, was introduced to India by the first Mughal emperor, Babur. It symbolised the four flowing rivers of Jannah (Paradise) and reflected the Paradise garden derived from the Persian *paridaeza*, meaning *walled garden*. In mystic Islamic texts of Mughal period, Paradise was described as an ideal garden of abundance with four rivers flowing from a central spring or mountain, separating the garden into north, west, south and east.

Most Mughal charbaghs are rectangular with a tomb or pavilion in the centre. The Taj Mahal garden was unusual in that the main element, the tomb, was located at the end of the garden. With the discovery of Mahtab Bagh or *Moonlight Garden* on the other side of the Yamuna, the interpretation of the Archaeological Survey of India is that the Yamuna river was incorporated into the garden's design and was meant to be seen as one of the rivers of Paradise. The similarity in layout of the garden and its architectural features with the Shalimar Gardens suggest that they may have been designed by the same architect, Ali Mardan. Early accounts of the garden describe its profusion of vegetation, including abundant roses, daffodils, and fruit trees. As the Mughal Empire declined, the tending of the garden also declined, and when the British took over the management of the Taj Mahal during the time of the British Empire, they changed the landscaping to resemble that of lawns of London.

The Taj Mahal complex was bounded on three sides by crenellated red sandstone walls, with the river-facing side left open. Outside the walls were several additional mausoleums, including those of Shah Jahan's other wives, and a larger tomb for Mumtaz's favourite servant. These structures, composed primarily of red sandstone, were typical of the smaller Mughal tombs of the era. The garden-facing inner sides of the wall are fronted by columned arcades, a feature typical of Hindu temples which was later incorporated into Mughal mosques. The wall was interspersed with domed *chattris*, and small buildings that may have been viewing areas or watch towers like the *Music House*, which was now used as a museum.

The main gateway (*darwaza*) was a monumental structure built primarily of marble which is reminiscent of Mughal architecture of earlier emperors. Its archways mirror the shape of tomb's archways, and its *pishtaq* arches incorporate the calligraphy that decorates the tomb. It utilises bas-relief and pietra dura inlaid decorations with floral motifs. The vaulted ceilings and walls have elaborate geometric designs, like those found in the other sandstone buildings of the complex.

At the far end of the complex, there were two grand red sandstone buildings that are open to the sides of the tomb. Their backs parallel the western and eastern walls, and the two buildings were precise mirror images of each other. The western building was a mosque and the other was the *jawab* (answer), whose primary purpose was architectural balance, although it may have been used as a guesthouse. The distinctions between these two buildings include the lack of *mihrab* (a niche in a mosque's wall facing Mecca) in the *jawab* and that the floors of *jawab* have a geometric design, while the mosque floor was laid with outlines of 569 prayer rugs in black marble. The mosque's basic design of a long hall surmounted by three domes was similar to others built by Shah Jahan, particularly to his *Masjid-Jahan Numa*, or Jama Masjid, Delhi. The Mughal mosques of this period divide the sanctuary hall into three areas, with a main sanctuary and slightly smaller sanctuaries on either side. At the Taj Mahal, each sanctuary opens onto an enormous vaulting dome. These outlying buildings were completed in 1643.

The Taj Mahal was built on a parcel of land to the south of the walled city of Agra. Shah Jahan presented Maharajah Jai

Singh with a large palace in the centre of Agra in exchange for the land. An area of roughly three acres was excavated, filled with dirt to reduce seepage, and levelled at 50 metres (160 ft) above the riverbank. In the tomb area, wells were dug and filled with stone and rubble to form the footings of the tomb. Instead of lashed bamboo, workmen constructed a colossal brick scaffold that mirrored the tomb. The scaffold was so enormous that foremen estimated it would take years to dismantle. According to the legend, Shah Jahan decreed that anyone could keep the bricks taken from the scaffold, and thus it was dismantled by peasants overnight. A fifteen kilometre (9.3 mi) tamped-earth ramp was built to transport marble and materials to the construction site and teams of twenty or thirty oxen pulled the blocks on specially constructed wagons. An elaborate post-and-beam pulley system was used to raise the blocks into the desired position. Water was drawn from the river by a series of *purs*, an animal-powered rope and bucket mechanism, into a large storage tank and this was raised to a large distribution tank. It was passed into three subsidiary tanks, from which it was piped to the complex.

The plinth and tomb took roughly 12 years to complete. The remaining parts of the complex took an additional 10 years and were completed in order of minarets, mosque and jawab, and gateway. Since the complex was built in stages, discrepancies exist in completion dates due to differing opinions on *completion*. For example, the mausoleum itself was essentially complete by 1643, but work continued on the rest of the complex. Estimates of the cost of construction vary due to difficulties in estimating costs across time. The total cost has been estimated to be about 32 million Rupees at that time.

The Taj Mahal was constructed using materials from all over India and Asia and over 1,000 elephants were used to transport building materials. The translucent white marble was brought from Rajasthan, the jasper from Punjab, jade and crystal from China. The turquoise was from Tibet and the Lapis lazuli from Afghanistan, while the sapphire came from Sri Lanka and the carnelian from Arabia. In all, twenty eight types of precious and semi-precious stones were inlaid into the white marble. A labour force of twenty thousand workers was recruited from across northern India. Sculptors from Bukhara, calligraphers from Syria and Persia, inlayers from southern India, stonecutters from Baluchistan, a specialist in building turrets, another who carved only marble flowers were part of the thirty-seven men who formed the creative unit.

Soon after the Taj Mahal's completion, Shah Jahan was deposed by his son Aurangzeb and put under house arrest at nearby Agra Fort. Upon Shah Jahan's death, Aurangzeb buried him in the mausoleum next to his wife.

By the late 19th century, parts of the buildings had fallen badly into disrepair. During the time of the Indian rebellion of 1857, the Taj Mahal was defaced by British soldiers and government officials, who chiselled out precious stones and lapis lazuli from its walls. At the end of the 19th century, British viceroy Lord Curzon ordered a massive restoration project, which was completed in 1908.

He also commissioned the large lamp in the interior chamber, modelled after one in a Cairo mosque. During this time the garden was remodelled with British-style lawns that were still in place today.

In 1942, the government erected scaffolding in anticipation of an air attack by the German Luftwaffe and later by the Japanese Air Force. During the India-Pakistan wars of 1965 and 1971, scaffoldings were again erected to mislead bomber pilots.

More recent threats have come from environmental pollution on the banks of Yamuna River including acid rain due to the Mathura Oil Refinery, which was opposed by the Supreme Court of India directives. The pollution had been turning the Taj Mahal yellow. To help control the pollution, the Indian government set up the Taj Trapezium Zone (TTZ), a 10,400 square kilometre (4,015 square mile) area around the monument where strict emissions standards are in place. In 1983, the Taj Mahal was designated a UNESCO World Heritage Site.

The Taj Mahal attracted from 2 to 4 million visitors annually, with more than 200,000 from overseas. Most of the tourists visited in the cooler months of October, November and February. Polluting traffic was not allowed near the complex and tourists either walk from parking lots or catch an electric bus. The Khawasspuras (northern courtyards) had been restored for use as a new visitor centre. The small town to the south of the Taj, known as Taj Ganji or Mumtazabad, originally was constructed with caravanserais, bazaars and markets to serve the needs of visitors and workmen. Lists of recommended travel destinations often feature the Taj Mahal, which also appeared in several listings of seven wonders of the modern world, including the recently announced New Seven Wonders of the World, a recent poll-with 100 million votes. The grounds were open from 6 am to 7 pm weekdays, except for Friday when the complex was open for prayers at the mosque between 12 pm and 2 pm. The complex was also open for night viewing on the day of the full moon and two days before and after, excluding Fridays and the month of Ramzan. For security reasons only five items: water in transparent bottles, small video cameras, still cameras, mobile phones and small ladies purses were allowed inside the Taj Mahal. Ever since its construction, the building has been the source of an admiration transcending culture and geography, and so personal and emotional responses have consistently eclipsed scholastic appraisals of that monument.

A longstanding myth holds that Shah Jahan planned a mausoleum to be built in black marble across the Yamuna river. This idea originates from fanciful writings of Jean-Baptiste Tavernier, a European traveller who visited Agra in 1665. It was suggested that Shah Jahan was overthrown by his son Aurangzeb before it could be built. Ruins of blackened marble across the river in *Moonlight Garden*, Mahtab Bagh, seemed to support this particular legend. However, excavations carried out in the 1990s found that they were discoloured white stones that had turned black. A more credible theory for the origins of the black mausoleum was demonstrated in 2006 by archaeologists who reconstructed part of the pool in the *Moonlight Garden*. A dark reflection of the white mausoleum could clearly be seen, befitting Shah Jahan's obsession with symmetry and the positioning of the pool itself.

No evidence exists for claims that describe, often in horrific detail, the deaths, dismemberments and mutilations which Shah Jahan supposedly inflicted on various architects and craftsmen associated with the tomb. Some stories claim that those involved in construction signed contracts committing themselves to have no part in any similar design. Similar claims were made for many famous buildings. No evidence exists for claims that Lord William Bentinck, governor-general of India in the 1830s, supposedly planned to demolish the Taj Mahal and auction off the marble. Bentinck's biographer John Rosselli says that the story arose from Bentinck's funraising sale of discarded marble from Agra Fort.

In 2000, India's Supreme Court dismissed P.N. Oak's petition to declare that a Hindu king built the Taj Mahal. Oak claimed that origins of the Taj, together with other historic structures in the country currently ascribed to Muslim sultans pre-date Muslim occupation of India and thus, have a Hindu origin. A more poetic story relates that once a year, during the rainy season, a single drop of water fell on the cenotaph, as inspired by Rabindranath Tagore's description of the tomb as *one tear-drop...upon the cheek of time.* Another myth suggests that beating the silhouette of the finial will cause water to come forth. To this day, officials find broken bangles surrounding the silhouette.

During the previous years some empty rooms, on an upper level of the Taj Mahal had been converted into small or medium sized, rooms dwellings for overnight stays.

*****

Agra was a city on the banks of the river Yamuna in the northern state of Uttar Pradesh, India. With a population of 1,686,976 (2010 est.), it was the 3rd most populous city in Uttar Pradesh and the 19th most populous in India.

The city finds mention in the epic Mahābhārata where it was called Agreva□a, or *the border of the forest.* Legend ascribes the founding of the city to Rājā Badal Singh (around 1475) whose fort, Badalgarh, stood on or near the site of the present Fort. However, the 11th century Persian poet Mas'ūd Sa'd Salmān writes of a desperate assault on the fortress of Agra, then held by the Shahi King Jayapala, by Sultan Mahmud of Ghazni. Sultan Sikandar Lodī was the first to move his capital from Delhi to Agra in the year 1506; he later died in 1517 and his son Ibrāhīm Lodī remained in power there for nine more years, finally being defeated at the Battle of Panipat in 1526. It achieved fame as the capital of the Mughal emperors from 1526 to 1658 and remained a major tourist destination because of its many splendid Mughal-era buildings, most notably the Tāj Mahal, Agra Fort and Fatehpūr Sikrī, all three of which are UNESCO World_Heritage_Sites

*****

The speech – which was confidential – was to be made before the citizens of Agra at the Sadar Bazar market square. As the speech was due to be made in March the temperature would be about 38 degrees Celsius, so the personnel and soldiers who went could expect hot warm weather with, possibly, a very slight chance of rain.

Leon opened up the fifth email it was just a status report from Ralph Williams in Scotland – nothing of real importance; however the last email intrigued the commander what with it having such a strange subject heading. Undeterred he opened it thus releasing the virus and duplicating the screen he was looking at, at *Proagnon* headquarters; as soon as Leon Bigship saw the mysterious and nonsensical words and numbers he wished he hadn't opened it.

*****

India, officially the Republic of India, was a country in South Asia. It was the seventh-largest country by geographical area, the second-most populous country with over 1.18 billion people, and the most populous democracy in the world. Bounded by the Indian Ocean on the south, the Arabian Sea on the west, and the Bay of Bengal on the east, India has a coastline of 7,517 kilometres (4,700 mi). It is bordered by Pakistan to the west; China, Nepal, and Bhutan to the north; and Bangladesh and Burma to the east. India was in the vicinity of Sri Lanka, and the Maldives in the Indian Ocean.

Home to the Indus Valley Civilisation and a region of historic trade routes and vast empires, the Indian subcontinent was identified with its commercial and cultural wealth for much of its long history. Four major religions, Hinduism, Buddhism, Jainism and Sikhism originated here, while Zoroastrianism, Judaism, Christianity and Islam arrived in the first millennium CE and shaped the region's diverse culture. Gradually annexed by the British East India Company from the early eighteenth century and colonised by the United Kingdom from the mid-nineteenth century, India became an independent nation in 1947 after a struggle for independence that was marked by widespread non-violent resistance.

India was a republic consisting of 28 states and seven union territories with a parliamentary system of democracy. The Indian economy was the world's eleventh largest economy by nominal GDP and the fourth largest by purchasing power parity. It had the second-largest standing army in the world. Economic reforms since 1991 have transformed it into one of the fastest growing economies in the world; however, it still suffers from poverty, illiteracy, corruption, disease, and malnutrition. India was a nuclear weapon state and had the tenth-largest military spending in the world. A pluralistic, multilingual and multiethnic society, India was also the home to a diversity of wildlife in a variety of protected habitats.

HART never recruited anyone from the country of India; as some members of the government of that country didn't – officially recognise HART as a proper fighting force, and never had.

*****

Ali Devisingh Akhbar (born 15 October 1967) was the 13th and current President of the Republic of India and youngest person to hold the office. He was sworn in as President of India on 10 September 2012, succeeding Pratiba Patil after her untimely demise at the peace conference. He had been a member of the

Indian National Congress (INC), as had Mrs Patil, and was nominated by the ruling United Progressive Alliance and Indian Left. He had won the presidential election held on 19 July 2012 defeating his nearest rival Bhairon Singh Shekhawat. Bhairon Sing Skehawat had also stood against Pratiba during the earlier election, in 2007.

Akhbar had represented Edlabad constituency in Jalgaon District, Maharashta as a member of the Maharashtra Legislative Assembly (1982–2000), and was deputy chairman of the Raiya Sabha (2001–2003), Member of Parliament from Amravati in the Lok Sabha (2004–2009), and the 24th, and the first youngest male Governor of Rajasthan (2010-2012).

Ali Devisingh Akbar was born on October 15, 1967 in Agra city of Utter Pradesh District, Maharashtra. Smt. Akhbar assumed office as the 13th President of India on September 10, 2012. He was the youngest man to have been elected to this august office. Immediately prior to the election as the President of India, Smt. Akhbar was the Governor of Rajasthan from November 10, 2010 till August 17, 2012.

Smt. Akhbar received his early education from RR Vidyalaya, Utter Pradesh and later obtained a Master's degree in Political Science and Economics from the Raja Balwant Singh College, Agra. Later, he obtained the degree of Bachelor of Laws (LL.B.) from Government Law College, Bombay (Mumbai). While in college, he took active part in sports, excelled in table tennis and won several shields at various Inter-collegiate tournaments. Even as an MLA, he pursued his studies as a law student.

Smt. Akhbar started his professional career as a practicing lawyer at the Utter Pradesh District Court and simultaneously devoted himself to various social activities, especially, for the upliftment of poor families.

*****.

At the underground bunker one of the computer operators called their leader over, "Sir! We're getting a picture."

Walker wondered over, "Don't touch anything," he said authoritatively. "Let's just observe for the moment; we don't want to alert HART to our presence, yet." They watched as Commander Bigship called up information on India, the Taj Mahal and the city of Agra.

"Now why would HART want information on India?" he wondered. Once he'd retrieved all the information needed Leon viewed the email from President Akhbar's office again. Mitchell ordered another duplication of the screen.

The operator pressed the *PrtSc* key – on the keyboard - thus creating a duplicate of the screen the HART commander was presently viewing, this would be used for reference later as would the duplicates of the screens containing the other information. "Let's see," Walker told the gathered technicians and computer operators in the room, "this speech is set to happen on the 18th March 2014 I believe we should send a *Proagnon* group over to assassinate this President Akhbar, as we did with his predecessor "

"But sir," one of the technicians reminded his leader, "he will have full protection from HART forces." He sat back down in his seat and awaited his superior's response.

"Ah yes," replied Mr Walker evenly, "I have thought of that. Do we still have that uniform from the HART soldier we killed?"

"You mean Captain Theresa Robins. I believe we do, and we can soon make up a false identity tag for whoever will be wearing the uniform," the same technician told Mitchell.

"Perfect," responded Walker, "I shall go back to my office now and select the squad we shall send. Patch the duplicated screen feed through to my office; I shall monitor things from there." With that he strode from the computer room and returned to the leader's office, where he switched on the computer terminal that would allow him to access the feed from the computer room. He, then, set about choosing four or five soldiers for the *Proagnon* assassination squad; once he'd made his selection he requested – via the radio communications system - that those personnel he had selected gather in the main meeting hall at 14.00. Although the speech was, more or less, three months away Walker liked to be prepared.

*****

Commander Bigship accepted the invitation from President Akhbar, he realised later on he probably shouldn't have without Commander Strobing's authorisation, but Leon was sure Ronan wouldn't mind; he was still puzzled by the *Good Day* email HART had received, it just seemed to be a load of gibberish but maybe it was a code – of some sort - so he left it on the system for Commander Strobing to look at when he returned. He then went, to the drinks cabinet, and poured himself a whisky and sat back down in the command chair to relax; as he sat there, sipping his drink, he began to wonder how Major Howell's daughter – Suki – was getting on.

*****

In the small pub – in Ardersier – Suki Howell climbed out of bed after her first night in Scotland, dressed and made her way downstairs for breakfast. As she was in a pub there were mainly men in the bar; there were a couple of young women sat at a corner table. One of the women's hair was dyed a bright pink whereas her companion's was a darkish brown with green streaks in. When the one with pink hair saw Miss Howell she shouted, "Get off back to your own country you fucking nigger." *So*, thought Suki, *there were still some people with racial prejudices*.

She ignored the woman and walked up to the bar. She asked the man who was working the other side, who she took to be the landlord, "Do you know anything about the sea fort in the Moray Firth or the Maxwell consortium?"

"Depends whose asking don't it," said the landlord – in a thick Scottish accent.

Suki thought quickly, "I just want a little information, that's all; plus I'm a student doing research on Mr Maxwell and his consortium." She hoped her response had sounded plausible.

The man rested his elbows on the bar and leaned conspiratorially forward, "All I know is that there's been strange things happening on that sea fort, of Maxwell there's no sign and nobody knows the identities of the other members of his consortium."

"Thank you," replied the young Japanese woman, "you've been most helpful." In fact he'd been no help, HART already knew most of the information but, still, she had to start somewhere; she asked the men – who were drinking in the bar – the same question but received more or less the same answer from each of them. Undaunted she had her breakfast, it was a cooked breakfast of Eggs, Bacon, Sausages, Black Pudding, and Beans.

Afterwards she had a cup of tea and then exited the restaurant to return to her room; there was no sign of the two women although the men were still gathered round the bar; Miss Howell ascended the staircase up to the first floor, upstairs was in near darkness – for some reason, maybe the overhead lighting had failed – so Suki had to feel along the walls to find her room.

She reached the old, wooden, door and was about to turn the handle to open the door when a torch snapped into sudden life, blinding her. Roughly she was grabbed from behind – a woman's arm went around her neck pulling tight so she was nearly choking, and then a knee was thrust into her back – winding Suki. Suddenly the Japanese woman's room door was opened from the inside and she was thrust inside. "Get in there nigger!" Suki recognised the voice.

Miss Howell was grabbed by another pair of hands that pulled her into the room, "Get on the bed," snapped another voice and then a fist connected with Suki's jaw – as the fist connected there was a *crack* and the Japanese woman fell back onto the soft sheets of the bed; as Miss Howell lay dazed, trying to recover, another figure entered the room and slammed the door closed. Suki opened her eyes and looked up at her assailants – she'd been right, the voices had belonged to *Pink* hair and *Green* hair.

"What do you want?" she managed to stammer – somewhat puzzled as to why these two had attacked her.

"Simple," replied *Pink* hair, "we don't like strangers – by the way I'm Claudia and my friend is Sharon," Sharon gave Suki a wave as if mocking her, "not that you'll need to remember our names. As I says we don't like strangers –

particularly slanty eyed niggers; oh and another thing shut your fucking mouth!" Miss Howell did as she was told, she now knew she was dealing with two, not very well educated, young girls – teenagers trying to act *big*; Claudia *Pink* hair grabbed the Japanese woman's hands in one of hers and held them above her head; Miss Howell gasped – in mild pain and surprise and tried to kick her assailant. "Hold her," Claudia called to Sharon.

The other woman came further into the room, round the side of the bed and lifted the Japanese woman's legs back onto the bed. "Spread em," commanded *Pink* hair; Miss Howell shook her head in a refusal gesture. "I said spread em bitch!" Again Suki shook her head, "Sharon," Claudia said to her friend, turning her head slightly, "as she won't spread em voluntarily you'll have to help her." Sharon smiled at her companion, walked round to the foot of the bed – grabbed one of Suki's legs in each hand and pulled them apart.

Miss Howell screamed, "You fucking bitch!" she tried to kick out but *Green* hair's grip was too tight. Claudia then produced four pieces of rope and a knife from her jeans pocket and she tied the Japanese woman's hand to the bedposts and then moved down to where Sharon was standing.

Claudia used the other two pieces of rope to tie Suki's legs to the relevant bedpost and then handed Sharon the knife saying, "You know what to do." The little Japanese woman screamed and shouted as she was tortured and her clothes were cut off her. Claudia *Pink* hair punched Major Howell's daughter – in the stomach, "Silence bitch or we simply stab you;" suddenly the knife, held by Sharon *Green* hair touched a spot on Suki's inner thigh –she quivered a bit.

"Patience nigger," Sharon told her victim, "I'm just warming up." Suki Howell managed to raise her head - an inch or two – and saw the knife clearly, for the first time. She turned to look at the girl named Claudia, who was holding her hands tightly; Claudia had a T-shirt on, despite the weather, so her arms were exposed – so the Japanese woman bit into *Pink* hair's flesh. Claudia yelped and as Major Howell's daughter hoped the grip on her arm's slackened. Instinctively Sharon withdrew the knife and letting go of Suki's legs she bolted round to her companion's side.

"I ain't urt," the older girl said sharply. "Finish er off." Meanwhile the Japanese woman swung her legs round and managed to catch the back of Sharon's knee – causing her to fall backward; she hit her head on the wooden wardrobe behind her and she lay still. "Get ta yer feet," Claudia raged but Sharon didn't move. "Gotta do everyfin mesen av I?"

However, Suki pushed upwards and managed to break free; "Get back bitch!" and the girl with *Pink* hair tried to push back but this time the Japanese woman was ready for her; she grasped Claudia's arm in a vice like grip with one hand, stood and faced the other woman and said quietly bet menacingly, "Don't mess with me girl!"

"Or you'll do what exactly?" *Pink* hair demanded. "Look at you; you're only a small nigger."

"This," answered Suki and punched her assailant. Claudia was both shocked and surprised at the power behind the Japanese woman's punch – she was slightly taller than most Japanese women but shorter than Claudia by a good couple of inches. "Now get out," demanded the Japanese woman, pointing the knife – which she'd picked up earlier – at Claudia, who looked at Suki. She could see the smaller woman meant it so she left and made her way downstairs.

Suki then turned her attention to *Green* hair – Sharon slowly opened her eyes and looked around her; seeing only the Japanese woman she said hesitantly, "Where's Claudia?"

"She's gone and left you," the other woman said, "now I suggest you follow her and leave me alone." She pointed the knife at Sharon who quickly got up and followed her *Pink* haired companion. "Here," called Miss Howell as Sharon reached the bottom step; she threw the knife down and returned to her room, Sharon caught the knife and left.

Suki cleaned herself up, the bruising from her wrists and ankles would come out eventually – once she'd cleaned herself up she grabbed the duffel coat Mr Williams had given her, along with some money, put the coat on and money in the pocket, descended the stairs and left the pub. She walked through the streets of Ardersier hoping to find somebody who may know something, however small, about the fort or the people who owned it.

Everyone she asked told her that they didn't know anything about it other than what she already knew. However, as she was passing the hotel a man emerged from inside dressed in, a light grey, pin-striped suit; Suki judged him to be in his mid to late twenties, again she asked about the fort and the consortium that owned it.

The man looked at her, somewhat suspiciously, for a moment and then said, "I cannot help you my dear," the Japanese woman sighed, "although if you will agree to meet me here for dinner tonight I will introduce you to somebody who can. By the way my name is Paul Pearman."

"I'm Suki Howell," she told him, "and yes I'll have dinner with you tonight. Shall we say around 18.30?"

"You're on," responded Mr Pearman to this Japanese woman and then turned and walked off down the snow covered street.

*****

Not knowing anything about what was happening in Scotland Commander Ronan Strobing climbed out of bed that morning, along with his sister-in-law, Melissa Stevens and his son; they all had a good breakfast, Simon having cereals while the two adults had a breakfast cooked by Melissa. Over breakfast Ronan told his companions, "I will go to the opticians this morning to collect my new glasses, and perhaps do a bit of shopping as I see we're running low on bread, milk and a few other things; and then this afternoon I was thinking of, maybe, picking your mother up Melissa and going to visit Arnold. Is everyone okay with that?"

"I am Dad," his son replied. Ronan turned and smiled at the boy, he seemed to become more and more mature every day – still he'd had a good deal to deal with these past couple of years – he would make a fine young man one day.

Melissa, on the other hand, said somewhat grudgingly – or so Ronan thought, "Okay then." It was understandable though, she'd never got on with her father that much – especially over her choice of men. They all went into the city of Hull, in Mr Strobing's Saab, and while Ronan went and fetched his new glasses Melissa took Simon into the Hull shopping mall to do the rest of the shopping.

There was one awkward moment when Miss Stevens bumped into Celia Most, who was out shopping with her son Mike. Simon ran straight up to Mike and hugged him – the older boy was taken aback; his mother said, "Why don't you take young Simon over to the magazine stand, see if he wants a comic or something."

"What a good idea," replied Melissa and gave Simon two pounds. "Will you fetch us a TV magazine as well." Mike could tell the two women wanted a talk but didn't want Simon to hear, so he led the young boy over to where the newspapers, magazines and comics were situated. "Now," began Miss Stevens, "I think we should talk."

"Yes I think we should," responded Commander Most, "what exactly is your interest in Commander Strobing?"

"Simple," answered Ronan's sister-in-law, "I love him and want to be with him. I'll admit I've made a few bad choices in men but my heart's always belonged to Ronan, plus I know he wants me." The last bit she said more firmly. "And what exactly is your interest in my brother-in-law?"

"Firstly," Celia responded, "he is no longer your brother-in-law – he was only related to you through your sister who's now dead; secondly he and I were in love before he met your sister."

"I don't suppose you believed me when I told you before that he proposed to me but I turned him down, but it's true. Face it, Melissa, he's not in love with you; I doubt very much if you actually know what the word love means."

Melissa looked at her rival for Commander Strobing's affections, "You don't know what you're talking about you dried up old hag; we sleep together whenever he's home in England, and the sex is really enjoyable – every night we do it."

Mrs Most considered her reply, "What about the night he slept with Maria Sanchez?"

"How do you know about that?" Miss Stevens demanded to know, her voice rising in anger. Mrs Most waited for her to finish before replying.

"Ronan told me all about it." She didn't say her son had received a similar letter, calmly she asked her love rival, "Did Ronan mention if he had sex with her?"

"He says he didn't but he can't remember everything that happened." Just then the two boys returned; Simon was clutching a copy of *TV Quick* and a copy of *Sherlock Holmes* magazine – which came out on a monthly basis.

Melissa led him from the shop forcing herself to smile at the other woman and say farewell; they left the shop and continued to do the rest of the shopping; after they'd finished Melissa – practically – had to drag Simon into a lady's lingerie shop, she picked out a red bra and panties set, and then she took Simon to the counter and asked the assistant to keep an eye on him; the assistant – a woman in her thirties – assured Melissa she would.

Reassured Miss Stevens went and tried the lingerie set, it fitted her perfectly; after purchasing the garments the two of them – aunt and nephew – left the store and went to meet up with Ronan, in a café. The two adults ordered beef lasagne, while Simon Strobing ordered burger and chips. Once they'd eaten they had cups of tea, Ronan paid the bill and the three of them left to return to the car. As they left the warmth of the shopping mall and emerged into the outside air everyone shivered – even though they were all wearing thick coats.

The three of them crossed the road and walked through the streets back to the Saab vehicle. Once they were all in Ronan started the automobile and drove, slowly, back home, where they dropped off the shopping before going on to the hospital.

*****

They picked up Elle Stevens and carried on to the medical building and took the lift to the third floor; exiting the lift they were informed that the doctor in charge of Mr Stevens case wished to see them; the four of them were directed to Dr Charles Lighten's office, they made their way over and knocked on the office door. "Come in," called a cheerful sounding voice – the four people entered the office to find Dr Lighten seated at his desk, consulting some medical notes relating to Arnold's case. "Please sit down," the doctor said to them. Everyone found a chair and sat down.

"Now," began the medical man, "we have had to move Mr Stevens."

"What is wrong with him doctor?" Elle looked very concerned at this latest bit of news, Melissa held her mother's hand.

"That's just it," Dr Lighten told them. "We've performed tests on him in these last couple of weeks and your husband – Mrs Stevens – doesn't seem to be improving yet, at the same time, he doesn't seem to be getting any worse so we felt he could be moved to a ward for the moment, wad 2B – which is located on the floor below - if you wish to see him."

"Too right we do," Melissa burst out. The doctor sighed.

Mrs Stevens spoke in a much calmer voice, "Yes we would like to see him Dr Lighten. Please forgive my daughter's outburst." The doctor nodded as if in understanding. Charles Lighten then led them from his office and down to ward 2B.

Once they all reached Arnold's bed Dr Lighten said to the other four, "As you can see he is still connected by tubes and wires to the various machines, but as we felt he seemed to have passed out of danger a few of the tubes have been removed. We're still pumping antibiotics into his bloodstream and his condition is getting no worse, he's stable."

Dr Lighten left them then; they all pulled a chair up to the side of the bed and Elle kissed Arnold, probably he knew nothing about it, and then said, "Arnold, I don't know if you can hear me but the four of us are all here, there's myself, Melissa,

Ronan and Simon. We're all worried about you, please come back to us soon."

"As it's nearly Christmas – doesn't time fly – I've brought some Christmas cards from our friends and some get well cards. I'm keeping all our presents at home, I won't open them until you come home – I promise."

Ronan then told his father-in-law about his new vehicle and how different it was from his last vehicle. Melissa then told her father she was sorry for all the arguments, in the past, and he'd been right – she had made some bad choices in men – but now she'd found the ideal man for her, and that was Ronan Strobing. Elle looked aghast at this revelation.

Simon then walked over to his Grandfather's side, kissed him and told him to hurry up and get better, he then held the old man's hand and jumped back as he felt his Grandfather's hand squeeze his. He turned quickly to his father, "Granddad squeezed my hand he's awake."

"I'm afraid he isn't," Ronan told the boy. "You probably just felt an involuntary movement of his hand, as the antibiotics kicked in. I'm sorry son."

Elle looked over at Melissa and said sharply, "You mean you and Ronan are seeing each other," the two of them nodded. "How could you? Your sister's only been dead just over a year, and anyway you're Simon's aunt; why spoil that?"

"Can we continue this discussion back at your house Mrs Stevens?" enquired Mr Strobing. "People are beginning to look at us."

Mrs Stevens looked around, "Okay," she said to them, somewhat calmer now. They all left the hospital, and Commander Strobing drove back to Elle's house where he parked up and they all got out. "Let me help you Mum," said Melissa, helping her mother out the car.

"Get off me," the older woman's sharp reply even made Ronan cringe, "I can manage." Once she was out she crossed to her front door and unlocked it; when it was fully open Mrs Stevens told her Grandson, "You can go and play, or read, upstairs. I just need to talk to your father and aunt." The young boy did as he was asked while Elle turned to Melissa and Ronan, "Come with me please."

The two of them followed Mrs Stevens through to the main living room, "Please sit down;" the seated themselves on the sofa, not too close and not too far apart. Now," began the older woman, "tell me again what you said earlier."

Her daughter looked across at Mr Strobing but couldn't read the expression on his face; turning to her mother she said hesitantly, "I simply stated that Ronan and I were together now. Is that a crime?"

"To me it is," snapped Elle. "This man was married to your sister for God's sake! A sister that is now dead. Admittedly if Ronan wants to move on then that's his choice, but – as I said earlier – you're Simon's aunt."

"And you," she snapped turning to Mr Strobing, "should know better! What would Mandy think of you, bedding her own sister; just the thought of it's disgusting."

"Hang on mother," her youngest daughter said taking the heat off Mr Strobing, "I believe you said that it's Ronan's choice if he wants to move on."

"Indeed I did – my girl – but you!"

"I believe that's my decision," her son-in-law piped up. "And whether my decision as well as choice of partner, meets with your approval or not is totally immaterial. I don't give a damn what you think – if Simon's happy with this, and he is, I don't think anyone should interfere. I could stop you seeing your Grandson, but I won't – on condition that you give us your blessing."

"Furthermore, Mandy would want me to be happy and if Melissa makes me happy I feel no-one should interfere." Mrs Stevens knew she could do nothing but she felt she had a duty to try and prevent it.

"Okay," she eventually sighed resignedly. "It's your life. I give you my blessing, though I still think you're making a big mistake."

"Thank you," they both said to the older woman. "Now with your permission I believe we should go home, before the weather gets too bad," continued Ronan – it had started snowing again. Once Simon reappeared the three younger people departed, after reminding Elle to keep safe and warm.

*****

Floyd Maxwell, watched by an anxious Carol Turnerr, had decided to leave the traffic computers alone as he had selected another target; he had decided to target the computers that controlled the oil rigs, out in the North Sea, Floyd knew this would prove difficult for most people but he had discovered a tiny *loophole* in the systems once when he'd tried – many years previous – and now decided to exploit this *loophole* further, thus bypassing the in-built security systems.

Slowly and carefully – so as to avoid the security system's suspicion – Maxwell keyed in the codes he'd discovered on his earlier visit, he'd only been 16 at that time and now was now double that age; once inside the master computer – which was linked to the main computer aboard each oil rig, there were now only 5 of them – the others had been shut down and dismantled, he hacked into the part of the master computer that controlled the drilling heads, on the rigs, and typed in the commands that would cause the drill heads to come to a standstill, thus ceasing all operations. Then he would commence the next part of the plan that Sandy (Carol) and he had come up with.

*****

Suki Howell met Paul Pearman in the lobby of the hotel, in Ardersier, at their prearranged time of 18.30; Miss Howell was wearing a white blouse and green skirt, along with some high heeled shoes, for the occasion. She recognised Paul immediately – even though his back was to her – as he was still dressed in the same light grey suit she'd seen him in earlier. At the moment he was talking to another man, the Japanese woman didn't recognise him, so Suki walked over – her heels making a *click-clack* sound on the polished hotel floor; she tapped him, lightly, on the shoulder and he turned round, as he turned she got a look at the other man – he was balding very prematurely – although he didn't look older than 35, she did concede – to herself – she may be wrong about his age.

"Ah hello again Miss Howell," Paul said upon seeing her. Next he introduced the other man, "I should like you to meet my brother, Grant, he can tell you more about that sea fort than I can." The two of them shook hands, Grant Pearman – Suki thought – had a much firmer grip than Paul in fact he seemed to have a grip like a vice; although he looked like a very gentle person. "Shall we go through for dinner," suggested Paul, "then, afterwards, I shall leave you two to discuss the sea fort."

They walked into the restaurant, only a few tables were occupied – the other guests, in the building, had either already eaten or had gone out for dinner though there weren't many places to go. The three of them had some slices of turkey – it was 23rd December – boiled potatoes, veg (broccoli, carrots and peas) plus gravy, which they all enjoyed immensely. After they'd had pudding (lemon slice and custard), two cups of coffee each and mints Paul Pearman said to them, "Sorry I have to go now, business meeting – even at Christmas," he smiled over at his brother. "Enjoy yourself."

"What did he mean by that?" Suki asked the other man as his brother left.

"Maybe we'd be more comfortable in my brother's room," Grant answered, "there's a drinks cabinet in there," he continued quickly as he saw the dubious look the Japanese woman gave him.

"Okay then," she sighed, knowing where this might lead and regretting what she'd just said instantly; she knew intelligence operations all had risks, and the sorts of dangers that were involved with them – her father had made sure of that – but if she didn't take this chance there may never be another one and she felt if it came to it she could handle herself well enough.

She followed Mr Pearman through a maze of corridors until he stopped outside a room door; taking a key card, similar to a credit card, from his jacket pocket, he inserted it into the slot; the door mechanism *clicked* open. Pearman pushed open the door and turned to Miss Howell, "Get inside," he said to her in something of a sharper tone than he'd used earlier. Suki hesitantly stepped inside, "Come on, I ain't got all fucking day;" to prove his point he gave the Japanese woman a shove.

Suki was aware of him coming in behind her and closing the door – there was another *click* which Miss Howell knew meant she was now locked in the room, with this man. "Turn around," he ordered her – she turned slowly to look at him. "You want information right?" Suki nodded, "Well you're gonna have to do something for me. I'll trade my information for items of your clothing; do you understand?" She was unprepared for such a trade, but Commander Strobing had given her the authority to get the information any way she could but could she do this?

Her hesitation seemed to annoy Grant Pearman, "Do you understand me bitch, you strip, I give you the information."

"I'm not prepared to do that. Either you give me the information I seek, or I leave right now," she suddenly remembered the locked door and cursed herself for being so stupid. She couldn't defend herself against him either. Admittedly she had been trained, by her father, but Grant Pearman was – evidently – more of a *brute* than his brother.

"Have it your way," he snarled, producing a gun from the same jacket pocket that had held the key card. He pointed the weapon at her head, "Now strip bitch or I kill you here and now!"

Knowing she was beaten; even though she was slightly taller than many of her fellow Japanese women she still had short arms and legs, so she couldn't grab the pistol or kick the weapon out Pearman's hand without him killing her so she simply said, "Where do you want me to start?"

"Your blouse," he replied. After each of her clothes came off he admired her body – he looked more like a schoolboy seeing a girl take her clothes off for the first time.; as each item came off he made her kick it over to him. Once she was fully naked he said, "Get on the bed and lay face up."

She was now aware of how small the room was becoming, in her mind at least, and of him leering over her; she knew he was going to rape her, and she felt so puny and defenceless. "Spread em bitch," Pearman commanded, grabbing her legs.

"No, you can't make me," she cried, knowing that he could but trying to put up some resistance. He simply grabbed her legs, once he'd got a good grip on each he pulled her legs apart and she howled in pain.

"Shut your filthy mouth," Pearman shouted at her as he pulled her down the bed; and then came the part Suki was dreading, as he forced himself upon her she screamed, and howled, in pain. Finally after a good quarter of an hour her ordeal finally came to an end. "On your feet," he commanded; Miss Howell felt so battered and bruised she just lay there. "On your feet or do you want more of the same?"

The Japanese woman looked up at him, "Please do what you want to me," she began weakly, "I don't care." With that he clamped one hand around her neck and dragged her off the bed, in his other hand he held his pistol.

"I could shoot you here and now," he snarled at the small figure before him, "but I'm not!"

"What are you going to do to me?" she asked him, her voice even weaker now.

"This," he told her and spun her round and then slammed her back into the wall; Major Howell's daughter fell forward onto the hard marble floor, "I ain't finished yet," and he rolled her over and punched her in both eyes, across the bridge of her nose – there was an audible *crack* – in the stomach, and on both sides of her chest – a *crack* was heard both times. Finally he forced her forward and smashed the butt of his gun across the back of her head, producing a trickle of blood.

Unable to stand anymore torture, from this animal, she said pathetically, "Please shoot me."

"I'm no killer," and Grant Pearman picked her useless body up and slammed her against the wall again – this time face forward. She screamed and slid to the floor apparently lifeless. "I'm going now," Pearman snarled, "but before I go I will tell you what I know, not that it'll do you any good, but there are scientists on that sea fort – I've heard the name Simon Forrestor

– supply ships go there once a week to take food and bring back crates of the new deodorant *Propower*, which I, and other employees of the consortium distribute. The Maxwell consortium only has two *real* members, Floyd Maxwell and another person; nobody knows who this somebody else is." Once he'd told her this he left – Pearman was probably hoping she'd die before anyone got to her

About half an hour after Pearman left Suki, who was still conscious – just, heard a *click* and then footsteps on the marble floor. *Maybe he's come to finish me off*, thought Miss Howell. A figure appeared in her vision and said, "My God, what the hell happened to you?" There was something about the voice, something Miss Howell recognised; it seemed familiar. "I'd better get an ambulance," he spoke into a hand held device; the Japanese woman could just about hear him. "Ambulance is on its way, now lie still. I left you with my brother and now look at you." Now she knew that voice belonged to Paul Pearman.

Approximately 5 minutes later paramedics arrived and put her in the ambulance. One of them said to the man in the light grey suit, "We'll be taking her to the women's department at Raigmore hospital, in Inverness, should you wish to visit the young lady."

*****

Raigmore hospital in Inverness was the main hospital in the South East Highland Community Health Partnership area of NHS Highland Health Board. It served patients from its own and adjacent CHP areas as well as those from adjacent *Health Board* areas. It was also a teaching hospital in association with the Universities of Aberdeen and Stirling.

Raigmore has been a hospital site since 1941. The single storey wartime wards continued to be used for a further three decades, until the construction of the present buildings. Amongst other medical services supplied during this period, the hospital provided the main maternity unit for the Highlands. In 1970 the first of a series of new buildings were opened, including an A&E department, radiology and radiotherapy, laboratory, out-patient services and a medical department.

The hospital had over the years taken over the provision of some or all of the services previously performed by older hospitals in Inverness including Culduthel Hospital (this was closed in 1989), Hilton Hospital (this was closed two years earlier, in 1987) and the Royal Northern Infirmary (since 1999 this had been a Community hospital, and this was where Suki was destined to end up).

*****

The hospital has a 32-bed Paediatric unit, where in-patient care in Medical Paediatrics; Oral Surgery, ENT (Ear, Nose and Throat) unit and Child and Family Psychiatry are based. Raigmore also contained a 57-bed maternity unit; specialist services such as cystic fibrosis, cardiology and rheumatology and the Birnie Child Development Centre for children with learning difficulties and special needs Raigmore Hospital was granted baby friendly status in November 2005 after a pivotal report.

Developments at the hospital have included the Wyvis Unit which was a recent development and refurbishment on the Raigmore Hospital site. The £600 million refurbishment project provided a new home for the re-located nurse-led pre-op assessment department and cardiac ultrasound service. The result had seen a decrease in the waiting time for a routine outpatient echocardiogram.

Pick Everard was selected by NHS Highland to build a new day service unit extension onto the main hospital site. Head consultant and architect, Keppie Design assisted in the mechanical and electrical engineering and building work side of the project. This new unit provided specialist renal and endoscopy departments, and was opened in 2009.

A Maggie's Centre, also known as Maggie's Highlands, could also be found on the Raigmore Hospital site, being one of the few existing in Scotland. Maggie's Highlands was opened officially on 7th June 2005 by the then Scottish Health Minister, Andy Kerr and Carol McGregor. The hospice was designed by Scottish architect, David Page of Page and nearby gardens by Maggie's husband, Charles Jenkins.

*****

In southern London, the virus hadn't spread belyond the river yet – but it was only a matter of time, Floyd Maxwell had keyed in the commands for the next stage of the plan he and Carol had worked out; all he had to do was press the *Enter* key. Leaning back he said to his female companion, "I believe the honour belongs to you."

Eagerly Miss Turner leant forward and pressed the relevant key.

CHAPTER 12

HAPPY CHRISTMAS?

As soon as Carol Turner relaxed her finger after pressing the *Enter* key a signal was sent from Floyd Maxwell's computer – via the internet – to the master computer that controlled the other computers aboard the drilling rigs; this signal passed to the machine on each rig overriding all other safety commands and one by one each rig exploded. The date was 24th December 2013 and aboard each structure the men, there were about 50 on each rig, were busy shutting various components down and each was looking forward to spending the next week with their families.

The explosion devastated each structure and turned each into a flaming torch that could be seen on land; the explosion also caught the boats that were on their way to collect the riggers from their platforms, each boat contained 4 personnel, so in all 278 men were killed – both riggers and sea sailors.

As the news of these explosions and the resulting devastation they'd caused – not only to humans but also to many species of wildlife, due to a resulting oil slick – many people were of the opinion that this was a sign of things to come and therefore Queen Charlotte should abdicate the throne of Great Britain and all its empires, although there were very few nowadays.

*****

These deaths weren't the only ones to occur around Christmas Richard and Julia Carcroft's children had informed their parents they wouldn't be returning to their parent's home in, Tiptree, Essex for the Christmas celebrations as they feared for their children's, as well as their own, safety now the *mysterious* virus seemed to be back with a vengeance. Richard and Julia respected their children's wishes and prepared themselves for a lonely Christmas. "I know," Julia said to her husband, "why don't we invite Miss Linden to join us – you've always been keen on her."

Mrs Carcroft had met Debbie Linden once at a party she and Richard had attended; she'd also noticed how her husband had looked at the young woman and how his gaze seemed to have followed her around the room, until she'd left at about midnight with a young man. Therefore, since her husband had started his trips to London to see an old friend – as he put it – she'd started to become a little suspicious, as the only person in London Richard knew was Debbie Linden. Perhaps it was a totally innocent arrangement but his trips had always seemed to have taken place after a row with his wife.

"I don't think she'd want to come up here my dear," replied Richard smoothly. "Anyway we've only met her once at that party, you remember, so I'm doubtful she'd even remember us." There was something in her husband's voice, as if he was pleading with her not to invite Debbie. Suddenly Julia noticed a sort of spot on Richard's lip that she'd never noticed before. It seemed to be leaking a horrible looking, yellowish, liquid.

"Open your mouth Richard," his wife said to him; Richard thought this was a strange request, but as his wife was a dental assistant at the local surgery he knew she wouldn't make such a request for nothing – so he, dutifully, opened his mouth. "Yuk," remarked Julia when she spotted the same types of spots all over his the inside of his mouth; "I think you'd better see a doctor Richard, those spots look nasty."

"What spots?" asked her husband, totally confused.

"The ones inside your mouth," Julia answered. "Can't you feel them?"

"No I bloody can't," he responded somewhat gruffly. His wife was probably worrying about nothing, as usual. She really was a worrier nowadays.

"I'm still going to make you an appointment at the surgery," his wife said, "in fact I'll phone them now," and she went through, into the hallway, to phone the surgery. Whilst she was gone Richard Carcroft sat back in a comfy chair to think about his mistress.

Suddenly he went into a spasm and started shaking – however hard he tried he couldn't control himself, "Julia, Help!" he cried. Rushing back into the room Julia saw her husband violently shaking and went white as a sheet.

"Richard! What's wrong?" she managed to ask, once she'd recovered from the initial shock. Richard was – usually – such a healthy person. Instinct suddenly took over, "I'll get an ambulance."

"No, Julia, please don't leave me." Slowly his spasm subsided and Richard slid off the chair and onto the floor. "Richard," Julia cried, "Richard!" He remained motionless and his wife, fearing the worst now, reached over to check his breathing, there was no breath; panic now setting in she felt for a heartbeat, or pulse, there was none. Her husband of 37 years was now dead!

It was then that Julia Carcroft started spasming and shaking, just as her husband had; knowing she had developed these things – in her mouth – and resigning herself to the fact that she was probably about to die she just sat next to Richard's body and held his, now, cold hand in her own. They had lived together, now they would die together!

*****

At the police station where James Andon worked – it was a month since he'd been at work – and every officer who knew him was beginning to worry. The next his mates down at the police station heard about him was when they read – in the newspaper – that their long time colleague, and friend, James Andon was dead!

Gareth Masters, the officer James had, inadvertently, infected was still at work though – somehow he'd built up some type of immunity to the virus – though some of the other officers he worked with had had to take time off.

*****

Debbie Linden, who had been Richard Carcroft's mistress, was out shopping – she was unaware of the fate that had befallen her lover – and had just left the supermarket, after buying food for the coming week, was walking down the street towards her apartment when her arm started shaking; it stopped, after about a minute, so she just kept on walking, she thought nothing of the shaking.

Suddenly it started again, Miss Linden wasn't sure what it was and began to feel a bit scared; passers by, on the street, simply looked at her as if she was mentally deranged and then stepped onto the road to avoid her – probably they thought she would hit them if they walked on the street. "Please help me," she tried to say but the words – more or less – came out as a whisper. Miss Linden tried to grasp onto a lady who was passing by but the woman shook her arm away.

"Get off me you freak!" It was then Debbie realised that everyone around was staring at her.

"Please help me," she pleaded again as she felt her legs begin to spasm and shake. Then all of a sudden Debbie dropped her shopping, pitched forward and fell onto the pavement – face first.

Later when a kind man turned her over it was discovered she'd stopped breathing, and had no heartbeat or pulse. "Perhaps we should've helped her," the man said to other passers by who had formed a circle round the body of the young woman.

*****

James Andon's partner, Sandra Kensindale, who had been having the affair with Miss Linden, was cleaning up at home when she began to spasm and shake; eventually she found she couldn't breathe and, like the others before her, collapsed on the floor.

When she was found by neighbours she was found to be dead – her mouth now full of the same spots that had been found in other victims.

All these deaths occurred just before Christmas 2013.

*****

Suki Howell was now in the women's department in Raigmore Hospital, due to the treatment she'd received at the hands of Grant Pearman, on her initial admittance it had been found that she had suffered some internal damage and had therefore had to have an emergency operation to repair the damage that had been inflicted upon her; it had also been found she'd had a very tiny foetus within her, this had had to be removed. Now she was beginning to recover from her ordeal, however she was still a little wary of the male doctors.

Once Miss Howell felt strong enough she'd asked for a sheet of paper, together with a pencil, and had written down everything she could – clearly – remember.

Upon hearing of the Japanese woman's predicament from Paul Pearman – who was a good friend - Ralph Williams had contacted HART and informed Commander Leon Bigship. Once he had been informed he summoned her father, Major Shinto Howell, and told him of his daughter's predicament. "I must go to her at once," the Major said once Leon had finished. "I knew it was a bad idea for her to want to go on this intelligence gathering mission, but I still let her go as she assured me that she could look after herself. Can a flight be arranged for me?"

Leon looked, across the desk, at the Japanese man who was, desperately, worried about his daughter's safety. With, what he hoped was, a reassuring smile he told the man seated opposite him, "I'll arrange for you to travel over there to be by her side. We'll *pull* her from this mission and place Alice Stronglove over there – upon her return. As soon as Suki is fit enough she is to return with you."

"One final thing," the Japanese man wondered what the commander was going to say. "You are relieved from your duties until you return, a temporary replacement will be found."

"Thank you sir, shall I go and pack now?"

"Yes you may Shinto. Dismissed," Major Howell saluted his superior, got up from his seat and left the office; as soon as he'd gone Leon picked up the phone and dialled the number for *Cointrin* airport.

*****

Commander's Most and Strobing, unaware of the deaths in Tiptree and London – and also unaware of Suki Howell's condition, watched the television coverage of the oil rigs blowing up; both of them were saddened by the loss of life, but neither of them, nor HART, could have done anything to save those poor people.

Suddenly the STU-8 in Ronan's study started warbling; dashing from the chair he was sitting in – Melissa was in the other seat while Simon sat on the sofa – over to the study he answered the phone like device. "Hello," he said into the receiver.

"Good evening Commander," replied Celia's child like voice. "Did you see the news about the oil rigs?" she asked her immediate superior.

"Indeed I did," he answered, "damn shame about it; I'll tell you, it has all the hallmarks of a *Proagnon* attack, but what I don't understand is how. I mean we saw no assault craft, air or otherwise, so how did they do it? Unless of course, there is somebody else linked to *Proagnon* and I think I may know who but I have no concrete evidence."

"Who do you think it is?" Celia enquired.

"One moment," answered Ronan and closed his study door so Melissa and Simon wouldn't hear. "Firstly let me ask you do you remember that CCTV footage that Dr Schaiffer got from Norwich hospital?"

"I do," the voice at the other end responded.

"Well I believe that a certain Mr Gareth Andrews was on the footage."

"You don't mean…?"" Commander Most let her voice trail off as if willing her superior to say it wasn't true.

Commander Strobing's reply was, "I'm afraid I do, though as I say I have no concrete evidence therefore I could be wrong." He could hear Mrs Most's sharp intake of breath and then she fell silent; after she hadn't spoken for, what seemed like, a minute – though in truth it was only half a minute Ronan said, "Celia are you still there?"

"What, oh yes sorry, it's just that's a great deal to take in; after all he is the queen's consort."

"I don't blame you if you don't believe me, the queen didn't either."

"You mean Queen Charlotte knows?" enquired Commander Most. "You've actually told her?"

"I showed her the footage, Mr Andrews was there as well, but she refused to believe me despite the similarities."

"I do believe you Ronan. However when we return to headquarters we'll review that footage again. Anyway the reason I called was to wish all three of you a happy Christmas! I admit I haven't seen eye to eye with Melissa and probably never will."

"And the same to yourself and Mike," Ronan was going to add that Peter would probably return soon but he didn't want to re-open any old wounds.

After he'd replaced the handset he sat at his desk and thought about all those families that had lost a loved one in that explosion: whether it was a brother, son, husband or lover. Then he asked himself a question that he thought he'd never have to ask himself: how many more deaths were there to be before the menace of *Proagnon* was utterly eradicated?

Putting these thoughts aside he opened his laptop, which was always on his desk, and thought if he continued work on his latest book that may take his mind off these other thoughts. In fact he was so engrossed in his writing he didn't see the study door open and close; suddenly a voice that he recognised as Melissa's, said to him, "Ronan darling, it's midnight, shouldn't we be getting to bed? Simon went a couple of hours ago."

Commander Strobing visibly jumped and he looked up at Miss Stevens, he wasn't aware of the time. "Of course my dear," he then saved his work, turned the laptop off and placed it in a drawer, in the desk, and locked it. He got up and followed Melissa from the study; they walked from the main room – Ronan switching the light off – and upstairs to the bedroom.

*****

Next morning, as it was Christmas Day, Ronan Strobing and Melissa Stevens were up early to gather all of Simon's Christmas presents together and make sure he had a perfect day; Ronan would be fetching Melissa's mother, Elle, over in a couple of hours; once both of them were certain they'd gathered all of Ronan's son's presents Mr Strobing and Miss Stevens sat, in the chairs, in the main room and had a drink each, the commander of HART had a whisky, his usual drink, while his partner had a sherry; and waited for the younger Strobing to appear.

Simon came downstairs at about 09.00, "Surprise!" called the two adults as he walked into the room; Ronan and Melissa, as well as gathering the boy's presents together, had also decorated the main room with streamers, balloons, a Christmas tree and various other decorations – Melissa had, actually, put a few up the previous evening whilst Simon had been in bed, and her partner had been working.

As with the evening before the STU-8 started warbling at around 11.00, Commander Strobing went across to the study, to answer it; he lifted the receiver, "Hello," he said.

"Good morning commander," replied Commander Bigship, "just to wish you a very happy Christmas."

"And the same to you Leon."

"Has anybody informed you of the latest development sir?" enquired Leon Bigship's firm, but also somewhat gentle, male voice.

"No they haven't, what is it?" As Leon told Ronan about what had happened to Miss Howell Commander Strobing's face grew pale; however he was informed that Suki was in Raigmore hospital and her father had flown out from Geneva's *Cointrin* airport the previous day to be with his daughter.

Leon then told his superior that this wasn't his fault he'd outlined the risks of what could happen to her and still gone ahead, regardless. So, no, it was not Commander Strobing's fault. He then rang off, and the overall commander of the HART organisation walked slowly back into the main room, his son had decided to unwrap his presents when his father had brought his Granny Elle over.

Ronan left the house in Hull and drove, in his Saab, to pick Elle Stevens up; however before he went to her house he drove to see Celia Most. When he arrived and knocked on the door Celia answered; Mr Strobing asked if he could be allowed in as he had something to tell her, so she invited him in saying, "Mike's gone round to a friend's house to wish them a happy Christmas, so we won't be disturbed. Come through to the main room," Ronan followed her through and the two of them sat down on the sofa. "Now this news, what might it be?"

"Well," began her superior, "you remember I allowed Miss Suki Howell to go on that intelligence gathering mission to Scotland?"

"I do indeed," responded Mrs Most, knowing Ronan had more to say.

"I received a call from Commander Bigship earlier and he informed me that Miss Howell is now in hospital. Apparently she was beaten up by Grant Pearman, his brother Paul – whose hotel room she was in when she was brutally attacked – found her body when he returned to his room; also he thinks she was raped by his brother who – incidentally – works for the Maxwell consortium." Ronan paused to let what he'd just said sink in.

"Her father," he continued, "flew over here yesterday to be at her side, until she is well again; Leon has given him leave on compassionate grounds, I just feel I should take some of the responsibility."

Celia told him, as Leon had before, he shouldn't feel responsible. Suki Howell had known what dangers she may have to face and had gone willingly. The HART commander knew she was right but still felt a degree of responsibility. "Now," he continued, "as I'm here I'd like to wish you a happy Christmas in person," and, for some reason, he leant over and kissed her; "Sorry," he apologised quickly, realising and regretting his mistake immediately, "that shouldn't have happened."

"I know it shouldn't have happened but I'm glad it did." Suddenly Celia's hands were locked behind her superior's neck, encouraging him to kiss her further; they found themselves kissing more and more passionately, they were both giving into their feelings that had begun in Iran – earlier that year.

Catching a sudden glimpse of his watch, it was 11.32, Ronan got up, quickly, and said, "I'm sorry Celia but I don't have time for this now. I have to pick up my mother-in-law." Despite Mrs Most's pleas for him to stay she could see his mind was made up and, he had made his choice, so let him go; but told him she'd always be there for him.

Ronan left the house occupied by Celia Most and her son; he did – secretly – hope that Peter Most, Commander Most's husband, was still alive. After all he was with Melissa now and didn't want to endanger that, he drove to Elle's house and picked her up; once he'd picked the older lady up he drove his vehicle back home, Melissa and Simon were both waiting. "What took you so long?" enquired Melissa, once they were both inside.

"Roadworks," her lover replied, "they don't seem to stop anymore for Christmas."

"I didn't see any roadworks," said Mrs Stevens casually.

"That's because I had to come a different way round to your house."

"Anyway," continued Mr Strobing, "now you're here may I take your coat Mrs Stevens?"

"Of course you may dear," the older woman replied. "Hello Simon, what's Santa brought you?"

"I don't know yet Grandma; I was waiting until you arrived before I opened my presents." Mrs Stevens handed the three presents she'd brought with her, one looked rather heavy, to her daughter who took them through to the main room, and placed them with the others.

"Dinner will be served at 2," Melissa told them once the four of them were seated on the main room. "Actually that reminds me I'll just go and check on it." So Miss Stevens got up and walked off in the direction of the kitchen. Mr Strobing poured Elle Stevens a small sherry, and passed it to her, which she accepted gratefully.

When Melissa returned a few moments later they all watched Simon as he opened his presents, when he unwrapped the present his Gran had got him his eyes almost popped out their sockets. His grandparents had managed to get him a copy of every Sherlock Holmes story; what was more they were all first editions plus they'd been signed by Arthur Conan Doyle – the signatures weren't real but that didn't matter to young Master Strobing. "Thank you Grandma," he said once he'd got over the surprise, "I'll treasure them forever;" and he got up, ran to his Grandmother and hugged her fiercely.

When he'd finished he returned to his final present, the one from his father and aunt, unfortunately the shape gave it away – it was a bike; however Simon tore the paper off to reveal a – gleaming, brand new – blue and red bicycle. He hugged his father and then Aunt Melissa. Ronan handed his son a small, box-shaped, present that was inscribed *Simon, hope you like it, Celia Most.*

"Hmph, what's she got him?" enquired a disgruntled Melissa. Simon unwrapped the present which turned out to be a train locomotive, "He doesn't even like trains anymore;" although, even she could see, he was holding the box very tightly.

Ronan then looked over at Elle, "Yes, thank you for the, wonderful, present you and Arnold got Simon. All those books must've cost you a small fortune." Miss Stevens got up and went through to the kitchen – just to check on dinner preparations or so she said, however Ronan knew she was fuming that Commander Most had bought Simon a present. He could imagine what his lover was thinking, *Was Celia trying to get round Ronan and win him back by buying his son a Christmas present?*

*****

Sandy Tulliver (Carol Turner) along with, the man she knew as, Floyd Maxwell had seen the news reports that had covered the destruction of the five oil rigs with a great deal of satisfaction. "Now all we need is for this virus, Simon Forrestor has developed, to strike down the commanders of HART and then our way will be clear; *Proagnon*, with us as its leaders, will be able to obtain world domination."

"Quite right my dear," Floyd replied; however there was something in his voice that seemed to ring alarm bells in Sandy's head. He got up from his seat, on the sofa, next to her and walked through to the kitchen from where he called back to her, "Time for a spot of dinner I think."

*****

In Scotland Major Shinto Howell was sat, on a chair, by his daughter's bedside.

He had arrived the previous day and had been allocated a family member room in a side building that adjoined the main hospital; he had asked the nurses who had been in attendance the day the young Japanese woman had been brought in what had happened, they'd all shaken their heads indicating none of them knew, however then one of them had remembered the note Suki had written later on and handed it to her father saying, "It's probably some gibberish; don't get your hopes up."

"Thank you," said Mr Howell, who was slightly smaller than his Japanese daughter. "It is much appreciated," and he gave a small bow in front of them. A couple of the ladies tried to stifle giggles whilst the others just smiled – after all he was only showing his gratitude. "Now if you will excuse me," he said to them, the appreciation in his voice, "I shall go and study my daughter's writings," and he wandered away in the direction of the *day room*.

Once he was sure there was nobody in the room with him, and he wasn't likely to be disturbed Suki's father crossed to the furthest corner of the room and slowly unfolded the piece of paper. In Miss Howell's neat handwriting were the words:

> *I think I have been beaten up and, quite possibly, raped by a man called Grant Pearman. However before I fell unconscious, or whatever, I think I heard him say that there are scientists aboard the sea fort, led by a man named Simon Forrestor, who are working on a new kind of spray/deodorant.*
>
> *Of course what I heard may be totally wrong or may be interpreted as the writings of a mad woman. However this may be what is happening, I do not know.*

Major Shinto Howell read these words twice over; his own daughter beaten and, maybe, raped, why had she not been better protected? He needed to speak to, who was her mentor whilst she was over here, Ralph Williams; that was it, and Shinto knew exactly where to find him.

HART had several safe houses scattered in many countries throughout the world, however the safe houses in the USA and Russia had had to be closed down since the election of each country's new president.

The safe house where Mr Williams was to be found was located just outside the small village of Arderseir; he lived in a remote cottage just east of the village. Having digested the rest of the words his daughter had written – some of it was faint in places but the meaning of her writings was indisputable. Suki's father pocketed the note and walked back to the nurse's station, "Excuse me," he said upon reaching the desk, "how would I be able to get to the village of Arderseir?"

"Sir," giggled a nurse. "Just catch a bus from the hospital's main entrance and inform the driver on where you wish to travel to. If it is not the correct bus the driver will tell you; they are most helpful nowadays." Then she realised her mistake, "Of course there are no buses running today, what with it being Christmas Day, but if you are prepared to wait my colleague here," she indicated a, young, dark haired nurse, "will drive you there as she, herself, lives close to the village."

The blonde nurse looked towards her colleague who nodded in confirmation.

"Thank you," announced the diminutive figure of a Japanese man. "You are most helpful and kind. I shall wait in the room I have just left," and then he turned and wandered back to the *day room* of the ward. The nurses watched him leave and smiled at his retreating back.

"What a strange man," remarked one of the young ladies, absently, once he'd left the main desk on the ward. "I just hope he finds what he's looking for," all the medical staff, at the desk, nodded in agreement.

At around 14.00 the four nurses who had been on shift started to pack their things away and changed into their everyday clothes, and then the dark haired nurse fetched Major

Howell from the ward's *day room*. They walked down the corridors, of the building, to the main entrance, as they walked the nurse introduced herself, "My name's Christine Woodward."

"Shinto Howell," the Japanese man replied.

"Tell me Shinto; is that your daughter or wife in our ward?" She smiled to herself.

"It is my daughter," he responded rather indignantly. "I do not have a wife over half my age." Christine apologised at once and led him from the main building round to a car park that was marked *Staff only*.

She led him to a maroon coloured Audi and said proudly, "This is my car, my own pride and joy." *Until somebody runs into it* thought the Major but said nothing, he didn't want to burst her bubble. "Hop in," and she opened the passenger door for him; hesitantly Shinto Howell climbed in, "I'll just put these in the boot, and then I'm all yours."

As Christine wandered round the back Shinto sat there thinking and found himself wondering if this young woman might be slightly deranged, but he had more pressing concerns at this moment; although, admittedly, even he found this young woman – probably not much older than his own daughter – reasonably attractive. She then climbed into the driver's seat beside him and said quite suddenly, "Where to my dark skinned friend?"

"Erm," he murmured, suddenly unsure but then realised better. "Let's just enjoy the trip to Arderseir." He knew the safe house would be located beyond the village and could probably only be approached by foot, he wasn't sure of the precise location but he'd know it when he saw the building.

His new companion looked at him and nodded, "Okay, you're the boss," and she reversed and then drove away from the hospital; funnily enough Major Howell didn't feel like any sort of boss, at the moment. Christine pulled onto the dual carriageway and started to drive, the vehicle they were in, like a demon – passing other motorists in slower moving cars and trucks.

Once they'd slowed down, to a more sedately pace, Christine informed him that she had her own house – bought for her by her parents, as was the car – but no male figure in her life; Shinto could almost tell why she'd just said what she'd said, and he was right, as Christine did say if he ever needed anywhere to stay he'd be welcome to stay with her.

It took about 7 minutes to reach the village of Arderseir. Miss Woodward asked him if he knew where he wanted. Shinto Howell replied, "I think it may be wise if you drop me at your place." His companion grinned across at him as if this was what she'd intended to do all along; she drove the Audi through the village and out onto some back roads – some no more than tracks. They drove up to a, stone built, cottage and Christine drove the vehicle into an adjoining outbuilding and parked up. "Come on," she said to her new Japanese friend and led the way round to the front of the cottage, closing the outbuilding's doors behind them.

"What about your uniform?" Suki's father suddenly asked.

"I can get that later," she responded quickly; once they were both at the front door of the stone building the lady of the house located the door key and opened the door. "My home," she told the amazed looking figure by her side, "please come in, let me make you a cup of tea, and then I'll give you the guided tour if you want."

Very hesitantly and not wanting to lose sight of the reason why he was in Scotland Major Shinto Howell of HART stepped, tentatively, inside.

He was in, what he thought of as, the living room; there was a settee and two, obviously, comfortable chairs; a television and DVD player were located in one corner; there was a fireplace on one of the walls, above which were some family photographs, whilst the back wall was completely dominated by a pine dresser. "Sit down," said a voice from behind him, "I'm just going to get changed and then I'll make us a pot of tea."

Mr Howell sat down and then suddenly remembered his own wife; although she was far away, in Japan, plus they were separated. However, if she could see her estranged husband now she'd disown and divorce him. Here he was, in a total stranger's house, and a female stranger's at that! Still how would she ever know? Shinto then decided he'd have a cup of tea with Christine Woodward, and then he'd go on his way. He sat back to wait for her.

About 15 minutes later she returned carrying a tray of tea things – as she placed the tray on the table between the settee and the chairs she made sure this Japanese man got a good look down her blouse top and saw what was available; as she straightened up he noticed she was wearing a pair of, figure hugging, jeans. When she turned the jeans certainly held very little back from the imagination, as they were blue but had been washed so many times they were now practically transparent.

Thankfully she seated herself on the settee – it was an old brown, patterned, one - and they made small talk whilst allowing the tea to brew in the pot, after about 5 minutes the small Japanese figure got to his feet and started pouring the tea saying, "I shall perform this task as you made the tea."

"Thank you Shinto," Christine said, gratefully, to her companion as he passed her the cup and saucer. She sipped her tea as the little man from Japan retreated to his own side of the table. "Mr Howell," she enquired, "how long do you intend staying?" A plan was beginning to form in her mind; as she'd invited her three nursing colleagues to a party, at her place, that evening.

"Well," he responded, "I had actually intended to leave once I've had my tea."

"Well Mr Howell, it is already reasonably dark outside and as there is snow on the ground it is safe to assume the ground might be slippery; plus you may get lost even if you think you know where you're going, and the ground round here can be very treacherous. Why not stay here tonight as my friends from hospital, you remember, are coming over later for a party, and then you can go first thing after breakfast tomorrow." What she didn't tell him was it was to be an all girl party.

"Won't that inconvenience you?" asked the HART Major, glancing out the front window and noting it was getting darker.

He knew he shouldn't but he was prepared to accept her offer, albeit with reluctance. Miss Woodward informed him it would be no inconvenience as her spare room was always made up; also she told him that his daughter wouldn't thank him for rushing off and perhaps falling, thus ending up in hospital.

Accepting what she'd said Shinto followed Christine out to her Audi and brought inside the things he'd brought with him, his walking cane and the backpack containing clothes and a small TAC-SAT. Once everything had been brought inside the house Christine showed the Major to his room; Shinto looked around the room; it contained a chair, a bed, a wardrobe and a bedside cabinet – there was absolutely no evidence of any wallpaper, however there was one framed print of a sailing vessel.

Miss Woodward saw the look of dismay on his face, "Sorry it's a bit basic but I don't have many guests."

"I'm sure it will prove adequate accommodation for my one night," the Japanese major informed her, not wanting to hurt her feelings. They had an evening meal together later, and then Major Shinto Howell informed his female companion that he was feeling tired so decided to go and have a lay down in his room.

At around 9 pm he was awoken, he hadn't realised he'd fallen asleep, by loud music, slowly he got off the bed and walked to the room door – he intended to tell them to keep the noise down. Shinto threw open the door to be greeted by the sight of the four nurses from the hospital dancing around, but they were all partly unclothed; one of them, the blonde, giggly, one was dancing on a table while the others danced on the floor. However what appalled him was that she seemed to be removing her own clothes, much to the other three's amusement; when he reckoned it was Christine saw him in the doorway she indicated that her friend dance for him, so the blonde turned and began to dance for him. The white T-shirt she was wearing was soon thrown off to reveal the naked flesh beneath.

Major Howell was shocked at this behaviour, some of the girls in his country behaved this way – he knew that – but to see a girl from this country behave this way, it was disgusting; that was one of the reasons why he'd joined HART, and taken his daughter with him – to stop her falling into this sort of trap, or perhaps worse.

He quickly turned, intending to retreat into his room and shut this spectacle out, but as he turned he caught his foot on the doorframe and winced at his stupidity. An arm caught him from behind and a voice said, "Going somewhere?"

The HART major thought he knew who the voice belonged to and tried to shake himself free of the hand that held him. He managed it and hurried inside the, bare, room; it was then he heard the door close and he knew he wasn't alone, turning he saw it was the blonde – still wearing next to nothing – who had followed him. She shoved him forward, against the bed, "On you get," said the voice from behind him; he fell onto the bed, rolled over and looked up – there she was smiling down at him, "Hello," she said. "My name's Jenny if Chris hasn't told you already." He suddenly noticed that she now seemed to be minus her underwear, "Now we're gonna get nice and comfy."

"No we are not," retorted Major Howell sharply. "Now get off me!" He struggled against her grip but she was holding his wrists too tightly; he watched with alarm as she began to expose his chest, revealing his dog tag – he'd forgotten to take it off.

"So what, or should I say who, have we here?" Jenny asked as she saw his dog tag – she seemed to be mainly speaking to herself. Carefully lifting the tag off the man from Japan's chest the young woman named Jenny leant forward so she could read what was written on the metal disc, her breasts were perilously close to Shinto's face so he closed his eyes. "Hmm," Jenny's voice began, "Major Shinto Howell of HART. So we've got us a real life major, I wonder what my friends would say."

Through clenched teeth and as menacingly as he could manage, given his predicament, Mr Howell said, "You tell them and you'll regret it." The woman leaned back, loosening her grip ever so slightly.

"Why?" she demanded to know. Suddenly the little man pushed her back off the bed, reached over the side of the bed and grabbed his walking stick, "Why?" Jenny asked again, in puzzlement

"Because of this young lady," and the HART major unsheathed the samurai sword that was integrated into his walking stick, he had never been a, true, samurai warrior but one of his ancestors had and so the sword had been passed down through the – male – Howell descendants; as the sword was now in the last of the Howell descendants hands – those that were male – Shinto had had the HART technicians integrate the samurai sword as part of his walking stick.

Major Howell wouldn't have used it on the young woman as he was a peaceful man by nature; the only time he would even be tempted to use it was if he was threatened by an enemy agent. Jenny, however, thought he would use it on her and backed away. "Please don't hurt me sir. I never meant any harm, I wouldn't have done anything."

Shinto Howell re-sheathed the sword and placed it by the side of the bed again, he could see she was scared now. "My dear young lady, I would never harm one hair on your pretty little head. I think you are a fine spirited young woman who would, quite probably, make somebody a good wife one day; I will admit you took me quite by surprise and I was reacting to that, maybe it was wrong of me to unsheathe my sword, therefore I apologise for my oversight." By now he'd managed to regain a seated position, on the bed, and patted the area beside him, "Come sit next to me, I am completely harmless."

"Okay," responded the girl named Jenny and put her underwear back on and then went and sat beside this strange little man. He reached for her hand and placed his around it – protectively – as a father would do a son or daughter; she didn't pull away as he expected her to.

"I apologise again if I scared you, as I have told you I would not have used the sword, it is mainly for ceremonial purposes now."

He then proceeded to explain about the samurai warriors and their place in Japanese history, plus his own family's part in that history. "So you see," he concluded, "the sword is now only of symbolic value and so I just carry it as a symbol of what my family once was."

"That is very interesting," announced Jenny. "But tell me what happens to the sword upon your ultimate death?"

"Ah," Major Howell began, "I was wondering if you'd ask me that. Upon my death, as I have no male heirs, I have made provision for it to be placed in the British Museum as an exhibit; and before you ask my daughter knows nothing of our family's past history. Therefore I am trusting you not to tell her, plus I have never spoken of my ancestor's involvement to anyone in the Western world."

"Your secret's safe with me," the young blonde woman assured him, "I shall tell nobody." Then with a wink and a smile she let go of his hand, and hopped off the bed, Shinto watched her retreating figure as she crossed to the room door and hoped he had made the right decision by entrusting this young nurse with his family's, personal, secret; he did trust her now that they'd talked properly.

She left the room and closed the door behind her; Shinto Howell then felt a wave of tiredness sweep over him and decided that the time was right to go to bed; therefore he undressed, down to his underpants, and was just about to climb into bed when he realised that Jenny may be alone out there, she'd tried it on with him at first but now they'd reached an understanding. Cursing his own stupidness he redressed and left the room, the main room which had been full of light and sound, earlier on, was now quiet and dark, "Jenny," he called. There was no answer. Suddenly the HART major heard the reassuring sounds of laughter coming from the other bedroom; there was a light on in that room.

Curious now he walked closer, his bare feet making no sound on the carpeted floor, he stopped at the room door, bent and peered through the keyhole; there were two single beds in the room and each one was occupied, by two of the nurses; not wishing to see any more he crossed back to his own room and, quietly, slipped back inside – where he undressed, again, and climbed into bed.

*****

Back at HART's main headquarters, in Switzerland, in the medical department Dr Hans Schaiffer was still trying to find a cure for this *myster*y virus, he'd tried all the antibiotics at his disposal – even combinations of them; also the medical man had, on occasions, had to import other newer drugs though nothing seemed to have any effect, it was as if they were something in the virus's make up that refused to acknowledge any antibiotic tried. Therefore, it seemed, if he wanted to find a cure he'd have to find a sample of the virus; yet where would he find a sample?

The main activity seemed to be over in Britain, mainly up in Scotland on that sea fort in the Moray Firth, though the infection seemed to be spreading rapidly; the last report he'd received had informed him that the effects were now being felt in London. Some people still appeared to be going about their everyday business; evidently they'd built up some type of immunity, but how? Thankfully, there was a medical conference being held at the *Memorial* hospital, in Geneva, in a couple of months.

Commander Bigship had also seen the news of the destruction of the oil rigs, via one of the satellite news channels; as with the other commanders he had felt saddened by the news and the loss of life that had resulted. He'd recalled the HART soldiers who had been on Christmas break, in case of any imminent attack; he could have called the other two commanders back but he'd felt that any attack would be easily repelled without any intervention.

*****

Commander Strobing took Mrs Stevens home when she decided to go. Ronan knew he could have asked Elle Stevens to stay for a few days; however she had been adamant that she wanted to return to her own house, the one she had – until earlier in that year – shared with her husband; as the Saab pulled up outside the little *terraced* house Mrs Stevens turned to her son-in law, looked him straight in the eyes and said, "Thank you for making this a most enjoyable Christmas, I know things can't have been easy for you since Mandy, along with Zoe, was taken from us, but you've done an excellent job bringing Simon up."

Ronan Strobing replied, "That is indeed praise and well received too. I will admit, though, that I've had plenty of help, from Melissa and Arnold, as well as yourself; so I've been very fortunate, plus Simon, although he doesn't know it, has helped lift my spirits."

"I know Arnold isn't here right now but I'm sure he would agree that you've done a fine job, and I feel – this is a personal decision here – that Melissa, little Melissa, has made a fine choice in you. I admit I know how it would look to some people and, yes, even I was a bit miffed when I heard about you being together."

She paused, unsure what to say next. Finally she said, "However, you are together and if it makes the three of you happy I give you my blessing and approval."

"Thank you Elle," he wasn't sure what else he could really say; he then helped Mrs Stevens from the car and across the snow covered path to her front door, she unlocked it and they went into the hallway.

"I'm fine now Ronan, oh please pass on my good wishes to my daughter and tell her what I've said. Anyway thank you again for a wonderful day, I will see you all again soon." Commander Strobing took that as his cue to leave.

He left the little house and climbed back into his vehicle, he sat there thinking – for a moment – about what Elle had said to him; and then he began to wonder if he ought to pop over and see Commander Celia Most, just to see if she and Mike had had a good day. He decided he might as well, since he'd got the car out already.

He drove the few streets and parked his, silver, vehicle outside the residence he climbed out, walked over to the door and knocked on it, the door was answered a moment later by Mike Most, "Hello Mr Strobing, if you've come to see my mother she's taking a bath."

"I'll wait for her down here then," then he noticed Mike Most had a fur lined, green, parka coat on, "Going somewhere?" he asked innocently.

"I've been invited to another party. I was going to lock the door behind me but now you're here. I'm sure you'll keep my mother company for a while."

Suddenly there was a shout from upstairs, "Who's at the door Mike?"

"It's okay Mum," her son shouted back. "It's Mr Strobing, he says he'll wait down here for you as I've informed him you're, slightly, busy at the moment. Anyway I'm off out now."

"Okay Mike, be careful but enjoy yourself," Celia's son handed the door keys to Ronan and then left. Once the younger man had closed the door Celia's voice came floating down the stairs, "Feel free to come up, I may need you to scrub my back."

Downstairs Mr Strobing hesitated – he would have gone up, gladly, if it had been Miss Stevens that had called for him, but this was his work colleague. Okay, so they'd had a relationship, years ago, and they'd briefly shared a bed in Iran, when HART was in that country, but both had been in the past. As much as Ronan was tempted to rekindle their relationship – he'd hinted as much in the past few months – he'd got a new lover now and didn't want to endanger that. "C'mon Ronan, I'm waiting."

He walked up the carpeted staircase but stopped when he reached the bathroom door, "I'm sorry Celia," he said pathetically. "But I don't want to scrub your back."

"In that case, I do understand you know, will you just come in and hand me my towel?"

Ronan thought about this and then responded, "I suppose it can't hurt so I will." Celia could hear the indecision and hesitation in his voice; she knew what he was going through, well maybe not exactly, but she had a good idea.

Slowly the bathroom door opened and framed in the doorway was Commander Ronan Strobing, his fellow commander noticed his eyes were fixed straight ahead, "Where's the towel?" he enquired.

"That big white one, over there," and Celia indicated the towel she meant. Ronan got the towel from the towel rail, and held it open for her but inclined his head upwards so his gaze was fixed on the ceiling. Gratefully she took the towel with one hand and placed the other on his, "Thank you Ronan. You may go now but lock the door and push the keys through the letter box."

Ronan Strobing left the house doing as he'd been instructed, and then climbed into his Saab and headed home.

*****

Up in Scotland Major Shinto Howell climbed out of bed, dressed, and then went through into the main room for breakfast, the four young nurses were already seated, in their uniforms, at the table eating a cooked breakfast of eggs, bacon, sausage, beans, mushrooms, black pudding and haggis. Two of the girls he knew but the other two – another brunette and a redhead – he didn't. "Good morning ladies," he said, as he approached the table.

"Good morning Mr Howell," said Christine. "I believe you already know Jenny," Jenny gave him a little wave, "However may I introduce Claire," the brunette, "and Michelle," Michelle shook her long red hair at the little Japanese man. "Please sit down, I'll just go and make you some breakfast. Anything you don't want?"

"Mushrooms, black pudding, but just a small piece of haggis," he replied to her question, and turned to the two new ladies while Christine disappeared into the kitchen; he shook hands with the other two girls and sat at the table, the four at the table chatted politely as they waited for their friend.

She returned with a plate of food for Shinto about ten minutes later, he ate steadily; when he'd finished he thanked his host for breakfast and for letting him stay the night.; the lady of the house smiled at Major Howell – Shinto thought she maybe wondered why he – along with his daughter – were in Scotland. Maybe she'd heard about the virus but there hadn't been that many cases in Inverness, where the hospital was located.

"Now Mr Howell I believe you said something about going to the village of Arderseir today."

The Japanese major looked up at his host, "Indeed I did young lady I should like to go whenever possible," indicating he thought she was offering to give him a lift. "Just to the public house which is located there."

"Hmm," murmured his host looking at the others, "I will take you there when I've cleared up. I'm taking my friends back and I'm sure they won't mind if you tag along." The other three women indicated that they didn't mind at all, so while Miss Woodward cleared the table Major Shinto Howell, of HART, returned to his room to finish packing his backpack. "Don't forget your walking stick," Jenny called to him.

"Very good of you to remind me," he called back. By about 10 am everyone was ready, Christine Woodward led the way out to her Audi, placed Shinto's backpack, along with his walking stick, into the boot of her vehicle and then the other three young nurses, Jenny, Claire and Michelle climbed into the back seat while the little Japanese man got in the front passenger seat.

Once they were all belted in the Audi drove off. Major Howell still had the piece of paper, with his daughter's writings on, tucked in his coat pocket; for the journey to Arderseir However, he suddenly thought, what if this Ralph Williams didn't live at Arderseir, he would be no nearer getting any answers, and then there was that other person Grant Pearman; who was he? He may find some answers at the pub in Arderseir, or he might not, still time would tell.

He was so engrossed in his own thoughts that he never noticed they'd reached the village that was their destination;

they pulled up outside the pub and Miss Woodward climbed out. "We've arrived Mr Howell," the Japanese man looked up in surprise.

"Right, thank you," and then he cheerfully said to the others, "Sayonara ladies." Thankfully all the nurses knew many different languages.

"Good bye Mr Howell," they each responded in turn as he climbed out. Christine gave him his backpack and walking stick, and wished him luck. Shinto thanked her and watched as she got back into her vehicle, started up the automobile and drove away; he crossed the street to the pub and walked inside. The three men, who were drinking, at the bar looked over at him as he entered. "Cold day outside," the barman said to the man from HART then he enquired, "drink sir?"

"Just a soda water please," was the response as Major Howell took in the room; it was fairly spacious with tables set round the edge of the room; the main bar ran along the opposite side of the room, plus a small restaurant was situated at the back. "Excuse me," he asked the man who was pouring his drink, "do you or your friends," he gestured to the men who were drinking, "know a Mr Ralph Williams?"

They all thought and then answered one by one, "I'm afraid I don't." The barman then handed Shinto's soda water over which he paid for and sipped thoughtfully, he then produced the note from his daughter, "How about a Mr Grant Pearman, or a man named Forrestor?"

"Pearman, that name rings a bell," replied the barman. "I think he's staying at the hotel."

"No," said another man at the bar startling the Japanese man. "That's his brother, Paul Pearman, nobody knows where Grant is."

"Wait a moment," the barman called as Shinto Howell finished his drink. He produced a *reservations* book and flipped through the pages, "Here we are, Mr Williams made a booking, by telephone, on behalf of a young lady."

"That would be my daughter," Major Howell said suddenly. "Did he leave an address?"

"I'm afraid not sir but, as far as I can remember, he and Paul Pearman are good friends, so I'm sure Mr Pearman can give you more information than I can." Major Howell thanked the man and headed for the door, "Wait sir. Don't you need to see your daughter's room?"

"That can wait," the Japanese man responded curtly, "first I need answers," and he left the building and crossed the street to the hotel. As he entered the, small, foyer everyone turned and looked at him; he walked over to the reception desk and enquired after Mr Pearman.

"I shall just ring his room, see if he's there, who shall I say is asking after him?" said the young man on duty.

Major Howell thought but then decided on the truth, "Mr Howell." The receptionist rung the room while Shinto went and sat in a chair.

The receptionist called over, "He's on his way down sir." The Japanese man grunted in reply, about five minutes later a man in a grey suit appeared at the desk and the receptionist indicated Mr Pearman's visitor.

The man in the suit, evidently Paul Pearman, walked over to his visitor, "What can I do for you Mr Howell? May I just say I hope your daughter's on the mend, such a sweet natured girl."

The Japanese man peered at him curiously, "She's doing well," he replied, "no thanks to your brother. I just need to know two things; where's Ralph Williams, and, where the hell's your brother?"

The Japanese man's sudden flare of temper took Paul Pearman by total surprise. "Mr Williams lives more towards Inverness, I can take you there if you like. As for my brother, Grant is away – on business – at the moment but will return soon."

So it was that after they'd had lunch they boarded Paul's car and made the journey to Ralph Williams house; it was as Major Shinto Howell thought, a HART safe house. Paul pulled up outside and the two of them crossed to the front door which Paul knocked on. A moment later the door opened and framed there was the figure of Ralph Williams. "Hello Paul, what a pleasant surprise, who's your friend?"

Shinto's fist shot out and struck Ralph Williams in the chest. Winded, he fell to the floor. "Greetings Mr Williams."

CHAPTER 13

ANSWERS & RETURN TO DANGER!

"What did you do that for?" Pearman demanded to know of the Japanese man.

"All will become clear my friend," Shinto Howell answered and walked on into the HART safe house, he seemed to act as if he owned the place, meanwhile Paul Pearman helped Mr Williams to his feet.

"Are you okay?" Paul asked his long time friend, concern in his voice, as he helped him to his feet and through into the main room – where they found the Japanese man was already seated. As Mr Williams and Major Howell had never met before so neither knew who the other was, it was Ralph Williams who finally broke the silence; his friend having gone to make them all some tea. "Just who are you?" a puzzled Ralph Williams asked the seated man.

"I am Major Shinto Howell of HART," was the answer that was given. Ralph looked somewhat surprised as he seated himself opposite the man. "Well?" demanded Suki Howell's father

"Well what?" Mr Williams asked, now totally puzzled. Paul Pearman returned carrying a tray with the tea things on it, plus some cakes; he placed the tray on the rectangular, wooden, table – which was situated between the two men, whilst Pearman seated himself on the sofa at the end of the table, he poured them all some tea and sat back, wondering why these two men seemed to be at loggerheads.

As the little Japanese man seemed unresponsive Ralph said, "I'll ask again, well what?"

"Why the hell wasn't my daughter better protected?" Shinto stormed.

Ralph protested, "She was. I gave her a recording device and told her to wear it at every meeting, plus I issued her with a *Sterling* submachine gun and other kit for her, personal, protection." He paused and then said angrily, "So don't you come in here and tell me she wasn't fucking well protected. If it's anyone's fault, it's through her own negligence."

Paul was shocked at all this, who were these men and that young woman. Shinto Howell saw the look on Pearman's face and said, "We are from an anti-terrorist organisation called HART (Human Alliance for the Retaliation against Terrorism). Mr Williams, here, is our Scottish liaison officer, and this," he gestured at the house around him, "is a HART safe house."

""Some members of the public know of our existence, but not always who we are. Therefore we are swearing you to secrecy," finished off Ralph Williams.

Paul just sat there, "Okay," he finally said once he'd taken everything in.

"Also I need to ask you a favour," Ralph said to the man.

"Ask away secret agent man," responded Paul.

Ignoring Pearman's remark about being a secret agent Williams continued, "May I ask you to leave and return to the hotel in Arderseir where you are staying, once you've finished your tea and cake, as I have a couple of things to discuss with Major Howell." Paul agreed and as soon as he'd finished his food and drink he said his goodbyes and left the other two men to discuss whatever they had to.

"Now," began Major Howell, eager to get down to business again. "You say my daughter was adequately protected. What do you think was the reason she wasn't protected that fateful evening?" Ralph noted Shinto's voice was a good deal calmer now.

"It would seem obvious, Major Howell that either she forgot to take protection with her, or she felt it wasn't necessary. I remember, though, telling her to wear the microphone/recording device for every meeting – whether she felt it necessary or not."

"So, if she had adequate protection but failed to use it where would it be now?" the Japanese man enquired thoughtfully.

"It must still be, in the room, at the pub."

"Shall we go then?" Howell said. Agreeing Mr Williams brought round his *Toyota* Corolla from the garage at the rear of the house and he and Shinto Howell climbed aboard – Shinto bringing his walking stick and back pack with him. Once they were both aboard the HART liaison officer started the vehicle and drove away, they reached the village of Arderseir after a good 10 minutes – their journey taking a minute or two longer than expected as a couple of the minor roads were still a bit slippery in places.

As they pulled up outside the pub the driver turned to his passenger and asked, "Have you got your HART identification?"

"Yes of course," answered his Japanese passenger. "Shall we go?"

Ralph Williams smiled and said encouragingly, "Right. Let's do it!" They got out and marched into the pub. As there was nobody at the bar Ralph marched straight up to it and banged on the top, "Service." The bartender, from earlier, rushed in.

"Ah yes, gentlemen, what can I do for you?"

Major Howell spoke up, "We wish to see the room where my daughter, Suki Howell was staying."

The bartender produced the *bookings* book, from a shelf under the bar, and turned to the relevant page, "That would be room 2A. Do you have the authorisation to do so?"

"HART," they both said, showing their I.D. "That is all the authorisation we need." The bartender, reluctantly or so it seemed, handed the key to room 2A over to Mr Williams.

Both men walked up the staircase to the landing above, the major located room 2A, and the liaison officer inserted the key and unlocked the door; turning the handle he pushed the door open to be met by the sight of a very tidy room. Suki had only unpacked the clothes she needed, and there under a neatly folded up pair of jeans was the butt of a gun; it was only just visible but would have gone unnoticed to the untrained eye, but Shinto Howell spotted it almost at once.

Ralph Williams, however, wasn't quite as well trained and only saw the object when Suki's father prompted him, they removed the weapon, it was – as Ralph had informed him – a *Sterling* submachine gun. Upon seeing this Major Howell said, "I am sorry I doubted you Mr Williams."

"Thank you," the other man answered. It was Ralph who finally located the microphone/recording device which was disguised as a brooch; it had been discarded on a side table. "Damn fool!" he exclaimed sharply.

Major Shinto Howell was folding up his daughter's clothes and putting them in the case she'd brought with her when he heard the other man's exclamation; in a much calmer voice than his companion, although he was angry inside, he said, "It could be worse, she could be dead."

Williams agreed then asked, "Why are you folding up her clothes and placing them in her suitcase?" He seemed puzzled by this activity.

"Once Suki is well enough," answered the Japanese man, "I intend to take her back to her home, in Japan. I have cleared this with Commander Bigship as the other two commanders are home for Christmas."

"I see," announced Ralph Williams. "Do you then intend to stay in Japan with your family?"

Shinto looked directly at his companion and said, "I have thought about it but have not fully decided yet." Once Major Howell had finished packing his daughter's belongings, he helped Ralph Williams locate all the items he'd given Suki on her arrival. Once Miss Howell's suitcase was packed and Mr Williams had retrieved all other equipment the two men exited the room, closed and locked the room door; then whilst Major Howell loaded everything aboard the Toyota *Corolla* Ralph went through into the bar area to finalise a few details; afterwards the two men then returned to the HART safe house.

*****

On 28th December Commander's Strobing and Most left their, respective, places of residence in Hull and drove back to *Robin Hood* airport to begin the flight back to Switzerland and HART headquarters, which was located just outside Geneva. The flight back to *Cointrin* airport, which all HART agents used, would take just over an hour but would seem more like 2 hours as Switzerland was an hour ahead of the United Kingdom (timewise).

Once the Gulfstream *G550* executive class, business jet landed at its destination and came to a full halt the two commanders descended the built in staircase, which had been lowered, collected their luggage and wandered over to the HART *Range Rover* which had been sent to collect them. The driver of the vehicle, Corporal Dennis Walters, helped them load their suitcases on board, and then he climbed in the driver's seat; once both his passengers were aboard he drove out the airport compound, made a left turn and drove southwards towards the compound which housed HART. "Pleasant trip sir, ma'am?" he asked them politely.

"Speaking for myself," began Commander Strobing, "it was very pleasant, catching up with my family."

"I agree, it was a most welcome break," commented Celia. "I hope Commander Bigship hasn't been working you too hard."

"On the contrary ma'am," Dennis said, his eyes never leaving the road. "Commander Bigship was good enough to let us have Christmas Day off. I think this was because he felt there was no imminent threat posed by *Proagnon*."

"Leon must be getting complacent in his old age," muttered Commander Strobing to himself. "I can see I will have to have words with him when we get back to base." Thankfully neither of the other two heard him; finally Corporal Walters swung the SUV into the compound and halted beside the residences.

"There you are commanders," he said and they all climbed out the vehicle; once the corporal's two superior officers had collected their luggage they went inside their, individual, residence buildings to unpack, whilst Corporal Walters took the *Range Rover* back to the garages.

A short while later the two commanders sauntered across to the main building that was their headquarters. "Let's see what Leon's been up to, in our absence," Celia said to Ronan.

"Or rather not up to," finished off Commander Strobing thoughtfully. They encountered Miss Stronglove, "Hello Alice," Ronan said and then called over to Celia, "you go on ahead, I'll catch up." Commander Most carried on while Ronan turned to Alice, "How's your mother now Alice?"

Alice was taken aback by her commander's question, as nobody usually asked about her family – let alone showed any concern. "She's much better now sir, thank you for asking," she answered and then said, "sir."

"Yes Alice."

"It's great to have you back," and she reached up and kissed him.

Ronan was completely surprised at this; did Miss Stronglove harbour feelings for him? He took a step back and said to her, "I'm sorry Alice but you know the rules, no relationship can ever be formed between us; we can only ever be friends."

"I know sir," the young woman apologised. "Sorry sir."

"Apology accepted," Commander Strobing said to her, "just try not to let it happen again."

"Yes sir," was the response. With that the superior officer carried on to the main headquarters building; once he'd walked past the two guards, on duty, he went inside and took the elevator upwards to the fourth floor where the main offices were located, as well as giving access to the medical unit, admittedly this was on the floor below but could be accessed using the back stairs. The overall commander strode into his office to find the other two waiting for him, plus a, brown, folder lay on the desk – it was marked NATO.

*****

The North Atlantic Treaty Organization (NATO) was an intergovernmental military alliance based on the North Atlantic

Treaty which was signed on 4th April 1949. The NATO headquarters are located in Brussels, Belgium, and the organisation constitutes a system of collective defence whereby its member states agree to mutual defence in response to an attack by any external party.

For its first few years, NATO was not much more than a political association. However, the Korean War galvanised the member states, and an integrated military structure was built up under the direction of two of the U.S. supreme commanders. The first NATO Secretary General, Lord Ismay, famously stated the organisation's goal was *to keep the Russians out, the Americans in, and the Germans down*. Doubts over the strength of the relationship between the European states and the United States ebbed and flowed, along with any doubts over the credibility of the NATO defence against a prospective Soviet invasion — doubts that led to the development of the independent French nuclear deterrent and the withdrawal of the French from NATO's military structure from 1966.

After the fall of the Berlin Wall in 1989, the organisation became drawn into the Balkans while building better links with former potential enemies to the east, which culminated with several former Warsaw Pact states joining the alliance in 1999 and 2004. On 1st April 2009, membership was enlarged to 28 with the entrance of Albania and Croatia. Since the 11th September attacks, NATO has attempted to refocus itself to all new challenges and has deployed troops to Afghanistan as well as trainers to Iraq.

The Berlin Plus agreement was a comprehensive package of agreements made between NATO and the European Union on 16th December 2002. With this agreement the EU was given the possibility to use NATO assets in case it wanted to act independently in an international crisis, on the condition that NATO itself did not want to act — the so-called *right of first refusal*. Only if NATO refused to act would the EU have the option to act. The combined military spending of all NATO members used to constitute over 70% of the world's defence spending. The United States alone accounted for about two fifths the total military spending of the world and the United Kingdom, France, Germany, and Italy accounted for a further 15%.

New NATO structures were also formed while old ones were abolished: The NATO Response Force (NRF) was launched at the 2002 Prague summit on 21st November. On 19th June 2003, a major restructuring of the NATO military commanded began as the Headquarters of the Supreme Allied Commander, Atlantic were abolished and a new command, Allied Command Transformation (ACT), was established in Norfolk, Virginia, United States, and the Supreme Headquarters Allied Powers Europe (SHAPE) became the Headquarters of Allied Command Operations (ACO). ACT was responsible for driving transformation (future capabilities) in NATO, whilst ACO was responsible for current operations.

As a result of post-Cold War restructuring of national forces, intervention in the Balkan conflicts, and subsequent participation in Afghanistan, starting in late 2003 NATO restructured how it commanded and deployed its troops by creating several NATO Rapid Deployable Corps.

Membership went on expanding with the accession of seven more Northern European and Eastern European countries to NATO: Estonia, Latvia and Lithuania and also Slovenia, Slovakia, Bulgaria, and Romania. These countries were first invited to start talks of membership during the 2002 Prague Summit, and joined NATO on 29th March 2004, shortly before the 2004 Istanbul summit. In the same month, NATO's Baltic Air Policing began, which supported the sovereignty of Latvia, Lithuania and Estonia by providing these countries fighters to react to any unwanted aerial intrusions. Four fighters were based in Lithuania, provided in rotation by virtually all the NATO states. *Operation Peaceful Summit* temporarily enhanced this patrolling during the 2006 Riga summit.

The 2006 Riga summit was held in Riga, Latvia, which had joined the Atlantic Alliance two years earlier. It was the first NATO summit to be held in a country that was part of the Soviet Union, and the second one in a former Comecon country (after the 2002 Prague summit). Energy Security was one of the main themes of the Riga Summit. At the April 2008 summit in Bucharest, Romania, NATO agreed to the accession of Croatia and Albania and invited them to join. Both countries joined NATO in April 2009. Ukraine and Georgia were also told that they would eventually become members. The official languages of NATO were English and French, the secretary general was Anders Fogh Ramussen, whilst the chairman of the NATO military committee was Giampaolo Di Paola.

Although HART had never been an officially recognised by NATO, as a *true* fighting force – though all that had changed the previous year, it had always been on hand, since formation in 2006, if needed.

*****

"I'd completely forgotten about this," said Commander Strobing as he flicked through the folder, "thankfully I've got another month before my report is due. Anyway what's been happening here while Celia and I have been away?" He turned to look at Leon Bigship.

"Well sir, it's been very quiet around the world over the Christmas period."

"Except the destruction of those five oil rigs, in the North Sea, and the deaths of those 278 rig workers and sailors; plus that mystery virus has now hit the city of London, forcing Buckingham Palace to be quarantined. You call that a quiet Christmas, I hear you even had the men stand down on Christmas Day; you're getting complacent Leon, Peter Roberts would never have stood for that, all I'm going to say though – consider this a friendly warning – is don't let it happen again." Leon was taken totally by surprise by his superior's reprimand.

"Sorry sir," the other commander apologised. "However, whilst you were away you received an email from the President of India's office, Ali Akhbar, requesting that HART provide the security for a speech he is to deliver, in the town of Agra – but why not the capital, New Delhi."

"Perhaps he feels that if he delivers the speech in a minor town such as Agra there is less chance of an assassination attempt or a terrorist attack," replied the man now seated in the command chair.

"Perhaps you're right," commented Celia.

"Perhaps," Ronan nearly exploded, "of course I'm flaming well right." Leon and Celia just looked at each other, the commander seemed to have a very volatile nature; admittedly they'd always known Commander Strobing had a bit of a temper but it appeared to be getting worse nowadays. Maybe the pressures of command were starting to get to him. "Anyway Leon did you answer the email?"

His subordinate answered, "I did sir, I said that we'd be more than happy to help," Commander Bigship looked first at Commander Most to gauge her reaction and then at Commander Strobing, who looked like he was ready to explode again.

"You mean to say you accepted without consulting me, yes I probably would have accepted but that is no reason for you," he pointed at Leon, "to go behind my back." Commander Strobing's voice then softened, "In light of these recent events I have decided to transfer you to the HART compound in Turkey; their base commander, John Craig, is due for retirement in a couple of months, and I want someone there who I can rely on."

Leon was shocked but knew Commander Strobing, like Commander Roberts, wouldn't make this decision lightly – however he felt this was similar to demotion; after all nothing ever happened in Turkey. "But sir," he protested but knew his superior's mind was made up.

"Dismissed for now Commander Bigship," and, gloomily, Leon Bigship left the office. Celia came and stood in front of the desk.

"Weren't you a bit hard on Leon?" she said.

"My dear Commander Most, Leon may feel a bit put out – at the moment – but he's got to learn two things; when a request like that comes in he should not go over my head, plus there is no place in an organisation like HART for complacency."

"Admittedly that is true but Turkey! It's so out the way, anyway why there?"

"Why not? It's better than the Arctic. Now let's look at the schedule for the next year; late January – report to NATO, February – the medical conference at the Memorial hospital, finally March – President Ali Akhbar's speech in Agra." He then looked at the details for that trip and began to laugh, looking up at his deputy he said, "Guess where we're staying?"

"I don't know. Please tell me."

Ronan grinned at her, "The Taj Mahal!"

Commander Most's face fell, "The Taj Mahal," she repeated, "but I thought that was a mausoleum."

"It is Celia, a tomb, we're sleeping in a tomb," he was laughing harder than ever now. "Sorry," he apologised, trying to keep a straight face, "apparently it's changed over the last few years; some rooms have been converted on one of the upper levels so we don't have to sleep with the dead." Just then there was a knock on the office door, "Enter," called out Commander Strobing. The door to the room opened and a haggard, looking, Dr Schaiffer walked in. "Hans, what news do you bring me?"

Dr Schaiffer looked from one to the other, "I'm afraid commanders I can only report that the medical staff, as well as myself, have been working hard on finding a cure for this virus but so far we have had little success. I may know more after February's conference."

"Very good Dr Schaiffer, you may return to your work." With that the German medical man left the office. "I think we should retire now Celia, I'll just consult the rota and see who's on reception tonight," he called up the duty rota on his computer. "I see it's our new receptionist Hanna Strong."

Ms Strong was a middle-aged woman in her forties, her husband Joe had passed away several years earlier, and she'd been recruited by HART to take the place of the deceased receptionist, Lisa Bell. However, even though she was in her forties she still dressed in tight fitting black trousers and green T-shirts, often giving the men of HART something to look at. Gwyneth Jones had given the new lady a friendly warning, but this seemed to have had very little effect; if this kept up Ms

Hanna Strong ran the risk of losing her job, especially now the overall commander was back.

*****

Over in England several doctors had noted the fact that some people seemed to have developed a natural immunity to this new virus despite the fact they had come into contact with someone, maybe several people, who had shown signs of the virus. Doctors were baffled, but had called in all those with this natural immunity; most patients went and had samples of blood taken, and were also swabbed for a sample of DNA; the results from each patient would be taken to the medical conference, in Geneva, in February and would be discussed at great length, also the medical personnel attending would merge the results to see if they could find a common factor. Plus, it was hoped, that Dr Hans Schaiffer – of HART – would be able to find a cure for the other, infected, patients.

*****

Over the last couple of days of 2013 still nothing happened, there were no terrorist attacks linked with *Proagnon*, there was absolutely nothing. Commander Strobing did wonder if *Proagnon* had, finally, given up; if so, why give up without a fight? They could be regrouping, he supposed.

*****

In the *Proagnon* bunker Mitchell Walker was plotting again. He was planning another attack but this time intended to use the newly built *Wolves* as well as the *Havoc* helicopters.

The *Wolves* were similar to tanks, being tracked on each side; they were a one man vehicle. However the main difference was that instead of a turret on top, towards the rear of the vehicle was an array of 16 small compartments, on a stand type of device; the stand supported 8 of the compartments – on either side – each small compartment housed a single missile capable of causing much destruction. These machines, coupled with the air support provided by the *Havocs* would, hopefully cause maximum destruction.

Being tracked meant that the *Wolves* were amphibious to a certain degree, although their speed was greatly reduced to just 8 mph in water compared to an extra 12 mph on land.

So it was, on New Years Day 2014 that the fleet of vehicles rolled out on the way to their final destination, Walker would follow in a Jeep when contacted by radio; the six *Wolves* rumbled on and took up positions surrounding Tehran's *Imam Khomeini* airport, the *Havocs* hovering in strategic positions; the Jeep carrying the deputy leader of *Proagnon* rolled up, and came to a halt outside the main terminal building.

"You are completely surrounded. We mean you no harm if you surrender now, however any resistance will be met with force," he called through a megaphone.

*****

At the headquarters of HART there was a knock on the commander's office door, "Enter," called Commander Strobing.

The receptionist on duty, Joshua Smith, almost burst into the office and said rapidly, Sir, we've just received a transmission from Iran. Apparently *Proagnon* have surrounded the *Imam Khomeini* airport with several vehicles that are similar to tanks."

"What are their demands?"

"That's just it, sir, they haven't made any yet."

The commander thought about this, and then said to the receptionist, in the form of a question, "Okay Josh, what assets do we still have?"

The man standing before his commander consulted a clipboard which contained a sheet of paper which was a list of all the HART vehicles that had been brought back from Turkey, plus the remaining troop numbers. "Well sir, see for yourself," and he placed the clipboard on the desk, in front of Commander Strobing; Ronan looked at it.

Once he'd read through it he looked up at Mr Smith, "Not brilliant is it?" he asked, it was more of a rhetorical question.

Even though he knew it was rhetorical Josh answered, "No sir." It was at that moment that the new receptionist entered the office.

"Yes Miss Strong," the commander said in a slightly annoyed voice.

"Sorry sir," she responded, "Mr Smith. It's just that we've received a transmission, from *Proagnon.* It seems that their commander wants to meet with you."

"So that's his game, he attacks *Imam Khoemini* airport holding everyone hostage knowing HART will respond thus drawing me out. Question now is why? If he'd wanted to kill me he could've done so, easily, back in England, yet he didn't. Why?"

"Perhaps he wants to do a deal," ventured Hanna.

"You could, very well, be right Hanna," replied Commander Strobing. "Still it wouldn't hurt to take a bit of backup with me; Hanna, have the other two commanders meet us in here at once."

"Very good sir," and she left the office. All the time she'd been in the room Commander Strobing had noticed what Gwyneth Jones had noticed.

Calling her back Commander Strobing said to her, in a voice that wasn't exactly angry but Miss Strong knew he was warning her, "Just a friendly warning, Miss Strong, but I would prefer it if you were more suitably attired for reception."

"Of course sir, sorry sir, I shall be more suitably attired for my next shift. I shall now fetch the other two commanders," and Miss Strong left the office in search of the others.

Mr Smith walked from the office as the other two entered.

"Leon, Celia, please take a seat," Commander Strobing told them; he seemed in a good mood but both of them knew it probably wouldn't last, both of them pulled up a chair. "Now as you may know *Proagnon* troops have surrounded Tehran's *Imam Khoemini* airport with Mi-28 *Havoc* helicopters and vehicles that look like tanks but are capable of firing missiles." He paused a moment and then continued, "Here is a list of all available HART vehicles, all that are currently undamaged, plus the number of available personnel. This excludes all medical staff, and the staff needed to run headquarters, plus us three," Ronan told the other two – although both of them already knew this information. "I should like to hear your comments and what course of action you think we should pursue." He sat back in the, leather, command chair and waited.

Both Celia Most and Leon Bigship studied the list then Commander Most asked, "You mean to say this is it?"

"I'm afraid so, not much is it?"

"No sir," she answered, bluntly. "Anyway have these terrorists made any demands?"

"Only one and that is that their commander wants to meet with me; before you ask I don't know why either." He then noticed Commander Bigship was studying the list very intently, "What are your thoughts Leon?"

"Sir," answered the older man, "I would say that the number of personnel on this list HART can never hope to beat *Proagnon*. The last war claimed too many casualties."

"Agreed." Suddenly there was a knock on the office door, "Come in," called the overall commander. Joshua Smith entered again and stood at the back of the room. "What is it this time Josh?"

"Sir's, ma'am," he began, "we have just received another transmission from *Proagnon*. It appears that the *Proagnon* leader, well deputy leader, Mitchell Walker, wishes to meet you – alone and unarmed – at the site of the *Imam Khoemini* airport, if he sees any further HART soldiers his men have orders to shoot you, on the spot."

"Reply and inform him that I agree to meet him."

"But sir," protested Celia, "this is suicide."

"It could very well be a trap," Leon concluded. He knew Commander Most thought the same.

"It probably is a trap which is why I will not go unarmed or alone. Suggestions on what vehicles we should deploy, along with soldier numbers." Mr Smith, once he'd delivered his message and received an answer, had quietly left the room.

"I believe," Commander Bigship began, "that we ought to use the C-130 *Hercules* to transport 4 of the *Apache* helicopters out there along with the C-141B *Starlifter* transport plane which will be carrying both of the remaining Bradley Infantry Fighting

Vehicles, the Dodge Ambulance, 2 HMMWVs and 2 soldiers plus us three."

He then passed the list over to Commander Most; she studied it and then said, "I agree but do we need to take both Bradleys? Plus wouldn't a couple of Jeeps serve us better than 2 HMMWVs?"

"Possibly we wouldn't need both Bradleys but we could take one of the new Strykers instead," conceded Leon, "or a couple of Jeeps instead. Ultimately the decision is yours Ronan."

"Thank you, both of you, for your suggestions and ideas but as you say the final decision is mine," Commander Strobing said. After a few moments he announced, "I have made my final decision and it is – we shall use the two transport planes we mentioned but we shall take 2 HMMWVs plus 3 *Apache* helicopters and the Dodge Ambulance aboard the Hercules, while aboard the *Starlifter* we shall send the final *Apache* helicopter, one of the Bradleys plus a couple of Jeeps. Is that okay?" Both of the others nodded. "The new personnel carriers will be brought into action should the need arise."

The two other commanders left the office when they were requested to. As Ronan settled back, in the command chair, he began to think about the dwindling number of HART soldiers.

*****

The M1126 *Stryker* was an 8x8 wheeled armoured machine in the long line of *Stryker* vehicles. The primary operational role of the M1126 was as an armed armoured personnel carrier that was able to ferry infantrymen and supplies to the front, or wherever needed, while providing a respectable level of firepower during the disembarkation process. The weapons of the M1126 can be made specific to suit the role of the operator and a particular mission. The *Stryker* essentially shares the same basic chassis as the LAV family of *Generation III* wheeled vehicles did.

Design of the *Stryker* was characterised its eight large road wheels, fitted four to a side. The on-the-fly adjustable suspension system allowed for 8x8 wheeled (full-time 4 x 4, selective 8x8) operation allowing the *Stryker* to operate effectively both on paved or unpaved roads as needed. Armoured surfaces were sharply angled at the front for the increased protection to the crew and important internal systems alike while its slab armour greeted the side views. The *Stryker* featured a broad glacis plate consistent with the *Stryker* family line of 8-wheeled vehicles. Seating was for two primary operators (driver and gunner) along with 9 combat-ready infantrymen and their applicable equipment. Infantrymen exited the vehicle through a large ramp at the rear of the hull. The multiple hatches atop the hull allow for crewmembers to achieve a stance position from within the *Stryker* body, though at the risk of exposing themselves to any enemy fire. Hatch positions were located for the Squad Leader and VC along with two rear-guard positions as well as a power access hatch on the left hull side just rear of the driver's position and an additional escape hatch for any passenger's rear of that. The driver was afforded a dedicated hatch complete with vision blocks at the front left of the vehicle. The surface area of the *Stryker's* upper hull was suitable for carrying various battlefield odds and ends.

A digital system onboard the *Stryker* allowed for a fully-interactive battlefield map to be used in marking targets of note and their respective positions. This information can then be utilised by other battlefield vehicles and commanders for more cohesive planning between units. Performance for the *Stryker* IVC comes from a single diesel powerplant developing 350 horsepower of output. The power to weight ratio is 15.8 kW/ton. A top speed of 62 mph was listed though speeds reaching 70 mph were possible. The operational range for the *Stryker* system is reported at 300 miles.

Armament for the *Stryker* is made diverse and mission-specific thanks to the universal soft mount cradle atop the hull centre. The cradle can accept the Remote Weapon Station that itself can fit a variety of weapons as required by the operator. The RWS is a product of the Kongsberg Defence & Aerospace company of Norway and this was represented on the *Stryker* by its US Army designation of PROTECTOR M151. The mounting could fit an M2 air-cooled, heavy calibre machine gun or the

MK19 series 40mm automatic grenade launcher. The turret system could also be fitted to fire up to 16 x M6-type smoke grenades. The M151 was a complete remote-controlled firing system meaning its occupants could engage enemy targets without exposing their upper bodies through a hatch to fire the weapon. All firing is handled from within the relative safety of the *Stryker* vehicle itself.

The *Stryker's* chassis makes up a wide range of mission-specific all-terrain armoured vehicles. This included the M1126 Infantry Carrier Vehicle, the M1127 Reconnaissance Vehicle, the M1128 Mobile Gun System, the M1129 Mortar Carrier, the M1130 Command Vehicle, the M1131 Fire Support Vehicle, the M1132 Engineer Support Vehicle, the M1133 Medical Evacuation Vehicle, the M1134 Anti-Tank Guided Missile vehicle, the M1135 Nuclear, Biological and Chemical Reconnaissance Vehicle and the prototype 105mm self-propelled howitzer system (development on this had been cancelled a few years back).

Stryker was a US Army designation name for the LAV series and the name itself was originally derived from the names of two unrelated US army medal of honour recipients (covering World War 2 and the Vietnam War) with the surname of *Stryker*. The USMC utilised the LAV family as the LAV-25, though a *Generation II* system.

*****

The other armoured personnel carrier that HART had managed to obtain from the United States army (before the USA became closed to the anti-terrorist organisation) was the M113A1 (a member of the M113 family).

*****

The M113 armoured personnel carrier could be regarded as one of the most successful post-war armoured vehicles. No fewer than 80,000 units were produced since the system made its way to frontline service in 1960 with over 50 countries utilising the form in some way around the world. The chassis, of the vehicle, proved highly adaptable and became the basis for many other defensive systems and specialised battlefield vehicles. The

M113 still remained in service with many fighting forces, as well as HART.

The first instance of the M113 was being developed as early as 1956, with the initial production models - the M113 - coming out in 1960. These initial models were fitted with a gasoline engine though the follow-up model - the M113A1 - was soon fielded in 1964 with a more powerful and efficient diesel engine. The improved M113A2 followed over a decade later and found its way into frontline service by 1979. Features incorporated into this variant included improvements to the suspension system and the cooling system. The M113A3 represented the M113 in its fully evolved form, this model being fitted with a turbocharged version of the diesel engine. Software updates and additional armour protection also rounded out the list of improvements from the basic M113.

The M113 was a highly identifiable piece of battlefield machinery, appearing almost as a featureless fundamental design. The front featured a sloping appearance whilst the rest of the vehicle was nearly box-like. The system could be crewed by a minimum of 2 personnel and an additional 11 passengers could be carried aboard. Armoured protection, at least in the earlier M113's, was kept light and was intended to protect airborne troop elements from any shrapnel injuries while delivering them into combat. Over the decades, the system had been reconfigured and retooled to fulfil a variety of battlefield roles.

Standard defensive armament for the M113 consisted of a 12.7mm machine gun, though this could be substituted for the operator's needs and the specified role of the vehicle. The chassis had proven highly adaptable and could be found in other roles such as that supporting an air-defence turret system as in the anti-aircraft missile-wielding M730 Chaparral or the gatling alternative in the M741 Vulcan. Additionally, many M113's were converted to battlefield ambulances, cargo carriers, mortar carriers, smoke dispensing systems, missile carriers and mobile command posts.

*****

As with most old military vehicles HART engineers and technicians had modified these vehicles to HART's specifications. Reaching a decision on the dwindling soldier numbers Commander Ronan Strobing activated the microphone on the intercom and called the receptionist, on duty, into his office. A few moments passed before there came a knock on the, newly reinforced, office door, "Come in," he called.

Hanna Strong entered the office, again dressed in clothes that were much too young for her as well as somewhat revealing. "Yes sir." Commander Strobing looked hard at her, his disgust at her appearance very much evident. "Oh dear," she said, suddenly realising why he looked so disgusted, "I've done it again."

Commander Strobing suddenly said, "Yes Hanna, now get those clothes off and wear clothes more suitable to your job; like a knee-length skirt, blouse and a jacket, and not skirts like the one you're wearing and short tops."

Miss Strong started unbuttoning her top, in front of him. "When I said get those clothes off I didn't mean in here, I meant in your – private – quarters," Ronan told her, and then said, rather sharply, "Now get out my office and send somebody, more decently dressed in. If you are not properly attired when you come on your next shift I shall have no choice but to dismiss you."

"Yes sir, sorry sir," and she, practically, flew out the door. About two minutes later Gwyneth Jones entered.

"Ah Mrs Jones, I require you to give the signal to the crews of the *Hercules* and *Starlifter* to load on board the following vehicles," and he handed her his final decision list. "Next I wish you to contact all HART agents, around the globe plus those on the reserve list, and ask them all to come here; if any refuse they need a very good reason."

"Oh yes, please advise the crew of the B-208 *Ultrafortress* to ready their plane in case it is needed."

"Right away sir" and Mrs Jones turned and walked, smartly, out the door.

*****

The B-208 *Ultrafortress* was a modified and more up-to-date version of the B-52 *Stratofortress*. It acted, now, more as a flying command centre if HART needed it; this was the main reason it had been undergoing repairs/modifications in the latter half of the previous year and it was now ready to fly again.

Although it now, primarily, served as a flying command centre it was still heavily armed but its armaments were rarely used now and its days as a strategic bomber were numbered. The armament suite on board the B-208 was still very similar to the armament suite aboard the original B-52; this consisted of (externally) 2 AGM-86B ALCMs cruise missiles, and 2 AGM-129 cruise missiles. Its internal armaments consisted of 20 AGM-86B ALCM cruise missiles, along with 20 AGM-129 cruise missiles; it could also carry about 31,500kg of mixed ordnance, bombs, mines and missiles in various configurations.

The general dimensions of the aircraft had also been altered; the height of the B-208 was now a full 20 metres, the length was now a full 50 metres, and the width was now 55 metres. Of course with these alterations being made the wingspan and the wing area had had to be increased to 59 metres and 400 metres squared respectively.

As this original B-52 had been increased in all dimensions another 3 members of crew were added to the original 5 and now consisted of 2 pilots, 2 co-pilots, 2 radar navigators (bombardier), a navigator and an Electronic Warfare Officer. Besides weapons the plane also had around 50 separate computer workstations – each had its own operator and helped to provide the HART mission with airborne support, providing them with tactical manoeuvres and different battle scenarios.

Basically it was a much improved aircraft with more speed, more flying time due to its larger fuel storage capacity, although its service ceiling of 15,000 metres was left unchanged.

*****

Commander Ronan Strobing turned his attention to the report, and dossier, he knew he had to compile, plus his recommendations, for NATO. These types of reports had to be compiled once every three years – therefore the previous two had been written by his predecessor Commander Peter Roberts.

*****

In Scotland, at the HART safe house, Ralph Williams was asking Major Shinto Howell what he intended to do once his daughter was well enough to travel; he'd asked before but couldn't remember what Shinto had told him. The Japanese man answered, "I intend to take her back to Japan and our ancestral home."

The house in question was presently occupied by Shinto's sister and brother-in-law as Suki's mother, Shi'lene, had died ten years earlier; as she had only been 10 at the time Shinto had asked Suki's uncle and aunt to move in with them because then, at least, there would be another female in the house – as well as somebody for Suki to look up to. Admittedly Suki's father didn't want his daughter to forget her mother, and so he kept a portrait of his wife in Suki's room, plus he placed various photographs of Shi'lene around the house. Suki's aunt and uncle didn't object to this as both of them knew not to object.

Several years later he had packed a case and flown over to Switzerland, taking Suki with him leaving the house in the capable hands of his brother-in-law and sister; another 8 years later, in 2011, when he deemed Suki to be old enough to look after herself he had joined the Human Alliance for the Retaliation against Terrorism (HART), their commander at that time, Peter Roberts, had quickly promoted Shinto – due to his outstanding achievements and bravery – to the rank of major. Now in 2014 Shinto was preparing to take his daughter, after her ordeal, and perhaps himself back to Japan – for good.

Ralph Williams had taken Major Howell – everyday – to visit his daughter; Suki Howell had been moved, from the hospital ward, into a recuperation unit which was also situated within the hospital grounds. Although Suki would always see her father she distrusted any other man who came near her, she just needed time the nurses assured Shinto, so Mr Williams always stayed in the car.

Suddenly the telephone rang startling both men; the Japanese man just hoped it wasn't a call from the recuperation unit informing him his daughter had had a relapse, or worse. Mr Williams answered the phone and said into the mouthpiece, "Yes, he's here. I'll just get him for you." Ralph then returned into the main room and said to Major Howell, "It's Gwyneth Jones for you, Shinto."

The little man, from Japan, got to his feet and hobbled through to the hallway. Picking up the handset he said, "Hello."

Gwyneth's strong Welsh accented voice came back loud and clear, "Major Howell, we have a problem, our personnel numbers are dwindling so therefore Commander Strobing is recalling all the personnel he can. Can he count on you to return?"

Shinto had been thinking more about Suki recently, due to her current predicament, and was also thinking that she'd need him more in the future and therefore he'd considered resigning from HART. No, suddenly, his mind was made up, "You may inform Commander Strobing that I shall not be returning in fact I am resigning to return to Japan with my daughter to take care of her. I shall leave my Beretta pistol and anything else that belongs to HART, including my dog tag with Ralph Williams. Tell Commander Strobing I'm sorry but my daughter comes first."

"I understand," Mrs Jones told him, "and I'm sure the commander will as well. Good bye Mr Howell."

"Good bye Mrs Jones," and he replaced the receiver. That was one of the hardest decisions Shinto had ever made, he turned to see the figure of Ralph Williams framed in the main room doorway. "You heard?" enquired Shinto Howell.

"I did indeed," replied the figure in the doorway, "and, personally, I believe you're making the correct choice." Shinto looked surprised as he hadn't expected Ralph – of all people – to be in agreement with him.

"My daughter comes first, I believed when I first joined HART I could prevent Suki getting hurt; however, I have failed in that task and now believe that I can better protect her by being by her side."

Ralph Williams smiled at his Japanese friend, "Most admirable of you. I suppose I would feel the same way if I had a daughter of my own." Ralph stepped aside as Mr Howell made his way past and walked through into the bedroom he was using. Approximately an hour later the diminutive Japanese man re-entered the main room with his rucksack and walking cane.

Seating himself opposite Williams he told his host, "It is done. I have left all property of HART through there, including my dog tag." Then Shinto asked Mr Williams a strange question "Now, after our evening meal will you take me to see Paul Pearman please?"

"But why?"

"I just want him to arrange a meeting between his brother and myself," Mr Howell responded.

"Why? Ralph demanded to know. "He told us he doesn't know where Grant is."

"I believe Mr Pearman was lying to us."

Ralph looked shocked. "And anyway, why do you want to see him?"

Casually the little man from Japan replied, "I simply want to know why he attacked Suki." This wasn't the whole truth but the Japanese man felt that if the Englishman knew the whole truth he'd refuse.

"I guess I will," Mr Williams said, "if you promise to leave your walking cane behind." He looked at Mr Howell to gauge his reaction, Shinto smiled at him.

"Of course I will my dear Williams," was the reply. "What do you think I intended to do, kill him?"

"That thought had crossed my mind," muttered Mr Williams. After dinner the English HART agent took the small Japanese man, minus his walking cane which Ralph told Shinto he could return for after the meeting. He got his Toyota *Corolla* from the garage and both men boarded the vehicle, once they were both wearing their seatbelts Mr Williams started the vehicle, turned the headlights on and drove, slowly, back towards the village of Anderseir.

After a little over five minutes they pulled up outside the hotel and the two men walked inside. They found Paul Pearman seated, in the lobby, reading a paper. "Hello Paul," said Ralph as they approached.

Mr Pearman looked up, "Oh, hello Ralph. I see you've brought your friend along," he smiled at Mr Howell, "and what do you want of me?"

Shinto spoke up, "I should like you to arrange a meeting between your brother, Grant, and myself."

"I've told you," protested Paul, "I don't know where my brother is," he looked up at Williams for support but no support was forthcoming. "I don't know."

Ralph responded, his face showing no emotion, "My friend, here, believes you do."

"How can I?"

"Tell me Mr Pearman, if you don't then how did you manage to arrange a meeting between my daughter and him?" Mr Howell asked.

"Okay, supposing I do," sighed Paul resignedly, "why do you want to see him, and where do you want to meet him?"

"I simply want to know why he did what he did. As for where I suggest we use the same place as where he met my daughter, my beloved Suki."

"I'll do my best, "he promised. "Will you be staying with Mr Williams?"

"I will," Shinto told him, and then he and Williams left the building, climbed back into the *Corolla* and Ralph drove them both back to the safe house.

*****

At HART headquarters everything was readied, in preparation, for the trip to Iran; all three commanders would be going along with Private James Shearman and a new recruit, Private Amy Tingle. Private Tingle and Private Shearman had been selected because of their marksmanship qualities as both had previously worked as police officers.

Once all the vehicles had been loaded aboard the transport planes and all personnel were safely aboard and strapped in firstly the *Hercules* followed moments later by the *Starlifter* rose into the cloudy sky and started their journey south-east towards Iran. After roughly 2 hours the first of the two planes touched down about 5 miles north of the airport so as not to alert the *Proagnon* force unduly and all vehicles aboard were unloaded. A few moments later the *Starlifter* came into land beside the smaller plane and all its cargo was unloaded.

Once Commander Strobing had devised a battle plan he climbed aboard a Jeep and went off for his meeting with Mitchell Walker, maybe it would be their final meeting. The other two commanders had taken the two soldiers, in the HMMWVs, round to the back entrance of the airport and they had entered through that entrance; this wasn't guarded. Leon had taken the chief security officer aside while the other three personnel had merged into the crowd of waiting passengers, "HART," he said, "We are in full control of the situation. Please inform your men to stand down." The security chief did as he was asked and the HART personnel took up strategic positions, on the upper level, where they could see the situation unfolding below them.

CHAPTER 14

THE MEETING, REVENGE & DEPARTURES!

The Jeep carrying the overall commander of the HART organisation rounded the corner of the main terminal building to be met by the lone figure of Mitchell Walker flanked by two of the *Wolves*, "Stop where you are, get out and face me like a man. If you do not the drivers of these vehicles have orders to completely destroy this airport and everyone inside it."

The HART vehicle pulled to a stop, Commander Strobing climbed out and began walking, hesitantly at first and then more steadily, towards the *Proagnon* leader; "Pull the Jeep further back and await further order from me." The driver nodded and started the vehicle up, and then drove further back.

"Very wise Commander Strobing," Walker said as Ronan neared him, Mitchell extended his arm to shake the commander's hand; Ronan took it and they shook hands. "Now commander," began Walker, "after our last encounter," Ronan remembered the massacre at the school where his son, Simon Strobing, was a student and the high speed chase that had followed as Walker had held Simon as a hostage. Mitchell continued, "As I was saying, after our last encounter I have been doing quite a bit of thinking about how senseless this war of ours is, it has claimed too many casualties on both sides already."

"Agreed," Ronan confirmed.

"Therefore my men and I have agreed to end all hostilities, for good." Commander Strobing was puzzled, why would this man suddenly decide to give up? Also Ronan had noticed a slight difference in Walker's voice, why was that?

The *Proagnon* leader suddenly pulled a pistol from inside his tunic, "If we are to end this here and now then one of us must die, you!" and he raised the *Glock* pistol and pointed it at the other man's head; Mitchell squeezed the trigger and a shot rang out.

*****

At Raigmore hospital's recuperation unit Suki Howell was discharged, her father (now resigned from HART) and Mr Ralph Williams collected Miss Howell, in his *Corolla* and drove her back to the safe house, Suki was a bit wary of Mr Williams but her father assured her that she could trust him.

That evening all three of them were sitting in the main room, watching television, when the telephone rang, Ralph got up and walked through, to the hallway, to answer it. He picked up the receiver, "Hello," he said into the mouthpiece.

"Hello Ralph it's Paul here, is your Japanese friend still around?"

"He is," confirmed Williams, and half turned to see Shinto Howell framed in the doorway.

"I have located my brother and he is willing to meet your Japanese friend. As before Grant wants the meeting to be in my hotel room, more private he says, anyway would your friend be okay to meet Grant tomorrow evening?" By this time the Japanese man had crossed to the telephone and had heard every word; when Paul had asked his question Shinto had nodded his head rather rapidly.

Ralph spoke into the mouthpiece again, "I believe that shall be suitable, shall we say about six?"

"Six will be fine, I'll let Grant know. Good bye."

"Bye Paul," said Ralph and then added, rather quickly, "and thanks for arranging this." He replaced the receiver and asked Shinto, "Are you happy now?"

"Very," replied Mr Howell, and then added mysteriously, "please don't tell Suki anything about this, she'll think I've gone mad."

*****

The next evening, at about half past five, both men began to get ready for the trip back to Arderseir's hotel. Suki noticed this activity and enquired of her father, "What's going on?"

Ah Suki, my dear, Mr Williams and myself are returning to Arderseir, just to check we've got all of your belongings. Don't worry my child."

"Can I come with you?"

"Not this time my dear, it would be better for you if you stayed here."

"But dad," Suki started to protest. "What about me?"

"Mr Williams will look after you until I return, trust my judgement in this instance please." He looked up as Williams entered, "Are we all set?" Suki, reluctantly, returned to her seat.

"We're ready as we'll ever be. Are you ready?"

Shinto answered, "I'm ready shall we go?" The two men exited the room; Shinto called back, "We'll lock the door. You'll be safe." The Toyota *Corolla* started up on the second attempt, once they were both safely aboard, and the vehicle moved off. After about five minutes the car drew up outside the hotel. "You get back to Suki, I'll be okay," the Japanese man reassured Mr Williams.

"What about when you want picking up?" Ralph asked his companion, his friend just smiled at him.

"I shall either call you or make my own arrangements when I wish to return," responded Shinto and turned to walk inside the building, it wasn't much to look at – it was more like a large house than a *proper* hotel.

"Okay," Mr Williams told him, "I'll see you later," and he drove away, in the direction of his home. Mr Howell entered the lobby and saw Paul Pearman among the crowd of people – though, in truth, there was never more than five people about – at most, there was another man with him that Shinto assumed was the man's brother. Grant.

He approached them, a little wary of the muscular man, and Paul introduced them to each other, and then he said rather hurriedly, "I have to go out now so I'll leave you two gentleman to get better acquainted." The two men then turned and sauntered off deeper into the hotel, Grant Pearman leading the way. Paul watched them go and then sighed to himself.

Grant led Shinto to his brother's room - they entered the accommodation and seated themselves, facing each other, on a couple of chairs. Shinto looked around him; the room was just a basic room; two beds with bedside cabinets, couple of chairs, TV, telephone, wardrobe, and en suite bathroom. Having taken all this in he turned back to face the, large, figure of Grant Pearman. To a lesser man he probably seemed scary – what with his large and muscular frame.

"Well," snarled Grant, "what do you fucking want with me?" A lesser man might've been intimidated by the man's aggressive behaviour but ex-Major Shinto Howell wasn't, despite his small size.

Mr Howell smiled, benignly, at the man, "I simply wish to know why you raped my daughter, Suki."

"Because I wanted to," began the bigger man. "Bloody foreign whore, almost begged me to do it to her."

"That's a lie."

"She spread her legs like the fucking prostitute she was, and she enjoyed it. Now if you've come hear to exact your revenge, little man, then let me tell you, little man, I ain't scared of you, in fact I could probably knock the living daylights out of you."

"I'd like to see you try," the Japanese man said, smiling. The next thing he knew one of Grant's mallet sized fists was heading his way; Shinto ducked and the fist flew over his head, and then stepping – nimbly – aside he watched as the bigger man's momentum carried him on and he fell over.

Quick as a flash Grant recovered his senses, looked up at Mr Howell and then got to his feet. "For making me look a fool I'm gonna fucking kill you," and a fight broke out between the two men, bedside lamps got smashed and furniture was broken; both men received their fair share of cuts and bruises during the course of things. Finally Shinto fell back and Grant picked up a broken bedside table and raised it above his head, it was evident that he intended to kill the small, helpless, Japanese man; luckily Mr Howell had brought his walking cane, as he'd told Mr Williams his back was playing him up, and it now lay beside him, before Grant could strike Shinto Howell withdrew the sword – in his walking cane – and held it out to defend himself. Unfortunately the downward momentum threw Grant Pearman forward and he fell onto the sword blade, the blade pierced his body and went straight through him; he howled in pain but all the little man could do was watch, totally dumbstruck, as the other, bigger, man fell towards him, he managed to roll out the way before Mr Pearman came, crashing, down to the floor.

Mr Howell was horrified, he'd never used the sword – he carried – in anger and had only brought it with him to, maybe scare this man who had raped his daughter if he had become violent; what had – now – happened was just a terrible and horrible accident; however would the authorities see it that way? Realising he had no option but to flee Shinto – managed – to lift the big man and heaved him onto his back, he withdrew the Samurai sword and replaced it in it's holder; looked at the dead body and felt sick, the floor was covered with patches of blood and there was a look of shock mixed with total surprise on Mr Pearman's dead face, Shinto knew he was dead just by looking at him. Taking the key card from Grant's pocket Shinto Howell took his walking cane and left the hotel room, the door clicking shut behind him.

He knew he was – quite probably – doing the wrong thing by just leaving the lifeless body, but if he stayed he would be accused of murder and placed in prison, and then where would his daughter be? Also if this came out there was no telling how she would react.

Shinto handed the key card to the man who was working at reception, and then walked into the hotel bar; he was surprised at the number of young people he saw in there; three – a couple, and a girl on her own. Spotting that the girl had a familiar face he got himself a drink and then went over to the table she was sitting at. "Hello Christine."

*****

Back at the HART safe house Suki Howell was beginning to trust Ralph Williams again, hadn't her father told her she could trust him not to harm her? However Mr Williams seemed preoccupied at the moment, whenever the Japanese woman asked what he was doing she was, simply, told that it was some important paperwork he had to do for HART.

"However I will need a photo of you and one of your father, when he returns," the Scottish agent told her.

"Where is my father?" she enquired.

"I believe he told you he was going to check and see if we've got all your belongings," he told her. "But as he's been gone longer than anticipated he may have met somebody he knows."

"Or, knowing Dad," Miss Howell began, "he may have run into trouble. It's close to midnight on a cold, snowy, evening, Dad's missing – yet you don't seem unduly concerned."

"Your father can look after himself," Ralph said gently but, at the same time, firmly to her. "Don't worry yourself."

*****

In front of Iran's *Imam Khomeini* airport the figure of Mitchell Walker fell, dead; as soon as their leader's body fell another *Proagnon* soldier raised his AK-47 and aimed it at Commander Strobing, "One more step and I kill you here and now," he said menacingly, and then he said to the driver of the *Wolf*, "arm your missiles, radio the other *Wolves* and inform them to prime and prepare their missiles for launch, and to await my command." He switched his attention back to Ronan, "So tell your men and vehicles to withdraw or I shall give the command for my fellow soldiers to completely destroy this airport, thus killing everybody inside it."

"You wouldn't dare, Commander Strobing retorted. "You'd kill your own soldiers as well." A silence fell over the area as the HART commander and the man from *Proagnon* faced each other, and eyed each other with suspicion. "Come on," he muttered under his breath; suddenly – about a minute later – a HMMWV roared into view and skidded to a halt between the two men.

"Get in sir," the driver of the vehicle said quickly to his superior, throwing open the passenger door. The vehicle had supplemental armour fitted on so Ronan was quite safe as a group of *Proagnon* soldiers appeared and fired their AK-47 assault rifles at the retreating HMMWV.

"One moment," the HART commander said, "do you think you can get as near enough to that body over there?" Ronan was pointing at Mitchell Walker, "There's something about that body that just doesn't seem right." He looked – hopefully – at Corporal Spriggins, who was the driver.

"I'll do my best sir," he responded and turned the vehicle, and drove – slowly – alongside the other man's body; Ronan opened the passenger door, not too wide for fear of getting killed, and looked down at Walker. There seemed to be something wrong with his face; therefore Ronan got the man into a sitting position, leaned out and touched his face – it felt rubbery Commander Strobing smiled to himself and, slowly, pulled at the face and as he thought it came away in his hand – revealing a much more youthful face underneath. "Hurry it up sir," the corporal urged, "that *Wolf*, I believe you called it, has just turned and is lining us up."

"Okay," the HART commander said, climbing back inside the HMMWV; once he was seated and had shut the door he said to Spriggins. "Go!" The driver accelerated away at the High Mobility Multipurpose Wheeled Vehicle's top speed of 55 mph. As they were moving away Ronan grabbed the radio microphone and activated it, he then bellowed into it, "Commander Strobing to all HART vehicles and personnel, open fire on the *Proagnon* forces."

Then all hell broke loose, the Bradley Fighting Vehicle rumbled – slowly – into view and opened fire on the nearest *Wolf*. Missiles and shells flew between the two vehicles but the missiles from the *Proagnon* machine either fell short of the BFV or missed completely. The HART vehicle's shots, though, mostly all connected – those few that didn't threw up sand, blinding the driver of the enemy vehicle and it spun off course and crashed into a rock – exploding instantly.

The other HART land vehicles had collected the rest of the personnel and was, now, speeding them away to safety; unfortunately Private Tingle fell from the Jeep that was carrying her, and by the time she'd recovered she looked up and came face to face with one of the *Proagnon* missile carrying vehicles, the driver was totally oblivious, to the fact, that she was there – so intent was he on making the HART BFV pay for destroying the other *Wolf*. Amy screamed but the driver didn't hear her over the – powerful and loud – diesel engine. The HMMWV carrying Ronan Strobing had halted and turned to face the battlefield; surveying the site through powerful binoculars he saw Miss Tingle and the danger she was in as the enemy vehicle rolled inexorably closer. "No!" he screamed, "We have to save her. Go Spriggins!" The driver didn't move, "Corporal Spriggins, I am ordering you to move this vehicle so we can save Private Amy Tingle!"

Spriggins looked at the commander and said, "With all due respect sir, I don't think we would reach her in time. I'm sorry sir, if we could reach her in time you know I'd go, but as I'm sure, even, you realise we can't." then he added, "I'm sorry sir, truly I am."

Ronan knew he was right, he just didn't want to accept it – since he'd been in command HART had lost many good men, and women. "Accepted," the commander eventually said in defeat, "take us back to the rendezvous point." As the vehicle, they were in, powered up and began to turn Commander Strobing saw – out the corner of his eye – the point at which the *Wolf* rolled over, and crushed, Private Amy Tingle. The HMMWV then drove away.

However, up above, the four HART *Apaches* had taken out the group of *Havocs*; afterwards two of the *Apaches* had flown down and taken out, using their *Hellfire* missile system, the remaining three *Wolves*. Once every enemy vehicle was destroyed the HART helicopters joined the other vehicles, and personnel, at the rendezvous site.

Once everybody had arrived back Commander Strobing called all the personnel to a meeting, "Today," he began, "we have triumphed in this minor, skirmish against the enemy; admittedly we have lost Private Amy Tingle in the fighting, her loss is felt mostly by me as it was me who ordered her to come on this mission."

One of the soldiers, who was standing in the group, suddenly spoke up, "Sir, it was my fault, she must've fallen out when I hit a rock. Don't blame yourself." Commander Strobing smiled across at the man, he knew that he was responsible – as commander – for all of the HART team, and he'd let them down, Amy most of all.

Silently the HART personnel loaded the vehicles they'd used on board the transport planes, and the two, huge, planes lifted off into the night sky. As it was dark many soldiers grabbed some shuteye while the commander, along with his two deputies, relaxed but kept alert – even Private Shearman shut his eyes; about two hours after they'd lifted off the planes – the *Hercules* leading and the *Starlifter* bringing up the rear landed on the runways which were located inside the HART compound.

Everyone exited the two transport planes, except the crews who taxied the two, enormous, aircraft to their - individual – hangars, for refuelling purposes. The vehicles were unloaded and taken to either the garages, or taken to the aircraft hangars for refuelling.

Commanders Strobing, Most and Bigship returned to their, separate, offices; once all three of them were back Joshua Smith – the receptionist on duty – strode over and knocked on the overall HART commander's office door. "Come in," called Ronan, still saddened by the death of Amy Tingle. *More paperwork for me to do*, he thought.

Joshua Smith entered the office and seeing the look on his superior's face, said apologetically, "Sorry to disturb you sir but Ralph Williams, in Scotland, needs you to contact him." It was then that he asked, "Did everything go okay in Iran?"

Ronan Strobing looked at Mr Smith, tears in his eyes, and his voice cracked as he spoke, "It didn't go quite as planned. We saved the airport and destroyed the enemy vehicles, however we lost Private Tingle; she was crushed under one of the *Proagnon* vehicles."

Josh knew the commander felt personally responsible for each death that happened; Commander Roberts had shown much less emotion. Maybe this show of emotion would, probably, be Commander Strobing's downfall. The receptionist watched as a solemn Commander Strobing took out a wooden cross from a box behind the desk, and then said quickly, "I'll come back in a bit," the receptionist told the commander, "when you've had time to collect yourself."

"That will be fine," responded the man behind the desk; standing up he placed Amy's dog tag, there was always a duplicate at headquarters, around the wooden cross and then took it down to the garden of remembrance and placed the cross alongside the others – there were so many now. Then he, along with the other commanders – who had joined him, said a silent prayer and returned inside; the others followed his lead.

What none of them noticed was Private James Shearman watching them; once they'd gone he walked over and knelt down – locating Amy's cross he produced a marker pen and wrote on it 'I will always love you. JS'. He smiled at the words he'd written, he'd never told Amy how he'd felt about her – he'd never really had the chance. After shedding a few tears over his loss he made his way back to barracks.

*****

Hearing her name spoken, by such a familiar voice, the young woman known as Christine Woodward turned and looked up, "Hello Shinto," she said in greeting.

"May I join you?" he enquired, knowing full well she was alone.

"But of course," was the answer he got. "Sit down and tell me all." Shinto seated himself opposite her and was about to tell her everything – well almost everything – when they were interrupted.

"Hi guys," called a light, airy, voice, "mind if I join you both?"

"Course not Jenny," Christine answered. "That's if Shinto doesn't mind." The, diminutive, Japanese man shook his head to say he didn't mind, so Miss Ramsay joined them. "Shinto was about to tell us everything." Ramsay, Shinto had found out, was Jenny's surname.

"Can't wait," the blonde woman blurted out, purely by accident.

"Well," began ex-Major Howell, "My daughter, Suki, is now safe. In fact I intend to take her back home to Japan – where I shall stay myself, as well, as I feel it is partly my fault she got herself into such a dangerous situation."

"But," began the blonde woman, "if you intend to stay behind with her, won't that mean you'll have to resign from HART?" As soon as she'd asked this question she realised – from her friend's look – that the brunette knew nothing of HART.

"I've already done that," Mr Howell said to Miss Ramsay, next he turned back to Christine. "Please don't tell anybody about HART; although some people know about us not everybody does. Can I trust you not to say anything?"

"Of course you can Mr Howell," the young, brunette, woman answered.

Jenny, again, spoke up, "You say you are returning to your home country with your daughter? I was wondering if I might come with you." Shinto had half expected something like this, but to – actually - hear those words had taken him aback; he told the blonde he needed a moment or two to think it over, he sipped at his drink as he considered her request.

"Jenny," Christine said to her friend, "why do you want to go to Japan?" The other woman just smiled at her female companion.

"It's simple," announced the young blonde, "I've had enough of nursing, in Scotland, and feel that I could, maybe, help more, or introduce new ideas, over there. Plus, as you know, I've always wanted to travel."

Shinto Howell looked up, after draining his glass, "I have reached my decision."

"And that is?" Jenny asked eagerly, Christine looked on in apprehension, and the knowledge, that she may be losing her blonde friend.

"Well," began Mr Howell, "I have no wife – as you know – and I would be pleased to have another companion in our house but," there was always a but, you are nearer to Suki's age than my age and I believe it would be good for her to have a companion more her own age; she has her aunt but as she is older Suki and her often clash, therefore, my dear Jenny, the answer is yes."

"Thank you Mr Howell, you won't regret it," Jenny enthused. "When do we go?"

"I'm not entirely certain myself," answered Shinto, "if you would care to leave me a contact number I will let you know." Rapidly Jenny wrote down her, mobile, phone number, and passed it across to the Japanese man. Once the two ladies had finished their drinks the three of them, Shinto carrying his walking cane left the hotel, boarded Christine's Audi and roared off into the dark, winter, night.

*****

When Shinto entered the HART safe house he was greeted by his daughter, "Dad, what's happening?" she asked.

"Ah Suki, my dear daughter, we are returning to Japan and our ancestral home in Tokyo; I have also arranged for a nurse – that looked after you in the hospital – to travel over with us, to help and be a companion to you, as she is more your own age." He walked on into the sitting room to see Ralph Williams, "Mr Williams, have you finished all the documentation my friend?"

"Yes I have," said HART's Scottish agent, "everything is completed and ready. When will you be ready to depart?"

Shinto considered the question, "Tomorrow evening. Are there any flights tomorrow?"

"Indeed there are, I have booked three seats on British Airways, flight 906, which leaves at ten tomorrow evening from Inverness airport. I had to go through my – special – contacts to get you both on board at such short notice." He paused and sipped at the whisky he'd poured himself, "I heard you speaking to Suki; it was lucky I had the foresight to book three seats. By the way who's the lucky lady?"

"It's not like that," protested Mr Howell, "her name is Jenny Ramsay and she was one of the nurses who looked after Suki during her stay in Raigmore hospital. And my thanks for booking the extra seat."

Suki Howell then joined the two men in the room, "So this Miss Ramsay is to be my companion. I don't think I need one but she can come with us, she may prove useful." Shinto Howell phoned Miss Ramsay and informed her to meet him, together with his daughter, at Inverness airport; she was to pack whatever she wanted to bring, and meet them at the entrance to the airport at half past seven, in the evening, the next day. She assured him she'd be there and gave a little giggle; Shinto, his job done, replaced the receiver, and then retired for the night; tomorrow would be a long day.

*****

Inverness Airport was an international airport situated at Dalcross, 13 km; (8.1 mi) northeast of the city of Inverness in Highland, Scotland. The airport was the main gateway for travellers to the north of Scotland with a wide range of scheduled services throughout the UK and Ireland, and limited charter and freight flights into Europe and beyond. 591,397 passengers passed through the airport in 2009 though that number had increased over the following four years. The airport was owned by the Highlands and Islands Airports Limited (HIAL) who also owned most of the regional airports in mainland Scotland and the outlying islands.

Flybe was the largest carrier at Inverness Airport. It operated the thrice-daily London-Gatwick service, inherited from BA Connect operated by a based Embraer 195 aircraft. The carrier also had a based Bombardier Q400 which operated routes to Manchester, Jersey and Southampton. There are also *Flybe* routes using a Q400 to Belfast and Birmingham.

The airport was a hub on the Highlands and Islands network where flights between the islands and the central belt connect. In the 1970s, *British Airways* operated Viscount services on the network, later this was down-sized to Hawker Siddley 748s. These were then replaced by ATPs. British

Airways continued to lose money on these routes and gradually transferred its operations to franchise carriers *British Regional Airlines* and *Loganair*. Today these services were all operated by *Loganair* under a franchise agreement with *Flybe*. Links to the central belt have recently been lost. There are no longer any direct services to either of Glasgow's airports after they were withdrawn by *Loganai*r. *Highland Airways* attempted to operate this service and this was subsequently short-lived. A twice daily service to Edinburgh was withdrawn in 2010 due to the lack of demand.

The airport terminal was notable as an early example of the Public-private partnership favoured by the UK Government, of that time. HIAL was criticised for a PFI deal signed to build a new terminal at Inverness Airport. The deal signed by HIAL meant it had to pay £3.50 for every passenger flying from the airport to the PFI operator. In 2006, the PFI deal was cancelled, costing the Scottish Executive £27.5 million.

*****

During the next day Mr Howell and his daughter did the packing for the, long, journey home. Shinto hadn't that much to pack neither did his daughter so they'd both finished within an hour. For the remainder of their time in Scotland Ralph took both of his Japanese friends round the, few, shops in Ardersier – explaining that most people did their shopping in Inverness as Ardersier was only a small village.

At about seven that evening they loaded the luggage aboard Ralph Williams Toyota *Corolla* and headed for Inverness airport, the journey took the three people, roughly, twenty minutes. Standing outside the entrance, awaiting their arrival and with suitcase in hand, was Miss Jenny Ramsay; once everyone was in the main, terminal, building Mr Williams bid his Japanese friends, along with their new associate, a fond farewell and returned to his car. He had a report to make, upon his return home, to the commander of HART.

Once inside the departure lounge Miss Ramsay asked Shinto Howell, "Where are we flying to?" Mr Howell looked, slightly, puzzled at first, and then realised what the young woman meant.

"We are flying, my dear Miss Jenny Ramsay, to Narita International Airport, and then when we leave the airport we shall travel by taxi to my home in Tokyo."

*****

Narita International Airport was an airport that served the Greater Tokyo Area of Japan. It was located 57.5 km (35.7 mi) east of Tokyo Station and 7 km (4.3 mi) east-southeast of Narita Station in the city of Narita, with some portions extending into the adjacent town of Shibayama.

Narita handled the majority of international passenger traffic to and from Japan, and was also a major connecting point for air traffic between Asia and the Americas. The airport handled 35,478,146 passengers in 2007 but more in the following years. It was the second-busiest passenger airport in Japan, busiest air freight hub in Japan, and eighth-busiest air freight hub in the world. It also served as the main international hub of Japan`s Flag carrier Japan Airlines, All Nippon Airways and Nippon Cargo Airlines. It also served as an Asian hub for the US based Delta Air Lines and as a focus city for United Airlines and Vietnam Airlines. Under Japanese law, it is classified as a first class airport.

The airport was known as New Tokyo International Airport until 2004, but was commonly called *Tokyo Narita* even before it was officially renamed to differentiate it from Tokyo International Airport, commonly called *Tokyo Haneda.*

*****

Ralph Williams headed back to Ardersier. Upon reaching the safe house he contacted headquarters, in Switzerland, to inform the commander of events. He was informed by the receptionist on duty, Joshua Smith that the commander, along with both his deputies, was away in Iran; he was then asked if he wanted to make his report anyway, but the Scot needed to speak to one of the three commanders personally, and so Mr Smith told him that Commander Strobing would be in touch when he returned.

*****

The non-stop flight from Inverness to Tokyo would be made aboard a *British Airways* Boeing 747-8I – British Airways had only been flying to Narita Airport for the last couple of years – and the flight would take about ten hours so with the plane's take off time of ten that evening the civilian flight would arrive at Narita airport at approximately eight the next morning. However with the time difference of nine hours the real time, in Japan, would be at around five the next evening.

At about nine forty-five the four hundred and sixty seven passengers were permitted to board the aircraft, and then, once everybody was seated, at just gone ten the four GEnx 2B67 engines were powered up and the air vehicle taxied to the top of the main runway; once a clear slot was found the engines powered up to full thrust and the aircraft thundered down the 1,887 metre, asphalt, runway and rose into the sky, to begin its long flight to the far east.

*****

At headquarters, in Switzerland, Commander Strobing – who had been reminded by Joshua Smith – walked back to his office and contacted Mr Williams in Ardersier. Luckily Ralph hadn't retired to bed yet answered, "Hello."

"I believe you wanted to speak to me," said Commander Ronan Strobing, in a friendly tone but one that was also authorative.

"Ah, Commander Strobing, yes I did. As you may know Suki Howell was raped just before Christmas."

"I had heard."

"You may also know that her father Major Shinto Howell came over to be by his daughter's side."

"Uh huh," Commander Ronan Strobing now sounded bored so Ralph decided to cut a long story short.

"Major Howell, now wanting to be with her more, has resigned from HART, and I have just driven them to the Inverness airport and I believe they're headed back to their home in Tokyo."

"Is that everything?" asked the commander of HART.

"Not quite sir, a friend of mine, Paul Pearman, has had his brother killed."

"What's that to do with us?" Ralph knew if he didn't explain quickly the commander would, possibly, explode.

"The only reason I mention it is because Paul's brother, Grant, was the one who was responsible for raping Suki, plus he met with Major Howell the night he was murdered." That grabbed the commander's attention, "So the question is sir, do we hand Shinto Howell over to the authorities?"

Commander Strobing's answer was, "Maybe it was deliberate maybe it wasn't. Admittedly HART doesn't condone that sort of behaviour but I believe that in this case it may be better that we should say nothing, as you say Shinto's resigned and there are rather a lot of men – who look very similar - in Japan. So even if we did inform the authorities it would be like looking for a needle in a haystack."

Ralph thanked Commander Strobing for his guidance in this matter, said his farewells and replaced the receiver. Ronan sat there, thinking about what he'd just told Mr Williams, and realised it had only been a month ago that he'd done a similar thing: he had shot and killed his sister-in-law's ex-partner simply because he'd aided *Proagnon* forces to find Ronan's son, and then they'd held a siege at the school. Commander Strobing had felt betrayed by Lloyd Edwards, the man had betrayed Melissa Stevens, Ronan's son Simon, and Ronan himself; admittedly Commander Strobing hadn't needed to kill Mr Edwards but he'd just felt so let down, and had – perhaps – let his anger boil over, in that instance. If he could undo it he would, still the past was the past.

Ronan was brought back to reality by a knock on his office door, "Come in," he called. The door, slowly, opened to reveal Hanna Strong – who was now wearing a grey trouser suit, more suitable clothing for a receptionist.

"Well sir," she began, "do I pass?"

"Much more suitable for your job; is that all you came in for?"

"No sir, I mainly came to ask if you'd seen the time?" It was then the commander turned and looked at the clock, 12:15, he'd been thinking for a whole hour – maybe a little less. Perhaps he'd dozed off, he wasn't sure.

"You're right Miss Strong," he told her even though she hadn't said anything, "I should be getting to bed. By the way who's on-call tonight?"

"Commander Bigship sir, though I don't really anticipate anything happening tonight."

"You're probably right, *Proagnon* are probably licking their wounds," he rose to leave and left the room. As he walked past Miss Strong he caught a whiff of her perfume, it smelt flowery. "I like the smell of your perfume, anyway goodnight Hanna."

"Goodnight sir," she responded, once he'd gone she – secretly – smiled to herself.

The next day Commander's Celia Most and Leon Bigship were up at six thirty, but there was no sign of Commander Strobing – perhaps he was already doing some paperwork that he hadn't finished the night before. As the two of them entered the reception area they were met by an irate Dr. Hans Schaiffer, "Where is Commander Strobing?" he blurted out then added, "I need him to sign some paperwork." Both commanders shrugged their shoulders.

"Perhaps I can help," said the voice of Miss Hanna Strong as her shift – on reception – had finished, and she was making her way back to her residence. "The commander left late last night, actually it was me who had to prompt him to go and get some sleep as he looked shattered; he's probably just slept in."

"Thank you Hanna," Celia said. "I shall take temporary, command. Please follow me Dr Schaiffer."

"Yes ma'am," replied the German doctor and followed Commander Most into the deputy commander's office. They sat at the, wooden, table, and Dr Schaiffer passed the paperwork over to Commander Most who studied it closely.

Reaching the end she looked up at the man seated across from her. "Are you sure these are all in order?"

"Yes they are," he responded. Celia looked - closely – at him; he had never lied about anything that pertained to medical records or any type of medical paperwork. So, knowing these were all in order, she signed the papers.

She passed them back to him, "There you go," she told him, "I don't pretend to know what it all means, but I know you wouldn't lie to us."

"Thank you ma'am," he said to her as he took the paperwork back. "The form you have just signed gives me permission to order and use a specialist drug that has recently become available."

"Hmm," murmured Celia. Once he was dismissed Dr Hans Schaiffer walked from the office and crossed to reception where he handed the order form to the receptionist on duty now, Ben Gillespe. "See that you order a large quantity of that, relatively, new drug. I have the commander's, albeit Commander Most's, full authorisation."

"Right away sir," said Ben. Dr Schaiffer then made his way back to the medical department.

*****

Commander Strobing awoke and turned over to look at the clock which read 09.00, aware of the fact that he'd overslept he roused himself, fully, dressed and hurried downstairs for some breakfast. Once he'd eaten he was just about to return upstairs and grab a quick shower when there came a knocking at his door; slightly annoyed he went and answered it, as it could be important. When he opened the door he saw Hanna Strong standing outside in a full length duffel, coat and a mischievous smile on her face. "Hello Miss Strong."

"Greetings commander, may I come in?"

"Actually Hanna I was just about to go upstairs for a quick shower," he informed her.

"Do you want anybody to scrub your back?" she asked him cheekily.

"No thank you," he answered politely. She then opened her coat to reveal she had nothing on underneath. Ronan gasped and started to turn away; before he could fully turn away Hanna grabbed him and kissed him. “Really Miss Strong,” but he found himself reciprocating. He pulled away and realised if anybody had seen them it may mean the end to his days as commander of the Human Alliance for the Retaliation against Terrorism (HART) forces.

However, unseen by both of them they had been observed, by a small figure, who was even now making her way across to the main headquarters building.

Hanna Strong, finally, fastened her coat back up and left Commander Strobing to take his shower, whilst she went back to her own residence to get some sleep.

As soon as he was ready the commander of HART crossed to headquarters and as he walked through the reception area Ben Gillespe said to him, “Commander Most’s been filling in during your, temporary, absence. Oh, and Miss Stronglove wishes to see you.”

“Very good Ben, carry on,” the commander replied, and then asked, “Do we have a file on Private Amy Tingle?”

“We do sir; I’ll locate it for you and send it in with Miss Stronglove.”

“Thank you Ben, I’ll buzz you when I’m ready.” With that Commander Strobing went inside his office. About five minutes later, when he was settled, the commander activated the intercom to reception. “Send Miss Stronglove in please.”

About a minute later there came a knock on the wooden, office, door, “Come in,” called the HART commander; Alice Stronglove entered the room carrying a – thin – folder. “Ah Miss Stronglove, please take a seat.”

Alice seated herself opposite her superior, “I believe you wanted this,” she said and handed him the, thin, folder. Ronan thanked her as he took the folder.

“I believe you wished to see me,” he stated. “I also wish to see you, but I’ll let you begin.”

Alice considered how best to put what she wanted to say, “Sir, earlier today I observed Miss Hanna Strong and yourself, at your residence, and you weren’t – exactly – exchanging pleasantries." HART's superior officer looked slightly uncomfortable at this revelation.

"And, what may I ask do you intend to do with this information?" Alice was rather surprised that he hadn't tried to deny this indiscretion.

"I could," Miss Stronglove said to him, "choose to keep quiet, or I could report this and have you removed as HART's commanding officer."

"You could," Ronan told her, "but don't forget about the time you kissed me, right here, in my office. How do you think that would go down?"

"You wouldn't."

"If you reported me I'd feel it my – moral – duty to report what you did," Commander Strobing reiterated, and then added, "I believe you could call that check-mate."

The figure seated opposite the commander considered what her superior had jus said, "Okay sir," she said finally, "what did you want to see me for?"

Alice's commanding officer said, "Suki Howell, who had gone to observe things in Scotland but put herself in danger and she ended up in hospital – with hindsight I think she was too young for this mission. This resulted in her father, Major Shinto Howell, having to travel over there to take care of her; now he has resigned from this organisation and taken his daughter back to Japan."

"What has that to do with me sir?" Miss Stronglove asked him.

"You were – originally – assigned to this mission but, unfortunately, your mother became ill so we had to send Miss Howell in your place. However, now your mother is well again, I wish you to go over to Scotland – see if you can learn any new information on this *Damancas* sea fort. I must ask if you still wish to take this assignment on?"

Alice smiled, "Yes I still want to take this assignment, and I shall not put myself in danger – well, nothing I won't be able to handle." Commander Strobing smiled back at her. He appreciated her enthusiasm. "Who will my contact be?"

"A man named Ralph Williams; he runs the HART safe house in a, small, village in Scotland called Ardersier. I shall contact him as soon as you are ready to leave for the airport." Once she was dismissed Alice returned to her residence to begin packing.

When she'd packed her suitcase she placed it in the boot of her Audi car and returned inside main headquarters to inform the commander she was ready to leave, he contacted *Cointrin* airport and let them know what was happening, and to have an aircraft standing by to take a single passenger to Inverness airport.

The airport staff informed him everything would be prepared and readied. Commander Strobing gave Alice Stronglove his authorisation, and she left his office.

As soon as she'd gone Ronan contacted Mr Williams and told him to expect another, female, visitor, and what time he should go to the airport to fetch her. He told the commander that he would be ready.

Alice arrived at *Cointrin* airport and entered the terminal building carrying her luggage; she was fast tracked through to the airside lounge where she awaited her air transport. Approximately twenty minutes later, at about 11.28, a Gulfstream *G550* rolled up and Alice left the lounge and climbed aboard the aircraft whilst her suitcase was placed in the – underside – luggage area.

Once Alice was strapped in and all the pre-flight checks had been completed the aircraft taxied to the top of the main, concrete, runway. Once a clear slot had been found the plane thundered down the runway and rose into the dull, overcast, sky to begin its one hour and thirty five minute flight to Inverness airport.

The plane landed on the asphalt runway at approximately one twenty in the afternoon – however due to the time difference it was only twenty past twelve in Scotland. Ralph Williams was waiting for her at the top of the runway, his Toyota *Corolla* parked up, ready and waiting. As the *G550* came to a standstill Alice Stronglove exited the air transport vehicle and crossed the tarmac to the man waiting beside the, dark green, automobile. "I presume you're my contact," she said to him. She had to shout to make herself heard above the roar of the plane's engines.

"You must be Miss Stronglove, I've heard a great deal about you."

"All good I hope," Alice shouted again.

"Apparently you're one of our best agents at gathering intelligence," the man from Scotland told her as her suitcase was taken out the aircraft's luggage compartment. Once he had put her case in the Toyota's boot, and she was safely belted in, in the passenger seat Ralph Williams drove from the airport compound to the safe house he ran in Ardersier.

The main reason Suki Howell hadn't been installed in the safe house straight away was because Mr Williams felt she may have learned more in the, local, pub; however that had turned out to be a mistake, nearly costing her, her life, on at least two occasions, as he'd been told about *pink* and *green* hair. Ralph had been informed that Miss Stronglove's safety was in his hands.

The car drew up outside the safe house and Williams carried Miss Stronglove's case in; he then gave her the same equipment he'd issued to Miss Howell: Sterling sub machine pistol, the radio transmitter shaped like a brooch, and any other equipment that may prove necessary. Plus he gave her the same advice he'd given the Japanese woman, not to put herself in any immediate or undue danger.

Alice then asked where the ships were leaving from that carried consignments of food, or supplies, to *Damancas*; this was the first sensible question Williams had heard, it was evident that this Alice Stronglove didn't hang about – he then wondered if Suki Howell had even thought of that.

Then he asked himself if Alice had been, very, well briefed or she just knew what questions to ask to help solve the mystery of if there was anybody aboard the sea fort – owned by the Maxwell consortium - in the Moray Firth.

Ralph confessed he didn't know off hand but he assumed any ships would probably be going from the main port in

Inverness. Alice expressed an interest in visiting the port, just to see; Ralph informed her he would take her there after they'd eaten and she'd unpacked – he'd put Miss Stronglove in the *guest* room.

*****

In his office, in *Proagnon's* underground bunker, Mitchell Walker was fuming over the failure of the *Imam Khoemini* airport operation – they'd been defeated by HART, their mortal enemies, again. He was also angry over the overlong absence of Sandy Tulliver – she may be his superior, but Walker would dispose of her – without a second thought – if he ever got the opportunity. How could Dr Q have even considered making her his deputy?

He contacted the radio room and demanded, "Have we heard from the bitch Tulliver yet?" Many *Proagnon* soldiers knew the contempt Mitchell had for his superior.

"No sir." The operator knew this would make him even angrier, but the operator was only telling the truth.

"Dammit! Where the hell is she?"

"We don't know sir," he reported truthfully.

"When she comes back, if she even dares, I'll kill the fucking bitch!" Walker was furious at the woman who was in overall command of the terrorist organisation.

*****

Unaware of the fury of her deputy Sandy Tulliver, or as she was known to her partner Carol Turner, was busying herself shopping for the man she knew as Floyd Maxwell. Maxwell had informed her that he was going to see a friend over the river, and while he was away – he'd be gone a couple of hours; as there was – now – little food in the house Sandy was shopping; she trusted Mr Maxwell and knew he would not let her down, after all it was he who'd suggested they – the Maxwell consortium – purchase the, disused, *Damancas* sea fort. However one thing still troubled her, where did he get the money to purchase the sea fort? He wasn't a millionaire, or if he was he kept it well hidden.

CHAPTER 15

NATO!

Commander Strobing was looking through Amy Tingle's personnel file – as she'd only recently joined and had no *real* combat experience, as had been proved, unfortunately, in Iran; the file mainly held it's first page giving her basic details; as he looked through it the HART commander noted that she lived in the town of Toledo, Spain.

She was the only daughter of Mr Horace and Mrs Sally Tingle – both he assumed had left the United Kingdom once Amy had been born. She also had a brother, Peter, though it appeared that Amy knew nothing of him as she'd never mentioned him to anyone – again whether she didn't know of him, he had been killed somewhere, or he was *the black sheep of the family* Ronan wasn't certain and he could hardly ask her now. Just the recollection of her being crushed under that *Proagnon* war machine made him shudder.

Still he had a duty to inform her parents so without further ado he filled in one of the condolence telegrams, and placed it in an envelope, on which he wrote the address. Having done that he *deleted* Private Tingle's file from the computer database of the organisation's personnel – although paper files were still in use he'd begun transferring all the information they held onto the computer, as he was doing it alphabetically on surname he'd only reached the letter P; therefore Amy's information hadn't been transferred yet.

*****

Toledo was a municipality located in central Spain, and 70 kilometres south of Madrid. It was the capital of the province of Toledo and also the capital of the autonomous community of Castile-La Mancha. It was declared a World Heritage Site by UNESCO in 1986 for its extensive cultural and its monumental heritage as one of the former capitals of the Spanish Empire and the place of coexistence of Christian, Jewish and Muslim cultures. Many famous people and artists were born or lived in Toledo It was also the place of some important historic events such as the Visigothic Councils of Toledo.

*****

Elsewhere in HART headquarters Dr Hans Schaiffer was preparing the things he would need for the forthcoming medical conference – which was to be held at UHHS Memorial Hospital, in Geneva. Many top doctors – from each country – would be there, plus many friends including Charles Lighten and Ming Honda; Ming wasn't a top specialist in the treatment of viruses but he would be there in case there was a sudden influx of cases at that hospital.

The other, specialist, antibiotics he'd ordered – a week earlier – had arrived, and so he had brought out the sample of blood he'd taken from Mr Stevens many months ago, and added a drop of the serum to the Petri dish containing the infected blood, moved it to one side and began to write up notes on what he'd just done plus the name of the serum he'd used; initially he'd figured it would be just a case of a blood transfusion, basically exchanging bad blood for good, but that had been tried in a French hospital – the patient had still died though. Afterwards a sample of blood was taken and it was found that nothing had changed – the infected cells were still there.

Evidently another solution needed to be found, and this antibiotic was the only one left to try. The German medical man was growing evermore frustrated; he was, after all, one of the top specialists – if not the top specialist – in the world. Once he'd written up notes on what he'd done he left the notes on the table so he could write up the conclusion when he returned from ward duties.

When he returned to his office two hours later he began by placing the Petri dish under the microscope and examining the effect the serum had had on the contents; he was astonished at the results he found, all the infection had - totally –disappeared. He quickly wrote the conclusion down and placed the sheet of paper in a folder that he would be taking with him, and then he placed the serum in one of the overhead cupboards - in the office - and locked the cupboard door.

Dr Schaiffer exited the office with a huge smile on his face, startling his colleagues; the man exited the medical department and made his way – up the back stairs and along the fourth floor corridor – towards the main HART headquarters.

*****

Upon reaching reception he breathlessly asked the receptionist on duty – Gwyneth Jones, "Is Commander Strobing still in?"

Mrs Jones looked up from the typing she was doing, "Yes he is Dr Schaiffer, I shall *buzz* him for you, please take a seat." As good as her word she *buzzed* him via the intercom, "Commander, Dr Schaiffer is here and wishes to see you. Shall I send him in?" A few moments later the woman from Wales said to Hans, "He will see you now, I shall come with you."

"Really there is no need," HART's medical man said to her.

"Apparently the commander has a job for me." Therefore, together, they crossed to Commander Strobing's office and the receptionist knocked on the door.

*****

"Please come in," called the commander of HART. Mrs Jones and Dr Schaiffer entered the, small but compact, office, "take a seat." Both people sat down, "Now Mrs Jones," Ronan said handing her an envelope, "please see that this gets delivered promptly, and please see if you can arrange a flight to Spain's Madrid airport as I wish, with the family's permission, I have enclosed a note, to attend the funeral of Miss Tingle."

"I will see to both matters straight away, actually sir Private James Shearman has made a request for a flight to Spain. I would guess he wishes to attend the funeral, probably for reasons of his own."

*****

Madrid-*Barajas* Airport was the main international airport serving Madrid, located in Spain. It was the country's largest and busiest airport, the world's 11th busiest airport and Europe's fourth. It was opened in 1928, and had grown to be one of the most important aviation centres of Europe. It was located within the city limits of Madrid, just 9 km (5.6 mi) from the city's financial district and 13 km (8.1 mi) northeast of the Puerta del Sol, Madrid's historic centre. The airport's name derives from the adjacent district of *Barajas*, which has its own metro station on the same rail line serving the airport.

The Madrid-Barcelona air shuttle service which was also known as the *Puente Aéreo* which meant literally *Air Bridge*, and it was the world's busiest route, with the highest number of flight operations. The schedule had been reduced since February in 2008, when the Madrid–Barcelona high-speed rail line was first opened, covering the distance in 2½ hours, and it quickly became popular. Barajas served as the gateway to the Iberian peninsula from the rest of Europe and the world, and is a particularly key link between Europe and Latin America. The airport was the primary hub and maintenance base for Iberia. Consequently, Iberia was responsible for more than 60 percent of *Barajas's* traffic.

*****

"Dr Schaiffer," Ronan began, turning to the other man, "what news have you for me?" Mrs Jones got up and left the office.

"Well," began the German doctor, "as you know I have been doing much research into this – *mysterious* – virus. I have finally made a breakthrough, as you know we, or rather I, thought a simple blood transfusion would help?"

"Indeed I do," remarked Commander Strobing as Commander Celia Most entered the office. "Dr Schaiffer," said Ronan quickly, "do you object to Commander Most hearing this?"

"Not at all."

"Please proceed."

"The blood transfusion method was tried, on a patient, in France but – sadly – didn't work. However a couple of days later the patient, who had been treated, died; afterwards another blood sample was taken and it was found that the infected cells were still there."

"Is this leading somewhere?" enquired Commander Strobing, the irritation evident in his voice.

"Yes, as I say I've made a breakthrough and if you come with me to the medical department I have something to show you."

"I hope you're not wasting our time," the HART commander said.

"I assure you sir, ma'am, I am not," responded Dr Schaiffer. Both commanders rose from their seats and followed the medical man back to the HART medical department. He unlocked his office door and went inside; Commander's Strobing and Most, again, followed the German inside. "Please be seated," he said, pulling up a couple of chairs for his superiors, once they were seated he brought out a second Petri dish that was labelled Arnold Stevens. This one had remained untouched; plus he also brought out the *Ansolid* antibiotic that he'd used earlier and filled a *dropper*.

The German also brought a microscope over so his superior's could view the change in the blood. "Now as you can see the *slide* contains a drop of blood, which I took from Mr Stevens a few months ago. Please note the infected cells." Although both Ronan and Celia had done this sort of thing many years ago neither was sure what they were looking for and told Dr Schaiffer, who said, Trust me it's there. Perhaps this will make it a little clearer;" he smiled to himself as he let a drop of *Ansolid* escape from the *dropper*. The change was almost instantaneous, the blood which before had been a darker shade of red had, now, lightened considerably. "This substance has now removed all traces of the infection. I did the test earlier so I know it's worked."

"How did you manage to get hold of this *Ansolid*?" asked Commander Strobing curiously.

"Ah," began the German, "Commander Most here signed a form, on your behalf, requesting that the drug company supply me with some. You were absent, at the time, or something similar. Therefore Commander Most signed the form for me."

Commander Strobing thought back, "That must have been the morning when I overslept. Anyway these results are incredible!" He passed the *slide*, together with the microscope, over to Celia so she could study the results; Celia, like Ronan, not knowing, really, what to look for just agreed.

"Thank you Hans," the male commander said, "I shall complete the forms so this *Ansolid* can be mass produced and sent to various countries." He then rose from his chair and along with Commander Most left to return to their – normal – duties. As the two of them re-entered reception Joshua Smith called over, Commander Strobing, a telegram has arrived for you."

Ronan walked over to the main desk, "What is it Josh?" asked the man in charge; Commander Most- meanwhile - made her way back to her office.

"Sir, it is a reminder about going to make your report to NATO."

"Damn!" the commander said firmly, "I'd forgotten about that, again. When is it Josh?"

"A week today at their headquarters."

"Can a flight be arranged for me?"

"Of course sir, I'll see to it at once." Then he said, "You do realise you won't be able to attend Miss Tingle's funeral."

"I realise that. Therefore Private Shearman will have to go on his own."

"Just before I go back to my office, may I ask if Mrs Jones managed to arrange a flight for me, to Madrid in Spain?" the HART commander enquired.

Joshua Smith looked at Gwyneth Jones's report, "She did sir. You will be attending the NATO conference next week, and then a couple of days after you return Private Shearman will be flying out for Private Tingle's funeral. Apparently he had deep feelings for her."

"I see," the commander told the receptionist knowing that colleagues – at HART – did develop feelings for each other, but they never showed these feelings should it compromise an assignment they were sent on.

*****

Over in Scotland both Alice Stronglove and Ralph Williams were searching the ports in Inverness to see if they could find out if any ships had been or were destined to take supplies to the *Damancus* sea fort. However their search had yielded no results, disappointed they returned, in Mr Williams *Corolla*, to the safe house in Ardersier.

As they were driving Ralph said to his passenger, "Well that's that. Inverness would be the most obvious port to use."

"Indeed it would," agreed Alice. "Tell me, Mr Williams, do you have any contacts who work at other ports, in Scotland?"

Ralph thought hard about the question he'd just been asked, "Well," he began, "I remember when I lived just outside Fraserburgh around twenty years back I had a friend – Will Macdonald – who worked at the port of Fraserburgh, as did I – and we, often, sent supplies to the sea fort. Although I lost contact with him when I moved; I still, think I've got his telephone number somewhere back at the house; although I doubt he still works at the port I could give him a call though, ask him to snoop around if you like you wee lassie."

It was the first time Miss Stronglove had been called a lassie, and a wee one at that. "Yes I would like that; it may lead us nowhere or it could yield some results." She sat back, "If there's any jobs going on the supply ships I'll take one."

"Not so fast Miss Stronglove," Mr Williams told her as they pulled up outside the safe house, "after all as you said it may lead nowhere."

Alice looked up at HART's Scottish agent, "Okay I'll try and contain my enthusiasm, but I have a good feeling about this." Alice followed by Ralph went inside where Ralph cooked them a meal.

After dinner Ralph Williams, helped by Alice Stronglove, started the search for Will Macdonald's phone number. They searched phone directories – Ralph must have had millions of address books that they looked through, though many were empty. The two of them turned drawers out – even his clothes drawers; finally at the bottom of the man's underwear drawer – Alice was looking through that, although it was, slightly, embarrassing for her – she found an old and rather battered, blue, address book. Carefully she thumbed through the pages and there it was – Will Macdonad's address and telephone number. "Found it!" she called then, carefully, she put Mr Williams's underwear back in the drawer and replaced it; again, carrying it with care Miss Stronglove took the address book through to where the HART Scottish agent was.

*****

Commander Strobing had placed all the necessary paperwork he would need for his meeting at NATO's headquarters – which was located in Brussels, Belgium – and had packed the clothing he would need for the trip; he was due to leave two days before the meeting and return to HART the day following the meeting, during his absence Commander Celia Most would be in charge.

When the day finally came Ronan was taken to the airport – in Geneva – in an *Apollo II* vehicle driven by Ben Gillespe, who was on a day's leave from reception duties. Although the flight between the two airports was only, a mere, thirty five minutes in the Gulfstream *G550* executive jet he wanted to be able to do a bit of sightseeing before the meeting.

Once he was securely strapped in and the pilot had gained clearance for take-off, the plane built up speed and took off – rising to a ceiling height of 45,000 feet. As the plane journeyed onward towards the airport at Brussels the HART commander checked he had everything he needed; the paperwork detailing the last war against *Proagnon* and how this war was going, plus any recommendations he had for the future. Once he was sure he had everything Ronan closed the briefcase and *snapped* it shut.

After about half an hour in the air Commander Strobing was advised to fasten his safety belt as they were coming into land at the airport at Brussels.

*****

Brussels Airport was an international airport 6 NM (11 km; 6.9 mi) northeast of Brussels, Belgium. The airport was partially in Zaventem and partially in the Diegem area of Machelen.

The airport was home to around 260 companies, together directly employing 6,000 people.

In 2005, the airport was awarded Best Airport in Europe by Airports Council International/International Air Transport Association (ACI/IATA), based on a survey conducted with over 100,000 passengers worldwide.

The company operating the airport was known as *The Brussels Airport Company N.V./S.A*"; before 19 October 2006, the name was BIAC (Brussels International Airport Company).

The airport was a particularly key link between Europe and Africa.

*****

When the jet had landed, on the concrete runway, and come to a complete standstill, the staircase was lowered and Ronan Strobing exited the executive jet, carrying his suitcase. His luggage was unloaded and the commander of HART walked through the main terminal and exited the building in search of a taxi; he found one, his luggage was loaded aboard and Ronan instructed the drive to take him to the *Royal Windsor Hotel*, which was a luxury hotel which was part of the *Warwick* group – as he was the HART commander no expense had been spared.

*****

The *Royal Windsor Hotel* was elegant and very sophisticated; the hotel boasts the best location in Brussels. Just off the world-famous Grand Place and only 150 metres from the *Square* congress centre, this Brussels hotel is within easy walking distance from Brussels' Central Station, the Antique Market on the Sablon, plus the Royal Covered Galleries and Brussels' Royal Palace Gardens. Brussels' Zaventem Airport is only a 20-minute journey away.

The *Royal Windsor Hotel* Grand Place is one of Brussels best hotels ideally located whether a person is on business or simply planning a vacation in Belgium for the holidays. After a completed three-year refurbishment plan, the hotel offered guests a blend of traditional values and the latest technology to ensure a carefree stay in the heart of Brussels. Simply put, the hotel offered the very best in Belgian lodging accommodations and is the ideal place to stay during Belgium holidays.

The hotel contained 266 rooms, including 16 suites and one royal suite; the *Royal Windsor Hotel* therefore guaranteed to provide its guests with attentive and personalised service. The combination of its sheer elegance with the latest sophisticated equipment such as three telephone lines, including a free high-speed SDSL line, or wireless Internet would be certain to meet all requirements of guests whether their stay in Brussels is for business or pleasure. Each guest had free access to this Brussels hotel's Fitness Centre, which included his and hers saunas.

The Royal Windsor Hotel's Chutney's bar-restaurant was considered by many people to be the best restaurant in Brussels; it offered a diversified menu and some memorable cocktails. The *Royal Windsor Hotel* also had a piano bar and a nightclub in the hotel that stayed open until dawn. This hotel also offered 24-hour room service.

Contained within are the ideal Brussels meetings facilities, the hotel offered 15 soundproofed and air-conditioned meeting rooms that can each accommodate up to 300 people, with natural daylight, as well as a Business Centre with staff assistance.

*****

Ronan had wondered why the NATO meeting couldn't be held in the hotel, as they had an abundance of conference and meeting rooms, but he had been assured that the facilities at the headquarters of NATO offered much more; therefore the hotel was okay for staying in overnight but not for this type of meeting. Anyway, the delegates would be better protected at NATO as there would be many soldiers to guard them.

So it was next morning that Commander Strobing got ready and then took a taxi to the main headquarters building, and then he took the elevator – once he'd been searched – to the floor where the large conference room was located; again he was searched before he went into the room. He didn't like being searched but knew that the soldiers were only doing their duty.

He entered the conference chamber and looked around the conference table; there were delegates from many countries that were part of the organisation, there were some familiar faces but there were many that were not. Commander Strobing seated himself at the table and listened - patiently – as each delegate had his or her turn at speaking; each delegate had a glass of water set before them.

Finally it came to Ronan's turn to speak, he got to his feet – he'd got his paperwork out his briefcase a few moments before. He then shuffled his papers into the right order and began, "Ladies and gentlemen. As you know HART's involvement in the war against *Proagnon* began after the ill-fated peace conference in the summer of 2012 which killed many of the world's dignitaries and most influential people. This war that followed claimed many lives; indeed at HART headquarters we have a garden of remembrance where we can remember those that lay down their lives, in the first war; nearly two hundred, in total, of HART soldiers, or indeed agents, were killed. Even our illustrious commander, Peter Roberts, was killed. Of course the war claimed many *Proagnon* soldier's lives as well; our battles took us to America, Russia; basically to many different countries throughout the world."

Commander Strobing took a sip of water before continuing, "In the end the conflict took us to the Middle East, and in question the country of Iraq where *Proagnon* soldiers, together with their leader – Dr Q, who turned out to be the son of a man Commander Roberts had helped imprison many years ago – and his deputy, Sandy Tulliver, took over the *Babylonian* palace of Iraq's former, and most ruthless, leader/dictator Saddam Hussein."

"Excuse me Commander Strobing," said the, female, delegate from the Netherlands – Heidi Peters. "But can you enlighten us on how Commander Roberts met his untimely demise?"

"Certainly if you so wish although my memory of the precise events is a little patchy in places."

"Go ahead please."

"Well, as I have told you *Proagnon* were occupying the *Babylonian* palace. HART soldiers, along with Commanders Roberts, Most, Lang, Bigship and myself stormed the building and killed many enemy soldiers; we took Dr Q/Adam Barker prisoner but Sandy Tulliver seemed to evade capture - somehow, we started to escort Dr Q out when the whole building started to collapse. Luckily we all escaped – relatively unscathed – and boarded the HMMWV that was in the HART convoy outside: there were two M151 Jeeps, an old cattle truck to carry the soldiers, plus the HMMWV. As we were preparing to leave a jet appeared overhead, whether it was one of HART's or not I don't remember; also a, rather, round clergyman appeared and tried to engage the driver of our vehicle in conversation." He took a further sip of water before continuing, "As he was speaking in Arabic our driver didn't understand a word, anyway suddenly the man opened up his robes to reveal the explosives he was wearing – he pressed himself against the side of the HMMWV and the vehicle exploded and started a chain reaction. All four vehicles, in the convoy, were completely destroyed; Commanders Bigship, Most and myself were thrown from the exploding vehicles and ended up a few metres away."

"When I finally recovered from my unconscious state I looked about me to see a column of smoke rising into the sky, the convoy of vehicles were burning, the plane that had been hovering overhead had departed, and there was absolutely nobody about. I saw a body laid near to where I was, I also saw, in my peripheral vision, a figure – dressed in black – walking towards us; as the figure reached us it pointed – what I assume was – a gun at both our heads, said something and then fired. Luckily the shots missed – not by much, maybe the shooter meant to miss us."

"Forgive me Commander Strobing," Miss Peters said again, Ronan looked up. "I believe you mentioned three people were thrown clear. What happened to the third?" There were nods from the other delegates as well.

"Ah yes I will come to that. The shooter then walked away, leaving us for dead. Again I lapsed into unconsciousness, later I awoke again and detected a shuffling sound; my companion was - seemingly – awakening. The third person was laid a few metres away, seemingly dead. Groggily my companion and I contacted HART HQ, in Turkey, the radio aboard the HMMWVV still seemed relatively operational; after waiting while forces arrived to transport everyone – including the dead – back to HQ in Turkey." Ronan paused at this point to let everything he'd said sink in.

He drained his glass of water before continuing, "Now I mentioned that was the first war; now we move onto the second, and latest, war with *Proagnon*. Once we were all back at Turkey each of the dead bodies was identified, as best could be done – Commander Roberts was one of them, and so I ascended to take over from him. Everyone that had taken part in the first war was taken back to the main HART headquarters in Geneva, where we set up the garden of remembrance."

"*Proagnon*, however, seemed to have divided – we didn't know this but we believe this time they are being helped by person, or persons, unknown. There is an old, abandoned, sea fort named *Damncass* – which is located just off the northern coast of Scotland and is owned by the Maxwell consortium, which seems to have suddenly sprung to life. A short time after this a strange, and mysterious, virus started to breakout throughout the United Kingdom. We, at HART, believe this virus is being produced aboard *Damancas*."

"Then why don't you blow the bloody thing up!" shouted one of the delegates, angrily.

"We simply don't have enough intelligence for that, yet. Suppose we do blow it up and kill lots of innocent people. HART would then just be as bad as *Proagnon*. Think about it."

"Of course, yes, apologies Commander Strobing," the delegate from Slovenia answered more quietly and then re-seated himself. Ronan knew how the man felt though, the lack of action – in this matter - got to him sometimes.

"Anyway whether by design or accident this virus seems to have started spreading into Western parts of Europe. Dr Schaiffer – HART's leading medical expert – believes, after many long months – he has found a cure; therefore this antibiotic, *Ansolid* it is called – is going to be mass produced and distributed throughout the world. Admittedly this might not be soon enough for some people, but we still wish to save as many lives as possible." He paused again.

"However the main body of the *Proagnon* forces keep making random attacks throughout the world, possibly to try and divert our soldier's attention away from their main priority."

"Do you have any agents, in Scotland, investigating this sea fort?" asked another delegate, possibly the Spanish one.

"As a matter of fact we have one agent, Ralph Williamson, stationed in Ardersier. He runs the safe house over there, and I believe one of our intelligence gathering experts – Alice Stronglove – is over there as well. So when she reports back to HART," he eyed the Slovenian delegate, "we shall decide whether we need to strike or not." Commander Strobing – of HART – then sat down.

"Thank you Commander Strobing," the secretary general said and then asked, "do you have any recommendations for the future?"

The commander thought about this before replying, "Indeed I do. We, at HART, have decided to develop the *Apache* AH-64 Longbow helicopter for better battle operations; we shall begin development on the British version of this helicopter in the next month or two. Also I would like to have permission to transfer Commander Leon Bigship to take over at HART's headquarters in Turkey on the retirement of the present base commander John Craig. The two main reasons for this are that I believe since we returned from Turkey he has proven to be the weakest link. Plus he also accepted an invitation to the president of India's speech without me knowing about it; don't get me wrong it's not that I wouldn't have accepted but for him to go over my head like that I don't find that acceptable."

"If there is no other business this meeting is over," announced the secretary general. The delegates and the commander of HART rose to their feet and filed out the conference chamber, where they were searched again.

CHAPTER 16

FRASERBURGH & *DAMANCAS*!

"Hello," the voice said on the phone. The voice had a good strong Scottish accent to it.

"Hello Will," answered the voice of Ralph Williams. "It's been a long time."

"Aye it has that," Mr Macdonald said, remembering the voice of his – old – friend and the times they'd shared some twenty years ago. Then he asked somewhat suspiciously, "And what do you want with me now?"

"Can we come over to see you and all will be revealed?"

"Really Ralph," Will sounded somewhat annoyed now. "You move away all those years ago, you never contact me; then out the blue you phone me and expect me to want to see you again."

"That was the general idea," the HART agent said, "well can we?"

"We you say. Does that mean there's a Mrs Williams now?" he asked curiously.

Mr Williams looked at Alice before responding, "No there isn't. One of my work colleagues is staying with me at the moment," he emphasised the words work colleagues.

"Aye, sure you can come see me, and bring yon wee lassie with you, I still live in the same house. It'll be good to have some company."

"Thanks Will, we'll come over tomorrow. Bye for now," Ralph listened a moment longer to the response from his old friend and then replaced the receiver. He then turned to Miss Stronglove, "You'd better get packing we're going to Fraserburgh tomorrow. Alice smiled and then went off to pack a case.

"How long are we stopping for?" she called over her shoulder.

Ralph thought a moment, "Pack enough clothes for ten days, hopefully we'll be able to wrap this intelligence operation up in a day or two but you never know."

"Will do,." Mr Williams then smiled to himself, Will Macdonald would enjoy meeting Miss Stronglove; and then he – himself – went to pack a case.

The next day, around mid morning, both people loaded their suitcases Ralph's *Corolla* and once they were ready they boarded the vehicle and Ralph started the engine up. Once Alice was strapped in he set off on the, roughly, two and a half hour journey from the village of Ardersier to the port town of Fraserburgh.

*****

As they entered the outskirts of the town Mr Williams pointed out many local landmarks; there was the lighthouse museum, the heritage centre and the variety of amenities and facilities, the famous Kinnaird Head lighthouse/castle. Fraserburgh also had a variety of churches that Ralph pointed out; these included the 3 Church of Scotland congregations, these were Old Parish, South Church and West Church, the 4 Pentecostal churches, these were Elim Pentecostal, Assembly of God, Calvary Church and Emmanual Christian Fellowship; as well as these were Baptist, Roman Catholic, Episcopal, Congregational, Brethren and Bethesda Evangelical Churches plus the Salvation Army. Also the community war memorial had been built by Alexander Carrick.

Of course Alice wasn't too taken by the churches but if they were the local landmarks so be it, although she was more interested to see inside the famous Kinniard Head lighthouse/castle; something about it aroused her curiousity. Therefore she asked her guide about it.

*****

HART's Scottish agent told her that the Kinnaird Castle was built – so it was said - in 1570 by Sir Alexander Fraser, who was the eighth laird of Philorth and then it was sold to the Trustees of the Northern lights in 1787, who turned it into a lighthouse. The last to reside in the castle were John Gordon of Kinellar and his wife, Henrietta Fraser.

The original lighthouse was no longer operational, this having been replaced by a new lighthouse on an adjacent site. The Museum of Scottish Lighthouses at Kinnaird Head incorporated the original lighthouse and a modern building that housed collections of lenses and other artefacts from many of the lighthouses across Scotland.

This museum also hosts a wide range of special events throughout the year, and included a cafe and gift shop.

Located approximately fifty metres away is a small three storey tower known as *The Winetower*. It was reputed that in the cave below, one of the Fraser family imprisoned his daughter's boyfriend, leaving him to drown there. The daughter then jumped from the roof of the tower. There is red paint on the rocks below to illustrate her blood. According to local tradition, the tower was said to be haunted. Of course Ralph had never really believed this tale.

As they got nearer to the house where Will Macdonald lived the *Corolla*'s air vent system pulled in the smells of the fish being unloaded from the ships in dock; the fish gave off a pungent aroma that filled the nostrils. Ralph, having worked here, many years ago, was used to the smell, but poor Alice wasn't.

Mr Williams parked up outside 28 Aberdonian Way, and went and knocked on the door; the door was answered – a moment later – by another man who looked, slightly, older than Ralph Williams, but was a few inches shorter – at least that's what Miss Stronglove noticed but, admittedly, she couldn't see that clearly.

Another minute passed and then Mr Williams returned to the vehicle. "C'mon Alice," he said opening the car door, "come and meet Mr William Macdonald." HART's intelligence gathering expert climbed out of the passenger side and walked up the path to meet Ralph's *old* friend. As she neared him she saw that, in truth, he seemed younger than Mr Williams; he kissed her – on both cheeks – and then stood aside to allow her into the house.

"The sitting room's through there," he said and pointed; it was then Miss Stronglove noticed he had very mischievous looking black eyes. "Ralph and I'll bring yon cases and bags in, tis no work for a wee lassie."

"Sexist pig!" She had met men like this Will Macdonald before.

Will looked at her, winked and said, "That's what I like to see, a lassie with fire in her belly." Alice wasn't sure if he was just teasing her or not. It was then Ralph unloaded his *Corolla*; after letting Alice past Will went to join his friend, and – between them – they brought the luggage inside. "I've put both of you upstairs, follow me."

A while passed before both men returned; they sat down, Alice had prepared some drinks of tea for them all. "Now Ralph," began the man named Will, "what's all this about?"

"As you know, when I used to work alongside you, supply ships used to be sent to the *Damancas* sea fort located in the Moray Firth."

"Aye," said Mr Macdonald.

"Well what I, sorry we," he looked over at Miss Stronglove, "would like to know is, are supply ships still being sent from the port to this sea fort?"

"Is that all you want to know, you could've asked me that on the phone," the Scottish man blurted out. Then he added, "Aren't you gonna introduce me to yon lassie?"

"What? Oh yes sorry, Will Macdonald, Alice Stronglove."

The two of them shook hands; it was then Will apologised for being a sexist pig earlier. Alice nodded as if accepting the apology. Then Mr Macdonald turned back to Mr Williams, "In answer to your question, my friend, we still do – God knows why – there hasn't been a soul on there for months. All I know is we suddenly received this phone call and then the port authorities ordered us to begin sending supplies again."

"Don't you find that a little suspicious?" asked Will's friend.

Will simply stared and replied, "As long as I get paid for it I don't find it suspicious. I'm not paid to be suspicious of why these things happen. Though, admittedly, I was a little surprised."

"My work colleagues believe that the fort has been reactivated and there are scientists aboard working on some sort of new virus."

"Aye a new type of virus did strike Fraserburgh a few months back, doctors were baffled – people who had it died. Anyway who are these – *mysterious* - colleagues of yours? You left us rather suddenly."

"Will, what I'm about to tell you is classified," Ralph began, "but since 2010 I have worked for an organisation known as the Human Alliance for the Retaliation against Terrorism, or HART as it's more commonly known; I usually take a back seat in this organisation but I'm always *on hand* if needed. This," he gestured to the woman in the other chair, "is Miss Alice Stronglove – HART's intelligence gathering expert."

"If she's so expert," commented Will, dryly, "why did you come to me?"

"Because, "Alice replied, "as you work at the port – plus you know Mr Williams – he thought you'd be the best person to ask." Will just nodded his understanding, "Furthermore," Alice continued, "I was wondering if there are any jobs going on these supply ships, for me."

"Don't be daft lassie. All the supply *runs* have a crew, but I'll check because you never know; you might be put on one of the relief crews."

"I'm willing to try anything once," the young woman told him, and then – instantly – regretted her choice of words when Mr Macdonald grinned at her.

"I bet you will," Ralph's friend said to her.

"Really Will!" Williams said. "She's young enough to be your daughter." Then the two men idly chatted about the past; Alice felt – slightly – out of place so took her leave of them and went upstairs to unpack. When she – eventually – returned downstairs, some fifteen minutes later, she found Mr Williams sitting in the main room – on his own.

As if reading her mind Ralph looked up and said to her, “Will’s had to go to work, some emergency or other, he doesn’t know when he’ll be back so if we get hungry we’re to help ourselves.”

*****

Over in Switzerland Commander Strobing had returned from his, successful, trip to Belgium; most of his colleagues commented that he seemed in much higher spirits than when he’d left a week ago, they wondered if the NATO conference had gone – particularly - well or whether there was some other reason.

When he entered the commander’s office Commander Most looked at him to see him beaming back at her; she wondered – like everyone else – why this sudden change had come over him. Deciding to get straight to the point she simply said to him, “Okay Ronan, spill.”

“I can’t help it if I’m happy,” he replied. “I’ve just spent a pleasurable few days in Brussels.”

His response only heightened her suspicions, “Yes I noticed you were gone an extra couple of days.”

“That’s the perks of being overall commander.”

“Yes okay,” she responded, “but what I’d like to know is why?” Ronan sat down - facing her – the smile never leaving his face.

“Would you believe the conference went very well?” The look on her face told him that that answer did not satisfy her, as she knew there was more than that to it. “Okay you win,” the commander of HART sighed, feeling deflated now, “I met a delegate at the conference, the female delegate from the Netherlands – Heidi Peters was her name, and she and I spent the night together.”

“What?” demanded Mrs Most; “Ronan, don’t you realise the consequences of your actions?”

"I do," her superior answered sheepishly. "I admit it should never have happened but it did, after all we're only human." Ronan felt a bit of remorse for his hasty actions now.

Celia looked across at Commander Strobing, "Okay putting that aside, did you make any recommendations for the future of HART?"

"Indeed I did. I recommended that we be allowed to develop the *Apache* AH-64 Longbow helicopter for better battle operations; the British version of this helicopter – the Augusta Westland Apache Mk1 – will be the first to be developed over the next couple of months. Also I recommended that Commander Bigship be transferred to take over at HART's headquarters in Turkey on the retirement of the present base commander John Craig. The two main reasons for this move are that I believe that since we returned from Turkey he has proven to be a weak link. Plus he also accepted an invitation to the president of India's speech without me knowing about it; don't get me wrong it's not that I wouldn't have accepted but for him to go over my head like that I don't find that acceptable."

"I see," responded his deputy, "but Leon won't like it, sir."

"Commander Most, need I remind you who is in overall command here? If Leon doesn't like my decision he knows what he can do."

"Of course sir," Celia said. "Did anything else come out of the conference?"

"Ah yes. One of the security guards; the head security guard as a matter of fact, from Nigeria, Zimba Mandango, came to see me after the conference and requested that she be allowed to join HART."

"And you said?" Celia asked.

"I told her that she could have a week's trial here, to see if she could handle the exercise routine. Even though she assured me she could I would still like to give her a week's trial. This trial will begin next week."

Commander Most nodded her approval – though she wasn't sure she did approve – and left the commander's office.

*****

At the residence of Floyd Maxwell – in southern London – Sandy Tulliver (Carol Turner) sat alone in the house as Mr Maxwell had had to leave to attend to some business over the river. She knew she should do some grocery shopping for the two of them as there was now very little food in the house, or she could simply stay in the house and use his laptop to try and get a message to *Proagnon*; of course Mitchell Walker would be furious at her continued absence, there again he might be just furious. Her third option would be to use the laptop to try and cause more mischief – after all her computer skills were only second to her partner's.

Deciding to do the grocery shopping she went upstairs and changed into, more, everyday clothing: jeans, t-shirt, jumper and trainers; once changed she took around £60 from the wallet he kept on his bedside cabinet, she didn't expect the groceries to come to that much – with the extra she'd probably treat herself to some new clothes. Once Miss Tulliver (Turner) – she would use her alias while out – had done everything she returned downstairs, grabbed a thick coat and left the house after locking the door; she then caught a bus into the shopping centre.

Later on Miss Tulliver (Turner) returned with the groceries, and then checked her mobile phone; she had two new messages, one text and one voicemail. Both were from her partner and said basically the same thing: *I'm sorry, darling, but I'm needed at the sea 4t in Scotland so i will b away longer than I 4t, I love u & will b back soon. Fxx.*

Fine! thought Sandy, *What does he expect me to do in the meantime? Sit here and twiddle my thumbs*. She was livid.

*****

Mitchell Walker was sitting – in his office – in the *Proagnon* bunker wondering why it was that HART kept defeating them so easily then it came to him, the *Proagnon* soldiers never took, or threatened, the right hostages.

He knew that there was a medical conference coming up to discuss this virus in Britain and some European countries; apparently the HART medical man, Dr Hans Schaiffer, had discovered that the new antibiotic – *Ansolid* – could help cure those who were infected. This information had come from his Dutch contact who'd been at the NATO conference with the HART commander, Ronan Strobing.

How Walker hated that man now; if he'd realised he'd hated Commander Strobing so much before he'd have shot the commander's son, after all Ronan's wife was dead, along with his daughter, so he should've shot the son – then one day he would've shot Commander Strobing thus wiping out the bloody lot of them.

Suddenly his train of thought was interrupted by his computer informing him that he had received an email; Walker was puzzled, who could've sent the email, after all a special password was needed to access the *Proagnon* system.

Intrigued he accessed his – personal – email account. There was no subject to the message; very curious now he opened up the message and read it, it was from Sandy Tulliver; she was just letting him know that she was in England, and staying with her partner. Walker'd never heard her speak of a partner before, therefore he'd assumed there wasn't one, but now knew differently; if he could capture this man he would have some leverage over his superior, maybe force her to relinquish command of *Proagnon* and he would take over.

Going back to the medical conference Commander Strobing had – unwittingly – revealed, to his informant, that this conference was to take place at the Memorial Hospital in Geneva; therefore if a group of *Proagnon* soldiers were there they may have a chance of eliminating this Dr Schaiffer, and perhaps also threaten to kill some of the patients if their demands were not met.

*****

In Fraserburgh Will Macdonald had returned home from his *emergency*; Alice hadn't believed there was any *emergency*, she believed Will was – secretly – ferrying extra supplies to the *Damancas* sea fort. She'd raised these suspicions with Ralph Williams but he wouldn't hear a word against Mr Macdonald.

Will returned and informed them that a gear lever bearing – aboard one of the ships – had needed changing, and as he was an engineer he had been called in to change it; Miss Stronglove still didn't believe he was totally innocent. However Will looked over at her and asked, "Do you still want a job on one of the relief crews?"

"I do," responded HART's intelligence gathering expert.

"Well there's a job going as a *relief* cook's assistant. You interested?"

"Of course I am."

"Well I put your name down lassie."

"Thanks Will," she said, got up from her seat and kissed him – on the cheek – lightly. Ralph just sat there remaining quiet for the moment – obviously thinking.

"Thank you Will," he said. "I expect you had to pull a few strings."

The Scottish man sat down on a vacant chair, "Actually Williams I didn't. I looked through the crew lists and noticed there was a vacancy for a cook's assistant so I enquired about it and then put Miss Stronglove's name down." When Alice heard this she wasn't sure if she believed him, evidently Ralph Williams did.

Later on they had an evening meal of Haggis stew, the female HART agent wasn't - exactly – taken by the taste but ate it all the same. Once they'd cleared away afterwards the three of them went through to the main room and watched some television for the rest of the evening.

Finally they went upstairs to bed; each of them had a single bedroom but the bathroom was a shared affair. After a couple of teething troubles, all three of them had a good night's sleep.

*****

A few days later Mr Macdonald returned home and informed Alice that she'd got the job as *relief* cook's assistant, and as the usual cook's assistant was on shore leave starting the next week she would be required to *fill in* for him.

So it was that Alice Stronglove started work on one of the supply ships the following week. Most of the crew were men – as Alice had expected – and appreciated having her around;

there was another female aboard but as she was chief petty officer, plus a bit sour faced, therefore most of the crew did their best to avoid her. In fact some of the men began to appreciate Alice a little more than she expected, and started being suggestive towards her; in fact this got so bad that on night time *runs* she would have to lock her cabin door if she wanted any rest. Thankfully, though, most of the *runs* were done during daylight hours.

Then came the day when the supply ship was allowed to dock alongside *Damancas* and the crew, plus Miss Stronglove, were allowed to board the sea fort and stay there overnight.

When Alice went below into the main structure she looked around in awe, the area they were all in was huge. It was then that she realised she still had her HART dog tag on – the crew, plus herself – were bound to be searched; if these men were to discover her dog tag and realise what it was she would be in trouble, to the crew aboard the supply ship she'd maintained it was just a type of necklace – nobody had questioned her further.

Thankfully she wasn't searched as she was just a *mere* cook's assistant although she had caught one man's attention – although Alice didn't know it; the man, in question, was called Simon Forrestor. The reason she'd caught his attention was simply because she didn't seem to fit in; admittedly she was probably on a *relief* shift, but still she didn't seem to fit in, he was sure – almost certain – that she'd never been on board a ship before, plus her hands had no callus's on them – okay she was a cook's assistant, allegedly, yet neither did her hand's look like they'd ever done any cooking.

His suspicions were heightened when Alice branched off from the main party and started to disappear down an adjacent tunnel, hurriedly he followed her. Before she'd got too far down the tunnel he caught up with her. "Going somewhere?" he enquired.

Alice turned and looked at him in shock, whether it was shock that she'd been discovered or whether her look was genuine Simon wasn't sure. "Sorry," Alice began, "I must've gone down the wrong tunnel." Simon wasn't sure whether to believe her or not.

Deciding to give her the benefit of the doubt – for now – he said, "Come on," and led this cook's assistant back to join the main party. When the whole party entered the main room Mr Forrestor requested that the crew sit down; once everybody was seated Simon addressed them, "You are now aboard *Damancas*, one of the last remaining sea forts around Britain, the fort is owned by the Maxwell corporation who have – kindly – hired it out to us scientists, we are working to develop a new deodorant here: the reason we are working away from the mainland is because we are using specialised chemicals and equipment, and don't want any *accidents*.

Poppycock thought Miss Stronglove realising now that HART were right and they needed to destroy this fort. It was then Simon Forrestor began to speak again, "Therefore we do not want anybody," he looked directly at Alice, "wandering off and getting lost. You will each be escorted to your rooms for your stay overnight – once inside your room the door will be shut and locked – and not unlocked again until tomorrow morning. Your rooms do have adequate toileting facilities – the toilet, as well as washing facilities are located one side of your room whilst the bed is located on the other; basically each room is similar to a prison cell, the window overlooking the sea has been boarded up to prevent anybody," again his gaze fell upon Miss Stronglove, "signalling to the mainland." Alice was convinced he knew she was a spy.

Once the meeting was over the crew from the ship were taken away – in groups of three – to their quarters. Alice got up to go with them but the man named Simon Forrestor simply said, "Not you. Sit down;" the HART agent did as she was told, "I have been watching you," Simon told her, "and you do not seem to fit in with the rest of the crew." He suddenly grabbed her hands, "Manicured nails, it looks like you've never done a day's work in your young life – therefore you appear to be a mystery," and then more firmly he said, "Come, I shall – personally - show you to your quarters;" plus to emphasise this he produced – from the inside pocket of his laboratory coat – a Walther *PPS* semiautomatic pistol, he pointed the weapon at her and said, "Move!"

Alice was led to her, prison cell, room; Forrestor forced her inside, shut and locked the door, luckily Alice had also been trained as a lock picker and was now quite an expert. Still just to keep up the pretence she undressed and climbed into bed and placed her hair clip on the side for later use. Managing to keep awake she waited until all was quiet and then climbed out of bed, slipped into her underwear – she was still wearing her HART dog tag – and set to work on the lock.

After several failed attempts the lock finally clicked open, peeking outside Alice saw nobody in the corridor. She'd noticed the radio room as Forrestor was forcing her to her quarters and intended to use it to try and radio the mainland, try and get the information she'd discovered to Will Macdonald so he could pass it along to Ralph Williams who would pass it on to HART.

The floor was cold to her bare feet as she padded along the corridor – as quietly as she could - towards her destination. Alice entered the radio room but didn't close the door, there were a couple of workbenches, in the room, and the – large – radio transmitter was set on the far wall; Miss Stronglove tried to figure out how to use the radio, once she felt she'd got an open channel she spoke into the microphone: "*Hello, hello, hello. Damancas calling Fraserburgh port, come in please.*"

Somehow she'd got the radio working properly as a voice said: "*Fraserburgh port to Damancas. Your signal is strong.*"

"I wish to pass on information that needs to be passed on to Will Macdonald."

"What is your message please?"

Before Alice could start her message a shot was fired from behind her, the bullet smashed into the radio. Alice turned to see the figure of Simon Forrester framed in the doorway; he stepped inside the room, pointing his Walther pistol at her; steadily he walked towards her. "I knew you didn't fit in, let's have a closer look at you," he walked right up to her, Alice felt very exposed – and it wasn't just through her lack of clothes, and grabbed her dog tag, "Hmm," he murmured, examining it more closely, "HART agent Alice Stronglove, I'm afraid – my dear – that you must be eliminated. Prepare to die," and he raised the pistol until it was pointed directly at her.

Alice Stronglove looked into the blackness of the barrel as he prepared to fire.

CHAPTER 17

SAVED & BETRAYAL!

As Forrestor lined up Alice – in the gun sights – when there was a knock on the door, "Sir," a voice called, "are you okay?" Momentarily distracted Simon lowered the pistol, as he did so Miss Stronglove rushed him.

Cannoning into him he fell backward, "Oof," Simon groaned as the wind was knocked out of him and he fell to the ground. As he fell he dropped the weapon he'd been carrying which the HART agent, gratefully, snatched up. The door opened and a *Proagnon* scientist was framed - in the entrance. The scientist raised his hands, in surrender, as the HART agent levelled the weapon at him.

"Let me past," Alice snarled – as best she could; "remember who's got the gun," she pushed past him and then shoved the second scientist into the room; he crashed into his superior and they both fell in a heap on the stone floor. Miss Stronglove slammed the door shut, just before the door was fully shut she called inside, "My name may be Stronglove but my love is too strong for either of you to handle."

With that cheeky comment she let the door shut fully and returned to her own room, and retired to her bed after relocking her door. Alice knew she hadn't – actually – achieved what she'd set out to do but, after all, she'd become slightly distracted.

In the morning the crew were let out their rooms and everybody ate a hearty breakfast of porridge Simon Forrestor eyed Miss Stronglove warily; as he was not, officially, a member of *Proagnon* he wasn't sure how far his authority extended. Admittedly he was chief scientist but there were also a few *Proagnon* soldiers aboard and they were the only ones with any *real* firepower. Did Simon have the authority to order them to kill her?

As they ate Simon looked across at the water vessel's cook and asked, "If you were to lose your assistant would you miss her?"

The cook looked across at Miss Stronglove and smiled, "To be honest with you Dr Forrestor I don't think I would." Alice had anticipated this and – luckily – written down her findings; sealed them in an envelope addressed to Will Macdonald; she'd also written that he should pass the information onto Ralph Williams, and then she'd passed the envelope to the chief petty officer earlier that morning.

Looking first at the cook and then across at Simon Forrestor she simply said, "I don't mind." This was a sudden change as the chief scientist had expected Alice to want to get away as fast as she could; yet here she was, practically admitting she wanted to stay. Why was this?

So later on that morning, the crew of the supply ship were escorted back to their vessel while Dr Forrestor led Miss Alice Stronglove to his personal quarters. As they were walking down yet another featureless corridor – on their journey – Alice said, "I may be an enemy of *Proagnon* with me being a member of HART but I'm curious as to know what you are doing here."

Simon didn't answer straight away but simply said, "I am not a member of *Proagnon* so you are not my enemy, I merely work alongside them anyway I have my own agenda." They reached his quarters then, "Come inside and I will tell you everything," he said in a pleasant voice. Alice hesitated, "What have you to fear?" the chief scientist asked her; the HART agent shook her head and entered the room, Forrestor entered after her, shut and locked the door.

This action immediately alarmed Miss Stronglove, "What are you doing that for?" she asked hurriedly.

"So we won't be disturbed," he answered calmly; this alarmed Alice even more. "Sit down Alice," so she seated herself on the edge of the bed.

He sat down beside her; "Now Alice," he began, "I was encouraged to help in this project by a Mr Floyd Maxwell – who runs the consortium that owns this sea fort, along with his business partner Miss Carol Turner, however to prove myself I had to inject this new virus into my wife. With me being a doctor I was convinced I would be able to cure her, but I injected her as instructed and about an hour later she died." He paused as the memories came back to him, "Anyway," he carried on, "I did everything as instructed and was brought here aboard a helicopter to begin work on this new strain of virus." He paused again, as if expecting Miss Stronglove to say something but she didn't "However when I realised that *Proagnon* were utterly ruthless I ordered a consignment of underwater mines be transported from the mainland; once they arrived I managed to slip away and attach them to the underneath of the fort, there are ten in all."

"Why are you telling me all this?" queried the HART agent somewhat curiously

"Simple," he replied, turning to face her, "I want you to know what's in store for you after I leave."

"What the hell do you mean?"

"Just this," and he pushed her onto the bed, Alice hit her head on something hard and fell unconscious; when she awoke she found herself strapped to the bed with rope, Simon stood leering at her. "Dumb bitch," he spat, "I trust you've sent a message to HART – may they all rot in hell – and when they act on the information and attack *Damancas*, probably blow the bloody thing out the Moray Firth – I shall be long gone." Alice knew then that she should never have trusted him, even for an instant.

"But what about the mines?"

"I shall detonate them by remote control, once I am far enough away, and help destroy this fort and everybody aboard it." Simon then slammed the door shut, locked it, and then got his wetsuit and a yellow dinghy – a rope was tied to it. Changing into the wetsuit – in front of her; he opened his room window that overlooked the sea and dropped the dinghy; it inflated and plopped quietly into the water below, once he was ready he said, "Goodbye Miss Stronglove. I won't say it's been a pleasure because it hasn't." Just before he left he placed a gag over her mouth to prevent her from crying out.

"Pig!" she spat through the material – at least it sounded like pig - as he turned and climbed down to the dinghy – which was attached via the rope to one of the steel rungs he was now climbing down. Once in the dinghy he attached an outboard motor to the rear of the sea vehicle, untied the rope and let it drop – harmlessly into the sea; Forrestor started the motor and raced away back to the mainland. There he intended to stay in his old friend's cottage, in Cawdor

*****

Cawdor was a village and parish in the region of Nairn which is in the Highland council area in Scotland. The village was situated 5 miles south west of Nairn, and 12 miles from the town of Inverness.

*****

The message Alice Stronglove had passed to the ship's petty officer had been passed to Will Macdonald who – knowing it was meant for Mr Williams – had placed it in his jacket pocket and begun his daily work; when the time for leaving came he changed out his overalls into his civilian clothes and, checking the envelope was still in his pocket, left to return home, he only lived a few streets away so he was one of the more reliable workers. Upon reaching home he passed the envelope, still sealed, over to Ralph Williams.

Ralph recognised Miss Stronglove's handwriting straight away and tore open the envelope; inside was a folded - single - sheet of paper which Ralph unfold quickly, "She's done it

Will!" he said enthusiastically. "Now may I use your telephone?"

"Of course you may," his friend said politely, "it is just through there, in the hallway." Ralph wandered through to the hallway and located the telephone.

He picked the receiver up and dialled the number that would connect him to the international operator; when the connection was answered he simply said, "HART headquarters please." He heard a noise behind him and assumed Mr Macdonald had come into the hallway, he was right.

"Just connecting you now sir," the operator's voice replied. The phone rung and then Williams heard a click behind him. He turned to see Macdonald pointing a pistol at him and sighed. "Come away from the phone Ralph or I kill you."

Williams stared at the gun, "Why Will?"

"I am also in the pay of *Proagnon* now, they knew about your involvement with HART and our friendship, and requested that I keep any busybodies away from prying too deep into *Damancas*."

Just then the phone – at the other end - was answered, "Hello," said Hanna Strong's voice.

"Hanna, tell Commander Strobing we were right about *Damancas* and to take the necessary action."

"I'm so sorry Ralph," muttered Will and pulled the trigger. The bullet entered Williams back – as he'd turned back to the phone; Ralph gasped, in surprise, and dropped the receiver, and then he collapsed to the floor, dead. Will replaced the phone handset, looked down at the body of his friend and kicked him, "You wouldn't listen Williams – you never did – and now you've paid the price."

*****

At HART headquarters, in Geneva, Hanna Strong heard the noise of the gunshot and then Ralph Williams strangled gasp, the receiver must've either fallen or been taken off him because a moment later somebody replaced the handset.

Realising what she'd heard was of vital importance she committed everything to memory and strode off to Commander

Strobing's office. Politely she knocked on the door and entered when instructed to, the commander was just wishing Dr Schaiffer good luck for the conference as the man was leaving that afternoon. "Good day commander, doctor," the receptionist said.

"Good day Miss Strong," answered the commander, he then turned to Schaiffer, "I hope your counterparts see sense."

"Thank you sir, I'm sure they will," with that he exited the office.

"Now Miss Strong, "what is your news?"

"We have just received a phone call from overseas, from our Scottish agent – Ralph Williams, he said and I quote 'tell Commander Strobing we were right about *Damancas* and to take the necessary action.'" Hanna's superior fell silent for a moment. "Also sir, Miss Zimba Mandango will be arriving tomorrow."

"Thank you Hanna, I will see you in a bit."

"Right you are sir." She wasn't sure what he meant; once the receptionist had gone he summoned his two deputies to his office and relayed the message to them, they both listened and then Leon spoke, "Well that's it, we can organise an all out attack on the fort."

"Yes," responded Ronan, "but one thing still worries me."

"And that is?" enquired Mrs Most.

"Why haven't we heard from Alice Stronglove. Miss Strong only mentioned Ralph Williams."

"She may have been captured, or even worse dead," ventured Commander Bigship sadly. "I'll admit it is very strange."

"Still we can't worry about it now. I'll contact RAF Lossiemouth tomorrow – have their fleet of Westland AH1 *Apache* helicopters readied for action. We shall send about twenty HART soldiers over there aboard a *Hercules* and then attack that damned fort." Commander Strobing then announced, "I will fly over to lead the attack personally, please don't try and stop me – either of you – as my mind is made up; now

Commander Most, would you deputise for me as I am retiring to my residence."

"Certainly commander, may I wish you a peaceful rest." Commander Strobing then left the office and met Hanna Strong, just leaving reception, "Hello sir, I didn't expect to see you so soon."

"I just felt like retiring to my residence early, do you want to walk with me?"

"If you want me to, I'll even come and have dinner with you if you so wish," the commander smiled in acceptance. "I've just got to go to the *ladies* sir, won't be a minute." So Commander Strobing sat – on a seat – and waited; when the receptionist returned, after about five minutes, she'd changed out of her work clothes and was now wearing her *tarty* clothes; Hanna had a long coat over the top but Ronan assumed she was wearing her *tarty* clothes. "Shall we go sir;" the two of them linked arms and left the building.

As they were walking across to the residence buildings Commander Strobing asked a passing soldier, "Did Dr Schaiffer get off alright?"

"Yes sir," the soldier replied and then looked at the two of them, his superior smiled and he and the receptionist carried on walking; they reached Ronan's residence and went inside, "Please make yourself at home," he said and he led her into the main room. "May I take your coat?"

"Sure," she answered, slipping it off; Ronan had been right, she was wearing some *tarty* clothes. Sighing to himself he took her coat and hung it up, and then returned to the main room and Hanna Strong.

He found, upon entering the room that Hanna had stretched herself out on the sofa but was propped up on one elbow; a couple of buttons – at the top of her blouse shirt – were undone, whether this was deliberate or not he wasn't certain. "Hanna," he began, uncertain where to begin, "you are a fine figure of a woman and a good receptionist. However, if you keep trying to seduce me – which I'm pretty certain you are -

then I will have no option but to terminate your employment here."

"Yes sir, my apologies sir."

"Furthermore Miss Strong, would you mind taking your shoes off the furniture." The receptionist swung her legs down and removed her shoes, and then for good measure removed her socks – she didn't wear stockings like Mrs Jones, said they brought her legs out in a rash though she had tried wearing stockings once or twice – then replaced her feet on the sofa. "Thank you Hanna."

Ronan then got them both a drink; of course he had his usual whisky while he got Miss Strong a drink of orange – as she didn't drink alcohol.

*****

Simon Forrestor powered his dinghy through the water until he reached the shores of mainland Scotland. He climbed out of the little, yellow, craft, deflated it and then carried it across to a small cave; once inside he stripped off his wetsuit and changed back into his doctor's clothes – which he'd brought across in a plastic bag. He placed his wetsuit and the deflated dinghy – once he'd folded it up into the bag and exited the cave, as he stood there surveying the scene he thought mischievously *I could detonate the explosive devices now, blow Damancas up with everyone aboard and save HART the bother, but I want to kill as many as possible.*

Forrestor then climbed the old and well worn, stone, steps up to the main headland; there he walked to the side of a road and put his thumb out to thumb a lift. Several cars passed him – not stopping – and then a rather battered looking Ford *Focus* passed him and slowed, it pulled over about a hundred yards ahead and Simon ran to it. He opened the passenger door, the driver of the vehicle was a big man with a hairy red beard, "Get in," he said; Simon knew that beggars couldn't be choosers and climbed inside. "Where you going mate?" asked the bearded man as the doctor buckled himself in.

"Cawdor," he answered, "one of my patients is sick." He placed the bag containing his belongings in the back.

The driver – as they pulled away – said, "I see you weren't expecting to be called out." He'd, evidently, seen what was in the plastic bag.

"No I wasn't," the other man answered, "I sometimes go out in my dinghy and wetsuit, but always take my mobile phone – just in case."

"Right you are sir," responded the big man; evidently Simon's answer had satisfied his curiosity. They drove on to the outskirts of Cawdor. "This okay?" queried the bearded man.

"Couldn't you take me a little further into the village?" asked the doctor; the man answered he would and drove Simon into the centre of the village. Forrestor thanked him, collected his belongings and exited the car.

As the *Focus* drove away Simon Forrestor began walking in the direction of his friend's cottage. Upon reaching it he ventured inside; there was a log fire roaring away and in one chair sat the owner of the dwelling, Paul Pearman. "Well Dr Forrestor?"

"Everything was going like clockwork, my dear Paul, until that HART bitch Stronglove turned up."

"I had to help Ralph Williams, another HART agent, but unfortunately he found out too much and I had to persuade one of my other agents to eliminate him." Simon sat down. "Did you deal with Miss Stronglove?"

"I tied her – tightly – to the bed in my quarters, aboard *Damancas* and then made my escape."

*****

Simon and Paul had known each other for about thirty years. They knew each other as Simon, and his late wife Rebecca, had often holidayed up in Scotland – particularly the village of Ardersier - where they had met Mr Pearman; they'd got chatting and found out that Paul, along with his brother Grant, owned this small cottage just outside Cawdor.

The Pearman brothers had rented their cottage out to the Forrestor couple whenever they stayed in Scotland; when Paul Pearman had found out that a certain Dr Forrestor was working aboard *Damancas*, which belonged to the Maxwell consortium, he had sent a message to Simon with one of the seamen aboard a supply ship offering Simon the use of this cottage whenever the good doctor came back to shore.

On one such occasion Paul had suggested placing underwater mines under the structure – just in case things went wrong for *Proagnon*. However, it seemed now that Grant – who was also in on the plot – had *mysteriously* disappeared, Simon wondered why. "Paul. I hope you don't mind me asking but where's Grant?"

Paul's face seemed to drain of colour as he replied, "He's dead! Killed by another of those accursed HART bastards, a foreign one at that, HART sent another agent over – before Christmas to find out information on *Damancas*. I introduced her to my brother, on the pretence that he could give her the information she sought; I told him to deal with her and so the fool went and raped her. I didn't know what to do; unwittingly, he was never big in the brain department, he had forced me into a corner."

He paused and then continued, "I, often, took Ralph Williams to see her, but then her father arrived – evidently Suki – that was her name – found a way to tell her father what had happened. Ralph Williams then asked me to set up a meeting between this foreign bastard and my brother; I had no idea what her father wanted – he was only small so I surmised if it was revenge he was after Grant could easily deal with him. I fixed up the meeting and went out for an hour or two, when I returned I found Grant lying in a pool of blood - he'd been killed by a sword, I think. Yet of the foreigner there was no sign. Therefore I assume he did this dastardly deed."

"Quite so," replied the doctor. "Tell me who killed Williams for you?"

"Ah," replied Mr Pearman, "I used one of his oldest friends – Will Macdonald. Apparently Macdonald received a phone call from Williams, who asked if he and a colleague could stay with Will. Knowing this had to be something to do with *Damancas* he phoned me asking what he should do. I told him to let Ralph, when he had the information, pass this onto

HART headquarters and then eliminate him. Actually I received a call from him about fifteen minutes ago informing me the job had been done."

*****

Next morning – at Commander Ronan Strobing's residence he awoke to find Hanna Strong lying next to him; *Not again*, he thought, his mind going back to the first night he'd spent with Lucy Lang and the regret he'd felt then – however, this time he didn't have a wife. As he watched her she – lazily – opened her eyes, "Good morning darling," she muttered, sat up and kissed him. Ronan climbed out of bed and, hastily, began to dress; "Come back to bed," she urged as she saw what he was doing.

"No," he responded, rather brusquely, and then almost snapped at her, "if you still want a job be downstairs in ten minutes."

"But Commander Strobing?"

"Ten minutes!" and he stormed down to the kitchen to prepare breakfast; about eight minutes later Miss Strong came hurtling down the stairs to join him in the kitchen.

"What was all that about upstairs?" she demanded hotly.

"I'm sorry Hanna it's just that every woman I've been with: my wife, my lover, my colleague, your predecessor – something bad has always happened to them. Face it, I'm a jinx."

"No you're not Ronan," the receptionist replied, put her arms round him and kissed him. They ate their breakfast quietly – for some reason the commander couldn't remember anything about the previous evening after he'd eaten the meal Miss Strong had prepared for them.

When he was ready he set off across to the main headquarters building – telling Miss Strong that he would phone when the coast was clear – once inside he journeyed up to reception to find an irate Gwyneth Jones rushing about and a tall, black, girl waiting in reception, he recognised the girl as Zimba Mandango. "She's late," said Mrs Jones hurriedly, "that Hanna woman, wouldn't surprise me if she's been entertaining a man friend." Ronan had to smile to himself.

"This way Miss Mandango," and he walked towards his office.

"Thank you sir," she said as she got up and followed him.

"Mrs Jones," he called over his shoulder, "please can you arrange a meeting of all, and I mean all, HART personnel in the conference room at eleven?"

"Yes sir, trust Hanna to be late today."

Commander Strobing, followed by the black girl, entered his office. "Pull up a chair, Zimba, and explain why you want to join HART." Miss Mandango explained everything she thought was relevant.

The HART commander listened intently and then said to her, "We have a big operation coming up and I would like you to be part of it if you want to. That is what the conference is about."

"I'll be there," she responded and knowing this meeting was over got up to leave. As she walked away Ronan admired the tallness of her, plus the way she held herself. Once she'd gone he rang his residence, using his office phone, and informed the latest receptionist that the coast would be clear at about quarter past eleven. She replied that she understood.

At eleven prompt all the HART soldiers, team leaders, commanders and reception staff met in the conference room. Commander Strobing walked in carrying a file, "Please be seated," he said, when everyone was seated he took his place at the head of the table. "Now as some of you know Alice Stronglove – HART's intelligence gathering expert – has been assigned to Scotland, to investigate the possible link between *Proagnon* and the sea fort *Damancas*. She managed to get a message back to us – by unknown methods but via a phone call from Ralph Williams – informing us that what we suspected is true, and we should mount a full scale assault as soon as we can. Then, according to Hanna Strong," he saw Gwyneth Jones look dubious, "she heard a gunshot and then the line went dead; I shall be contacting the base commander at RAF Lossiemouth once this conference is over – to inform him of our impending arrival."

He stopped and looked at the sea of faces around him, "The reason I have called this conference is to decide who will be going on this operation. Commanders Bigship and Most, plus the reception staff are free to go at this point as none of you will be going along." Once they'd left the room the commander looked round again, "I need nineteen people as I will be going as well; are there any volunteers?" Hands shot in the air, Ronan looked around, "Right, 1 - Ronan Strobing, 2 - Zimba Mandango, 3 - James Shearman, 4 - Dave Newbend, 5 - Samantha Goldsmith, 6 - Larry Sanders, 7 - Mary Bishop, 8 - Harry Jones, 9 - Paul Todden, 10 - Alan Fitzgerald, 11 - Dean Whiteman, 12 - Oliver Banks, 13 - Simon Hawks, 14 - Kevin Limpton, 15 - Barry Tompkins, 16 - Charles Manton, 17 - Ryan Silverton, 18 - Fred Deanman, 19 - Chris Sutton, 20 – Nigel Hargood."

Once he'd written the last name down he looked up at them, "This mission won't be an easy one, in fact I'd be lying if I told you that we'd all return alive because chances are we won't. If any of you wish to change your mind you may." Nobody moved, "Well," their commander said "in that case I thank you all for volunteering."

*****

Dr Hans Schaiffer had arrived at the UUHS Memorial Hospital the previous day for the conference. There were many friends there as well as some new faces; among the doctors present were Charles Lighten from England, Ming Honda from Switzerland, Juan Canton from Spain, Pierre Holstey from France and many others. However Hans knew the doctor from Germany very well, it was his own son Heinz Schaiffer – Heinz was to replace Hans - at HART – when he retired, which was not that far away.

"Gentlemen," the elder Schaiffer began. "Each of our countries has felt the effect of this new, mysterious, virus; however the effects seem mainly focused on Britain, so I will hand you over to Dr Charles Lighten."

"Thank you Dr Schaiffer, as you've already been told the virus is mainly affecting Britain though the effects have been felt in the more western fringes of Europe. I still have in my care

- at Hull hospital – the man who first caught this virus, well a strain of it, a Mr Arnold Stevens. When I say he is still in my care I mean his condition hasn't improved, yet it hasn't deteriorated either, it is as if he is in a comatose state." Dr Lighten sat down as Dr Hans Schaiffer got to his feet.

"Thank you Dr Lighten, now since this virus first came to HART's attention, Mr Stevens is Commander Strobing's father-in-law, I have put in many hours work trying to find a cure, but nothing I tried worked. I believe Dr Holstey that a blood transfusion – which I thought might work – was carried out on an infected patient, yet they still died?"

"That is correct Dr Schaiffer," answered the French doctor.

"Well I tried further combinations of antibiotics but all to no avail," everyone looked crestfallen, "that is until I heard of a new antibiotic called *Ansolid*." They all looked up again, "and this time it worked. The results were almost instantaneous."

The window Hans had his back to faced the window of a disused warehouse, Dr Canton stood to say something – he was seated opposite the doctor from HART. Some instinct made Dr Schaiffer dive to his left and a shot rang out hitting Dr Canton who fell, blood coming from a wound in his chest; it was then that Dr Schaiffer realised that bullet had quite probably been meant for him. As the Spanish doctor lay there Hans shot round the table, "Hold on in there my Spanish friend."

"I fear my time is up," Juan replied pathetically, a moment later his head fell to one side and he lay still, he was dead.

*****

Once the sniper had seen one of the men, in the medical room, fall he had raced down the stairs inside the warehouse, exited the building and crossed to a *silver* Mercedes van – which was parked just outside the hospital grounds. "Job done," he told the other three who were waiting for his return, and the van started off. What the shooter forgot to tell the others was that he wasn't certain whether or not it was Hans Schaiffer who he'd shot – all foreign doctors looked alike to him.

CHAPTER 18

HART: ATTACK!

The C-130 *Hercules* that would carry the sixteen male and the three female HART soldiers, plus their overall commander, from HART's main headquarters, just outside Geneva, to fly to RAF Lossiemouth in Scotland; in addition to the plane being prepared the HART operatives were also readying themselves by donning their *Kevlar II* body armour and their takedown uniforms, along with utility belt which contained their grenades – two smoke, two *flashbang*., and two ordinaries.

Also each soldier would be armed with a Beretta M12 submachine gun plus a Beretta 8000 *Cougar* semiautomatic pistol. Alan Fitzgerald – who had, temporarily, replaced Shinto Howell as major – carried the TAC-SAT, in his *Kevlar II* lined backpack as he was he had now replaced the, diminutive, Japanese man as major of HART. However, Ronan would be taking his 9000S pistol instead of the M12 submachine gun.

The plan – when they got there was to use the MK 1 *Apaches* to attack the sea fort – thus distracting the men aboard - whilst the HART soldiers flew over in the base's squad of five *Blackhawk* helicopters, slid down the zip-wires and entered *Damancas* by the main staircase; once down they would only kill the men aboard if fired upon first. James Shearman, along with Zimba Mandango, had also been assigned with the task of finding and recovering Alice Stronglove.

Once all the nineteen soldiers – plus the HART commander – were properly kitted out and ready they made their way across to the C-130 *Hercules* transport aircraft, which had just been brought out its hangar – by a tug vehicle, for the long journey to the Royal Air Force station in Scotland. When all personnel were aboard Commander Strobing revealed the battle plan for their forthcoming mission.

While Commander Strobing was away Commander Bigship would be in charge, this was because Ronan didn't want to be seen to be favouring Celia over Leon all the time, plus it would be good to have a new face at the helm – so to speak.

The *Hercules*, once everyone was seated, and strapped in, went through the standard pre-flight checks; the pilots then started the great four Allison T56-A-15 turboprop engines and began the – standard - take-off procedure; slowly the aircraft rose into the air to begin the two and three quarter hour journey to RAF Lossiemouth.

*****

Dr Hans Schaiffer – along with the other doctors at the medical conference – had been shaken by the death of their Spanish colleague, Dr Schaiffer even more so as he knew the bullet had probably been meant for him; Heinz was trying to comfort his father – as best he could – he led Hans into a side room while the main conference room was cleared. It was there where Hans broke down and confessed to his son that he believed that bullet had been meant for him – somebody had, evidently, betrayed the anti terrorist organisation, and Dr Schaiffer (senior) intended to find out who before he, finally, retired.

He suddenly looked up and asked his son, "How's your mother?" Hans and Helga Schaiffer had separated when he had joined HART; luckily Heinz had already been a junior medical doctor so it had not affected him that much.

"Oh she's okay, she still misses you Dad, but – I think – there's a new man in her life," Hans's son responded. Hans had guessed there was probably a man on the scene, just to fill the gap he'd left; he was pretty sure that this wasn't a permanent arrangement. At least he hoped it wasn't.

"Do you miss me not being around?" Hans knew his son had – probably – anticipated this question, but knew his father had to ask it nonetheless.

"Not as much as I used to," was the answer he got. "You see Dad I have become, very, friendly with one of the female junior doctors called Olga. We're thinking of taking things further, and – possibly - marrying." This response shocked

Hans, he knew things had to move on but now it appeared his own son didn't need him anymore. The young German saw the look of dismay on the older man's face, and quickly said, "I'm sorry Dad, I'll always love you but life goes on."

The older man smiled across at his son, "Yes, I suppose you're right," and then Hans and Heinz hugged. "I've missed out on so much, in your life; I hope you forgive me."

"Of course I do Dad," and father and son embraced again. The two medical men then gathered their briefcases up, and departed - from the hospital – with the others.

*****

In the cottage owned – solely now - by Paul Pearman, outside Cawdor, there was another knock on the door. "Expecting someone?" Simon asked Paul

"No. Nobody," his host answered, "still better see who it is," and he walked, slowly, over to see who was at the door; standing outside was a rather bedraggled looking Will Macdonald. "Will, what a pleasant surprise. Do come in," though Simon detected sarcasm in his host's voice.

Will walked inside carrying a duffel bag, evidently he was planning on staying. "Will," said Paul as Simon Forrestor walked over to join them, "may I introduce you to Doctor Simon Forrestor; he's been working aboard *Damancas*." He then turned to Simon, "Simon, may I introduce Will Macdonald," the two men shook hands.

"Will," said Mr Pearman as Dr Forrestor re-seated himself, "what brings you here?" The two men seated themselves as Will explained that since he'd killed Ralph Williams he'd felt that he wanted to get away from Fraserburgh until the police search died down; he knew Mr Pearman owned this cottage and so had come here, plus he'd been surprised to find lights on in this – out of the way - dwelling.

Just then they all heard an aircraft fly overhead, it sounded very large; their host and owner of the cottage crossed to the window, seeing it was a *Hercules* transport aircraft Paul turned to the others and simply said, "It looks like HART have arrived." Both of the other men were over, in a flash. "It seems they are heading for Lossiemouth and – quite probably – the RAF base," continued Paul.

"I have a little surprise for them on *Damancas*, one they will never forget," Dr Forrestor told his two companions; when asked what he had lined up Simon refused to tell them. Mr Macdonald then prepared the three of them a lunch of Haggis, potatoes, vegetables and gravy – all three of them ate heartily and then washed the meal down with some traditional Scotch malt whisky.

A couple of hours later they were sat doing a jigsaw puzzle when they heard the low drone of a helicopter; Forrestor got up from his seat and told the others, "Time for me to leave, I think."

"Why?" asked Will and Paul, both were astonished at Simon's, sudden, strange behaviour.

"You'll see," answered the doctor. "Now Paul, is there anywhere I can view all the main action from?"

Paul Pearman and Simon Forrestor exited the cottage, and Paul led his friend to a piece of the mainland from where he could get a good view of *Damancas*. The helicopters he identified as MK 1 *Apaches* combined with four, what looked like or very similar to, *Blackhawk* personnel carrying helicopters. "Have you everything you need?" asked Mr Pearman.

"I think so," was the answer; Simon then felt his pockets – his remote control was in one, and a pistol and mobile phone in the other. "Yes I do," he confirmed, "I'll call you when I'm ready."

"Okay," answered Simon's friend and started to make his way back to the cottage he owned.

*****

Commander Strobing had elected to stay behind at the Royal Air Force base – not because he was scared but he just felt that, for some reason, this mission would end in tragedy. Admittedly if he was killed in action Commander Most would take the helm as commander of HART, and she'd, probably, do a bloody good job; but, after all, Ronan was the present commander and if - for whatever reason – he had misgivings about a mission he didn't have to go.

*****

In the commander's office, at HART headquarters, the STU-8 warbled. Leon Bigship – who had been left in charge – answered it, knowing that whoever was on the other end was one of the select few who could call this office direct. "Hello," he said into the mouthpiece.

There was a thirty second delay as the signal was first encoded then decoded at the other end – this delay, supposedly, meant that hackers couldn't listen in.

"Hello Commander Bigship," said a male voice, "Commander John Craig here," the voice announced. Then he asked, "Is Commander Strobing there?"

"I'm afraid he isn't John, he's on a mission in Scotland. Is there anything I can do for you?"

"I'm not sure," answered John, "I just wanted to know if he's got a replacement commander for the HART headquarters in Turkey yet."

Leon studied some paperwork Ronan had left behind, "He has got a replacement for you lined up, John, but he doesn't say who it is. I'll query him about it when he returns."

"Right you are, thank you Leon, goodbye."

"See you John." There was a click at the other end as Commander Craig replaced his handset so Leon did the same.

It was then that there came a banging on the office door, "Come in," bellowed Commander Bigship, the door flew open and an irate Dr Schaiffer burst in, slamming the door behind him. "What's up?" Leon asked but he could see something had unsettled the German.

"They're after me! They tried to assassinate me at the conference!" was the hurried answer.

The commander looked at the frightened man, and then reasserting his authority said, "Sit down and relax, have a drink of water and then tell me all about it." He got the doctor a glass of water and once he was calm Dr Schaiffer explained to Leon everything that had occurred at the medical conference.

Once Hans had come to the end of his story Commander Bigship asked, "And who do you believe *they* are?" It was a pretty obvious question, and the answer didn't surprise him.

"I believe," announced the HART medical man, "that the gunman was a *Proagnon* agent – and the only reason I can think of is – somehow – *Proagnon* have found out about this *Ansolid*."

"Maybe so, but how did they find out? You believe there's a traitor within our ranks."

Dr Schaiffer had considered this fact, "Maybe not among our ranks, it could be somebody close to this organisation, or perhaps somebody one of us has been in contact with."

"But my dear Hans, when we join HART we are all made to sign the official secrets act."

Again Dr Schaiffer had considered this fact, "True, but we may still tell a high ranking government official." He leaned back and smiled, knowing he had scored a point. The question was now how Leon would react upon hearing the doctor's next statement. "Like somebody on the United Nations security council."

"Commander Strobing did attend the January meeting, and I'll admit he, probably, got friendly with one or two of the delegates. I believe we should get Commander Most in here," he then summoned her using the intercom. When she entered Leon invited her to sit down; she pulled up a chair so she was facing him, and then Commander Bigship got straight to the point, "What – exactly – did Commander Strobing tell you happened at the UN security council meeting?"

"He just made his report and recommendations, listened to what the other delegates had to say, and then everybody left the council chamber; he was approached by Zimba Mandango, who requested a job at HART."

"I don't think she would betray us to *Proagnon*," Leon told Dr Schaiffer. "Did he say what went on later?" he asked Celia.

Celia thought about this and smiled, should she tell them? Yes, she decided. "He did tell me that he'd got a little drunk and spent the night with Heidi Peters, the Dutch delegate, why?"

"Ma'am," Dr Schaiffer began, "when I was at the medical conference I believe somebody tried to assassinate me; the reason I believe was because *Proagnon* had found out about *Ansolid*. Commander Bigship, along with myself believe that somebody, maybe on the UN security council, has betrayed this organisation."

"I do see your point," conceded Celia Most, after careful consideration, "but we can't, really, go accusing delegates without knowing all the facts. This Heidi Peters may be totally innocent." After more discussion both Commander Most, along with Dr Schaiffer, left the room.

*****

Aboard the Victorian sea fort, in the Moray Firth, the first the assembled group of *Proagnon* scientists, plus the small group of armed soldiers, knew of the attack by the airborne war machines was when a missile from one of the four *Apaches*, a standard *Hellfire* missile thudded into the platform above their heads, and the lights flickered. "We are under attack," screamed one of the men.

"Calm down," growled one of the armed soldiers, "nothing can harm us down here. Get on with your work." Not feeling that reassured but seeing that none of the other scientists were panicking he carried on working. A second missile struck then a third and a fourth. "I suppose we'd better see what's going on," said the soldier who'd growled at the scientist. He was the group's leader, "You two," he indicated two other soldiers, "with me, while you," he indicated the youngest of the group, "stay here and guard them."

The younger man nodded whilst the other three raced in the direction of the stairs; although all the scientists had been issued with handguns nothing could be left to chance. Suddenly from above came the screams of dying men and the sounds of machine gun fire, the younger man ran across to the stairwell and shouted up, "Is everything okay up there?" His words were met with…silence; just then several *thuds* were heard from up above.

On the helipad nineteen soldiers were donning their gas masks as instructed to by their leader, Major Alan Fitzgerald. Once everybody – in the group of HART soldiers had donned their masks the major threw a couple of smoke grenades down the stairs, into the lower levels, as soon as he'd thrown the grenades down the soldiers began their slow descent – their M12 carbines at the ready, "Remember," Fitzgerald said into the helmets built in radio, "don't fire unless they fire first." As this was *standard* HART policy all the soldiers understood this.

As the soldiers rounded the bottom of the stairwell they came under fire – it wasn't heavy fire, just shots in the dark; despite the randomness of the fire four of the HART team went down, these were Mary Bishop, Simon Hawks, Chris Sutton, plus Harry Jones, whether this was due to being shot or just a stumble Major Fitzgerald wasn't sure – he soon got his answer when he saw the blood on their uniforms. "Bastards!" Alan shouted and returned fire, his bullets finding three of the scientists.

Suddenly Zimba Mandango and James Shearman shot past the main group and down a side tunnel, Fitzgerald knew what was happening, that these two had been asked to locate and rescue, if they could, the organisation's intelligence gathering expert.

*****

Simon Forrestor - just - stood watching, on the mainland, as the helicopters gathered around *Damancas* and the soldiers from HART descended into the sea fort; he placed his hand around the remote control and extracted it from his pocket. He looked at it, *Just a few moments longer*, he thought, *and then HART, plus Proagnon, are in for one hell of a surprise*.

*****

Back aboard the sea fort the fighting continued as more gunfire was exchanged between the two opposing forces; meanwhile Miss Mandango, followed by Mr Shearman, was racing down the corridor of closed doors, "Miss Stronglove," she shouted, "Alice!"

"She's in here," announced James, halting outside one of the doors, "I'm sure I heard a muffled cry."

"Try again," Zimba said, coming back to him; James called her name again and, again, heard a muffled response from inside – the black woman tried the door, it was locked.

"Stand back," James told her and kicked at the wooden door, it splintered, *Must be because it's an old door*, he thought, "C'mon Zimba, give us a hand." Zimba Mandango took her uniform tunic off, revealing the white T-shirt underneath, and dropped the tunic top on the floor.

Ignoring the look James gave her she said, "Right, let's get started," and she hammered her shoulder against the door, after about two minutes the locked door flew open to reveal Alice Stronglove – bound to the bed, and gagged. There was a breeze, in the room, as the window had been left open. Alice was mumbling, something, rapidly through the gag.

"What's that Alice?" asked Private Shearman. Suddenly there came a rumbling from underneath them.

By that time James had removed Alice's gag, "There's a bomb underneath us, several bombs. Save yourselves." Alice looked at them both as if telling them to hurry up and go. "Leave me," she said to them, "I got myself into this mess, now I must face the consequences of my misguided actions."

"She's right," Zimba said, "c'mon James."

"You heartless bitch! You can go – if you like – but I'm going to do my best to help a fellow comrade." Miss Mandango, totally unemotional, climbed up to the open window, peered outside, and jumped. Back inside Mr Shearman was unfastening Alice's bonds as fast as he could.

*****

On the mainland Simon judged it was time and detonated the explosive devices; as he watched there was a gigantic explosion and the fort exploded, killing everybody aboard. The flames from the explosion rose into the sky and downed seven of the eight helicopters – the one *Apache* not caught by the flames began to *limp* home, it had been at the outermost fringes of the explosion and had only been *licked* by the flames but hadn't been downed.

Dr Forrestor watched the destruction of the structure, no emotion showed on his face, and then sat on the ground to wait; he produced his own pistol from his pocket, just in case. He watched the sole remaining airborne war machine *limp* back to base – it was no threat anymore.

It was then that he heard a noise coming from the waters below; he looked down and saw Zimba Mandango as she swam back to the, rough shingle, beach at the base of the cliff. Smiling evilly to himself he crouched down and waited – he phoned Paul and Will as he was waiting and asked them to meet him, with a vehicle, at this point.

After about ten minutes Zimba began to appear over the cliff top – Simon kept out of view until she was on the top; he noticed she'd removed her T-shirt exposing the flesh beneath. "Which way to go now," she murmured to herself.

"Not so fast sweetheart," announced the doctor, coming out of hiding and pointing the pistol - he was carrying - directly at her. "Now be a good girl and walk towards me." Zimba, knowing this man meant business, slowly walked over towards him, as she moved Simon moved behind her and placed one arm round her throat and placed the pistol barrel against her head with the other. "My friends will be here soon and then we're going on a, nice, long journey."

"Who the fuck are you?" the black woman demanded to know.

"That's no way for a lady to speak," Simon said. "Still you're no lady you're just a bloody member of that pathetic organisation known as HART." Suddenly he noticed she was shivering, "What's wrong my pretty one?"

"Well," began Zimba, "I'm wet, I'm cold; at least let me put my T-shirt back on. Please?" Just then the Toyota *Corolla* that had once belonged to Ralph Williams rolled up, Paul Pearman and Will Macdonald climbed out the vehicle.

"Tis another wee lassie," said Will. "Prettier than ta last un." Both Paul and Simon just looked at him agog, as if he were mentally impaired. "What?" he demanded.

"Nothing," the others answered; Simon spoke up, "This woman belongs to HART so we have a captive. Now, the question is, what shall we do with her?" he asked nobody in particular.

He then answered his own question he pointed the weapon he was holding at Miss Mandango and snarled, "Get in the car bitch!" Reluctantly and at gunpoint she made her way over to the Toyota. "You two as well," said Forrestor. All three men and one woman – practically half naked – boarded the *Corolla* and they began the short distance to the cottage outside Cawdor that was owned by Mr Pearman.

When they reached their destination the four people exited the car, Paul and Will went inside; Simon forced Zimba in by pushing the barrel of his Walther pistol into her back; once they were all inside the owner slammed and locked the door, "Now what do we do with her?" asked the good doctor – still pointing his gun at the black girl.

"Lock her up," said Mr Macdonald simply.

Dr Forrestor considered this, "Yes we will, but first my dear," he said addressing Zimba, "would you like to take a bath and clean yourself up?"

The black woman considered this, why was this man – it was obvious he wasn't a friend – being so kind to her. She decided to press her advantage, if she had one, "I think I would, after swimming from *Damancas* to the mainland I think I deserve it; plus it'll give my clothing chance to dry out."

Paul Pearman, who was watching this exchange, suddenly snapped, "Cut the speeches. She is your prisoner Simon, if anything happens you will be held responsible." Forrestor nodded to show he understood and then led Miss Mandango to the bathroom. Pushing her – roughly – inside he slammed and locked the door behind them.

Zimba suddenly became fearful, "What are you doing?" she asked. Simon told her to shut up as she was wasting time and just get a bath. "With you in the room?" she queried.

"Don't worry I've seen it all before," he answered. Still unsure about this Zimba ran the bath, took off what was left of her clothes and climbed in the bath to have a soak; she was aware of Forrestor watching her every move but she didn't really care anymore.

Afterwards she dressed feeling completely refreshed, and then the man that had been guarding against her escape led her – at gunpoint again – back into the, main, dwelling interior. "Where the hell should I lock her up?" he asked his host.

"In here," answered his host – opening a door that led into an extra bedroom. "I have prepared the *guest* room for her. In you go," and he pushed HART operative Zimba Mandango into the room and closed the door then locked it. "She'll be secure in there, she can't escape – the only window in there is reinforced. Grant and I changed everything when we bought the place." With that Simon and Will sat at the table for their evening meal, Paul Pearman told them he would be eating in his bedroom – with that he disappeared into a darkened recess.

*****

At RAF Lossiemouth Commander Strobing awaited news of the nineteen men, and women, that had come on this mission; he'd seen, and heard, a rather large explosion and assumed that *Damancas* had been destroyed, yet there was no sign of the HART soldiers. Just then a radar contact was picked up on the scanner – it must be a helicopter, assumed the commander of the anti terrorist organisation, but which sort was it and why was it moving so slowly? All would be revealed when it landed.

Slowly, almost painfully, Ronan watched as the airborne vehicle came inexorably closer – Commander Strobing then left the radar room and went outside to greet the crew of the helicopter, and any passengers aboard; he saw – with the assistance of some binoculars - that it was a MK1 *Apache*, it looked damaged though; he watched as it finally came in to land, and then rushed over to the crew; he pulled open the door and – shouted - he had to shout over the engine and rotor noise, "Where is everyone?"

"They're all dead!" the pilot shouted back simply, "They were all aboard the sea fort when it blew."

"Surely you're mistaken," Ronan said but he knew, deep down, that what he'd been told wasn't a mistake – he probably just didn't want to believe it.

"No mistake sir," the pilot told the HART commander as he unbuckled himself. "I'm sorry. My companion thought he saw somebody in the water, but it could just as easily have been a piece of debris, and we didn't have the fuel aboard to check. Sorry."

Commander Strobing just fell to his knees and cried, "No!" Then the tears started to flow.

*****

The next morning, at the cottage, Simon Forrestor and Will Macdonald woke and got up – they dressed and went and had some porridge, Simon went and roused Miss Mandango; yet of Mr Pearman there was no sign.

"Let's get her to the car," Simon told Will. The previous evening all three men had decided that their next move should be to travel south.

"Right you are," Mr Macdonald answered. It was then that a shot was fired.

CHAPTER 19

THE FINAL MISSION & HOSTAGE!

Zimba Mandango screamed as Will Macdonald suddenly pitched face first onto the floor, the 9mm bullet smashing into his skull; from a darkened recess – in the wall – Paul Pearman stepped forward, the barrel on the Walther *PPS* pistol smoking. "Shut her up Forrestor or I'll put a hole in you."

Simon pressed the hypodermic he'd taken from his lab coat pocket into Zimba's neck; almost immediately – though he did note there was some resistance – she fell limp, in his arms, slowly he let her slide to the floor – unconscious. It was then Simon asked his host, "Why did you kill him?"

The answer shocked him, "I hated him," announced Mr Pearman, totally without emotion, "I tolerated Mr Macdonald, I even let him think he was useful. However, now his use is at an end, as we are leaving, I decided to dispose of him – permanently." Then Paul looked at Simon, "In case you haven't already guessed, I have my own agenda." Simon realised now – fully – why he'd killed Will Macdonald. "Let's get her aboard and go."

"You mean you're coming with me?" asked Dr Forrestor somewhat surprised.

"Of course I am," Paul responded as if the doctor was stupid. "I want to get away from this hell hole." He could see his friend was slightly shocked, "The cottage will be dealt with when we leave; as I told you earlier I have my own agenda."

Simon knew he probably shouldn't ask but did anyway, "Which is?"

"I think my employer, Floyd Maxwell, and I ought to have a little talk, that's if I can find him." Dr Forrestor suddenly realised he'd heard that name before – now where had it been, had he met this man? It seemed possible but also it seemed highly unlikely; still Simon was certain he knew the name. Seeing this look Mr Pearman enquired, "And what's up with you?"

"Nothing," answered the doctor, suddenly coming back to reality, "just a vague recollection." Then he followed up by saying, "Best not worry about it now, let's just get her aboard the *Corolla*;" so between them they carried Zimba's body outside to the waiting vehicle – opened the rear passenger door and placed her across the back seats.

"How long will her induced state of unconsciousness last?" Pearman wanted to know.

"Oh, several hours yet," answered Forrestor, glad to have scored a point against the elder Pearman brother – in fact the only brother left. "So she poses no – real – danger to us. I see our bags are already in the car so we can go when we're ready."

"That we can," responded his host, "I've just got to go back and get something, you wait here;" Simon waited – patiently – and after about five minutes Mr Pearman returned carrying a box of matches, and a crumpled piece of paper. "Okay, when I say go, go." Paul then lit the paper, pushed it through the letterbox and then rushed to the motor vehicle – getting in the passenger seat he almost shouted at Forrestor, "Go!"

Simon pulled away as fast as he could, noting the urgency in the owner's voice. They heard an explosion behind them and saw flames reach into the sky; momentarily stopping the vehicle the two men both turned and saw the cottage – or rather what was left of it – burning away. "Well that's that," remarked Simon, "where to first?"

"I think we'll make for Carlisle for a start, we shall stay overnight there and continue our journey in the morning." So they began the five and three quarter hour journey to the Carlisle Southwaite Travelodge, arriving at about five pm.

*****

At HART's main headquarters Commander Strobing was seated in his office, writing out a report on what had gone on in Scotland; laid on the desk before him were twenty crosses to remind him of the nineteen soldiers that had been lost, plus an extra one for Alice Stronglove who he'd also thought had been aboard the sea fort. He intended to plant the crosses in the garden of remembrance once he'd written his report and filled in the slips informing the member of personnel's family that they had been killed in action.

As he was writing there came a knock on the office door, "Come in," announced Ronan without looking up.

The door opened and Commander Leon Bigship walked in, "Sir," he said.

"Sit down Leon," the overall commander of HART replied in a, rather, deadpan voice. Leon pulled up a seat and sat opposite his superior.

"Sir," he began, "I don't pretend to know what went on in Scotland because you just won't talk about it. For the past few days since your return you have shut yourself away, either in here or in your residence, not speaking to anyone about it. Enough is enough I – for one – would like to know what went on."

Ronan stopped typing, closed his laptop computer and looked straight at his *old* friend. "All the soldiers that went with me are now dead, blown up aboard *Damancas*; I made a grave error of judgement, in fact I should've gone with them but figured that they'd be okay – it was a simple enough mission, find and retrieve Alice Stronglove, kill anybody who stood in our way and then get the hell out of there – evidently somebody had some other ideas."

"It wasn't your fault sir they knew the risks when they joined the HARTorganisation."

"Maybe they did, Leon, but I still feel partly responsible," said the HART commander. Leon knew the commander of HART was responsible for the welfare of the soldiers - under his command – but if they chose to place themselves in danger, and subsequently got killed, that was their own fault. "Anyway," Commander Strobing continued, "what has happened while I've been away?"

"Well sir," began Commander Bigship, "Commander Craig called to ask if I knew if you'd got somebody to replace him."

"And you said?"

"I told him I believed you'd got a replacement lined up but didn't know who it was. Was I right?"

Ronan smiled, "You were, in fact – you might as well know – I have decided to replace him with you; give you more responsibility etc."

Leon almost exploded, "In a dead end country like Turkey? Sounds more like a demotion rather than a promotion."

"Look at it this way," his superior said, "you'd be closer to the main *Proagnon* base; our first line of defence if you like. Anyway, you're going and that's an end to it. Any other news?"

"Yes sir. Dr Schaiffer returned from the medical conference a, very, frightened man. It seems that whilst he was there somebody, unknown, tried to assassinate him. He thinks it was because we knew about *Ansolid* and its ability to cure this virus."

"Did he say who he thought it was?" the superior commander asked.

"Commander Most and I had a talk with him, and Dr Schaiffer thinks it was probably a *Proagnon* agent. He also thinks - although this is pure speculation you understand – that somebody from the UN conference passed the information to *Proagnon*."

"Impossible!" exclaimed Commander Strobing, "The only person I – really – discussed that with was Heidi Peters, the Dutch delegate, when we were in bed."

"And you don't think she might have passed the information on?" persisted Leon.

"Certainly not," snapped his superior, "I am very particular who I share a bed with. However, I will admit that, I found her lovemaking rather vigorous "

"Okay," replied Commander Bigship, only too aware of his superior's temper. It was only too evident, when somebody disagreed with him. "But if we do find out it was her then you will have some serious explaining to do, like, why did you tell her – in such detail – in the first place."

"I know the procedure," remarked Commander Strobing tersely, "anyway I mentioned *Ansolid* to all the delegates, and the breakthrough it could give us." Ronan then heard a *bleep* come from the computer so he opened it up to see what the noise was. "Oh heck," he muttered when he saw what it was. "In three days time we fly out to India to protect their latest president as he gives his speech, A mission which you agreed to without asking me, not that I'd have said *no* but it would've been nice to be asked."

"I apologise for my oversight sir, anyway who's going?" Leon enquired.

Ronan called up the list, on his computer; "Let me see," "Ah yes, all three of the HART commanders and around seven of the soldiers; yes I know, only a small group so as not to arouse too much speculation as to why we're there. We shall pose as people on business and arrive a couple of days before the speech is due to be given and we'll leave once President Akhbar is back, safely, in the custody of his private bodyguards."

"Who'll be in charge while the three of us are away?"

"Yes I was wondering that as well," said a voice from the doorway; both Commander Bigship and Commander Strobing looked in that direction to see the figure off Commander Celia Most, how long had she been standing there? "Well sir, who will be in charge in our absence?"

Ronan looked at them both, "I'm going to ask our receptionist, Joshua Smith. Are there any objections?" The other two shook their heads. "Right, that's settled then, you two go and pack what you think you will need for the trip whilst I go and ask Mr Smith."

The other two left and Ronan followed them out; he went and asked Joshua as he'd just come on shift, Joshua agreed to *hold the fort* while the others were away, "We shouldn't be any longer than three days – at the most," explained the HART commander and then he followed the other commanders from the building.

He was walking in the direction of his residence when he heard a noise behind him; pulling the Beretta 8000 *Cougar* from inside his tunic pocket and ensuring it was loaded he swung round to face behind him. A startled looking Hanna Strong was revealed to be approaching him. "Well, well, well," murmured the HART commander, replacing the semiautomatic pistol back inside the pocket of his tunic, after first making sure the *safety* was back on. "Miss Strong," he said as she caught up, "what can I do for you?"

"It's more what I can do for you sir. I know you're going away for a couple of days, so I've come to offer to help you pack."

"There's really no need," Ronan said, but knew that Hanna wouldn't accept *no* as an answer so he relented. "Okay then, follow me," he sighed.

"With pleasure," she said – Ronan wasn't sure if she was being cheeky or not, but decided to say nothing. So followed by Hanna he carried on to his, private, residence.

Once inside Hanna started up the stairs, "Wait a moment," her superior said, "who told you, you could go up there?"

"Nobody," she responded, "I just assumed all the stuff was upstairs." Commander Strobing knew she – really – wanted to go upstairs for a, completely, different reason, but he didn't want that. He led her upstairs and into the – main – bedroom, he got his suitcase out the wardrobe whilst Miss Strong – as she'd been here before – produced items of clothing, from his chest of drawers, and held them up so he could say *yes* or *no*. Commander Strobing wasn't – ecstatically – happy with a woman finding him clothing to wear on this trip, but figured it was a good thing to have a woman's opinion; after all he wasn't exactly up on fashion these days, it was more a woman thing. Finally he got his business suit out of the wardrobe and laid it across his bed. "There we are. My thanks to you Miss Strong."

"It's been a pleasure," she replied and than added, somewhat cheekily Ronan thought, "there's not many men would allow me to rifle through their drawers." Despite whatever misgivings the commander had about Hanna Strong he smiled across at her. The two of them then left the superior officer's residence; while Miss Strong started back towards headquarters Ronan turned and walked over to Commander Bigship's residence, he had some *bridges to mend* with his colleague. Noting he wasn't following her she looked back and called, "Are you coming?"

"I'll be along shortly," the commander called back. "I've just got to see Commander Bigship."

"Okay," and Hanna continued in the direction she had been walking. Once he had prepared himself for what might be ahead he knocked on the door; after a few moments Leon answered the door, when he saw who was outside he invited his superior in straightaway.

"What can I do for you sir?" asked the older man as he led the other into the main room where they both found seats to sit on.

"Leon," began the superior officer, "I feel that our friendship has become –somewhat – *strained* over the last couple of months, and I believe I know why." Leon just sat there and listened to the – overall – HART commander.

Finally he said, "I admit it has, tell me why you think that is?"

Now it was the commander's turn to act surprised, "You admit there is a problem. I think it has to do with me reposting you to Turkey, would I be right?"

"Yes sir you would," answered his colleague. "It's just really shocked me, just because I answered that email."

"That, I suppose, is one reason but as I've explained I see it as giving you more authority, a headquarters you can be in full command of. I admit I'll still be in command of you but it would be your headquarters and I'd interfere, if you want to put it that way, as little as possible; admittedly it'd be a new challenge but I hope you can rise to it."

"Is that it sir, what if I don't want to go?"

"Then I shall have to order you – as your commanding officer – to go, and I don't really want to do that," responded Ronan, and then asked, "So what do you say?"

"I'll go," answered Leon and then added, "might give me chance to top up my sun tan, get bits brown I don't normally get brown." He smiled at his superior's look of horror.

"Leon!" exclaimed Ronan, "This isn't meant to be a holiday, although I see nothing against it when you're off duty, but remember work comes first."

"I will sir, but to see the look on your face – it was a picture." Both men smiled at each other and then Commander Strobing left, happy in the knowledge that the two men had managed to mend their *strained* friendship. As he walked back to headquarters he caught up with Commander Most and told her what had gone on.

She looked at him, "So things have worked out for the best after all. I wish things would work out for me."

"I'm sure they will Celia," he said as they wandered inside. "Once this mission is over and I've tied up a few other loose ends we shall have a months break from this place, go on holiday if you like – how about it, just you and me like the old days – that is if your husband has succumbed to this virus."

"I'll go, on one condition."

"Name it," her superior said as they crossed reception; he was in a much happier mood now, she noted.

"'I'll go if you bring Simon along, and I get to choose our destination."

"That's two conditions."

"I know," answered Celia. "Take it or leave it."

"That's fine," announced Ronan, "as long as you don't pick Russia." With a grin they went into their, separate offices. "Now," Commander Strobing mused to himself, opening up his laptop and switching it on, "where were we?"

*****

At the *Proagnon* bunker Mitchell Walker had selected the squad that were to fly to India and would, hopefully, eliminate President Ali Akhbar – whilst he was delivering his speech in

Agra. Unlike the HART soldiers the, terrorist, assassination squad would pose as tourists on holiday; whilst there they would be staying at the Hotel Mughal. So about five days before the date of the speech the four man squad carrying suitcases for their stay – and smaller briefcases containing sniper rifles, dressed as tourists, made their way from the underground bunker to Tehran's *Imam Khoemini* Airport.

In one of the men's suitcases was the uniform from the dead HART captain, Teresa Robins, however the name had now been changed to Robert Marx.

They were booked in on the *Nippon Airways* Boeing 747-F flight to the *Indra Gandhi* International airport in Delhi; a journey that would take approximately three hours maybe a little less. From there the four men would travel the one hundred and ninety five mile journey to Agra *CANTT* railway station aboard the intercity express train; stopping at the stations at H Nizamuddin, Okhla, Tuglakabad, Faridabad and Faridabad New Town, Ballabgarh, Asaoti, Palwal, Hodal, Kosi Kalan, Chata, Mathura Join, Farah Town, Raja Ki Mandi, before finally arriving four and a half hours later at Agra *CANTT*.

The four man assassination squad flew out of Tehran's airport at about nine thirty in the morning on that morning; each knew that, as they would arrive at approximately twelve thirty, they would have a spare five hours before boarding their train. So it was that at around a quarter past five – that evening – they boarded the train that would take them to their final destination of Agra, and then they would find a taxi to take them to the Hotel Mughal.

At last they reached Agra *CANTT* station and found a line of taxis waiting outside. The leader of the squad chose the third taxi from the front and asked if the driver if he could take them to the hotel where the four men were staying.

The driver said – in perfect English, which surprised the men, "I will be only too glad to take you, and your companions, to the hotel of which you speak – for a mere 120 Rupees." The men loaded their luggage – assisted by the driver – into the rear compartment of the taxi and then climbed aboard the vehicle.

The four then passed around the sandwiches which they'd purchased – with the help of a knife, killing the owner instantly – from the *Comesum* food court inside the station.

As they drove on the driver explained about his upbringing in Agra and how he'd come to be a taxi driver; the men listened, taking none of this information in. Finally they reached their hotel – the men from *Proagnon* very thankful as they didn't have to listen to anymore of this man's prattling – they couldn't stand much more anyway. "That'll be 120 Rupees please unless you prepaid at the station which I didn't see you do."

"Rot in hell," said the group's leader, rather gruffly, and then produced the *bloodied* knife and stabbed the driver – leaving him to slide, gently, down the side of his taxicab. As it was getting late there was nobody about except a few drunks.

*****

At the Carlisle Southwaite Travelodge Dr Simon Forrestor, along with Paul Pearman, rose from their night's sleep – they'd left Zimba Mandango in the back of the *Corolla* – alive but heavily sedated; the two men grabbed a, light, breakfast and a drink, went to toilet, and then went out to their vehicle – Zimba Mandango was still laid across the back seats – totally unconscious – the only sign she was still alive was the rise and fall of her chest. "Get in and give her some more, we don't want her waking up on the journey."

"I fear I've sedated her enough already."

"Just do it!" snarled Paul, producing his Walther *PPS* pistol and pointing it at Simon.

"Okay, okay," replied his companion producing a hypodermic from inside his laboratory coat pocket, he stretched inside the car, leant across Miss Mandango and then injected her – in the top of the arm – with the hypodermic. He then looked back at Paul, "There, happy now?"

"Perfectly," answered Pearman and climbed in the driver's seat. "Get in if you're coming!" Meekly Forrestor climbed in the passenger seat and fastened his seatbelt; they then began on the rest of their journey to the *John Groggins* hospital in Norwich. About six and a half hours later the *Corolla* pulled into the hospital's parking lot – Simon was glad to see his, trusty, Renault *Megane* was still there.

They pulled to a standstill, "What now?" Simon wanted to know.

"Simple," Paul responded, "you go in, grab a wheelchair and then you wheel her," he indicated Zimba, "inside. I will follow you." Forrestor, reluctantly, fetched a wheelchair from inside and helped Mr Pearman to transfer the, unconscious, form of Zimba Mandango into the wheelchair.

"Now what?" he demanded to know.

"You wheel her in and take her down to your laboratory. I shall follow – as her concerned partner, but don't forget I shall be holding a gun on you all the time so don't think of trying anything."

"Don't worry I won't," replied Dr Forrestor and began to wheel Zimba inside. As he wheeled her to the lift he said to any nurse - or doctor - who stopped him, "I'm taking this patient, to my office, to perform a few tests on her, which her partner will confirm, as she suddenly fell ill at home." Pearman confirmed this story.

The three of them went down to the level, in the hospital, where Dr Forrestor had his office. They entered the office, Paul closing the door behind them. "Now where is this laboratory?" he wanted to know.

Simon pressed a button – situated behind a medical chart – and the bookcase, at the back of the room, slid back revealing another lift, "My laboratory is under the hospital. Shall we go?"

"Yes," was the answer Paul gave and Simon wheeled the chair into the second lift, closely followed by Pearman and the lift descended into the bowels of the medical building. The lift stopped and they got out – Paul Pearman looked around him, dominating the main area - of the room – was a, large, rectangular, table surrounded by several chairs, along the two side walls was an array of computer systems, and on the farthest wall was what looked like a set of manacles – for both arms and legs – set into the rock wall. "My God Simon, you've certainly been busy."

"I'm glad you appreciate it; it's taken me three years to put everything together. Now let's take her over to the manacles."

*****

The HART soldiers, plus their three commanders arrived at Agra Air Force Station – which doubled as the airport of Agra – aboard a Gulfstream *G550*. They had used their own pilot, Dan Marshall, who had filed a flight plan to their destination, but had never – fully – declared it to the, civilian, flight authorities. They were greeted by businessmen from India, who took them to waiting transport, a bus that would ferry them to and from the Taj Mahal.

President Akhbar, so the superior HART commander learnt, was staying at The *Royal* hotel, in the presidential suite. On its journey the bus passed through the main market of the city, "Here is where our president will make his speech."

"Why here," Ronan asked their guide, "and not Delhi?"

"The president is a simple man he was brought up in Agra, and therefore feels safest delivering his speech here. It is only his maiden speech, as he is only a mere thirty years old he could be delivering speeches, here and elsewhere in India, for the next, say, forty years or longer."

"Agreed," Commander Strobing said and then asked, "the thing is why does he want security from HART, wouldn't his own – private – bodyguards suffice?"

The Indian considered the question, "Normally yes," he answered, "however as I say it is his maiden speech, and so he felt that an outside organisation be brought in for his protection; of course his own bodyguards will be *lurking* in the shadows."

As long as they're the only ones lurking in the shadows, Ronan thought to himself and then asked their guide, "Yes I can understand now why he wants an outside organisation to protect him but why HART?"

"HART are meant to be the best there is, anyway our own army, as are many others, is woefully understaffed due to cuts in our defence budget." The bus, finally, arrived at the Taj Mahal and the team from HART departed to find the rooms where they would be staying.

All the rooms were single rooms but the three commanders had marginally larger rooms than the soldiers. During the days leading up to the speech the HART group explored the main sights in and around Agra such as Agra Fort and various tombs, as well as other buildings.

The day of the speech dawned hot and bright and the HART group were up early; admittedly the speech wasn't due to be given until the afternoon so that gave them a little more time for sightseeing. The afternoon arrived and the personnel from HART found themselves vantage points, among the crowd and in the surrounding buildings, so they would – hopefully – spot any signs of trouble; each soldier had been issued with a two way radio so they could keep in contact with each other.

At just before two pm the three HART commanders emerged into the market square with a, reasonably, tall Indian man of some importance, this was denoted by the jewel encrusted rings, and the robes, he was wearing, this was President Ali Akhbar. He was then led across the square to a stage that had been set up to deliver his speech to the crowd that had gathered there; he stood and spoke into the microphone, "Ladies and gentleman, I am President Akhbar – the latest ruler of this country. I became president when our last president, President Sungi Sinitra, was brutally murdered a few months back whoever did this terrible deed still remains a mystery. As some of you know I was born and raised in this city so that is why I am giving my first speech here instead of in Delhi, I moved into politics at the age of twenty three and have for the last four years served in President Sinitra's government."

Suddenly Commander Most looked up at one of the buildings – she didn't know why – and caught a *flash* of some sort; she guessed it may be a telescopic sight on a rifle and was just leaning over to tell Commander Strobing when a shot rang out.

*****

In his underground laboratory Simon Forrestor and Paul Pearman had attached the clamps, on the manacles, around Zimba Mandango'sa rms and legs – thus fastening her to the wall; as she was still sedated she just flopped forward – her outer tunic had been removed leaving her chest covered by her vest like garment exposing her arms, also her boots and socks had been removed to prevent her kicking them with her feet. "What you going to do with her now?" Pearman demanded to know as the doctor placed the key to the restraining clamps on top of one of the computer workstations – Zimba would be able to see it but not reach it, however much she tried.

Producing a bag from under the table he produced from it a machine with wires attached to it, on the ends of the two wires were tiny metallic clamps. The main machine had a dial and many assorted buttons on it; next he produced a hypodermic needle with a syringe attached, the syringe had an *orange* liquid in it, the needle was new so it was still in its clear *sterile* wrapper. "When she regains consciousness I intend to ask her to divulge the information so I can contact HART headquarters."

"If she refuses to talk what do you do then?"

"I attach, with your help, each of these - minute - clamps to each wrist and then select a setting, and turn the dial. She will, slowly, be wracked by pain; the more our Miss Mandango refuses the more pain I shall inflict."

"She'll die before she tells you," commented Paul, a trace of dry wit in his voice.

"I have thought of that," replied Simon, "therefore I intend to push her to *red* level 5, if she still won't talk I intend to inject her with this truth serum."

Paul looked at him in amazement, "You've thought of everything haven't you?"

"I like to be prepared," said Dr Forrestor dryly. "When I learn the number of HART I intend to contact and inform them that Zimba Mandango is still alive and if they want her back they must send their *accursed* commander – I assume there is one – to come and fetch her."

"And you intend to hand her back, just like that. You've got a screw loose."

"No my dear Paul, I intend to inject her with a – more – concentrated version of the virus we've used; I was working on it aboard *Damancas*, my own secret project; before her commander's eyes, and she'll die – quite quickly I should imagine."

"That's brilliant!" Pearman enthused, "you think of everything."

"I try to," sniffed Dr Forrestor. "There are two single bedrooms down here as well."

*****

In Agra President Akhbar fell to the floor, a bullet wound in his head; one of the bodyguards called the emergency services whilst the other stepped forward, "What happened?" he demanded to know.

"Your president has just been shot, an assassination attempt I believe."

Just then the dying president started to murmur something; the bodyguard bent his head lower, "Go ahead sir;" he listened for a minute then looked up at Commander Strobing, "He wants to speak to you."

Ronan bent his head lower, "Yes sir."

He had to listen carefully as the words sounded like that of an old man – not that of a man so young, "My time is up in this world, you are a good man so I hope you catch my killer."

"I'm sorry our security wasn't good enough," apologised the commander, but the president was already dead. The medical staff confirmed that fact when they arrived.

Commander Most, together with Commander Bigship and four HART soldiers were, already, in the building where Celia had glimpsed the brief *flash* – the building turned out to be a deserted flat above a baker's shop. The six of them thundered into the room to find a rifle, mounted on a tripod, but nobody in the room; Leon noted the barrel wasn't smoking so – curious now – he went over and felt the rifle, "It's cold," he said to the others, "it was just a decoy."

"But," protested Celia, "if that's a decoy where was the *fatal* shot fired from?" She moved over to the window that overlooked the square and saw – to her horror – there was another window almost opposite the stage. Why hadn't anybody noticed it before? "There," she called – triumphantly to her colleagues, who came over to stand beside her, "didn't anybody check it?"

"I did," answered Leon, "about a minute before we led the president out. There was nobody there so whoever did this must have been quick." The HART personnel all returned to the Taj Mahal later that afternoon after the three commanders had made statements to the *local* police.

The three commanders met later in Commander Bigship's quarters – as his room was slightly larger than the other two's. "How the hell did it happen, and who did it?" Commander Strobing asked.

The other two looked at each other before Celia replied, "I think we are agreed it must've been a *Proagnon* agent."

"Agreed," commented Ronan, "but how the hell did they know we were coming?" Then he added, "Only the three of us knew about this mission, we only picked the soldiers a few hours before we came; and I told Joshua Smith we'd be away a couple of days, I didn't tell him where we were going. I'll admit Miss Strong knew I was going somewhere but I didn't inform her where"

Both Leon and Celia looked at each other, dumbly. "Neither of us can answer that, sir, but perhaps that Indian chap can," Leon announced to the superior officer.

"Hmm, maybe," answered Ronan, "I'll quiz him on the journey back to the air force station. If he knows nothing when we get back to headquarters I will have – all – our computer systems shut down, yes I know the risks, and have the technicians, fully, check the system out."

"Yes sir," the other two replied in unison. It was then that the bus to take them back to the air force station arrived and the, downcast, HART personnel boarded; once they were all aboard the bus set off on its journey to the air force station, Ronan then took their Indian guide aside and told him who they believed was responsible for the president's death and also asked him who – on the Indian side – knew that HART were coming to protect the president.

The guide told the commander that only the president and the workers at the presidential office knew, and they were all trustworthy. In fact the two of them talked at great length about this matter; but neither could come to a satisfactory conclusion.

The bus reached the air force station and the HART personnel all got off, and then wandered over to the same Gulfstream *G550* that had brought them to this country. As soon as everybody was seated, fastened in, and the luggage stored satisfactorily the Indian guide came aboard to wish them well and farewell, and then Commander Strobing stood and said, “We thank you for all your hospitality, and are sorry something went wrong with our security. We have let India down and apologise; I know President Akhbar’s death will be on my conscience, if not all our consciences, for a long time. Farewell Imram Gandhi.” The Indian then left the plane and the door was closed behind him. Ronan then turned to face the HART personnel who had come on this *fateful* mission, “We have suffered a setback today, as we suffered a setback in Scotland a week ago; I’m sure we will take this in our stride, I know one death is one too many” With that he sat down and the executive jet began its journey back to Geneva’s *Cointrin* international airport.

*****

Sandy Tulliver (Carol Turner) had watched the assassination of President Akhbar on one of the news broadcasts – she knew there’d be some red faces at HART now, plus she – like Commander Strobing wondered how *Proagnon* had got the information.

As Floyd Maxwell was still away, he’d suddenly been called away on business or so he’d told her, Sandy had used his laptop to send an email to her deputy, Mitchell Walker, congratulating him on a well executed operation. She’d also noticed that a few days prior to his leaving Mr Maxwell had seemed to start to doubt, or mistrust, her – for some reason; however much she tried Sandy could not work out the reason why.

CHAPTER 20

RETIREMENT & A RACE AGAINST TIME!

The HART team returned to their headquarters – some seemed disillusioned whilst others seemed unusually upbeat – where their superior commander went into his office to begin the task of trying to figure out what had gone so wrong. He was joined, a few moments later, by the other two commanders; as their Indian guide had not been able to offer them any answers, or indeed any hints, on what had gone wrong. Commander Strobing called all HART personnel: this included all four of the receptionist, every soldier (even those on guard duty) and commander, plus – finally – the whole of the medical staff, to a meeting in the conference room. Once everybody was present and was seated Ronan stood up to address them all. "Ladies and gentleman," he began, "due to recent circumstances and the lack of answers to certain questions I have decided – against my better judgement I might add – to close down the entire HART computer network. I know the risks and the danger this will put us in, but I am sure if we all remain vigilant we should get through this period without incident; may I request you back up, or transfer, all necessary files to your computer's *memory* sticks, as the network will be closed down in two hours time."

"The network will be checked, this checking shouldn't take longer than an hour, for any *rogue* anomalies by our highly trained technical staff," he concluded and sat down. Everyone left the room then apart from the three commanders and Dr Hans Schaiffer.

The doctor approached his friends and said to them, "As you know sirs, ma'am," he said, "I am due for retirement in a few weeks. I would prefer no fuss – on that occasion – to mark this event, I just want to slip away quietly that day."

"That is understood Dr Schaiffer," Ronan said, "no fuss, none at all."

"I shall introduce my son as my successor before I leave though. Remember Commander Strobing, no fuss."

"Right you are Hans," and then they left the conference room. "Celia, Leon, my office if you please."

"Yes Commander Strobing," they confirmed and followed him into his office; their superior first backed up some computer files to a *memory* stick then and switched off his laptop, closed it and unplugged it. "Please be seated," he told the other two. They looked at each other, both wondering what their superior was going to say to them and pulled up a couple of chairs. He asked them both, "Do you really think I'm going to let Dr Schaiffer go without throwing him a retirement party?"

"We did wonder why you agreed – so readily – to let him go without a fuss. Now we know why, it was all a ploy," remarked Commander Leon Bigship. Celia just nodded her head to show she agreed with her colleague.

Ronan then opened the locker behind him and produced a box full of *party* items. "These have been ready for ages. They were intended for use when Commander Roberts was due to retire, but, unfortunately, he was killed in action. So this is the first retirement we've had at HART, most of the others have left us – in a box." Ronan knew he shouldn't have phrased it that way but his colleagues knew he could be – rather – blunt at times. So preparations, and plans, were made for Dr Schaiffer's leaving party.

*****

One person who wouldn't be able to attend Dr Schaiffer's party was Zimba Mandango, who was chained up in Dr Simon Forrestor's, secret, underground laboratory. "What is the contact number of your headquarters?" Simon demanded to know.

"I won't tell you," cried the black girl, "you or your friend."

"You'll save yourself a lot of trouble in the long run."

"I'm ready for whatever trouble you mean," she retorted. "I would rather die than tell you."

"As you wish," the doctor said and produced the *tiny* clamps. Handing one to Paul to attach to her other wrist he attached his to her left forearm, once Paul had done the same – on the right - the two men stepped back and Forrestor turned the torture machine on. "Last chance, what is the contact number of your headquarters."

"Go to hell," was Zimba's response.

"Okay, I did warn you," replied Simon and began to turn the dial – at level 1 Zimba never flinched, level 2 she felt some mild discomfort, level 3 slightly more discomfort, level 4 she gave a few cries, but on level 5 she started screaming. "I have another three levels to try yet."

"No," said Pearman hurriedly, "you said you'd only go up to level 5."

"I changed my mind," the doctor answered and turned the dial up to level 6. Zimba's screams became louder and Paul began to fear discovery, and voiced his fears; "Don't worry," his friend said, "nobody has found this room before."

He then looked at Miss Mandango, "Had enough yet?" He brought the dial back to level 1 as he asked his next question, "Are you willing to talk yet?"

"I've had enough," replied the black girl, "but I still won't tell you anything."

"Like I told you," Pearman suddenly said, "she won't tell you anything." He looked very smug.

"We'll see," his companion responded producing the syringe that contained the *truth* serum; carefully he opened the *sterile* packet containing the hypodermic needle and connected the two objects together, once he was ready he turned back to the black girl and said to her, "Now this won't hurt – much." He then selected an area of her upper arm and, gently, broke the skin; Zimba didn't even murmur. Next Simon slowly pushed down on the plunger so the *orange* liquid within could enter her body; he noticed that her eyes began to water and paused, "Anything you want to tell us darling?"

"N, N, No," she stammered. Simon knew the serum was beginning to have an effect by the way she stammered out the word.

"Give her it all," Paul said angrily. He could see Simon was faltering – he had no such scruples, "make her talk, or I'll do it myself." Luckily Simon just kept the syringe out of his reach.

The doctor turned to look at his companion – a look of thunder on his face, "Who is doing this, me or you?" Pearman shrank back at Simon's venomous tone; he'd never heard his friend speak like that before.

"You are," he replied meekly.

"Remember that in future," Forrestor told him then turned back to their hostage, "shall we try again? Is there anything you'd like to tell us?"

"No," said Miss Mandango more firmly.

"Suit yourself," the man holding the syringe said and pressed the plunger again. This time Zimba Mandango started to tremble, a sure sign she was about to *crack*.

"Okay I'll tell you."

"Told you it'd work," Dr Forrestor announced triumphantly to Mr Pearman; he removed the syringe from her arm. "What is the contact number of your headquarters?" She gave him an international phone number which he wrote down. "Thank you my dear, you've been most helpful. Now you may rest awhile." The black girl slumped back, totally exhausted.

Simon Forrestor turned to Paul, "Guard her I have some work to do." Pearman told the doctor he would, and then Forrestor entered the lift and went back up to his office; once inside he called the number Miss Mandango had given him. "Hello," said the *male* voice of Ben Gillespe, "HART headquarters."

"Ah hello," replied Dr Forrestor, "I'd like to speak to whoever's in charge."

"Commander Strobing doesn't wish to be disturbed – at the present, may I take a message?"

"You may," Simon answered and relayed his message, and all other relevant information, to the receptionist, plus he gave his name.

*****

As he listened Ben's eyes grew wide, they thought everybody on board *Damancas* had died when it had exploded; now this one man claimed that Zimba Mandango, HART's newest recruit, was still very much alive and he, along with another unknown person, was holding her hostage. "Thank you sir," said Ben, and then replaced the receiver.

Whether this information was correct or not it should be brought to the attention of the superior HART commander. Mr Gllespie took the notes he'd made and crossed to Commander Strobing's office, and then he knocked on the office door. Hastily Ronan hid the *party* decorations and called out, "Come in."

The door opened and the receptionist entered; he saw the other two commanders were there as well he wondered why but decided not to ask. "Sirs, ma'am," he began, "I have just received a phone call from a Dr Simon Forrestor, he claims that our colleague – Miss Zimba Mandango – is still alive." The HART commander smiled at this news. "Furthermore," continued Ben, "he claims that he, together with another person, is holding her hostage in his - secret – underground laboratory at *John Groggins* Hospital in Norwich."

"Okay Ben," Celia said to him, "what does he want?"

"That's just it, he will release her – alive – if Commander Strobing goes over, personally, to fetch her. However, he also stated that the commander must go – alone and unarmed."

The other two looked at Ronan, "Surely you're not going to agree to this?"

The superior officer looked back at them – thoughtfully – and then replied, "If there's a chance he will release her then I feel it is my duty to go, whatever his terms, after all I got her into this."

"Sir if I may offer an opinion," the receptionist said, "how do we know this man will release her safely?"

"Can you get Dr Schaiffer in here Ben?" The receptionist left and returned – a few minutes later – with Dr Hans Schaiffer, who asked what the commander wanted, "Can you recall ever meeting a Dr Simon Forrestor?"

The HART medical man thought back, "I can't recall meeting him, maybe I did, but I recall that my friend Dr Lighten met him once. Simon even stayed a night with Charles and his wife."

"Did your friend tell you what he was like?"

"Yes sir," Dr Schaiffer said, "Charles described him as a very sincere man and good doctor, but his wife told him she thought he had a darker side to him. Mind if I ask why you want to know about him?"

Ronan looked at his other two colleagues as Ben Gillespe had departed to continue his shift on reception. Their looks told him the doctor ought to know. "It's just that Ben Gillespe took a phone call from him, a few minutes ago, and he claims to be holding Zimba Mandango – who went on the ill fated mission to Scotland – and he has requested that I go to his laboratory, which is under *John Groggins* Hospital in Norwich to get her. Now I ask you, do you think I should go?"

"If I were in your position sir I would; if there's a chance she is there and unharmed then I would go for it."

"Thank you Dr Schaiffer, you may return to your medical duties now." HART's doctor left the office. Commander Strobing looked at the others, "I will go over there; I admit it may be a trap but if I don't go I won't know. Until such time as I return I leave you in command Celia. However as your superior I order you to stay here."

"Yes Ronan." The superior commander then got up from his seat and exited the office to pack for his trip home to England. As he walked through reception he said to Mr Gillespe – who was on duty for another quarter of an hour, "Please contact *Cointrin* and have them ready a Gulfstream *G650* for flight to England's Norwich *International* Airport. I will be there in about half an hour."

"Right you are sir," replied Ben, picking up the phone before the commander had left him. "I'll tell them to expect you." The commander thanked him and then left to pack as he figured he may have to stay overnight whilst he was there.

About twenty minutes later he placed his suitcase in his *Apollo II* car, climbed in and drove off to Geneva's *Cointrin* Airport. When he arrived he showed his HART pass and was ushered through to the *airside* lounge; after a couple of minutes the executive business jet rolled up to receive its, sole, passenger; once Ronan was aboard and his luggage was safely stowed away the two pilots welcomed him aboard. Once introductions were over Commander Strobing settled back in his seat whilst the pilots went through to the cockpit to complete the pre-flight checks, when these were completed the two Rolls-Royce Deutschland BR725 turbofan engines were started and the plane powered up.

As soon as it was cleared for take-off the business jet thundered down the runway; once it had attained maximum speed the nose, of the aircraft, rose into the sky and the plane began its fifty minute journey north westwards to England – Ronan had requested they use maximum speed all the way, which was 530 knots, 610mph, or 982 km/h (each was equivalent to another) as he wanted to reach his destination as soon as possible.

Around forty five minutes later the commander of HART was informed they were approaching their destination and to prepare himself for cabin depressurisation as they descended; although he'd been on many aircraft journeys before he'd never got used to depressurisation when the aircraft's cabin resumed, normal, ground pressure. Once the depressurisation period was over the three sets of dual wheels were lowered (one set below the nose with the other two sets toward the rear of the fuselage) using dual hydraulics; Ronan peered out the oval shaped window, to his right and saw the Norfolk coastline. "40 metres to landing," the pilot's voice said over the intercom loudspeaker, "30, 20, 10, 5," then there was a *bump* as the jet landed on the runway and *bounced* off. Then there came a second *bump* and this time the plane stayed on the runway.

The engines then started to *whine* and *scream* as reverse thrust was applied to slow the executive jet down; when it had finally come to a – complete – standstill the HART commander unbuckled his safety belt and then once the staircase had been lowered using hydraulics Ronan almost shot out to claim his luggage and darted into the airport.

He raced through the building, startling people who were moving the other way – even startling the security personnel, outside he located a taxi cab, got inside and said, quickly, to the driver, "*John Groggins* Hospital and step on it."

The driver was rather taken aback but moved off in the direction of the hospital Ronan had requested, "Going to see somebody sir?" the man asked jovially.

"In a manner of speaking," answered the HART commander bluntly.

"Sorry sir, I only asked." The vehicle drove through the streets of Norwich until they reached they destination. "That'll be £5.60," the driver said. Ronan shoved a £10 note in the man's hand.

"Keep the change," his passenger told him and then darted out with his luggage – leaving a, rather, startled looking taxi driver. Commander Strobing could only guess at what the man was thinking. He placed his suitcase outside one of the out buildings for collection later, lucky the grounds were covered by CCTV; he then noticed a Renault *Megane* and a Toyota *Corolla* parked side by side – one must be Simon Forrestor's car, but which one, and who did the other belong to?

Leaving this question for the moment he entered the main building and enquired after Dr Forrestor. "I'll just *page* him sir if you'd like to wait over there. What name shall I give him?" the nurse on duty said.

"Ronan HART," he answered. The nurse then *paged* Dr Forrestor and gave him the information she'd been given; the doctor told her he was on his way up.

When he arrived the nurse indicated Mr HART. "Ah Mr HART, I take it you've come to see my patient, this way please," and Dr Forrestor led Commander Strobing to the lifts. "My office is downstairs," he told the HART commander, "Miss Mandango, I assume you've come to get her."

"You know fucking well I have," blustered Ronan.

"Okay, okay, calm down." The lift stopped, "Here we are," said Simon cheerfully, "come along." Commander Strobing just growled at the doctor; he followed the man to his office, "Through here," the medical man told him and pressed the button that operated the bookcase mechanism, and a second lift was revealed. "This one's to my – secret – laboratory," he informed the other man; Ronan knew Simon held all the cards, at the moment, so he had no *real* option but to play along. They boarded the lift, the doctor pressed the *down* button and the lift descended to the laboratory.

Upon exiting the lift Forrestor walked, swiftly, towards his captive; Commander Strobing looked over at her with sadness in his eyes, "Oh Zimba I'm so sorry."

"Behind you," her - weak - voice called. Before he could turn a pistol barrel was pushed into the HART commander's spine.

"Move and I'll kill you," hissed a voice behind him.

"That's it, you hold him Paul," announced the doctor, "I have a task to prepare for." He then produced a, hermetically, sealed metal box from a storage cupboard and opened it; inside was a syringe containing *green* fluid and another hypodermic needle. He fitted the two together, "Now Commander Strobing, I believe, the fluid contained within this syringe is a concentrated version of the virus we have been using, I intend to inject your colleague with this fluid to see how it affects her – again I believe it will induce a quick death for her."

"You'll never get away with this."

"And how, my dear commander, do you intend to stop me? After all you are alone and unarmed." Suddenly Ronan thrust his elbow back into Paul Pearman's stomach, and he fell; the commander grabbed the man's Walther *PPS* and raced toward

Simon – hoping to knock the needle and syringe out his hand – he knew he could just have shot the man but he may have hit the black girl as well.

Simon looked from Commander Strobing to Zimba Mandango – Paul was of little help as he was just regaining his feet. Dr Forrestor, having made his choice, plunged the needle into Zimba's neck, she screamed, and started to depress the plunger. Commander Strobing pulled the trigger on the pistol and shot Dr Simon Forrestor, who started to collapse but his finger was still depressing the plunger, the black girl was really screaming now. Ronan pushed Forrestor away, and pulled the needle from Miss Mandango's neck; to his shock he found the syringe was now empty, "Behind you sir," rasped, a very weak sounding, Zimba Mandango; the HART commander spun round to see Paul Pearman rushing at him, without thinking Commander Strobing pulled the trigger and killed the man.

Locating the key he undid the restraining clamps and said to her, "Can you walk?"

"No sir, I'm sorry,"

"I'll carry you then," Ronan told her and hoisted Miss Mandango up, into his arms and carried her across to the lift; setting her down – for a second – he pressed the *up* arrow and the lift ascended back to Simon Forrestor's office. The two members of HART left the lift and Ronan seated Zimba, in a chair, whilst he searched Simon's coat – he had to act fast as he could see the black girl's health was deteriorating fast now. Finding the doctor's car keys, it was he who owned the Renault *Megane*, he helped Zimba to stumble to the door of the office; he found a wheelchair in the corridor and lowered her, gently, into it.

Zimba smiled weakly at her superior as he pushed the wheelchair from the hospital. "Excuse me sir, you can't take this patient out," the nurse told him.

Ronan thought quickly, "Dr Forrestor has performed his tests on her, and believes she needs more - intensive – medical care and has requested that I move her myself. He has even allowed me, personal, use of his car."

The nurse – evidently she was new – believed what she was being told and allowed Commander Strobing to wheel Miss Mandango away. "Phew," he sighed once they were out in the open air, "at least we got away with it;" there was no reaction from the black girl. "Zimba," Ronan called, leaning over and seeing she'd closed her eyes, "stay with me."

Her eyes fluttered open, "Sorry," she said to her commander; he unlocked the *Megane* and lifted her out the wheelchair, he hugged her to him – ready to turn her and place her in the passenger seat when she rasped, "No."

"No what?" asked Commander Strobing totally baffled.

"Commander Strobing, Ronan, I am sorry but I won't be returning with you; my time is done. But there is one thing I never told you, I love you." She moved in and the two of them embraced passionately; when he felt her body go limp he knew she was gone.

He lowered her back into the wheelchair and broke down, "I'm sorry Zimba, I shouldn't have brought you to Scotland. Now you're dead because I failed you. So long Zimba Mandango, rest in peace, I did love you." It was then he saw, possibly he imagined it, a faint smile cross her lips.

Wheeling her body back inside he said to the nurse, "She didn't make it." It was such an easy thing to say; leaving the wheelchair – with the lifeless body in it – in the nurse's custody he left and, after getting his suitcase, he climbed aboard the *Megane* and drove away, to find a place to stay.

Ronan, saddened by the loss of HART's newest recruit, drove around the city of Norwich until he came across the *Quality* Hotel. He pulled up outside and switched off the engine of the Renault car; he then went inside and enquired about the availability of rooms, he was informed by the receptionist – a pretty girl – that as they had had a late cancellation there was one single room available in the hotel. He couldn't believe his luck; he told her he'd take the room – after all he'd only be stopping one night; the receptionist told him the price for a one night stay was £25 including breakfast which was, in the dining room, at 8am.

The HART commander fetched his case from the car and went up – in the lift – to find room ten, where he was staying. He unpacked, had his evening meal and then went out to explore the surrounding area; returning later Ronan had a couple of drinks, in the bar, and then went up to his room. Whilst he'd been out he'd been approached by a couple of – what he assumed were – common prostitutes; he'd refused them and gone on his way.

Now he was back in the hotel room, he undressed and went to bed.

*****

At HART headquarters plans were well under way for Dr Schaiffer's retirement party, which would be held the first week of May which was only a month away – Commander Craig would be retiring and handing over to Commander Bigship on the same day, so the celebration would be a joint one. John and Leon would then travel back to Turkey, where John Craig would hand the running of the base over, officially, to Leon Bigship.

*****

Over the next couple of weeks workmen would be removing old piping from the old air force base at Diyarbakit in Turkey; these workmen were from a company that was used regularly by HART for all their maintenance requirements, once the repairs were completed Commander Bigship should have been installed as the base's latest superior officer. However unknown to HART or Commander John Craig the maintenance company had been infiltrated by *Proagnon* agents, and these agents had been instructed to help bring down HART.

*****

At the Maxwell residence Floyd had returned to his house and told his partner, Carol Turner, that he had a rather large surprise lined up for her; Sandy Tulliver (Carol Turner) wanted to know what this surprise was but Floyd told her he had to make sure it was right for her. Reluctantly his partner agreed to wait and see how things turned out, however Mr Maxwell did hint that the surprise may mean her staying in England.

Sandy (Carol) was overjoyed as she assumed this meant Floyd Maxwell was going to ask her to marry him – in fact he'd already, recently, asked somebody else to marry him – he was keeping Sandy as his mistress, for the time being

*****

Commander Strobing awoke, at six, the next morning in the single room; for one moment he couldn't recall where he was, or how he'd got there. Then slowly he remembered why he was there and the death of Zimba Mandango at the hands of Dr Simon Forrestor; as he remembered this he became depressed again, but there was nothing he could have done to prevent it – he might have been able to prevent it if things had been different.

Dragging himself back to the present he climbed out of bed, washed and dressed and then packed his dirty clothes; he was down for breakfast at seven thirty. Once he'd eaten and had a quick drink of tea, and loaded his suitcase aboard the Renault, handed the room key back into reception and the left to begin the journey back to HART headquarters in Switzerland – he was out of the hotel at just gone nine.

He had the receptionist phone the airport before his departure to advise them to ready the Gulfstream *G650* for his return journey. He drove the vehicle to the airport, got his luggage out – what there was of it – placed the keys in the glove box, and then locked and shut the door; Dr Forrestor wouldn't be requiring his vehicle anymore, and walked into the airport. Again he was taken through to the *airside* lounge; at approximately ten past ten the business jet rolled up; Ronan was allowed to board and his luggage stored away, and they began the one hour (approximately) flight home to Geneva's *Cointrin* Airport. The plane was flying back, this time, at its cruise speed of 488 knots, there was no rush now.

About half an hour after the plane had landed Commander Strobing was back behind his desk; the other two commanders, in the office, seated opposite him. "How did it go sir?" Commander Most asked; the HART commander had been very quiet – almost subdued – since his return.

Ronan looked up at them, tears in his eyes, "It was a failure, I failed Zimba as Forrestor killed her – right in front of me. It was all a trick he never intended to release her. She was chained up, like a dog. What hurts most is that just before she died she told me she loved me – Zimba Mandango loved me and I never knew."

"We're very sorry sir," she said to her superior, looking across at Leon who nodded. "How did it happen?"

Ronan explained – as best he could and then finally said to them, "I got her outside but as I was transferring her to the car I'd acquired she died in my arms." However in a more upbeat tone he asked, "What's been happening while I've been away?"

"Well sir," Commander Bigship said, "preparations for the retirement party of Dr Schaiffer, as well as that of Commander Craig are well under way. We've even managed to contact Shinto Howell and persuaded him to fly back for the celebrations. Work on replacing the old piping at our Turkish establishment is under way as well."

"What work?" asked the commander of HART, "I gave no such order."

"Perhaps Commander Craig did."

"Maybe you're right and I've just forgotten about it," responded Ronan.

*****

The next few weeks passed without incident and, finally, the date of the party arrived; Shinto Howell arrived that afternoon from Tokyo and was met by Commander's Strobing and Most while Commander Bigship met Commander Craig who arrived a little later.

Dr Hans Schaiffer and Commander John Craig had to meet with Commander Strobing – in his office – to sign some paperwork that would make their retirements official. To Mr Hans Schaiffer Ronan said, "Your son arrived earlier and awaits us in the conference room, so as soon as you've finished signing may I suggest all three of us join him?"

"Why do you want me along?" John asked his superior.

"Just for a farewell drink with everybody, let us all toast your health on your final day." Commander Craig accepted this and readily agreed; so once the two men had signed all the paperwork to make everything official they exited the commander's office and walked to the conference room doors which Ronan threw open.

"Surprise!" called all the assembled HART personnel, including Mr Shinto Howell and Dr Heinz Schaiffer; and then the party started; Music started playing, there was plenty of food and drink to go round; streamers were thrown, party poppers went off, there was balloons, everything a party needed. People began dancing to the music; Dr Schaiffer was persuaded to dance with Mrs Gwyneth Jones while Commander Craig was dragged onto the dance floor by Commander Most, to say both men wanted no fuss they both seemed to be – thoroughly – enjoying themselves.

By the end of the party both men were thoroughly exhausted. After some speeches the two left quietly; one to fly home to Germany, whilst the other was to fly back to Turkey with Commander Bigship. Before he left Hans was assured – by his son – HART was in safe hands.

LOOSE ENDS, REVELATIONS & DEATH OF A FRIEND!

So it was that after the retirement party every member of HART personnel – that wasn't on duty – left to retire to bed.

*****

Around the world the antibiotic *Ansolid* was mass distributed by the World Health Organisation (WHO). Doctors in each country injected every member of that country's population with this new antibiotic – admittedly for some people it was too late.

Over in England Dr Lighten injected the antibiotic into Arnold Stevens, he wasn't certain if it would help or if the virus had taken too much of a hold already. A couple of days Mr Stevens began to recover and by the next week he was fit enough to return home, Elle was overjoyed, Arnold soon returned to his old – crotchety – self.

*****

At her flat in Amsterdam there came a knock on the door, to the apartment, of Heidi Peters; she got up to answer it, curious as to who could want her - at this hour. Standing outside was a man dressed in a pin striped suit, he was slightly taller than the United Nations Dutch delegate. "May I come in?"

"Who are you?" she asked.

"I believe we have something in common," he told her.

"Such as?" she asked.

"Let me in and I shall tell you."

"Okay come in, it's just I'm not used to strange men turning up on my doorstep," she told him. He smiled innocently at her.

The man walked in and seated himself in one of the chairs, in the main room. She seated herself opposite him and asked again, "You said we had something in common, well what is it?"

"*Proagnon.*"

"I never want to hear that name again. Please go."

"I am one of their emissaries and I bring you a gift from them."

"What is it?" Her curiosity was piqued now.

"This," and he produced a *Glock* pistol and shot her dead. Then he hurried from the apartment, leaving the door open, he bolted down the stairs – almost colliding with a young couple coming up. He apologised and then walked out the entrance door and disappeared into the Amsterdam night.

*****

In his London house Floyd Maxwell had enough evidence to reveal his *big* surprise to Carol Turner.

He invited her out to dinner one night and drove her – in his Vauxhall *Vectra* to a, rather, upper class restaurant in the main city. "Darling," said Carol, "how can you afford to bring me here when you don't work?"

"I have – good – credit at many places like this," he answered simply. What he meant was his alter-ego, Gareth Andrews, as the queen's consort did. He took her inside – he had a briefcase with him. The head waiter met them at the door.

"Good evening sir, ma'am. Your usual table, in the corner, has been prepared for you Mr Maxwell." The head waiter watched the two people walk towards a table at the rear of the restaurant; he'd never seen the young lady before, was she just a friend or something more?

Miss Turner and Mr Maxwell seated themselves, and Floyd placed his briefcase on a vacant seat, they ordered their meal and wine. It was then that Mr Maxwell opened the *combination* locks on his case and removed some documents which he placed face down – on top of the briefcase until they'd eaten; Sandy (Carol) looked at the sheaf of documents, they were bound together using something like *silk* ribbon. She was just about to query her partner about this when their meals arrived.

Once they'd eaten and all the plates had been cleared Floyd picked the papers up and undid the ribbon – it was very official looking – he turned the first document over and began, "Now Miss Carol Turner, or should I call you Sandy Tulliver?"

Sandy was shocked, how had he found out her real name? Still it didn't really matter, now. "Call me Sandy Tulliver," she told him.

"Well Miss Tulliver, I have done a great deal of research on you and it appears that Mr and Mrs Tulliver – your parents – were never your *real* parents. Plus Sandy Tulliver was never your *real* name."

"Oh yes," she began, she was shocked at these revelations; was Floyd simply trying to play with her mind or was everything he telling her the truth? "Do carry on," Sandy eventually said, "if you know so much then please tell me my *real* name?"

"That one," he told her, "was the hardest part of my investigation." She then realised why he'd been a bit *off* with her these past couple of weeks. "But after much searching I have discovered your birth name, your *real* name if you like, is Angela Pendragon." He paused to let that bit sink in, "It appears you were born to the queen's father and one of his many mistresses; therefore you are Queen Charlotte's half sister and the throne of Britain may not rightfully be yours but I think you could take it, with my assistance." She had turned quite pale now.

The head waiter hurried over, "Are you okay Miss?"

"What? Oh yes, just a spot of trapped wind," she lied. "Could I have a glass of water?" The waiter brought her one over. Angela looked directly at Mr Maxwell, "Are you telling me the truth or is this all a pack of lies?"

"No my darling," it was the first time he'd called her darling; he passed the papers over, "It's all there in black & white."

Angela read each document thoroughly, "Where do we go now?" she queried.

"Back to my car," he suggested. Floyd placed all the papers back in his case and they left the restaurant; Angela had never touched her glass of water, the waiter bid the two of them farewell and then set about clearing the tables.

Once they were in the Vauxhall Floyd looked over at Angela, "I have another surprise for you, and that is my name is not Floyd Maxwell but Gareth Andrews and I am Queen Charlotte's consort." With that they kissed and then drove off into the night – it was raining as usual.

*****

Over in Turkey Commander Bigship had settled into his new post; the staff at the base liked him and he liked them, of course he felt there were a few things that could be changed and he would put forward these recommendations – in his first report to Commander Strobing. Although Ronan had told him, about a month back – possibly two, that he could change what he wanted Leon felt it was best to ask before making any *drastic* changes.

He wandered back to the commander's office – passing many HART personnel on the way – to write his report and make his recommendations, when he felt the whole base structure shudder. "What is happening?" he enquired.

The two guards replied, "We don't know sir. We've never felt anything like this before." Then – totally without warning – the base exploded, huge columns of fire and smoke rising into the air. Hovering overhead was an orbiting *GlobalHawk* Unmanned Aerial Vehicle (UAV); this relayed pictures of the explosion to the main headquarters.

"Sir!" shouted Gwyneth Jones into the intercom that connected reception to the commander's office, "we have a situation in Turkey!"

"Patch it through Mrs Jones," called back the commander and then turned, in his chair, to face the screen on the back wall. As soon as he saw the first picture he, almost, shouted into the interconnecting intercom, "Most! Get in here, now!"

Celia hurried through, "What is.....?" she stopped speaking as soon as she saw the pictures being transmitted, "Oh shit!" she exclaimed. "Leon's there! Is anybody left?"

"Evidently not," answered her superior, and then called through to reception, "Mrs Jones, was that a recording?"

"No sir."

"Oh," Commander Strobing sighed. "They're all gone, killed in that one explosion."

"It would appear so sir."

"*Proagnons* Revenge," the superior officer said simply, stood and placed his arm round his deputy. A few days later the two commanders left to return to England for their *annual* holiday, both were saddened by recent events.